EWB

Enemies with Benefits

N.R. Walker

Copyright

Photographer: Xram Ragde
Cover Artist: N.R. Walker
Editor: Boho Edits
Publisher: BlueHeart Press
EWB © 2023 N.R. Walker

Warning

Intended for an 18+ audience only. This book contains material that is intended for a mature, adult audience. It contains graphic language, explicit sexual content, and adult situations.

Characters also partake in light, consensual degradation and humiliation. There is also undiagnosed disordered eating.
Reader discretion is advised.

Blurb

Marshall

I hate Valentine Tye.

I've hated him since we were ten years old. I hate everything he is, everything he stands for. Even the mention of his name gets my back up.

And when I see him?

My blood boils. My jaw clenches and my hands curl into fists. That's how much I hate him.

I want to cause him pain. I want to hold him down and actually hurt him.

And if that's not bad enough, that's exactly what he wants me to do to him.

Valentine

I know what people think of me. I know what they assume. They all think I'm some spoiled rich guy who's had everything handed to him.

They don't know me at all.

Behind my carefully constructed walls is an emptiness so dark it scares men away. I like pain. I like being used. For some messed up reason, it validates me. I don't need love or affection or, hell forbid, emotional attachment.

What I need is a man who hates me, a man who despises me.

A man like Marshall Wise.

Because never in a million years would he ever feel anything for me.

Right?

ENEMIES WITH BENEFITS

N.R. WALKER

CHAPTER 1

MARSHALL WISE

I HATED VALENTINE TYE.

I hated him with every fibre of my being, with the raging fire of a thousand burning suns. I hated him in ways I couldn't even describe.

Why, do you ask?

Let me count the fucking ways . . .

It began in primary school. Yep. I've hated that fucker since then. Year five, Under 10s Rugby Union Grand Final. He was the captain of his team. I was the captain of mine. He scored the winning try, taking his school to the state finals. Half my team were crying to their parents whereas I just glared at him. And you know what he did?

The fucker smiled at me.

Enter high school. Year seven, St Ignatius Boys School. One of Sydney's more exclusive private schools, where Valentine Tye and I would be classmates, teammates on the rugby team. He was team captain, because of course he was. Perfect grades, perfect hair, perfect face.

I might have even liked the guy.

Until two weeks out from the finals. I got home and my

parents sat me down. Mum had been crying, Dad was quiet, sullen. Devastated.

I had to change schools and move house. Dad had lost his business and I'd have to attend the local public high school. They couldn't afford the tuition because my father's much-loved hardware store had been squeezed dry and sold for pennies to none other than hardware giant Tye Corp.

Valentine fucking Tye.

Fast forward to eighth grade rugby semi-finals. North Ryde Public High versus St Ignatius; public poor boys against the rich preppy snobs. My old school, my old friends, and my new arch nemesis.

Ten minutes into the second half, we were up by four. Valentine made a break down the sideline, about to score for sure. I lined that fucker up, cleared half the field to smash him into the ground. I took out his legs and drove him over the sideline. I stopped him scoring and saved the game. Everyone cheered and I was named player of the match. But I couldn't even gloat since I had to go to hospital because, when I'd tackled him, I'd broken my arm.

Missed the grand final because of him.

I hated Valentine Tye. I hated him because I'd let my team down, and I hated him because he was still at the private school and I was at the public Shithole High.

I hated him the most because my dad struggled so damn much. He was never the same after that.

Fast forward again to grade ten. Sydney's high school rugby carnival. I never actually got to play against him, but I saw him. In his preppy school team gear, with his rich girl-friend and her long hair and pretty smile. I hated that he had the perfect life—an easy life—while I kept my head down, trying not to be obvious about checking guys out in the dressing rooms.

Shirtless, sweaty, hot.

I hated that I noticed him. He was tall, lean, fit. His dark floppy hair, his pale skin and flushed cheeks.

I fucking hated him for making me want him.

With no hope of going to uni, I left school at the end of grade ten and took a building apprenticeship. I enjoyed it, and was good at it. I got to hang out with my mates. I still played rugby on weekends, but I was out of the school division, so I never played against him again.

I saw him though, at a game here and there.

He got even taller, filled out more. With his still-floppy hair, high cheekbones, and sharp jaw, he was hot enough to be a model, and he turned heads wherever he went.

I fucking hated him for that too.

Then I didn't see him for a few years. Maybe he went to uni. Hell, he could have been on a runway in Milan for all I fucking knew. But it was hard not to be reminded of him when his family's mega-hardware company had gone national and had ads on every-fucking-thing all the damn time. TV, radio, internet. That damn advertising jingle grated on my every nerve. I hated it too.

Despite all that, there were about two years of my life where I never thought about Valentine fucking Tye.

Two blissful years of working hard and playing hard, both on and off the field.

Monday to Friday I was the site manager for my building crew. Saturday afternoon was game day or training, and Saturday nights I spent drinking with mates and usually ended up in a drunken fist fight or being balls deep in some guy's ass.

Two blissful years of no Valentine Tye.

Until the new rugby season started. A trial game against

the Lane Cove Tigers and *who* should run out on the field as one of their starting centres?

Valentine fucking Tye.

He looked good too. Real fucking good. And I did get the satisfaction of him doing a double take when he saw me. His eyes locked with mine and that asshole smirked around his mouthguard.

And all that bitter rage just bubbled right up to the surface. I'd never wanted to hurt someone so bad.

Just a few minutes in and he had the ball. I tried to take him down. I dived for his legs but the slippery fucker was fast. Then we were locked in a scrum, shoulders pressed in hard, and that fucker mumbled something.

"Got something to say, princess?" I snarled.

He laughed. He actually laughed.

I broke the scrum and grabbed his jersey, pulled my fist back, ready to get my fight on. I was gonna smash his perfect fucking nose. He came back at me too, sneering as he swung for me—but our teams pulled us apart.

My best mate, Taka, had a hold of me. "Take it easy, bro," he said, dragging me away.

"I hate that motherfucker," I bit out, trying to contain my anger.

"I know you do." Taka had been my best mate since the day I'd started at Shithole High. He knew my story. He knew why. "Just let it go."

Typical Taka. He was a giant of a man, a six foot four tall, three foot wide Samoan. He could stop a freight train on the rugby field. Off the field, he was the softest, gentlest man you'd ever meet. The only thing bigger than his smile was his heart.

I was more a hold-a-grudge-forever kind of guy.

The game ended and the fact we'd won on their home

turf made up for the fact I didn't get to punch the shit outta Valentine. Afterwards, we went back to the pub, the sponsor of their team. They sat around some tables in one corner; we sat in the other. I tried to shake off my anger, but I couldn't help glancing over every now and then at you know who.

In his preppy expensive sweater that matched his dark hair and made his skin look extra pale.

Taka knocked his knee to mine. "Stop it."

I hated that after two years, Valentine goddamn Tye was under my skin like he hadn't missed a day. Needing to clear my head, I stood up. "It's my shout." I went to the bar, ordered a round for my table and handed out everyone's beer. I took a long pull of mine. "I gotta take a piss," I said.

"Don't go startin' nothin'," Noah said. Another mate of mine, and a guy who always had my back when someone needed a lesson in manners outside a bar at two o'clock in the morning.

I grinned at him. "Course not."

I went to the men's room, took a piss at the urinal and when I was washing my hands, who should walk in?

Yep.

Valentine fucking Tye.

He stopped when he saw me, and then that fucker smirked.

My body's reaction was visceral and instant. My blood caught fire, rage burned through me, my hands clenched into fists. "What the fuck do you want?"

Before he could answer, there was a loud bark of laughter just outside the door. Valentine turned at the sound before he shot a panicked look at me, grabbed me, and shoved me into one of the stalls.

I almost fell, my hand on the wall to stay upright. "What the f—"

But in the blink of an eye, he shut the door and kept his forearm across my chest, his other hand over my mouth. "Shh."

I tried to shove him off as one of the guys walking in spoke. "Yeah, it's Marshall Wise."

Me?

With Valentine's hand still over my mouth, he pressed his body up against mine, and he put his finger to his mouth in a *be-quiet* way. His eyes were so dark brown they were almost black, his lips were the same pink that ran in blotches down his cheeks.

My god I hated him.

Hated how my body reacted to him.

Hated that he could probably feel it.

"Well, he's a piece of shit," another voice said at the urinal. "See how he almost punched Tye? Fucker'll get what's coming to him."

I tried to push Valentine off me, but he shoved harder against me.

"Apparently he fights pretty good," the first guy said. "For a gay guy."

"He's gay?"

My chest heaved and Valentine's eyes darted between mine. He shook his head.

"Yeah. Fucks anything, fights anything. He's a piece of shit."

The urinals flushed and the other guy said something about how I should watch my back, and I would have laughed if Valentine's hips weren't pressed up against mine.

If I couldn't feel his dick rubbing against mine. Felt good too.

What the fuck?

Then I remembered who it was. I tried to shove him off me again, but then, with his hand still over my mouth, he slid his other hand down and palmed my dick. He cupped my balls and squeezed, then massaged my cock. A little too hard, a little too rough.

A little too good.

"What are you—" I tried to say behind his hand. I wasn't fighting him anymore, and he knew it.

He moved his hand to my throat, squeezing a little. "Keep your mouth shut," he whispered.

Threatened.

I shouldn't have liked it.

I hated that I liked it.

Then he raked his hand down from my neck, down my chest, lower. He undid the button on my jeans and unzipped the fly. With a flash of warning in his eyes, he sank to his knees.

When he saw my traitorous cock, he made the softest grunt. Then he gave me the best blow job of my life.

He used his hands, his mouth, his tongue.

All I could do was fist his hair and concentrate on not making a sound while he worked me over.

He made me come so fast, so hard. He swallowed around me, then swallowed every drop.

And while I was slumped against the wall with my jeans around my thighs, my head spinning, and my bones made of jelly, without a word he stood up and walked out.

For a minute or two, I wondered if I'd imagined it.

But my very happy dick, the buzz in my blood, and my empty balls told me it was very real.

After putting myself back together, I went back to my table, to my friends.

"You okay?" Taka asked me.

"Yeah, I'm good," I said, swigging my beer.

I was so fucking good.

But I watched Valentine across the bar as he drank his beer and laughed with his teammates. Then I watched as he left with them, and he never once turned around. He never once looked at me.

He just walked out like what he'd done meant nothing at all.

Yeah. I really hated Valentine Tye.

CHAPTER 2

VALENTINE TYE

I'D HEARD RUMOURS ABOUT MARSHALL WISE.

I'd heard he was gay, out and proud since high school. I'd also heard he had a huge cock and he had skills that kept men begging for more.

I wasn't surprised by this. I'd seen him in high school in the change rooms in nothing but briefs or tight shorts. Even when we were teenagers, he'd been packing. I could only imagine it got better now that we were grown men.

And he'd certainly filled out nicely.

He was a solid build. Shorter than my six two by a few inches, but he was broader than me. Muscular. He clearly worked out or worked hard.

And the rumours about his cock?

All true.

At least nine inches long, thick enough that I could barely get my fingers around it.

Or my lips.

I didn't know what made me do it.

Well, I did . . .

I'd heard those rumours too.

That he liked to fight and fuck, and it wouldn't have been the first time he'd had his dick out in the bathroom at a pub.

Given the grapevine had claimed he was hung like a horse, I wanted to see for myself. I'd also heard he never did the same guy twice. An aversion to commitment or something. Which was perfect for me. Just what I wanted.

Needed.

It'd been far too long since I'd tasted dick.

Months since I'd left Melbourne. Months since I'd taken over as a managing director of the Sydney office under the watchful eye of my father.

I'd been too busy and too closeted to go looking for a gay fix. And so when I had the chance, I was going to take it.

It didn't hurt that Marshall Wise looked at me as if he wanted to kill me.

I found it incredibly provocative.

Arousing.

And he'd always looked at me as if he hated me.

Maybe he did.

He'd certainly tried to take my head off on the rugby field every chance he got.

God help me, I loved it every time.

So why did I push him into the bathroom stall? Because the guys on my team wanted to punch his head in, and if they'd found him alone in the men's room, it would've been an unfair fight and a bloodbath. And we'd have all been kicked out of the pub and got our sponsors offside before the season had even begun.

Why did I care if he got his head smacked in?

I was still asking myself that.

Guilt, probably.

Not that I regretted what I'd done. Not one bit. Given

the opportunity, I'd do it again. Hell, with that cock and his burning hate for me, I'd let him do whatever he wanted.

In the last few days, I'd jerked off twice to fantasies of his fat cock inside me.

"Valentine." Dad's voice startled me out of some very filthy thoughts. "Did you hear what I said?"

Thank god we were in my office alone and not in a full board meeting. "Sorry, I was thinking . . ."

"About?"

I lied. "This merger."

"And?"

"And I think we're ready."

He smiled at me in a way that made me uneasy. "Good. I expect the report on my desk by Friday."

———

ACQUISITIONS WERE something we did a lot of. Where smaller companies were absorbed into Tye Corp, allowing us to achieve asset and economic efficiency, mitigate weaknesses, and diversify risks. It also allowed us to obtain qualified staff who required little to no industry training.

Of course, not everyone saw it like that.

The cold reality of business was sometimes a bitter pill to swallow. Especially those who'd had to swallow such bitter pills before.

I walked into Kaplan Constructions at 9:00 am sharp the following Monday morning with my legal and finance team, just in time to catch the tail end of what I could only assume was the current CEO notifying his staff of his intent to sell the company.

Well, intent to sell was incorrect. To notify them that his company had been sold.

There was loud muffled shouting, then the office door almost being sheared from its hinges as someone ripped it open.

Marshall Wise stormed out only to stop cold when he saw me. His chest heaving, murder in his eyes. He pointed at me. "You! It had to be fucking you."

Then he started for me, and he probably would have killed me if he'd got to me, but he was stopped by a very large man whom I recognised from Marshall's rugby team. Taka, I think his name was.

He collected Marshall in much the same way I would assume a handler would manage attempting to put a feral cat in a cage. Marshall fought him the whole way out, but Taka was too strong.

Half my legal and finance team had taken a few steps back, but not me. I did manage to lock eyes with Marshall before he was hauled out the door, and there was nothing but unbridled hatred in his eyes.

I liked it.

I might have smiled at him as he was being dragged out.

Mr Kaplan was now at the door, saying goodbye to his other managers, and with a sigh, he gestured to the room behind him. "Apologies. Please come in."

His legal and finance teams were waiting for us and pleasantries were exchanged. All fine-print details had been gone over and accepted by both parties, contracts had been signed, and all that remained to be done were mere formalities.

Mr George Kaplan had aged out of the game. His words, not mine. He'd worked hard his entire life to grow his construction company from the ground up—and he'd done it very successfully—but he wanted to sell while he was still young enough to enjoy his spoils.

He was about to retire a very wealthy man, and we were about to collate his business into our ever-growing corporation.

"I take it not everyone is pleased about developments," I said, nodding to the door, to the fact that Marshall Wise needed to be restrained and removed.

Mr Kaplan sighed as he waved his hand. "Ahh. He's one of my best. He's . . . passionate."

I almost snorted. Passionate. That was one way to say fiery, pig-headed, and unable to contain his emotions.

"He's not too happy, no." Mr Kaplan met my gaze. "But he's signed on as site manager for the Mercer contract. Mercer wasn't too happy about the change of ownership as it was, but I assured them nothing will change—it's business as usual. They insisted the current manager and his team stay for the duration of the build. They like him." He sighed. "But as of close of business this Friday, that'll be your call."

Mercer was a massive industrial construction contract and including it was a hefty sweetener to this acquisition deal. If this contract was completed successfully, then we would perhaps secure future industrial developments with them as well.

I wouldn't risk souring any such lucrative deal. My father would kill me.

"Then we should make sure the site manager is happy to stay," I said with a smile.

He was going to fucking hate it, and he would absolutely lose his shit. I wanted to witness it.

"Should we call him back?" I suggested. "Or perhaps arrange a meeting with him at a more suitable time?"

Mr Kaplan smirked. "How about we give him a day to calm down?"

I doubted his rage at me would be dissipating any time soon.

"That's fine," I said. "Just let me know."

I was half expecting Marshall to be waiting for me outside his head office. I was half expecting to get charged at, yelled and sworn at, possibly even have punches thrown at me.

I was a little disappointed when it was clear that he was gone.

I was also a little disappointed he didn't turn up at the pub after rugby training on Thursday night. Not that he normally drank at our local, but he surely knew I'd be there.

I'd hoped he'd want to speak his mind before our meeting around the boardroom table first thing Friday morning.

But no.

He didn't show.

But he was there before me on Friday, sitting at the oval-shaped boardroom table with his arms crossed. He wore a company polo shirt, long work cargos, and dirty work boots. He was a tradesman, after all, but other team managers were there in dress pants and business shirts.

Perhaps it was a testament to Marshall's willingness to actually work on-site and not just supervise. Perhaps it was his way of saying he didn't think enough of me to dress for the occasion. I assumed it was the latter.

Everyone stood when we walked in. Everyone except Marshall. He sat there with his arms folded and his glare aimed right at me.

Good.

Mr Kaplan made introductions, pleasantries were exchanged, and my team gave an extensive rundown of Tye Corp's business model and mission statement. We explained that for them, Kaplan Constructions would stay exactly as it was—all staff from the office managers to janitors; all workplace agreements would transfer over. They would lose nothing. It was to make a seamless transition. We wanted happy employees, after all.

"Though if anyone would like to resign their employment," my legal manager added, "they will be able to do so without question, all benefits paid in full."

My gaze cut to Marshall, and his glare was still burning holes into my skull with laser precision. His jaw ticked and his nostrils flared.

But he stayed silent.

So he *was* staying.

Loyal to the people who worked with him and under him and to the company depending on him to complete the job.

And just like that, this game we played—where he hated me and I got off on it—entered new ground.

And all I could think about during this very important transition meeting was how I'd been on my knees for him and how much I wanted to suck his dick again.

"Anything to add, Mr Tye," my legal adviser asked.

I smiled at them all, my gaze landing on Marshall last. "I look forward to working with you all."

SATURDAY'S GAME was against Epping, and we played okay for the first game of the season. All the training and preseason prep didn't compare to actual match fitness.

But it felt good to run, to expend energy, to tackle, to get tackled.

By the time we were showered and back at the pub to

celebrate our win, I'd shaken off a big week at work and was feeling pretty good.

Lleyton put a beer in front of me. "Holy shit, is that an actual smile?"

"Fuck off."

He laughed. "Just kidding. It's good to see." He knocked his bottle to mine. "It's been a while."

I took a swig of my beer. It had been a while. Not since I'd come back from Melbourne. Not that I'd been too happy in Melbourne either, but I was freer to be more myself there, as opposed to here.

Not that I could be openly gay in Melbourne, but at least my father wasn't there watching everything I did, monitoring my behaviour and reputation. Sure, I'd had one-nighters and a few discreet regulars.

But nothing close to permanent.

Nothing close to fulfilling.

Here in Sydney, I had even less freedom.

Sure, I had a lot of good things. I had money, I had a nice apartment, a nice car. I had a job that challenged me, and despite the fact I worked for my father, I did need to prove myself.

Constantly.

I lived under a radar of expectations—probably more so than anyone else who worked for Tye Corp.

My father hadn't built an empire by not expecting perfection.

From his children, especially.

"Work okay?" Lleyton asked.

God only knows how long I'd zoned out for.

"Uh, yeah," I said. "It's going well. Just closed a big job."

"Nice."

I nodded, taking another pull of my beer.

Lleyton was the closest thing I had to a best friend. He was my best friend, even if I probably wasn't his. He was my only friend, if I was being honest.

I'd known him since we were seniors in high school, all through university, and I told him most things that were going on in my life. Most things. He knew my secret, that I liked men. And he kept my secret. I trusted him.

When I'd come back to Sydney after three years in Melbourne, I'd simply slotted back into groove with him. Rugby, and a few beers. It was all I had time for.

At least that's what I told myself.

Yet I had needs that weren't being met, a need for physical release, and I tried to keep a lid on it. Tried to tell myself being alone was fine. And I did like my own company; I had no problem with being alone. I just needed someone to scratch an itch that, for me, wasn't only physical.

It soothed an emotional itch too.

A secret I'd never told anyone. A few men had been a temporary fix, but to ask for a permanent fix meant disclosing my sexual needs. That meant exposing my vulnerabilities and risking too much.

Not even Lleyton knew.

Because the eldest son, the heir and likely successor to the Tye Corp empire, couldn't be anything less than perfect.

And gay, as my father would like to remind me, was not perfect.

And being gay wasn't even my darkest secret.

Lleyton knocked his knee to mine. "Looking for someone?"

Shit. I'd zoned out again. "What?"

"You keep watching that door like you're waiting for someone to walk through it."

I scoffed at how ridiculous that was, but then I glanced at the door.

He laughed. "Okay, spill."

"It's not like that," I said, dispelling his innuendo implying that I was waiting for a romantic interest to walk in. Then I sighed. "The company we acquired, the big job I closed?"

"Yeah?"

"It was Kaplan," I said quietly. "And I'm expecting some retaliatory backlash from one of my new site managers."

He snorted. "For real? Like they're gonna track you down on the weekend, follow you here, and do what?"

I shrugged because it did sound ridiculous. "Well, I'm pretty sure he wants to kill me."

He sputtered. "What the fuck! Who is it? Fire his arse."

I laughed. "I can't." Well, technically I could, but I wouldn't. "It's Marshall Wise."

He stared, mouth open, his bottle halfway to his lips. "You serious?"

I tapped my bottle to his in a cheers fashion and drank. "Yep."

"The guy that these guys"—he pointed his chin to where half our team sat at the next table— "wanted to kill the other week."

"Shh, keep your voice down," I hissed.

"Do you think he'd turn up here? Is that why you keep watching the door?"

"He could," I said with a shrug. "He knew I'd be here."

"Yeah, but he wouldn't . . ."

I drained my beer. "He was pretty pissed. You know the big Samoan guy, Taka?"

Lleyton nodded. "Nice guy."

"He had to drag Wise out of the office."

His eyes widened. "Holy shit. What did you do?"

"Smiled at him."

Lleyton laughed and shook his head. "Then let him come and try his luck. Until then, it's your shout."

A few more beers later, Lleyton glanced over my shoulder. "Ah, shit. Don't look now. But someone's here to try his luck."

I turned and, sure enough, half the North Ryde rugby team walked in—we'd heard they'd had a convincing win—and a drunk Marshall Wise was front and centre.

He scanned the bar, found me, and tried to straighten up. His smile died and his eyes hardened. His big mate, Taka, put his arm around him and steered him to the bar.

"Jeez," Lleyton mumbled. "He really hates you, doesn't he?"

I smiled, that fire in my chest burning a little warmer. "I'm counting on it."

"The fuck are you smiling at?" Marshall yelled from the bar. He was glaring at me, fire raging in his eyes. "You wanna fucking go?"

Grinning, I stood up—along with my entire team who now stood behind me—and I put my beer down. "You have no idea how much I want you to try."

He launched for me, but two of his teammates stopped him and security threw him out. His mates threw him in a cab, and I probably should have been glad no punches were thrown.

But honestly? I was disappointed.

Work on Monday was going to be interesting.

CHAPTER 3

MARSHALL

HONESTLY, FUCK VALENTINE TYE.

Fuck him for ruining rugby. Fuck him for ruining my Saturday night.

Fuck him for ruining my life.

I wasn't letting him ruin my job as well.

I was good at my job. I worked hard and did everything within my power to be the best. I was the youngest site manager at one of Sydney's best construction firms for a good fucking reason.

Well, Sydney's best construction firms until Tye Corp bought them out.

Fuck Tye Corp especially.

It wasn't bad enough that they'd monopolised the entire hardware industry in Australia, but now they'd begun branching out into construction companies, trying to sew up the entire fucking industry.

And if Valentine thought I was answering to him on any fucking thing, he was in for a rude shock. I'd fill in my reports, I'd tick all the boxes, like I always did. But I was on-site manager. Not an in-office manager.

I would keep my arse on the construction site and only set foot in their new fancy head office if I was dragged kicking and screaming.

Which was working just fine until Wednesday morning when a car pulled in. A very expensive car that I assumed belonged to my client. The Mercer bosses had the kind of money for Lamborghinis, so I dusted off my hands and began walking out to greet them.

Until Valentine got out of the car, in his expensive suit with his perfect hair.

I stopped walking, snarled at him, turned on my heel, and walked back inside.

"Mr Wise," he called out.

I stopped walking.

He'd called me Mr Wise. No doubt a reminder of the professionalism that was expected of me.

And this *was* my job. And possibly my way out. Because at the end of this contract, when the Mercer bosses were impressed with me, I'd be asking them for a job.

So I had to do the best job I could. Which meant not getting fired before then.

I turned around to find him closer than I'd expected him to be. "Mr Tye," I said with as much contempt as I dared.

He smirked.

I hated that smirk more than anything else.

Don't punch him in his stupid mouth. Don't punch him in his stupid mouth.

"I'm busy," I said, turning around and walking away.

I didn't stop until I got back to my work bench, which was a sheet of plywood across two sawhorses with blueprints and spreadsheets sprawled out. My tape measure was my paperweight.

I wanted nothing more than to flip it and fucking scream, but I took a deep breath and put my head down, grasping for composure.

"You're so angry." His soft voice was far too close behind me, and when I turned around, he was standing right fucking there. In his expensive suit, smelling of expensive cologne. His jaw bulged. His eyes flashed with . . . something.

Then his gaze dropped to my lips.

What the fuck?

"You're damn right I'm angry," I said. The way he was looking at me put me in a tailspin. Then I remembered him on his knees with my cock in his mouth, and my gaze cut to his.

I would bet money his thoughts had gone to the same place.

He licked his lips.

Like it was his ploy all along to throw me off my guard.

"You were expected to report into the office on Monday," he said, his tone annoyingly neutral.

"We were laying concrete," I said. "If you knew anything about construction, you'd know I had to be here."

"I know," he said, like he knew very well, and he couldn't care less.

"They finished yesterday," I added.

"I know." He studied my face. The tip of his tongue wet the corner of his lips. "Yet you didn't show this morning either."

"I'm busy. I forwarded the reports. Check your inbox."

"I did."

I turned back to my paperwork. "Were they wrong?"

"No. Everything was perfect."

"Then what are you doing here?"

"I thought you might have felt bad after your outburst on Saturday night."

I spun to face him, anger bubbling right under the surface.

He chewed on the inside of his lip, his eyes darting to my mouth and back to my eyes. There was something in his gaze, something in those dark eyes that looked a lot like excitement. Daring. Desire.

Like my anger aimed at him was turning him on.

He was getting off on this?

Then I understood.

He wanted me to hit him so he could fire me. Press charges, probably. Ruin me like his father ruined mine.

"If you want to fire me," I murmured, "just do it. You think you can hold this over me like some kinda power game, you're dead wrong. Because I don't give one fuck. And as much as I'd love to punch your fucking head in, I won't give you the satisfaction of taking me to court."

He seemed pleased by this. "I don't want to take you to court, Marshall. That's not how I play."

"Then what do you want?"

He looked at my mouth again, then that fucker looked down at my dick before his eyes raked back up to mine. "I think I want to play this game a little bit longer. It's fun, don't you think?"

What the fuck?

"Is my life a game to you?" I asked, my voice deathly quiet. I stepped in close, my eyes lasering into his. "You think this is funny? Do you *want* me to lose my shit with you?"

He grunted quietly. Not a scoff or a grunt of disgust.

Oh no, this was a grunt of desire.

Holy shit.

He licked his lips again, then his lips parted, and he inhaled like he was just about to say something—

"Everything okay in here?" Millsy said from the end of the room. Taka was right behind him. Both of them looked at us with wide eyes.

Valentine took a small step back. "Everything's fine. Mr Wise was just explaining concreting to me."

What the actual fuck?

"Yeah, I was getting to the part where he should know better than entering a construction site without the proper occupational health and safety gear." I collected a helmet off my table and threw it to him.

He caught it easily and smiled. "So true." Then he gave me a nod, then nodded to Millsy and Taka on his way out. "Keep up the good work."

I watched that fucker walk away until I couldn't see him anymore. Even then, my blood was still just under the boiling point, my chest heaving.

"What was that about?" Taka asked.

I looked up at him, then back out to where Valentine had gone. "I wish I knew."

Rugby training went well and, considering I never saw Valentine for the rest of the week, work went well too.

Everything was on schedule and on budget.

By the time Friday night came around, I was looking forward to a quiet night in with a few beers and a pizza and whatever Netflix had to offer.

I didn't want a big night. I needed to be on my game tomorrow. We were playing Randwick and they were always tough. They'd made the quarter finals last year, so I was excited to see their form this season.

I needed to be on my game.

And I needed to *not* think about Valentine goddamn Tye and how he looked at me with those dark eyes, at my mouth like he wanted to devour me, how he made that noise.

And how he looked on his knees in that bathroom cubicle with those perfect lips around my cock.

No. *Stop it*.

I needed to think about my rugby game. Not whatever game he was playing and how he was messing with my head.

God, how I hated him.

RANDWICK WAS TOUGH. I got hit hard, copped a swinging arm to the chin, and saw stars for a second, but thankfully, I didn't hit the deck. I also got flattened in a ruck and would have some nice sprig marks across my ribs.

But I gave as good as I got.

Crawford, the guy who'd tried to break my jaw, would have a nice shiner tomorrow, and I wasn't one bit fucking sorry.

And we won. Nothing like adding insult to injury.

But oddly enough, the Randwick guys were good value. We all went back to their local pub for a few beers after the game and I laughed with Crawford, even bought him a beer.

After that, a few of the guys wanted to head to Bondi. I knew there was a good chance of seeing Valentine there— they'd played at Bondi—and I'd had enough alcohol and a decent knock to the head to make me think that was a great idea.

It was late and there was a different vibe than there had been at Randwick: a lot of side-eyes and a glaring lack of sense of humour. The boys didn't stay long but I wanted to kick on. The band was great, and there were a few guys who gave me a second look, and with the potential for a hook-up, I stayed.

It had nothing to do with the fact that Valentine was there with his preppy mates, and it had absolutely nothing to do with the fact I'd caught him looking in my direction.

So I might have wanted to antagonise him a bit. Sue me.

After I'd had enough beer and was two vodkas deep, I decided that maybe hooking up with some stranger in front of Valentine was in order.

I wanted to see how he'd react. See if he cared.

And when a pretty little twink gave me a shy smile, I nodded his way. He blushed and I happened to like how it looked, so I lifted his chin for a closer inspection.

Except, apparently pretty twink's boyfriend didn't like that. He got in my face, and there was pushing and shoving, and security gave me a private escort out onto the street.

It certainly wasn't my first time.

I tried to get an Uber, but at two in the morning on the weekend in Bondi, that was like winning the freaking lottery.

And then, to make my night a whole lot more fun, a group of guys decided I was easy pickings. They shoved me into the alley behind the pub. "He's the fag from the bar," one of them said.

Oh, so that's what this was? A hate crime.

There were four of them, and I liked my chances of taking two of them, at least. Bolstered by the shots of courage and lime, and with my back to the wall, I sized them up, raised my fists, and grinned at them. "Yeah. So tomorrow you can tell all your friends you got your shit clapped by a fag."

I fucking smashed the first guy and one of them got a hit on me from the side, so I swung at him, and another guy came at me, but then suddenly there was a whole fucking crowd in the middle of us. I thought for a second that I was probably gonna die in a wild brawl . . . until I realised they were on my side.

Well, not really.

But they stopped the fight.

And some familiar guys were dragging me up the street. It was the Lane Cove Tiger boys. "Just put him in my car," a voice said.

"You sure?"

There was mumbling, but then I found myself being thrown into a very familiar black Lamborghini. "The fuck?"

"Shut up and put your seatbelt on," one of them said. I think his name was Lleyton. Then the door was slammed shut and my blood was still pumping from the fight. And then Valentine Tye got in behind the wheel.

Valentine fucking Tye.

"What the fuck?" I said.

"Put your seatbelt on," he snapped, then whipped the car out onto the street.

"Fuck you."

He smirked.

God, I hated him.

We drove past the hotel where the crowd was now being dispersed. "Those fuckers deserve a good beating," I said.

"And you were going to give it to them? Five to your one?"

I tried to remember. I thought there was only four . . .

What the fuck ever.

"Yeah, I coulda taken them."

He glanced over at me, then went back to looking out the windscreen. Fuck I hated that his side profile was so fucking good. All sharp lines and angles, with his perfect fucking hair.

He weaved us through traffic, probably way too fast. Or maybe it was just this car.

I hated that I liked his car.

The inside was all black, everything was sleek, and I hated that it suited him.

"Nice car."

A brief pause. "Thank you."

My eye was starting to hurt now. Well, more to the point, I was starting to feel it now. And it was wet.

I touched it and there was blood on my fingers. "Fuck."

He gave me another unimpressed glance. "Hm."

I pulled the visor down to check in the mirror, and yeah, it was split at the corner of my eye, under my eyebrow.

We were going through the Harbour Tunnel and the silence and smooth purr of the engine was enough to lull me to sleep.

Maybe it was the alcohol. Or the two decent knocks to the head I'd had today.

But the next thing I knew, I was being hauled out of the car and led to an elevator. *Where the hell am I?*

"I don't live here," I said.

"No. I do."

I focused on the voice to find who it belonged to and groaned.

Him, again.

Or still.

Whatever.

"What the fuck are we—"

Then the elevator opened, and he took my arm down a short hall. There were only two doors. He stopped at the one on the right, unlocked it, and pushed me inside.

Or maybe I fell.

Then I was being shoved into a seat at a dining table. The room was dark, but I could see it was huge, with massive floor to ceiling windows. A light came on, partly illuminating a sleek designer kitchen, and a black cat that watched me, judged me, from the floor near the fridge.

It was jet black, with long legs and a pointy face, and it was looking at me with as much disdain as Valentine often did.

It was the most Valentine-looking cat I'd ever seen.

"What's your cat's name?"

"Enzo."

I snorted. I had no clue what an Enzo was, but it suited it. "He looks just like you."

Valentine was now sitting across from me, his knees against mine. He had a first aid kit on the table and a wet cottonwool ball in his hand, his gaze fixed on the corner of my eye.

I pulled my head back. "The fuck are you doing?"

"Hold still," he said. His voice was so quiet, so calm.

He dabbed the cottonwool at my skin, and it stung but I didn't flinch. I didn't want to give him the satisfaction.

After a few swipes, he inspected it. "You shouldn't need stitches," he said. Then he went to put one of those butterfly clips on it, but I grabbed his wrist.

"I don't need that."

His dark eyes cut to mine. "It's either this, or I take you to hospital. Your choice."

I snarled at him and let him put the stupid clip on me.

He packed up his first aid kit. "You can sleep here tonight," he said.

What?

"Why would I do that?" Or more to the point . . . "What makes you think I'd do that?"

"Because you've been drinking, you took a hit to the head, and you kept losing consciousness in the car."

"I did fucking not."

He gave me another one of those unimpressed looks and stood up, then walked to the kitchen. "You can take the couch. Or the floor. Choice is yours."

I didn't lose consciousness. I was falling asleep.

Maybe.

"My choice is my own place," I said, then stood up. I wasn't that drunk. I'd certainly been a lot more intoxicated than this.

But then for some reason, Valentine had hold of my arm and the room was all funny angles.

Shit.

Maybe I *was* drunk.

But it still annoyed me. His hand on me. His body so close to mine. Those eyes.

That mouth.

"Fuck."

He hummed, a real low, filthy sound. "I would say *yes, please,* but you're not in any state."

What the . . . ?

"My dick works just fine."

He studied my face and then got real close, his nose an inch from mine, and he palmed my cock.

Holy shit.

It took a second for my brain and body to catch up to each other, and even though my brain was like *hell no, not him*, my dick was definitely on board.

My dick was always on board. A whiff of attention and it started to thicken.

Valentine smirked, his eyebrow flicked upward, and he began to massage me through my jeans. "Hm. Maybe . . ."

"The fuck do you mean *maybe*?" I said. I batted his hand off my dick. "Like I'd fuck you anyway. I fucking hate you."

His eyes flashed with black fire and he licked his lips, still far too close. "Good. That's what I'm banking on."

What the actual fuck.

He pushed me against the table, his body pressed against mine. "I want you to hate me. I *need* you to hate me." Then he popped the button on my jeans and wrapped his fingers around my cock, pumping me rough and hard. "And when you fuck me with your monster cock, I need you to *hate* me as hard as you can."

CHAPTER 4

VALENTINE

IT WAS A NOW-OR-NEVER SITUATION. HE'D HAD ENOUGH to drink that he'd either agree with me or punch me in the mouth. I wouldn't have minded either, but I was hoping for the former.

He was also intoxicated enough that if he did agree, he'd be free of inhibitions and maybe it'd hurt more.

For longer.

I had nothing to lose and very little likelihood of having this opportunity again.

Not with him, anyway. Someone who hated me and had a cock that size . . .

I had to put the offer out there.

And his cock was interested.

I didn't care if he was drunk, and I didn't care about the cut above his eye. It'd stopped bleeding and, to be honest, a little bite of pain made it fun.

So maybe if he didn't want to fuck me, I could suck him dry again.

I wouldn't have minded that either.

"The fuck is your problem?" he asked, his voice rough. He made no attempt to remove my hand.

I thumbed his slit, smearing precome, and twisted my hand back down his shaft so I could pump him again. *My god, the size of him.* "I want you to fuck me . . . hard. And my problem is that I'm not face down on my bed with your horse-cock inside me, that's what the fuck my problem is."

His mouth fell open.

"So, you either follow me to my room and have the best arse you've ever had," I said. I let go of his cock and turned, walking to the hall. I didn't turn around. "Or, if the answer's no, you can call yourself a cab or sleep on the couch or the street. I don't care."

I got to my room, my heart pounding.

This was it.

This was the moment.

The sleeping-on-the-street comment was probably a bit much but I needed to remind him that I was a piece of shit and he hated me.

I threw lube and condoms onto the bed, pulled off my shoes and took off my jeans. I was pulling my shirt over my head when my door swung inward, and he stood there with his huge, erect cock still hanging out of his pants.

But his eyes.

He was wild.

And pissed off.

I smiled and, dropping my shirt to the floor, I knelt on the bed.

And I waited.

My chest heaving, my blood burning hot. It had been too long, far too long, and I needed this too much.

When I heard the foil wrapper being torn open, I could have wept. Then when his knee pressed onto the mattress behind me, I lowered my head to the bed and stretched my back like a cat.

He still wore his jeans, undone and open. He still wore his shoes and shirt, as if I wasn't worth his time to take them off.

I preened a little.

A quick squirt of lube, but no prep, no warning.

He simply gripped my hips and drove himself into me. I thought he might split me open. I thought he was too big, and I couldn't take it. I bit out a cry, a groan.

"This what you wanted?" he asked, his voice rough.

"Yes," I cried out, gripping the bed covers. It was exactly what I wanted. What I needed.

He pushed all the way in. All the way, I was sure of it. And when his hips met my arse, he hit that wall inside me and I bucked up, crying out.

He pushed my head back down to the mattress, rough and strong, his big hand holding the back of my head down. His cock was buried so far in me, the pain of it was exquisite.

"Stay the fuck down, you piece of shit," he said. "You want me to fuck you like I hate you?" He pulled out and drove back into me. "Because I fucking do."

He fucked me. Hard, rough.

Yes, yes. Just like this. This is what I needed.

"You're good for nothing," he bit out as he fucked me over and over. "Piece of fucking shit."

Yes. *Yes.*

Then his hand was on my shoulder, pressing me down, and his other gripped my hip, his nails biting into my skin, holding me so he could fill me how he wanted. He leaned over me, driving his cock into me deeper, at a much better angle.

So much better.

Fuck, yes.

His hot breath on the back of my neck, the scrape of his teeth. His cock incredibly hard, hitting the very places inside me that craved this.

"Look at how you take my cock," he grunted. "Like the fucking whore you are."

That serenity I'd been craving, searching for, been desperate for, settled over me.

And I came.

My cock untouched. Just pure bliss.

My release was intense, physical, and emotional. I let go of it all and that cloak of darkness that had been wrapped around me for too long was gone. It was better than I'd imagined it could be. So utterly perfect.

He came with a roar, pushing me down on the bed and ramming into me, his thick cock pulsing inside me, filling the condom.

God, I could feel it.

Every spurt.

It was heaven.

He shuddered and groaned, but then he pulled out of me.

I was bereft by his absence, hollowed out and empty. I wanted him to stay inside me. I wanted him to stay inside me until he was ready to fuck me again.

I wanted his seed inside me. So he'd know he owned me, and he could treat me as if he owned me anytime he wanted.

I wanted it to never end.

With a groan, I fell to the mattress. The gape of my ass, the residual pain and pleasure had my thighs quivering, my body jerking.

I felt so unbelievably good. That fire in me, a mere burning ember for now, glowing warm and lovely. I dared to roll onto my back, to face him. To face the consequences, perhaps. And to ask him to do it again.

But he was already gone.

I SPENT Sunday soaking my sore and used body in a hot bath, only leaving my apartment to collect a grocery delivery from the foyer in the evening.

I also spent the day relishing every ache, every twinge. The high of the incredible fucking I'd got last night lingered on every nerve.

I was lounging in front of the TV with Enzo asleep on me when I got a text from Lleyton.

How was drunk Rocky in the car? I'm assuming you survived?

Drunk Rocky. I snorted at that, but to answer his question, I did more than survive. I'd never felt so good.

I sure did.

Monday morning arrived and I wasn't surprised that Marshall didn't show up to the managers' meeting. He should have, but he'd made it pretty clear that he thought his time was better spent elsewhere. And I did have his paperwork and reports, so him sitting in head office for an hour probably wasn't the best use of his time. But it wasn't an optional invitation.

Other managers had to comply, and so should he.

His insubordination reflected poorly on me, and I needed to lay down some rules.

Rules *and* boundaries.

Because I also needed him to fulfil my other needs, so

this was a minefield to navigate, and it wasn't a minefield I'd ever walked through before.

I was aware there were lines being crossed, and this had *bad idea* written all over it, and I also knew the scales of privilege were weighted in my favour.

I knew all of that.

And yet I didn't want to stop.

When the staff meeting was over, I buzzed my assistant, Shayla. "Can you please set up a meeting with Mr Marshall Wise in my office at five o'clock today? Thank you."

"Sure thing," she replied.

I doubted that. He would probably rather walk through lava than have a meeting with me, but this was a work issue.

Yet sure enough, at two minutes after five, Marshall Wise arrived at my office. His eye was a little swollen at the corner, but the cut was healing. He wore his long cargos and work boots, and he was covered in what appeared to be dust and dirt. He offered no apology for making a mess on my office furniture and I could deduce that was because he wasn't the least bit sorry.

His jaw bulged and those fiery eyes lasered into me.

"Thank you for coming in," I began.

"Like I had a choice."

I bit back a smile because, oh boy, his anger aimed at me was so good.

"We need to discuss your absences from our team meetings," I began. He went to speak, opened his mouth to do so, and I raised my hand. "It's a requirement of all site managers and giving you an exemption is not fair on the others, and it reflects poorly upon myself."

"No, making it a requirement to waste a site manager's time is a poor reflection on you."

I could barely hide my surprise, but . . . was he wrong?

I wasn't sure he was.

"Do you have any suggestions for workplace communications that better suits everyone's time?"

He squinted at me. "Are you taking the piss?"

"No. It's a serious question. If you can put forward a better option, I'll be happy to hear it."

He stared at me—clearly not expecting me to ask this—then his gaze went to the window and around my office, then back to me. "I'll . . . I'll have to have a think. But not meetings. You got all the information you need in our reports and sh—stuff. And on a Monday morning of all days. That's the worst. When does a client wanna see something or make changes or request my time? Monday morning."

"Okay, fair enough. I look forward to hearing some alternatives."

He squinted at me again as if he was trying to figure me out.

Good luck with that . . .

"Sooo," he hedged, about to stand up. "Is that it?"

Here goes nothing . . .

"Matters pertaining to work, yes."

He was halfway standing when he cut me an oh-shit look. He got to his full height slower, his face a stoic mask. "Ah, yeah, about that—"

"I won't discuss personal matters here," I said sharply. "Though I would like to talk, yes."

"And if I don't want to?"

"I can't make you," I said, looking up at him, my expression neutral. Thank god he couldn't hear my heart knocking against my ribs. "But if you're interested in hearing my proposal, be at my place at nine."

"Proposal?"

"Nine o'clock."

His nostrils flared and the loathing in his glare made my blood warm. I wanted to tell him to save his anger, to lock it down tight until I was ready for him to unleash it, but I was serious about not discussing personal matters at work.

A boundary more for his protection than mine.

He turned and left without another word, and I had to wonder if he'd show up. I hoped he would, though part of me questioned his defiance and how perhaps he wouldn't show up purely out of spite.

But I had a feeling he'd show. A burning feeling low in my belly that reminded me of hope.

———

By EIGHT THIRTY, my nerves were almost electric. By eight fifty, I'd convinced myself he wasn't coming, and when nine o'clock came and went, I was disappointed.

But not surprised.

I poured myself a glass of red wine as some kind of consolation prize when the intercom buzzer went, and I smiled when I saw it was him on the camera. It was ten past nine and I had to wonder if he'd made me wait on purpose.

Probably.

I buzzed him through and, leaving my front door open for him, I took a mouthful of wine for courage. I heard the elevator but still jumped at the gentle knock on my door. "Come in."

He came to an awkward stop near the couch. He wore jeans and a hoodie, and he shoved his hands into his pockets.

Instead of any kind of greeting or smile, I gestured to the bottle. "Would you like a glass of wine?"

"No."

Okay then.

I took my glass and opted for the couch, hoping it was more casual than the dining table. I sat, and he waited for a few beats, clearly unsure of what to do.

"Take a seat," I suggested.

He came around the couch, awkward and uncomfortable, and sat down at the same time Enzo saw me and decided to jump onto my lap. I ran my hand from his head down his back and he sat and stared at our company.

"Did I come here so you can *both* judge me?" Marshall asked.

"I'm not judging you," I said.

Marshall nodded to Enzo. "He is."

Then, like the treasonous fleabag he was, Enzo stepped off me and padded across the distance between us to curl up on Marshall's lap instead.

He made a face. "Uhhh."

"I see now why his full pedigree name is Enzo the Traitor."

Marshall's gaze cut to mine. "Was that . . . did you just make a joke?"

"Maybe." I sighed and sipped my wine. "Your eye looks good. No swelling, slight bruising. I thought you'd have a black eye for sure."

He stared at me, his jaw ticking. "You said you had a proposal," he said, cutting right to the chase.

No small talk, then.

Good.

"Yes. About what we did on Saturday night."

His eyes widened and his cheeks bloomed with colour. "Ah, yeah, about that." He fixed his gaze on the window, flinching with uncertainty. "I, uh, I'm not entirely sure what that was."

I never took my eyes off him and sipped my wine. "It was exactly what I wanted you to do."

His eyes cut to mine and his lips parted. He was clearly unsure of what to say. Or perhaps he was unsure of what to make of me. "You, uh . . . you—"

"I'd like you to do it again," I said, as if I was discussing the weather.

He stared at me as though I'd just asked him to rob a bank with me. "The fuck?"

"Yes. Thoroughly and with as much contempt as you can holster."

He dumped Enzo onto the couch and walked to the end of the room, then turned to face me, his hand to his forehead. He looked a little pale, or perhaps it was the low lighting. "What—and I mean this with as much sincerity as possible—the actual fuck? You want me to hate-fuck you?"

Hate-fuck.

That made me smile. "Yes."

Now he looked at me as if I'd lost my mind. Maybe I had.

"So that's your proposition?" he asked. He was very obviously stunned. "You want me to . . . like *Indecent Proposal* or some freaky shit? What the hell is wrong with you?"

"That list is quite long."

"Exactly. You don't want me to fuck you, you need a therapist."

"I had one. He assured me my methods were, if safe and consensual, perfectly fine."

Marshall gawped at me. It was almost comical. "Then you need a new therapist."

I had one of those too. I'd had several therapists, psychologists, and even one psychiatrist. I knew what my issues were, I knew from where they stemmed, and I knew all too well how to soothe them.

"No, I need someone who can't stand me to hold me down and fuck me."

He stared at me, then he laughed. "You're . . . you're . . ." He shook his head. "What makes you think I'd be even remotely interested in fulfilling your fucked-up fantasies? Why would I do this for you?"

"Because you hate me. You look at me as if you'd like to strangle me or beat the shit out of me." I sipped my wine again, meeting his gaze. "Plus, you have a huge cock, and you know how to use it."

His mouth fell open.

"And you have to admit," I said with a hint of smugness. "I have a great arse, and I would be a sure thing twice a week."

"Twice a week?"

"Yes. Once a week would be anal, just like you did on Saturday night. The other night, whichever night you choose, you can use me for whatever you want."

He stared at me, obviously trying to gauge my sincerity, and when he saw I wasn't joking, he let out a laugh. "Holy shit, you're serious."

"Yes."

He turned to face the wall of glass, his hand fixed in his hair. It gave me a wonderful side view of his body. Strong, fit, and— Was that a bulge in his jeans?

It was honestly difficult to tell, given the size of his dick.

I gave him time to think this over, though I was fast losing hope. I knew it was a long shot at best.

"As for work," I added, "nothing changes. You still do

your job, and I do mine. You get no special favours, and I still expect you to meet all your duty requirements. No more, no less. And you should expect me to still be fair and reasonable, as I am with all other managers. No more, no less." I shrugged. "And we tell no one, of course."

"You know that's real easy for you to say. You're the boss. Nothing *would* change for you. But when your 'proposal' ends badly—which you know it fucking will, right?— I'll be thrown under the bus."

"How?"

"You can't see the power exchange here? Jesus Christ, you know what? The fact you can't see it is reason enough for me to tell you to fuck off." He shook his head. "This is insane."

"The power exchange is in your favour," I said. It wasn't exactly true, but I held his gaze. "You get to treat me like garbage. You can walk in here whenever you want, throw me down, put a load in me, and walk out."

His mouth opened wider, as did his eyes.

I shrugged and sipped my wine.

"Are you . . . ?" He shook his head, words clearly failing him.

"Insane? No. Serious? Yes." I looked down at his crotch. "And I can tell you like the sound of it."

He adjusted himself. "Jesus Christ."

I put my wine glass on the coffee table and crossed my legs. "Your job will not be affected. You have my word."

"That's not good enough."

"What else do you want?"

"I don't know. Christ." He ran his hand through his hair again. "You know there are clubs for this kinda shit? Sex clubs or whatever. They do this shit."

"I've tried them," I replied. "They only play the part.

They don't *really* hate me. You, on the other hand, don't even try to hide it."

"Why should I hide it?" he said. That look of utter contempt for me was back. It made me feel . . . something. "It's no secret what your family did to mine. People should know what a fucking piece of shit you are."

I bit back a hum and tried not to smile as his insult sent a shiver through me. "Yes," I murmured. "And wouldn't you like me to pay for that? By holding my face into the mattress while you rough-fuck me, to prove again and again that you're—"

He put his hand up. "Yeah, that's enough. I'm done here."

He got to the door when my voice stopped him.

"I'll give you a week to think about it. No strings attached, no questions asked, just sex and nothing more. Like friends with benefits—"

With his hand on the door handle, he gave me a snarl over his shoulder. "We are *not* friends."

I smiled at him. "And that makes it so much better."

CHAPTER 5

MARSHALL

Valentine fucking Tye was messed up.

I knew there was something lurking under that perfect façade. I just didn't know how messed up it'd get.

There was something between us. An undeniable spark. A spark that I thought was pure, unadulterated hatred.

Turns out, he thought it was something else.

And okay, I'll admit . . . when I was drunk and at his house, that burning desire to punch the shit outta him was a thrill. He put my senses on high alert.

Then he asked me to fuck him. Rough and hard. Fuck him with every ounce of hatred I could muster.

And I was drunk enough and turned on enough to do it.

I fucked him *hard*.

I'd never been so rough with anyone in my life. Never during sex, anyway.

I'd pushed his face into the bed and pounded into him as if my life depended on it. I wanted to hurt him, and I wanted to show him his place.

That I was better than him and that I was in charge, and I'd fuck him into submission.

It had to have hurt him.

I had plenty of guys refuse to take my cock or stop halfway because I was too big.

He took me like a champion.

And even though I knew I had to be hurting him, I couldn't stop. I *wanted* to hurt him. I wanted him to beg me to stop. I wanted to hear the pleading in his voice.

I would have stopped—if he'd asked.

But he never did.

Oh, no. In fact, he'd begged for more. And when I shoved the back of his head and held him down, calling him a piece of shit, he came all over himself.

I didn't care at the time. It was so fucking hot, and his arse . . .

Christ.

When he'd said his arse was good, he wasn't lying. Hands down, the best piece of arse I'd ever had.

Tight, all the way in. And he took all of me. And when he came, his body milked me. It was exquisite.

I came so fucking hard.

When I pulled out of him, I expected anger or tears, threats, or something.

But his whole body was shuddering, he'd come all over himself without even touching himself. And the look on his face . . . There were no tears, no shock, no anger.

Oh no. He had a look of serenity on his face. Like I'd dumped his body at the gates of heaven.

So, yeah. Valentine Tye was messed up.

And then he asked me to go to his place. He had a proposal, he'd said.

I wasn't gonna go. I was certain he was going to tell me I'd hurt him and I was fired or some-fucking-thing.

But he'd said *proposal*.

So I went out of morbid curiosity, and out of all the things I'd imagined him saying, what he'd come out with was nowhere on my list.

He wanted me to do it again.

Once or twice a week.

He wanted me to use the hatred I felt for him to hate-fuck him as hard as I dared. The harder the better, even.

You can walk through that door anytime you like, put a load in me, and walk out.

Put a load in me.

Oh yeah. He was messed up, no doubt about it.

And the even crazier part?

I was considering saying yes.

Actually, I was pretty sure I was going to say yes, I was just waiting for the voice of reason to overrule my dick.

And waiting.

But it never came.

No, because instead of the voice in my head saying, *this is the reddest flag to ever exist* and *this will end so badly there will be no survivors*, the voice in my head was saying, *you get to show that motherfucker what a piece of shit he is twice a week* and *you can own him with your cock and treat him like the garbage he is.*

And I kept hearing him say *put a load in me* over and over and my dick had never wanted something so bad. I'd had a near permanent semi since.

Christ.

I was going to say yes.

Taka clicking his fingers in front of my face snapped me out of my head.

"You in there?" he asked.

We were at work. It was Friday, just before lunch, and god only knew how long I'd zoned out.

"Shit, sorry. What's up?"

He nodded to the parking lot. "You got company."

I turned, and sure enough, there was a black Lambo beside the work trucks, and Valentine was walking over.

Fuck.

Dressed in his stupidly expensive suits, tailored to fit his body like a glove. Carrying a laptop, or something. Though at least this time he had a workplace helmet under his arm. He put it on as he strode over, his long legs making short work of the distance.

God, I hated him.

My blood ran hot, and my hands were automatic fists. I had to make a concerted effort to unclench my jaw.

Even just seeing him made me mad.

"Morning," he said, more to Taka and Millsy than me. Then he looked at me. "Got a minute?"

My stomach twisted, certain he was about to ask me for my answer. Certain he was about to tell me to forget it. Certain he was going to tell me it was a joke.

We walked over to my makeshift desk, and he opened his laptop.

He discussed a new shipment delay, a trade-off for stock between us, and another worksite to keep both of us pushing forward with the least amount of disruption. It just meant we had to focus on the electrical fit-out instead of insulation next week, but we should be back to normal schedules the following week.

He never mentioned anything else.

Nothing personal, just like he'd said.

I wasn't sure why that bothered me.

I hated that he rattled me so easily.

He closed his laptop and put it back under his arm, thanked me for my time, and left.

I was sure he was purely making a point so I wouldn't forget his offer. Like him turning up here in those suit pants that hugged his arse like that would sway my decision.

I didn't need swaying.

Or maybe he turned up here knowing it would stoke my fires of hatred some more.

I didn't need any help with that either.

Because I hated him enough to sustain me for three lifetimes.

"Everything okay, boss?" Taka said.

"Yep," I replied, not taking my eyes off Valentine until his pretentiously expensive car was out of the lot. "Everything's fine."

"You know," he replied with his usual grin. "When we play his team in rugby, I think you might wanna sit that game out?"

I shot him a look. "Why?"

"Because I know you. You will try and take his head off, and that won't end well for you."

I grinned at him. "But it'd be so worth it."

"Yeah, but one of their guys will hit you back, then I gotta get involved. The whole team'll get involved, then their whole team'll get involved. There'll be black eyes and sin bins everywhere."

I laughed. "Sounds like fun to me."

He shook his head. "You need to find a better way to deal with your anger, my friend."

Like walking into Valentine's place anytime I wanted, putting a load in him and walking out.

"I'm working on it," I said.

"Good. Let's work on some lunch first. I'm starving."

WE PLAYED Leichhardt at our home field on Saturday, and we won, of course. I managed to keep my cool during the game—I might have tackled harder than was completely necessary and mouthed off a bit—but there was no push or shove, no fists thrown.

And I was even on my best behaviour at the pub afterwards.

I got drunk enough for two men, but all in all, it was a good night. We laughed, we watched the Waratah's game on the big screen, and I was home in bed by midnight.

Alone.

On Sunday, I woke up hungover and figured a good wank in the shower would make me feel better. It usually did.

I could normally pluck any memory of any sexual encounter and bust a nut pretty quick, but this time a certain someone starred front and centre.

Of him bent over on his bed, his tiny arse taking every inch of me, buried deep and tight. Of me pushing his head down, holding him down, fucking him relentlessly while telling him how much I hated him . . .

Yeah, I came just as hard that time too.

It was starting to mess with my head.

No, *Valentine* was starting to mess with my head.

So I went about the rest of my day as I did every Sunday. Laundry, groceries, housework, and dinner with my parents.

I had dinner with my parents every Sunday. Mum would cook up a feast and tell me to come around. I usually ate until I wanted to puke, then she'd give me enough left-overs in containers to do me for a week.

It was hardly a chore. I loved spending time with them.

Mum would sometimes drop past my unit uninvited, and we'd have a cuppa. We were a close family. After everything we'd been through . . .

"I'll be around next Sunday," I said as I got into my dual-cab ute, leftovers on the seat beside me. And I got back to my place feeling pretty good . . .

Until I got into bed and snaked my hand down towards my cock, and my thoughts took a nosedive into Valentine territory.

I let go of my dick in frustrated disgust because god fucking dammit, he was ruining my life.

I was *letting* him ruin my life.

Maybe if I fucked him twice a week, my body would stop craving it and my mind would stop thinking it.

What about your job, Marshall? You know this won't end well.

Yeah, but I had no intention of sticking around after this Mercer contract was finished anyway. I'd see out these next six months, fuck him twice a week for the duration, then turn around and leave him when I was finished with him.

Use him, play him, wreck him.

My grand master plan.

So, putting my plan into action and needing to take back some control—and needing to maybe throw him off his game a little—I decided I'd be a good little site-manager employee and turn up for the meeting first thing Monday morning.

I had no delivery to be on site for anyway, and my team could handle themselves for an hour.

It was worth it just to see the surprise on Valentine's stupid face.

I never contributed to the meeting at all, none of us did.

It was more Valentine discussing the last week's issues, delays, budgets, yadda yadda yadda.

It just made my point. These meetings were nothing but a fat waste of everyone's time.

I liked watching him talk though. His carefully chosen words, his long, elegant fingers, his chiselled jaw, and sharp, dark eyes. Because I liked knowing that I'd been inside him, that I'd fucked him. That I'd fucked him so hard he came all over himself.

And no one here had any idea.

To them, he was so cool, calm, and collected, so superior and commanding of respect.

To me, he was nothing but a whore for cock, who had a world of issues that Freud himself wouldn't be able to fix.

So yeah, I liked sitting there knowing all this.

"Mr Wise?" Valentine said. Shit, I'd been zoning out again. Christ, I needed to focus. The others looked ready to leave. "Anything to add?"

I dropped my pen onto my blank notepad. "No. Nothing."

I was about to add that this had been a huge waste of time, but I didn't want to be disrespectful. Not in front of his staff, anyway. I respected *my* work enough to show some manners.

He called the meeting done and everyone stood up.

"Marshall, a moment," he said quietly.

I scored a few wary glances from the others as they walked out, but I stayed seated and smiled.

When the door closed behind the last of them, he waited a few seconds to speak. "So you *can* bite your tongue," he said with a smirk.

I met his gaze. "What?"

"You wanted to add something at the end there, yet you chose not to."

"Because you'd wasted enough of everyone's time already and they wanted to leave," I said flatly.

He stared, then chewed on the inside of his mouth. Was he trying not to smile? It was hard to tell.

"So have you given any further thought?" he asked.

I shot him a look. We were *not* going to discuss personal shit here . . .

"About what we could do to improve staff meetings," he added.

He was playing me.

God, I hated him.

"Yeah, we could not have them. This meeting today?" I gestured to the now empty table. "Biggest fucking waste of my time."

His face, his eyebrows, did some brief flick thing. It was hard to tell if he was surprised or offended or amused.

"This coulda been an email," I added. "Or if you *have* to do face to face meetings, have them every second week. And if your aim is to make this some team-building bullshit or if you want to find out what's really going on, I dunno, maybe include a breakfast afterward. Bacon and egg roll and a coffee. You'd be surprised what people will actually discuss in an open conversation around the breakroom. Because sitting at a table like this feels like a lecture or an interview. We're not business corporate types like you. We're builders, tradies. We don't do whatever the fuck this is."

He stared at me and a slow smile spread across his face. "Thank you."

And while I was on a roll and needing to still be the one calling the shots, I scribbled on a piece of paper from my notebook. I stood up and slid the note across the table to him.

I walked to the door, not game to turn around, though I did catch a glimpse of him when I pulled the door shut behind me.

He read the note and smiled.

9pm
Your place

I KNEW in all likelihood Valentine expected people to be on time, so I sat in my car a few extra minutes and buzzed his apartment at 9:06.

Spite and loathing were a powerful thing. Petulance too, but if this was some fucked-up game we were playing, I had to play smarter.

I wanted to make him wait longer, but my dick was fully aware of what was going to happen tonight, and it basically *made* me get out of the car.

My brain, on the other hand, spent the elevator ride telling me this was a bad, bad idea.

But still . . . it didn't stop me.

He opened the door before I could knock and stood there with a towel around his neck. He'd clearly just showered, wearing expensive lounge pants and a simple black T-shirt. It looked expensive too, the way it clung to him so perfectly.

God, I hated that he was so good looking.

He smelled good too, which I also fucking hated.

He stood aside, a silent invitation, and he closed the door behind me. He walked to the kitchen, rubbing his hair with the towel. "I've not long been home," he said. Like I cared. "I have training sessions on Monday nights, but you said nine o'clock. Can I get you a drink?"

If I cared at all, I'd have asked him what training sessions he had—it wasn't rugby training because I knew that was Tuesdays for him—but I didn't care, so I didn't ask.

"No, I'm fine. Thanks."

He poured himself a glass of water from the tap and gulped half of it, then walked to the couch and sat, looking at me expectantly to follow. I'd have preferred to sit at the table where we had a buffer between us, but that wasn't the case. So I sat on the opposite sofa. "So, your proposal . . ."

He sipped his water this time, his expression unreadable. "Yes or no?"

It rankled me that he was so blasé about it but maybe the no-nonsense, no small talk was part of the appeal.

"I have questions. And conditions."

There was the barest hint of a smile as he slid the glass of water onto the coffee table. "Good. So do I."

"You said twice a week."

"Yes. Anal sex once, the other however you see fit."

Christ. He was so methodical about this.

I ran my hand through my hair. "However I see fit is very open."

He stared, studying my face for a second, then let out a quiet sigh. "If you'd prefer I lay down some ground rules, I will," he said, so matter of fact.

I would prefer that. You seem to have some perverse requirement. I'm just here to fuck.

"Twice a week. Saturday night and Wednesday night works for me but I'm open to your schedule. I'd prefer Saturday night to be the night you fuck me because it gives me Sunday to recover."

"Recover?"

"Yes. Your cock is a lot to take, and I want to relish the aches and pains."

Jesus Christ.

"That being said, if you want to fuck me on Wednesdays as well, I won't object at all. You can, after all, do what you want."

Fucking hell.

"I like rough sex. I like to be held down and fucked hard."

"Ah, yeah, I remember."

"What you did that night was perfection. It's why I proposed this . . . arrangement."

"Pure sex."

"Nothing else," he added coldly. "I would prefer no condoms, but that would require full testing for both of us beforehand should we engage in that. Which also means you can't engage in any kind of sexual relations with anyone else for the duration of this agreement. If you do, it's over. If you meet someone you want to date, this is over. If this isn't working for either of us, it's over."

God help me.

I wasn't looking to date anyone, so that wasn't an issue. And I got tested regularly, so that wasn't an issue either. But sweet Jesus, the idea of fucking him bareback.

You can walk through that door, put a load in me, and walk out.

Yeah, my dick was well and truly on board.

"Do you have any questions about any of that?"

I shook my head. "No."

"So," he added, "while I say you can do whatever you want to me, and yes, I like to be held down and fucked hard, I don't tolerate cruelty or abuse. I expect you know the difference."

Christ.

"Yeah. You want me to tell you what a piece of shit you are while I punish you with my dick?"

His eyes flashed with desire, and he tried to hide it, but it was too late. I saw it.

"Yes," he breathed.

"And you want me to muster every ounce of loathing I have for you while I do it?"

He smirked, his eyes fixed on mine. "Yes."

"That won't be difficult."

Because I did hate him. The longer he sat there, looking all kinds of perfect in his two-million-dollar apartment, I hated him a little bit more.

He smirked at me like he'd just read my mind. "I won't tolerate rudeness or lateness," he said with a slight flicker of his eyebrow. So yes, my waiting in the car for a few extra minutes had annoyed him. Good. "I won't be shared. You only come here alone. No filming, no photos. No means no. If I say stop, you stop. Understood?"

"Perfectly."

"If you need to change the day, just ask. This is a mutual agreement, not a legally binding contract. We need to be flexible because real life happens. We will converse only via text, not at work. This is never discussed at work. Even if it's just the two of us in a room or worksite."

"Good," I said. "And if I ever feel like this is compromising my job, or if I'm treated unfairly or if I'm treated better than anyone else, this is finished."

He gave a nod. "Likewise. I expect your treatment of me at work to remain the same. I'd like to be able to say you'll remain respectful, but you don't show me respect at work as it is, so if that were to change, people might suspect something is going on."

"I show you respect," I replied. "You should hear the shit I don't say out loud."

He stared at me, raising his chin a fraction, his gaze full of humour and heat. "New rule: we don't discuss work here. At all."

I smiled at that. "Agreed. To be honest, moving forward in this agreement—" I gestured between us. "—this is the longest conversation I want to have with you."

Holding my gaze, he crossed his legs like he was trying to tempt me. Like now the rules had been discussed, the game could play on.

And this was a game I could play.

"If we're done," I said, standing up, "I'll be off."

His gaze drifted down to my semi-hard cock and his nostrils flared.

I palmed myself and rearranged my junk, then smirked at him. "Shame it's not Wednesday."

His eyes drew back up to mine, and that fire was back. "Hm."

I wasn't giving in though. Suddenly the wait until Wednesday seemed like more fun. I got to the door.

"Wait," he said.

I thought he was going to ask me to stay, to fix him up tonight instead of Wednesday, but he met me at the door with his phone. "Your number."

"You can get it from work," I said, my hand on the door handle.

"No. I won't use my position as employer to obtain personal information. You either give it to me, or we don't do this."

Fuck.

Okay, so maybe that was fair.

I gave him my number and he thumbed out a text, and a second later my phone beeped.

I didn't bother reading it. I liked being in charge, I liked being one step ahead in the game. So I opened the door, having to step into his personal space so I could swing it wide. "See you Wednesday," I murmured.

And much to my dick's dismay, I walked out.

Yeah, waiting until Wednesday was going to be so much fun. The anticipation, the thrill, the knowing . . .

Until I got into my car and read his text. No hello, no preamble.

Forward sexual health test results to this number.

Did that put him ahead of me in this push and pull game? I wasn't sure. But as soon as I got home, I made an online appointment at the clinic to get tested.

ASA-fucking-P.

TUESDAY AT WORK was just like any other day. Busy as hell, and I absolutely was not disappointed at the end of the day when Valentine hadn't shown up at my job site.

I drove straight to the clinic after work. Got tested and swabbed for everything, went home, and got changed for rugby training.

Training was always a good distraction. It felt good to let off steam, to run laps and clear my head, and to have a laugh with the boys.

I got home, showered, and deliberately didn't jerk off. I wanted to save it.

Wednesday couldn't come quick enough.

Was this part of the game he was playing?

Toying with me, making me think about nothing else.

Making me count down the goddamned minutes, so when nine o'clock rolled around, I'd almost burst through his door to give him what he wanted?

I was desperate to give him what he wanted.

I didn't even care if it made him happy or scratched some perverted itch he had.

Because, holy fuck, I wanted it too.

What I really wanted to do was throw him down and bury myself inside him, but he'd said he'd prefer that was a Saturday night thing. He also said I could do it on a Wednesday if I wanted, but he'd made a point of saying what *he'd* prefer . . .

So I'd respect that.

At this rate, with how much overthinking what I was doing—and thinking about nothing else—I was so turned on I was gonna last a max of thirty seconds.

At seven o'clock on Wednesday, my phone beeped with some results from my test. Twenty-four-hour testing was now a very convenient thing. But it wasn't the results of all the tests I'd had done; some took a little longer, which I was sure he was well aware. I'd had a negative result on the HIV rapid test before I'd even left the clinic, but I wanted a full lab test done as well. I'd never had unprotected sex before—not including blowjobs—but never penetrative sex, and I wanted to be certain.

I sent him the results, and he replied with his five minutes later. He'd had his tests done last week . . . like he'd been anticipating this. Like he knew I'd agree, like he knew I'd be an easy target.

God, I hated him.

I managed to eat some dinner and pretended not to watch the clock, and I arrived at his place at ten minutes to nine.

There was no waiting in the car this time. And it wasn't because my waiting a few minutes had pissed him off last time, it was purely because my dick wasn't playing games.

I wasn't sure how this would go down. I had no idea what to expect. But there was no courting, no prelude, no conversation required, apparently. I pressed the button for his apartment and he buzzed me through.

Christ, I was actually doing this . . .

I'd never had a 'sex agreement' before. Never even had a friend with benefits.

Not that Valentine and I were friends. We were the opposite of that.

We were *what* with benefits? Enemies?

Was 'enemies with benefits' a thing?

I smiled at that thought as I rode the elevator up. He opened the door before I could knock, though he didn't invite me in. He didn't even say hello. He just opened the door, turned around, and walked towards the kitchen.

He was still wearing his suit pants and shirt, top buttons now undone, sleeves half rolled up. His dark hair looked like he'd ran his hand through it a dozen times.

I hated that he was sexy.

He looked like he'd had a really shitty afternoon and that gave me a small flicker of happiness.

"Want a drink?" he asked. He picked up a whiskey glass from the table and took a mouthful.

"Bad day?" I asked.

He shot me a dirty glare and put the glass down. "Are you gonna do what you came here to do? Or you just going to stand there?"

I bit down on the flare of anger that bloomed in my chest, though my voice was rough and I spoke through clenched teeth. "Get on your fucking knees."

His demeanour changed in an instant. There was no spark of fire aimed back at me, no barbed reply. Instead, he exhaled and a look of calm washed over his face. Even his shoulders relaxed.

And ever so slowly, he sank to his knees.

Holy fucking shit.

My cock throbbed at the sight and my feet moved on instinct. I stood in front of him and he looked up at me, a glazed look in his eyes. He kept his hands on his thighs, and I realised maybe it was because I hadn't told him to touch me.

I undid the button on my jeans and slowly unzipped the fly, and he sighed.

Jesus, this was hot.

I pulled my cock out, hard and aching. After three days of torture, it was finally going to get what it wanted.

Valentine licked his lips, and fucking hell, he was almost panting now.

"Open your fucking mouth," I murmured, my voice rough.

He smiled before he opened wide, and I tapped his bottom lip with the head of my cock.

"Tongue it," I ordered.

His warm, wet tongue licked the slit and lapped at the beads of precome.

"Now suck it," I said crudely.

He took me in, sucking on the head. He had to open wide to get around me, but his tongue flicked the frenulum while he sucked. His mouth, hot and wet, and the suction was so, *so* good.

But I knew he could take more of me. Like he had in the bathroom stall that night.

I fisted his hair and he groaned. Christ, he really loved this.

"Take more like the cock whore you are," I said, sliding in, feeling my cock hit the back of his throat. "Open up," I said, forcing him by his hair. "All the way up. I know you can take it."

He gagged but quickly swallowed and never once did he pull back. He grunted and hummed, so I pulled his hair harder and thrust in a few times.

I wasn't going to last, and it was probably just as well, because I wasn't sure how much more he could take.

When he put his hands on my thighs, I thought he was going to push me back. But he slid his hands around the backs of my legs to keep me right where I was.

"You're such a fucking piece of shit," I said, pulling his hair and sliding in and out of his throat. "Gonna make me come too fast."

He gagged and I held him on it.

I dared to look down, and seeing *the* Valentine Tye on his knees with my cock jammed in his throat was so fucking hot.

"You want me to come?" I asked.

He hummed, moaned, even.

So, with both hands holding fistfuls of his hair, I pulled back. He looked up, almost sorrowful that I'd rob him of my come.

"Dirty fucking whore," I said. "You don't get it down your throat. I want it in your mouth, I want you to taste it. Taste my come, you piece of shit. Suck it out of me."

His eyes closed and the fucker smiled, tightening his lips around me, and sucked.

Oh, holy fuck, did he suck.

He took me over the edge, taking every drop I gave him.

I convulsed and tried to remember that I was holding him by his hair. But my fucking god.

Best blow job of my life.

He continued to suck me until I couldn't stand it. I pulled out of him and let him go. He fell back on his arse, and I was almost too afraid to look at him.

That had been rough and brutal.

What I'd said to him . . .

But then he wiped his chin, the movement drawing my eyes to his face.

His hair was a mess, but he was smiling, serene.

Peaceful.

Christ, was that a wet spot over the bulge in his pants?

He'd come all over himself again.

Oh god, help me.

I tucked my still half-hard dick back in my jeans. "Ten o'clock on Saturday night. Have your arse ready for me."

He smiled and let his head fall back, as if I'd just told him he'd won lotto or something.

I saw myself out, not entirely sure what to make of anything that had just happened.

His behaviour.

Mine.

Christ almighty, I'd never treated anyone like that before.

And fuck, he'd loved every second of it.

Maybe I would have felt bad if I hadn't seen just how much he'd enjoyed it. But he had come, his dick untouched. Again.

And if I thought my dick would be happy with the best blow job ever, it wasn't. Semi-hard the whole way home, fully hard by the time I stripped off, and I had to jerk off in the shower.

To visions of Valentine on his knees, his pink lips around me. To the sounds he'd made, and the things I'd said to him, what I'd called him—a dirty whore, a piece of shit—so many horrible things. And I came again.

Just as hard, just as mind-blowing.

I fell into bed, unable to keep my eyes open a minute longer. I wasn't sure what to make of anything that had happened with Valentine, but I knew one thing...

Waiting until Saturday was going to be torture.

Chapter 6

Valentine

It took every ounce of self-control I had not to call into Marshall's job site. I wanted to walk in and see the look on his face, see how he acted, and see the brief moment of fear in his eyes as he wondered what I'd say.

Oh, how I wanted to see that, very much.

So I tortured myself by not doing it.

A small self-sacrifice to punish myself, to keep myself in check. To not give into whims and practice self-discipline was something I'd prided myself on.

After all, torturing myself was a skill I'd perfected years ago.

I'd had a terrible afternoon. Probably not undeserving, but being the target of my father's ire was something I'd had to endure all my life.

Unrealistic expectations, inevitable disappointments one after the other. Right foot, left foot, it was how my father operated. A march of regret he reminded me about every chance he got.

Whatever I did was never good enough, would never *be* good enough.

I could so easily take it out on those around me. I had a few hundred people on my payroll I could take my frustrations out on. So many yes-men who would do whatever I told them, who would wear any tirade of misdirected anger I sprayed at them. But I refused to be like my father.

So I aimed my arsenal inwards where it belonged.

And Marshall knew as soon as he saw me that I'd had a bad afternoon. Did he falter and ask me if I was okay? No. Did he ask me if I wanted to talk? No, thank god.

He did exactly what I needed him to do.

Ordered me to my knees and made me suck his dick.

And what a glorious dick it is.

Better this time than the bathroom stall incident. This time he'd fisted my hair and drove himself into my throat, making me choke, and called me a whore and a piece of shit while he skull-fucked me.

He was relentless.

He was perfect.

I'd gone to bed feeling lighter and less stressed, as if he'd shared the weight of my burdens. My throat was sore the next day, and every time it pained me to swallow or talk, I flushed at the memory.

I wanted him to do it again. Every night, even.

And then he'd texted me the full results of his bloodwork. Condoms were now officially optional.

Fuck, yes.

I wasn't sure why I wanted that so badly. I'd never even considered it with anyone else.

Part of me wanted him to own me so badly, I couldn't even think straight.

Waiting until Saturday was a different kind of torture. The anticipation was delicious, and it made every minute more gratifying.

I hoped he thought about nothing else. I wanted him so on edge by the time he walked through my door, he'd simply shove me over the back of my sofa, rip my pants down and impale me.

So, while I *wanted* to see him at work, see his face, see him squirm, I hoped my absence served a greater purpose.

I wanted him to think about nothing else. To want nothing else.

I wanted him to suffer as I did.

So I stayed away.

I knew he'd be playing rugby at Sutherland and the likelihood of seeing him at all before 10 pm was miniscule, so I was quite surprised when Connor—who was sitting by the window at the bar—said, "The Ryde boys are here."

Shit.

It was almost nine o'clock. I'd had maybe three beers all night, not anywhere near my usual amount after a win. And my nerves ratcheted up a notch when half of Marshall's team bustled through the door in a burst of noise, laughter, and bad language.

But no Marshall.

And suddenly my nerves were something else.

Unease? Concern?

Disappointment.

He knew I'd be here, so maybe he didn't want to see me. Maybe he was getting shitfaced somewhere else and had no intention of being at my place at ten o'clock. Maybe he—

"Look, dickhead, just sit the fuck down."

Or maybe he was the last guy in, helping one of his injured teammates into a seat.

His friend, one of their team's big burly forwards, had his ankle strapped and looked incredibly drunk.

Marshall, on the other hand, appeared to be completely sober.

He had a red mark on his cheekbone and a bump on his eyebrow, common war wounds of a rugby game.

"Hey, Wise," one of them yelled. "Whaddya want to drink?"

"Nothing," he replied. "I'm all good, thanks."

"Oh, come on, ya soft-cock," another one of them added. He was staggering, drink in his hand. "Since when do you not hit the piss after a game?"

"Since I had to drive you fuckwits," he replied.

"Well, you can have one now," Taka said, putting a bottle of beer in his hand.

Marshall's gaze ran across the crowd, finding me. I hid my smile behind my own beer as I took a sip, and then he looked up at Taka. "Fine. One drink."

Was he not drinking because of our arrangement?

I liked to think that was the reason. That he was being considerate, courteous. That he didn't want to jeopardise his plans for fucking me later.

I'd like to think I was the reason, even if I knew it wasn't likely.

I nursed my last beer, keeping one eye on Marshall while pretending to ignore him. For all of twenty minutes, anyway . . .

"Oh look, it's Rocky Balboa," Chris said. "Last time I saw you, you were about to get your head smacked in by five guys in Bondi."

"Correction," Marshall replied. "They were about to get their heads smacked in."

Chris snorted. "Yeah, right. If Valentine didn't save your arse, you'd a went home in an ambulance."

I turned at the mention of my name.

"He didn't save my arse," Marshall said.

Chris looked over at me. "Ain't that right, Valentine?"

"Something like that," I replied.

I met Marshall's gaze. Only he and I really knew what happened that night, what he'd done to me . . . how much I loved it. And what he'd be doing to me tonight.

I just needed to rattle his chain a little.

So I made a point of looking him up and down with as much distaste as I could manage, and I caught the bulge of his jaw before I turned back around.

He was so easy. Like waving a red flag at a bull. He really did hate me. Just one look and it was enough to piss him off.

Oh, I *needed* him angry.

I smiled as I drained the rest of my beer, and then I stood up. "That's my cue," I said, throwing a couple of twenties on the table. "Have a round on me."

"Aw, come on," Lleyton said. "One more. Don't go just cause these guys turned up."

"Nah, that's not it," I said. "Though the stench sure is something."

"The fuck d'you say?"

I turned at the familiar voice, and sure enough, Marshall was staring at me. He put his beer on the bar, then his steely eyes lasered in on me. "Wanna say that again?"

I grinned at him and he took a step towards me, then suddenly there were a wall of guys between us. Lleyton grabbed me and led me towards the door. "He's not worth it," he said.

But he had no idea.

It was going to be so worth it.

"Save it for work on Monday," he said as we stepped

outside into the cold air. "Make him redo every single bit of paperwork or something."

Oh, I was gonna make him do something, believe me . . .

"It's all good," I said, walking to my car. "Want a lift home?"

He looked back at the bar. "Nah, I'm gonna kick on. One of us has to hold up the team, and it's clearly not you. I can't believe you're pikin' out on me."

I smiled at him over the roof of my car. "See you Tuesday."

He pointed at me and shook his head. "It's *that* smile that makes Marshall Wise wanna punch your head in."

I laughed. *It was why I did it.* "Night, Lleyton."

I got in my car, buckled up, and drove home. I had about forty-five minutes before Marshall said he'd be here.

If he was still planning on it.

Maybe I'd crossed a line . . . It was in front of our team-mates, after all.

So I took out my phone and shot him a text.

When you requested my arse be ready by 10pm, how ready is ready?

I should have specified in my rules or asked for clarification before now. I'd just assumed it meant douched and lubed, but I shouldn't assume anything.

I could see that he read the message, but he didn't reply. So I went about my bathroom-business, figuring if he was a no-show, I'd just use one of my toys.

But fifteen minutes later my phone rang. It was Marshall's number, and I almost didn't answer it. We'd said we'd text, not call, and I was certain he was calling to tell me our deal was over.

Maybe I'd deserve that.

I hit Answer, and his voice was low and commanding in my ear. No hello, no anything.

"I don't give a fuck how ready you are," he murmured. It sounded like he got into a car. The wind was gone and then his engine started. "I'm fifteen minutes away and then your arse is mine. Ready or fucking not."

The line clicked off and it sent a jolt of pleasure through me. His words, the authority.

The ownership.

It warmed me through; my blood hummed, and my skin prickled in anticipation.

I already started to relax, knowing what was going to happen. That peacefulness only this could give me.

Thoroughly cleaned, I lubed myself and stretched my hole as much as I dared. I didn't want to overdo it because the stretch of him was part of the pleasure for me. But he was *big*, and he sounded somewhat impatient. I didn't want him to waste time by getting me ready.

When I'd said I wanted him to walk in, put a load in me, and leave, I hadn't been kidding.

I pulled on grey trackpants just as the intercom buzzed. I let him in, heard the elevator and that thrill of anticipation, of blazing desire, pooled low in my belly. I was already hard; the expectation, the knowing what I was about to get.

I'd never wanted anything so bad.

I opened my door for him, and he stood there, fire and loathing in his glare. He looked me up and down, his gaze lingering over my nipples, clearly liking that I wore nothing but grey tracksuit pants.

I smiled and turned around, walking slowly to the couch. I put a towel down and dropped one knee on the sofa, right next to the bottle of lube.

He closed the door and watched as I made a show of

kneeling on the seat, my forearms on the backrest. He stood there, not moving, so I slid my pants down a little, revealing the top of my arse, and that made him move.

He strode over, determined and mad. Mad at me, or mad at himself, I didn't care.

I stretched my back, sticking my arse out, and he undid the button on his jeans. The sound of his zipper made me moan.

"You're such a whore," he bit out, and with his hand gripping the back of my neck, he forced my head down to the seat of the sofa so my arse was sticking up. "Stay down."

Oh, yes.

Then he pulled my trackpants down. "You lubed yourself?"

"You said you wanted me ready," I said, muffled into the sofa.

He groaned. "You want it that bad, huh?"

He pressed the length of his hot erection along the crease of my arse. "God, yes."

He picked up the lube but then he stopped. "No condoms?"

Christ, he was taking forever.

I pulled myself up using the back of the sofa. "You can if you want. I thought you—"

He gripped my throat and pulled me back against his chest, his erection pressed hard against my lower back, his breath hot in my ear. "You have no idea how bad I want to fuck you raw."

Holy shit.

I was panting, my cock leaking precome. I moaned.

Then he shoved me back down, his hand on the back of my head, his cock pushing against me. So close, yet so far. "I said, stay down," he bit out.

My heart was thundering but when I heard the pop of the lube bottle, that blanket of calm washed over me. He drizzled more over my arse, and I could hear the wet, slick sound as he covered his cock.

Oh, yes.

Yes, yes, yes.

He tapped his blunt cockhead against my hole and pushed into me.

I'd thought I was prepared . . .

I was not prepared for this.

The stretch, the burn. The size of him, the heat of him. So, so hot. I groaned into the sofa, my hands trying to find purchase on anything.

He pushed all the way in, letting out a cry as he did. "Fuck, fuck," he groaned, his voice strained. "Oh god. So fucking tight."

I was panting, taking in the pain, and fighting the urge to resist. Letting it consume me instead. I was so full. He was in so deep.

Taking him bareback was everything I'd hoped it would be.

Then he began to move.

Sliding out and pushing back in, slow at first. Then, like he'd remembered who he was fucking, he gripped my hips and slammed into me.

I cried out and he pushed down on my back. "Fucking take it," he growled. "Like the slut you are."

Then he leaned over me and took a fistful of my hair as he pushed my face into the sofa. It hurt and, god, it felt so good at the same time. It also changed the angle inside me, and I saw fireworks behind my eyelids. "The way you looked at me tonight, trying to make me hate you. Well, guess fucking what?" He slammed into me over and over. "You got what you wanted."

He fucked me so hard, so deep, and so brutally perfect. The fingers of his left hand bit into my hip and his right hand held me down.

"Now take what you deserve," he said, fucking me into submission. Harder, faster, he owned me, treating me as though I was nothing but a means to an end. My god, I loved it. Then, with a loud cry, he slammed into me one final time as he came. And god, I could feel his cock pulse.

I could feel him come inside me.

Now take what you deserve . . .

Oh, believe me. I took it. I took every drop.

He groaned with each throb, until his body twitched and his thighs shook, and then slowly he pulled out of me.

I missed his cock already.

His hands stayed on my hips, and I was breathing hard. I felt good, used for his pleasure, and his pleasure only. I hadn't come, and even though my dick was hard, the high I felt was enough.

I waited for him to walk out . . . but he didn't. He kept his hand on my arse, and I realised, somewhat belatedly, that he was admiring his handiwork. At the wet I could feel leaking out of me.

"Fuck yes," he whispered.

I lifted my head, pushing myself up, but he was quick to grab me. One hand on my hip, one around my throat. "Where do you think you're going?" he asked, his voice hot in my ear. "I'm not done with you yet."

I shivered, goosebumps erupting over my whole body.

"Can you take more?" he asked, his hand at my throat, tightening just enough.

"Always," I whispered. It sounded like a prayer.

"Your arse looks so good," he murmured against the back of my head. "My come running out of your open hole." He pulled me back so he could rub his still-hard cock against my hole until he was nudging the back of my balls.

"Oh god," I breathed. I gripped my dick, pleasure rippling through me.

"Fuck, I'm gonna need to come again." Letting go of my throat, he took my hips in both hands and drove his cock back into me.

I cried out in pleasure and pain, so entwined I couldn't tell them apart. I gripped the back of the sofa to balance myself and he impaled me, holding my hips and rocking me on his cock.

God, he was so far inside me.

"You're such a slut," he bit out. "Taking my cock like this. Good for nothing, letting me fuck you like the piece of shit you are."

Oh god, yes.

I stroked my erection, desperate for release. But he let go of my hips and drove my face into the backrest so he could hold my arm.

It hurt so good.

"You don't touch," he barked, ramming into me and pinning me to the sofa. Then he reached around and under, tweaking my nipple. "You open the door without a shirt for anyone? Or are you just a worthless whore for me?" Then he twisted my nipple, pinched, and pulled it.

I cried out, pain and ecstasy shooting through me, from my nipple directly to my balls, and I came. He held my hips and fucked me as my orgasm tore through me, and in that moment, his massive cock was almost too much to take . . .

Until he roared, pulsing inside me again and again.

He held me still until he caught his breath, until he

began to soften, and then he pulled out. He pushed me down onto the sofa and he stuffed his cock back into his briefs.

I was in that blissed-out state, that place between heaven and hell where I knew I was going to hurt in the best of ways, and I longed for it.

The sound of Marshall's zipper snapped me back to reality. He put his hand on the side of my head and held me down, not rough but certainly not gently. "You look like a used whore full of my come," he whispered. He gave me a little shove. "Be ready for the same again on Wednesday." He turned and walked out, leaving me alone in the aftermath.

Tonight had been so much better than I'd ever expected. He said I looked like a used and worthless whore, and my god, I felt like one.

I was so full of his come.

He'd claimed me. Owned me like I was something to use and throw away.

I smiled into the silence.

CHAPTER 7

MARSHALL

THERE WAS NO WAY I WAS MISSING THE STUPID Monday morning meeting at head office, for no other reason than to see Valentine's face. I wanted to smile at him the entire time, only the two of us knowing what I'd done to him, how I'd left him on Saturday night.

It'd been the hottest sex of my life.

I hadn't come twice that close together since I was seventeen.

But holy hell, he did something to me.

Maybe he was onto something; maybe hate-fucking was my kink. He'd certainly known how good it could be and I had to admit, I agreed with him.

I'd also never had unprotected sex before, so that was new too. And so unbelievably good.

I'd never experienced anything like what I did with him.

Walking out of his apartment, knowing he was a quivering mess on the couch with two of my loads in him, like I owned him ... Jesus Christ. That was the hottest thing ever.

And the way he'd smiled when I said he could expect the same on Wednesday night . . .

So yeah, excuse me for being a tad smug. But I was going to sit in on this waste-of-time meeting just so Valentine fucking Tye would be reminded of who owned his arse.

So he'd *know* I owned him.

He was a few minutes late to the meeting, but he rushed in, apologising and taking his spot at the head of the room. "Thank you for waiting," he said, putting his iPad on the table. He looked around the room, his gaze falling to me for a beat too long, then on to the next person.

Yeah. He knew who owned him.

And damn if my dick didn't want another go at him.

Christ. Think of something else. Do not get a hard-on here.

Because then who owned whom?

Goddammit.

"It was suggested to me last week that perhaps a breakfast meeting would be more appropriate," Valentine began. "So I've arranged for fresh coffee and bacon and egg rolls, that kind of thing, to be served in the breakroom when we're done."

Everyone perked up immediately, moods lifted all around, and Valentine smiled. He didn't look at me directly, and it was probably just as well. I'd have hated for him to see the shock on my face.

Because *I'll be damned*. He actually did what I'd suggested.

"I'm open to any other ideas," he added. "On efficiency and how we might better spend our time. Please feel free to see me after we're done." He clapped his hands and gestured to the smart board. "Okay, I know you're all busy, so let's get started . . ."

That meeting was done and dusted in twenty minutes.

Man, I hated that he actually listened to me. I hated that he implemented something so easily just because I'd told him he needed to do better. I hated that he could streamline a meeting so it didn't actually suck.

What I hated most of all was that I hated him a little less.

What I didn't hate was how he filled out those suit pants and how that white button-down shirt was tailored like a freaking piece of art. I hated his perfect hair, and I hated his pretty face.

But damn, I loved knowing how his cheeks flushed during sex, how he groaned and whined, and that I could make him come with just my dick in his arse and a hard tweak of his nipple.

"Great, so if no one has anything to add, please enjoy your refreshments in the breakroom."

Okay, so I'd missed the last few minutes of the meeting. My mind had definitely gone down a very pleasant path instead of paying attention.

Damn.

I picked up my unopened notebook and pen and followed the others out. I caught up with Carl and Jaman while we ate our breakfast rolls and croissants, and I deliberately kept my back to Valentine.

I could feel him in the room though.

Like my Spidey-senses knew he was close. That little know-where-your-enemies-are radar in my head was pinging.

"So, who d'ya reckon told Tye to feed us?" Jaman asked quietly.

"Uh, it mighta been me," I admitted, sipping my coffee. "I told him last week these things were a waste of time."

Carl almost snorted his coffee. "You what?"

I shrugged. "It's true. And I told him to feed us. Christ. If he wants builders to talk about shit, there's gotta be food."

Jaman knocked his coffee to mine. "Cheers to that." He shoved the rest of his bacon and egg roll into his mouth and spoke around it. "It's good too."

The coffee was the expensive stuff.

I hated that he did this right.

But we talked about Carl's work—there'd been nightmare soil-engineering issues in the beginning—and then Jaman told us of a funny story with the council inspector who'd been a total dick but then got bogged when he'd tried to leave.

I also heard Harris and Andrews discussing shipment issues and workarounds with Valentine.

Not that I was listening. Not that I cared.

But he wanted his people to talk to him, to open up about job-site issues and to have think-tank discussions, and he was getting that now.

He might know corporate bullshit, but I knew builders. I'd worked with these other site managers for years. Hell, old Robbie Harris had been my boss when I was an apprentice outta high school.

And I'm not gonna lie. Watching him laugh with Valentine kinda irked me.

I don't know why, which pissed me off more. That Harris liked Valentine, or that Valentine was smiling for him.

Christ.

I downed the rest of my coffee. "Okay guys, I gotta go. Have a good week," I said, clapping big Jaman on the arm as I left.

I didn't turn around to see if Valentine was watching

me leave. While I'd have liked to see him notice, I really didn't want to see him *not* notice.

God, I hated him.

Getting to work and making myself busy was a great idea, and I trusted my team to get shit done when I wasn't there. I could also trust that they'd rib me for bailing early on Saturday night.

"Oh, here's the piker himself," Taka said as I walked in.

"Yeah, the only time he ever bails on us after a game is when he gets a better offer," Millsy added.

Taka grinned. "Must have been a real good offer, my friend."

It didn't take much for my mind to replay vivid scenes from Saturday night. "It was." I held up two fingers. "Two offers, actually."

Okay, so it wasn't technically *two* offers, but I took him twice. It was kinda the same thing.

Millsy gave me a shove with a laugh. "Christ. I'd have bailed on us too."

I snorted. "Okay, what are we up to with the specs?"

And just like that, I didn't give Valentine Tye one more thought.

Well, until I was in the shower after work . . . and again when I was alone in bed.

Was I really gonna fuck him again on Wednesday like I'd said I would? Even though he'd said before he'd prefer anal sex to only happen on Saturdays? But then the way he'd smiled when I'd told him to expect it on Wednesday . . .

With his flushed cheeks and messed up hair, and that glazed-over look in his eyes.

I really hated that he was so fucking hot.

I hated that he was taking up so much room in my head.

And again all day at work on Tuesday. I wanted him to

show up at my worksite. He didn't, and I hated him for that. I wanted him to text me, and he didn't.

I hated him for that too.

By the time Wednesday finally rolled around, my dick just wouldn't quit. It knew it was having another taste of Valentine and, so help me god, I hated him for that as well.

Having a permanent semi was something I couldn't easily hide in my work pants. They were long navy-blue cargos, kinda snug too, and wearing a tool belt only seemed to make the bulge more noticeable.

I considered taking care of it on my lunch break but, damn, I wanted to save it.

Maybe I could do him twice again tonight.

I had to wonder if he was suffering as much as me. I mean, his arse would be sore for a day or two, and that was suffering enough. But did he think of me as often as I thought of him?

And that's when it occurred to me . . . was he doing this to fuck with my head?

Was this mind game his way of torturing me? Did he hate me that much that he'd do this just to mess with me?

I wouldn't put it past him.

Because at the end of the day, Valentine Tye never did anything that wasn't self-serving.

So, if he wanted to play mind games . . .

I took a photo of the bulge in my pants. It was very obvious what it was, but it was just a crotch-shot. No boots, no background. And I very carefully made sure it was in *his* messages.

I typed out a message.

You better be ready for this

And I hit Send.

It gave me a thrill, a buzz. This game of cat and mouse, tit for tat. I waited for a reply . . .

And waited.

By three o'clock, I could see he hadn't opened it yet, and it stupidly bothered me that he was winning the mind game, and he wasn't even playing.

God, I hated him.

I hated that I was letting him get to me.

But then at ten to five, when I was pissed off and packing up—and even when I knew my work team was avoiding me because of my mood—my phone beeped.

Seven o'clock

I grinned. He didn't want to wait either.

"Oh, someone finally replied, huh?" Taka asked as he threw his toolbox into his ute. "You've been checking your phone all afternoon."

I pocketed my phone. "Shut the fuck up."

He laughed. "See ya tomorrow."

Smiling, I gave him a nod.

I shouldn't be this happy. I shouldn't let Valentine fucking Tye consume me so much.

I shouldn't have even agreed to this fucked-up arrangement. I shouldn't actually like fucking him hard and telling him what a piece of shit he is.

I shouldn't like that he craves it as much as I crave giving it to him.

I shouldn't like knowing I'd be leaving him tonight with an arse full of my come.

But damn . . .

That's what I liked the most.

I PRESSED his intercom at five to seven. Did I hate myself for being early?

Yes.

But I hated him more. For making me desperate. For making me so on edge, my balls were so full and my cock was so hard it was almost painful.

I'd never wanted sex so badly. Never like this.

It was his fault, and I hated him for it.

And I fully intended to make him pay.

He opened his door and turned around, walking over to his dining table. He still wore his work clothes: suit pants, fitted button-down shirt, and his tie was pulled loose at his open collar.

He looked like he'd had a rough day. A bad day, even.

And I might have asked him if he was okay, if he was up for tonight.

But that's not what this arrangement was.

And I didn't care about Valentine fucking Tye. I didn't care if he'd had a shitty day.

With his back to me, he poured himself a scotch. "Want one?"

I closed the door behind me. "No."

He downed a shot and poured himself another. "Thank you for coming earlier tonight."

His voice was flat, detached. He really hadn't had a good day.

"If you're not up for tonight—"

He shot me a glare over his shoulder. Ice cold and lethal. "I need it tonight more than ever." He downed his drink. "And from the photo you sent me today, I'd say you do too."

I walked slowly to him, saw the cat was having his dinner on the floor in the kitchen, so I was fairly sure Valentine had been home for all of five minutes. He knew he'd be getting home just before seven, and he wanted me here at the same time. So yeah, he must have had a real bad day.

I took the glass out of his hand. I put it on the table and ran my hand up his back. "My cock's been hard since I walked out of here on Saturday," I murmured. He leaned into my touch, and I gave his shoulder a squeeze.

He was so tense, so stressed. He tried to roll his shoulders, tried to let go of the tension, but in the end, he growled and turned to face me. "Whatever you intend to do to me, make it good."

Jesus.

"I think you should get on your knees and stop talking."

His eyes flashed with black steel; his nostrils flared. "No. I don't want to suck your dick. I want you to fuck me."

Oh, I see how it's gonna go . . .

I smiled at him and gently loosened his tie a bit more, and when I went to pull it over his head, I got to his mouth and slowly cinched the tie so tight, it gagged him.

"I said stop talking," I murmured.

His nostrils flared again, but this time his eyes flashed with desire.

Then I pulled him by his tie and led him to his bedroom. His room was dark grey, his bed covers varying shades of charcoal, and a slab of dark grey granite covered the wall behind his bed. No two ways about it, he had expensive style.

I left him standing there while I took the lube from his bedside table and threw it on the bed. He made no attempt to move or to remove his tie from his mouth.

So I took my time unbuttoning his shirt. I left it open, running my palm up his ribs and squeezing his pec. His nipple hardened at my touch.

Christ, he was so responsive.

Then, holding his gaze, I unbuttoned his suit pants, and he moaned around the tie that gagged him.

"You're such a whore," I whispered.

His eyes closed and he breathed in deep, the set of his shoulders relaxing already.

God, he wanted this so bad.

Needed it.

I turned him to face the bed and, pushing him to bend over the edge of the mattress, I spread his legs with my foot.

He grunted and lifted his arse. Christ, he was desperate.

"You need it so bad, huh?" I asked. "You want me to prep you at all or just force my way in?"

He answered by fisting his bed covers and whining. His shirt rode up, exposing the small of his back, the pale skin, and the hint of his briefs.

God, he was teasing me. Like he knew every box to tick, every one of my kinks, my fantasies. I leaned against his arse, pressing my hard-on against his crack, and I took both his wrists, stretching his arms up above his head. "Keep them there."

He fisted the bed covers right where I'd put his hands. "Good whore," I murmured and kissed the back of his neck, biting down on his shoulder.

He arched his back at the sting of it and, of course, rocked against my cock.

I leaned back and pulled his pants and briefs down, exposing his perfect arse, and as much as I wanted to ram into him, I couldn't do it. I'd literally tear him apart.

So I poured some lube down his crack and gave him a rough finger. He lifted his head, complaining around the tie in his mouth, so with my free hand, I shoved his head back down and continued to finger him. "Stay down," I barked.

"You'll get my cock soon enough. You that fucking desperate for it?" I added a second finger, rough and without warning, just how he liked it, but it was still better than no prep at all.

He lifted his arse and moaned, clearly eager for more.

I hated that I was going to give him what he needed. I hated that I needed it too.

I pulled my hand free and undid my jeans and took out my aching erection. I smeared lube over it, slicking myself up real good, then adding more to his arse before smearing it over his hole with my cockhead.

"You want it this bad?" I bit out. "You want this as bad as I do?"

He lifted his head to mumble something around the tie still gagging him, and I pushed into him.

All the way in.

He screamed around the gag, white-knuckled fists in the bedcovers.

But my god, he took all of me.

So hot, and so fucking tight.

I was never going to last. I wanted it to last all night, I wanted this pleasure to never end, but he felt far too good.

"Fuck yes. That's what you wanted," I said with a strained groan. With my hands on his shoulder blades, I pushed him down and slammed into him a few times. "Take it like the piece of shit you are. You think you can make me think of nothing else every minute of every fucking day. How much I want to sink my cock into you, up to my balls like I am right now."

I rolled my hips a few times to prove my point and slammed into him again. "All I think about is this," I ground out. "So you'll fucking take it like the whore you are."

And he did. He took it all. Moaning and whining,

holding onto the bedding while I fucked him hard, lifting his arse for more. He kept his head to the side, gag still in his mouth, while I pinned his shoulders down and gave it to him even harder.

And when he got that glazed-over look in his eyes, that serene look of when pain becomes pleasure, I put my hand on his head and held him down as I came inside him.

Fuuuuuuuck, he felt so good.

I wasn't ready for this to be over.

Not even close.

I stayed inside him and pulled the tie off. He licked his lips, the corner of his mouth red.

I didn't want to pull out. I wanted to stay right where I was until I was ready for another round. But I needed to think of him.

I pulled back, such an exquisite slide, and watched as his body released me. His beautiful arse, his pale white body, lean and strong, yet pliable. So very seductive.

Yeah, I was nowhere done yet.

"Stay right where you are," I ordered. "Don't move."

I walked out to the kitchen and opened the fridge. He seemed the type to have bottled water on hand, and he was. I took a bottle, cracked the lid, and went back to his bedroom.

He hadn't moved.

I knelt on the bed beside him and put the bottle to his lips. It was awkward and he spilled some, but he drank it, licking his lips again. "You can leave it on the bedside," he said, his voice hoarse.

I put the bottle where he'd said, but I chuckled as I ran my hand up his back. "Oh, I'm not done with you yet," I said, massaging his back, his shoulders.

It didn't hurt that my dick was back between his arse

cheeks as I leaned over him, kneading his tired muscles in my hands.

"And you didn't come," I whispered into his spine. Then I scraped my teeth along his shoulder blade and bit him again. Not enough to draw blood but enough to make him groan.

I massaged down his back to his arse, spreading his cheeks and, sure enough, he was beginning to leak my come.

It was the hottest thing I'd ever seen.

But I wanted to do things differently this time. So I pulled his suit pants and briefs all the way off, and I flipped him over. His shirt was open. He was almost naked before me, so fucking beautiful, but he immediately drew his arms in. A defensive move: he was vulnerable like this, facing me, exposed, and I could see every flicker of fear and panic in his eyes. But there was something else there too. Pleading, imploring, and honesty.

Even though my jeans were still on, I pulled off my sweater and shirt so I was as exposed as him.

I took his dick in my hand and began to stroke him. I ran my other hand up to his chest, rubbing over his nipple and pinching the nub hard enough to make him hiss.

"Is that the best you can do?" he bit out through his clenched teeth.

Was he trying to regain some control? Was he trying to goad me?

"I thought you'd be a better fuck than this," he added, and he tried to push me with his knees.

Yeah. He wanted to push me, all right. Right over the fucking edge.

I gripped his thighs, holding him tight enough to leave bruises, and lifted them up towards his chest, and then I pushed my cock against his wet hole and drove all the way back in. "A better fuck than this?" I rasped.

His breath caught, his eyes rolled back, his neck corded as he groaned.

I rammed into him again and again. "You should be careful what you wish for. Think you can handle this? You think you're so good?" I squeezed his nipple, and he cried out. "You're good for nothing."

I gripped his throat then, squeezing hard enough to make him gasp. His eyes widened and rolled back, a wicked smile on his lips. Still with my hand around his throat, I pulled his head forward, and crushed my lips to his, sinking my tongue into his mouth.

Then his body went rigid and he came, spilling come over his stomach and chest. His body milking mine, his pulse throbbing under my hand against his throat, his low groan vibrating under my touch.

Like his orgasm beckoned mine, like it sang for me, I came inside him again.

My forehead to his, my mouth against his. Our breaths hot and heavy, and when the room stopped spinning, when I remembered where I was, I opened my eyes and he was staring at me.

I pushed myself up and off him, slipping out of his body, and I stood there, panting, still dazed.

That orgasm had rocked me.

Valentine rolled over and slowly got to his feet, as if he had to reassemble himself. He walked to his ensuite with a slight limp and I was about to ask him if he was okay . . .

"Lock the front door on your way out," he said, and the door closed behind him.

Right, then.

Mr Cold and Calculating was back.

I redressed, took another bottle of water from his fridge because he wouldn't fucking miss it, stopped to give Enzo the cat a scratch—he was perched on the arm of the sofa watching me, so it'd have been rude not to say hello—and then I locked the front door behind me when I left.

I tried really hard not to think about what I'd done.

Not the rough, hard fuck, not the throat grabbing, not the two best orgasms of my life . . .

I'd kissed him.

I'd kissed Valentine Fucking Tye. Not that he'd specified kissing was not allowed, but I'd assumed it wasn't something we'd be doing. Like crossing some forbidden line, because our agreement certainly wasn't about intimacy.

And kissing was intimate, right?

And I tried really hard not to think about how he'd tasted of expensive scotch with hints of honey and malt. And I tried to forget how he'd kissed me back and how he'd come when I'd sucked on his tongue.

I shouldn't have fucked him on his back. I should have just kept him face down, arse up, and shoved his face into the mattress in that fucked-up way he liked.

Christ, Marshall.

Stop overthinking it. Stop thinking about him at all.

Yeah right, like that's gonna happen.

I showered when I got home and fell into bed with a very happy dick and a confused, heavy heart.

What have I done?

CHAPTER 8

VALENTINE

ON THURSDAY I HAD DISCOMFORT WHEN I SAT DOWN and bruises around my neck. It was winter so no one questioned my turtleneck, and I spent all day in my office with instructions to be left alone.

I cited being too busy for anything else, which wasn't exactly a lie. But it was more to the point that no one would notice my breath catch every time I moved in my chair, and so I could touch the heated finger marks on my throat in private.

Reliving the pain, the ache.

The lingering memories of his body in mine I could still feel.

It was utter bliss.

He'd fucked me so good.

I wasn't sure about the second time, being on my back underneath him. It was not my favoured position. I felt awkward and vulnerable, and he seemed to realise this. He'd stripped off his sweater and then, so it didn't feel too intimate, he held me down and proceeded to fuck me.

I got to see his clenched jaw, the determination on his

face to prove how worthless I was, that he could use my body for his own pleasure and disregard me when he was done.

His muscular torso, his bulky arms and strong hands . . . testament to the marks he'd left on my neck, to the bite mark he'd left on my back.

My blood warmed at the thought of it.

And he'd kissed me. Well, he'd smashed his mouth to mine and forced his tongue inside.

I should be embarrassed to admit that was the tipping point that made me come. I'd been close the whole time, but with his hand around my neck and his massive cock buried to the hilt, and then his tongue?

But I wasn't embarrassed.

I refused to feel shame for whatever turned me on.

I knew it wasn't everyone's cup of tea, and most men I'd encountered weren't up for how rough I liked it.

But Marshall had no problem with it.

The bonus of him hating me, I guess. The silver lining of my father ruining his father's business—a transaction I had no part in—but he hated me for it all the same. I couldn't say I blamed him. My father ruined a lot of people's lives.

I wasn't excluded from that.

No one was.

I wondered briefly if I should tell Marshall about the marks on my throat. Should he know? Probably. But I could only imagine he'd probably freak out, apologise profusely, and promise to never do it again.

And I wanted him to do it again.

What if he freaked out to the point where he called off our arrangement altogether? What had he called it? Enemies with benefits?

It would be the gallant thing to do, perhaps even the right thing to do. And Marshall Wise would do the gallant thing.

So no, I wouldn't be telling him.

My office phone buzzed and my assistant's line lit up. "Mr Tye, your sister is here to see you."

I refrained from sighing. "Okay, thank you. Send her in."

A few seconds later, Brooklyn walked in. She was the picture of elegance and grace, her dark pant suit was well fitted to her too-thin body, her camel-coloured coat matching her expensively bleached high ponytail.

She walked straight in and sat down opposite me. "Morning," she said.

"You should have called."

"You'd have told me not to come."

"For good reason. I'm busy."

"You're always busy."

"And so are you."

"I make time for you. Unlike you, since you returned from Melbourne."

I sighed, then. "Nice coat."

"Thanks. Nice turtleneck."

"Thanks. Can I get you a coffee?"

She relaxed a little then, even afforded me a smile. "No." And then she swung her axe. "I spoke to Dad."

I rolled my eyes. "Before we get into this, are you on his side or mine? It helps to know where thine enemies lay in wait."

She smirked, her pale pink glossy lips softening her face. "Your side. Always."

I smiled back at her. She was perhaps the only person in

the world who truly understood me. Not that she knew *everything* about me.

Not that anyone did.

Except for the men I'd asked to hate-fuck me.

Except for Marshall.

"So," she said. "Dad?"

I sat up straight in my chair and regretted it immediately. I didn't quite hide the wince from the sharp reminder my arse gave me.

"You okay?"

"Yeah, overdid it at rugby training," I lied.

"Why on earth you volunteer to be pummelled into the ground by sweaty men, I'll never know."

If only she knew . . .

"Yes, what did father dearest have to say about me this time?"

Now it was she who rolled her eyes. "Nothing really. Just how no one stacks up to his god complex. The usual. He was wondering if bringing you back here was the right move."

What?

"It was his idea," I said.

"I know."

"Moving into the construction industry was his idea. You know, in his quest for global domination. If his projection figures aren't what he was hoping for, he should have hired better analysts who'd tell him the truth instead of fucking yes-men."

She smiled. "I know that. Everyone does."

"Except him."

She nodded and sighed. "Anyway, I just thought you should know that was today's morning-meeting rant."

Ridiculing his son in a meeting with his board of directors. Nice. "Thanks for the heads-up."

She sighed and was quiet for a moment. "How's it going here anyway? Glad to be back?"

I wasn't sure why my mind leapt straight to Marshall Wise, as if he was the one good thing in my life. I shook my head. "Uh, yeah. It's fine. Lleyton got me straight back into rugby and training. It's helped."

"Don't miss Melbourne life at all?"

I didn't have to even think about it. "Not really."

"And how's Enzo? Did he handle the move okay?"

That made me smile. "He doesn't care where he is, as long as his bowl is full."

"Good." She studied me for a long second, and I recognised the look of guarded sadness in her eyes. So similar to my own. Before either of us could say anything too meaningful, she stood up. "Have lunch with me on Sunday. Just you and me at my place. One o'clock."

I'd have preferred dinner, given my plans for Sunday morning now revolved around a long soak in a very hot tub. But this was Brooklyn asking, and I could never say no. "Okay. One o'clock."

Her smile was bright before she schooled it away. We'd never been good at showing emotions. For anything or anyone. "There's a new Nepalese momo place that has the best dumplings in the city, apparently. I'll order in."

"Perfect."

With a nod and a swish of her ponytail, she was gone. How she could walk, let alone glide, in those heels, I'd never know. But she was the picture of poise and refined grace which most people mistook for conceitedness. Much as they mistook the same in me.

If only they knew it was an artfully mastered emotionally detached state of being from having one fucked-up childhood.

After all, people tended to leave you alone if you appeared unapproachable.

Despite all that, I felt better after her visit. We weren't close, not by any stretch, but now that we were both adults, perhaps I could make more of an effort. She was basically the only family I had.

Technically, I still had both parents, but I wasn't sure I could call them *family*.

Whatever that word meant, I wasn't completely sure.

I skipped lunch and managed to get a great deal done with zero interruptions, but I couldn't ignore my stomach forever. By four o'clock, I was starting to feel a little ill and shaky, so I wandered into the staff breakroom in search of something . . .

To find none other than Marshall Wise laughing with Olivia from accounts. Olivia saw me, ducked her head, and made a run for the door, but Marshall stood there leaning against the counter with his feet crossed, stirring a cup of tea.

He smirked at me . . . until he saw my face. "You okay?"

"I'm fine. Just need something to eat."

He put his cup down and then thought better of it and handed it to me. "Drink this. I just made it. White tea with two sugars." He turned and opened a cupboard door and produced a pack of plain biscuits and a small bag of grain crisps. "Have these. When did you eat last?"

I shrugged and was about to tell him I'd had coffee for breakfast after missing dinner last night too, but I stopped myself when I realised it wasn't any concern of his. I sipped his tea instead and was surprised by how good the sugar was.

I normally didn't have it, but it made me feel better almost immediately. I opened the biscuits and nibbled on the end of one, then washed it down with more tea.

"I just got busy," I said, feeling bad for not replying.

He seemed concerned and crossed his arms, waiting for me to finish the biscuits, apparently.

He was wearing his work pants, his dirty work boots, a company T-shirt with a flannel jacket. It bugged me that he made construction work so sexy.

"What are you doing here?" I asked, finishing the second biscuit.

"Had to drop off some invoices," he replied. "Got talking to Olivia."

"You two seemed cosy."

I regretted saying that the second it was out of my mouth.

He smirked and took back his half-drunk tea from out of my hands. He sipped it, smiling. "I've known her for years, and believe me, she knows she'd be wasting her time trying to grease my wheels, if you know what I mean. I drive in the very gay lane."

I shot him a glare, then went to the fridge in search of something else. Some juice, maybe. I found none. "Christ."

Just then, my assistant rushed past the door. "Shayla," I called out.

She stopped and came back, surprised to see me, clearly. "Oh. Yes?"

"Can we please order some small bottles of juice or lemonade to have on hand for whoever . . . ? And maybe some of those oat and yoghurt bars. Some fresh fruit."

She nodded. "Yes, of course," she said and was gone.

When I looked back at Marshall, he was fixing another

cup of tea. He turned and handed it to me. "Have this."
Then he opened the crackers. "Need me to hand feed you?"

I glanced around. We were very much alone, but
still . . .

I took the crackers and ate one, the salt bursting on my
tongue, and washed it down with more tea. I was about to
thank him for making it—his concern was polite but not
necessary—but he spoke instead.

"Nice sweater," he murmured behind his cup of tea. "I
didn't realise the Steve Jobs look was in this season."

So much for his concern.

"Thanks. It's to hide the bruises on my neck you
gave me."

I also regretted saying that the second it was out of my
mouth, but his reaction almost made it worth it.

He choked on his drink and coughed. "Are you serious?" I peeled back the tight-fitting neck and his eyes
widened. "Holy shit."

I sipped the tea and ate another cracker. "Don't be
sorry," I added casually. "Because I'm not."

He seemed to consider something for a second. "Well, I
dunno what's more concerning. That I'm not sorry, or that I
find it incredibly hot."

Not the reaction I expected from him, and it
pleased me.

"Hm. Anyway, it's not something we should be
discussing here."

"Ah, yes, your rules. In my defence, I didn't come here
to see you and I had no intention of paying a social visit.
You came in here all pale with your hands shaking, so I was
just making sure you didn't die. You're welcome, by the
way."

"My blood sugar drops when I forget to eat," I added lamely. "It's nothing serious."

"Forget to eat often?"

I rolled my eyes. This was not a conversation I was having with him. Why was I having a conversation with him at all?

"Thank you for the tea," I said, taking a step towards the door and stopping dead in my tracks.

Because there in the doorway, in his grey Italian long coat and his cold eyes, stood my father. Shayla stood behind him, shaking her head and mouthing sorry, which meant he more than likely just strode past her desk without even acknowledging her.

"Surprise visits always pay off," he said. "I'm not keeping you busy enough, I see."

I heard Marshall make a huff of disgust, and without a word, he walked out, staring my father right in his face as he went past. No greeting, no smile, just a sneer and a death stare. Right in my father's face. A lesser man would never . . .

I could have laughed.

Maybe Marshall Wise wasn't so bad after all.

My father stared after him, no doubt about to ask for his name and employment position, which I had no intention of giving him.

"I wasn't feeling well," I said, putting myself into my father's firing line instead. It worked because his laser stare zoomed in on me. "Thought I'd try a cup of tea. Shall we go into my office?"

I'D BEEN in a bad mood since the run in with my father on Thursday. On Friday, I'd asked Shayla to screen all calls, hold all meetings, and basically make me unavailable to everyone. Including my father. Not that he called or cared.

But by Saturday, I was looking forward to rugby. And to also getting railed afterwards, but running hard and playing a physical game was exactly what I needed.

We were playing against Burwood, and we'd had a great first half. We were up by twelve, and I'd had two try assists and I'd had a good run of metres and made plenty of tackles.

It felt good.

The physical output, the burn in my legs and my lungs.

Twenty minutes into the second half, Lleyton threw me a short offload, and I took off. I dodged their inside centre and tried to fend off their fly half. He grabbed me around the legs, and as he was taking me to the ground, a swinging arm came and collected me.

I don't remember leaving the field.

I came to in the dressing shed with the team strapper and the medic peering down at me. I was on my back, I couldn't see very well, and I tried to sit up, but the medic stopped me. "Stay there," he said. He was holding something to my eye, and it stung.

"You're okay, Tye," the strapper said. "You got coat-hangered, that's all."

"How's your neck?" The medic was peering into my eyes. "Do you have any pain?"

He kept asking me question after question, but the only thing it accomplished was annoying me.

"I'm fine," I said. "How's the game? How long have we got to go?"

The strapper laughed but the medic shook his head. "You're not going back out there. You gotta pass a head injury assessment with a fifteen-minute clearance. The game'll be over by then. Just relax."

He took the swathe away from my head and I could see the bloodied gauze. He inspected it. "Shouldn't need stitches. I'll put a clip on it. But you're gonna have a helluva black eye."

My eye was already swollen. When he'd taken the swathe away, I still couldn't see any better and it was because my eyebrow was now twice its normal size.

Great.

The medic did what he had to do: flushed it, cleaned it, stuck a butterfly clip on the cut, and wrapped my head. And by the time I'd cleared the concussion tests and he let me leave, I only got to see the last few minutes of the game.

We won, but it was bittersweet.

Their number four got the remainder of the game in the sin bin, and I got a swollen eyebrow, a bleeding cut, and a cracking headache.

But I wasn't averse to a little pain.

Nothing a few post-win celebratory drinks at the pub wouldn't fix, anyway.

I'd only intended to have one or two. I needed to get home and get myself ready for my nine o'clock appointment with a different kind of pain.

The bar was pumping; music was loud, laughter even louder, and I knew before we'd even walked in that the Ryde boys were there. They'd played Newport and had to literally drive past our pub to get back to theirs.

And from the noise, I could safely assume they'd won.

I saw Taka first. He was hard to miss. The man was a mountain. And, of course, wherever Taka was, Marshall was never far away.

He was standing there, a beer in his hand, laughing at

something. He wore jeans and that woollen sweater that suited him so well; it was a creamy brown like his hair, it was soft and cosy, well-loved.

And then he saw me.

He tried to hide his reaction, and maybe no one else would have ever noticed. But his jaw ticked and his eyes hardened. Now, he'd looked at me with the hatred of a sworn enemy a thousand times. I was no stranger to Marshall's contempt.

It was my favourite thing about him. The man hated me.

But this look was different.

I still had the bandage around my head, and I could only see out of my right eye, but I saw that look just fine.

I just didn't know what it meant.

Lleyton handed me a beer and I tried to laugh with them, but the truth was, my headache was kinda bad, and I couldn't focus. The beer didn't help at all.

I stood up and Lleyton grabbed me. "You okay?"

"Yeah, just gonna take a piss."

I weaved my way through the crowd, earning a few comments and nods from the Ryde team about my bang up. I finished at the urinal and washed my hands, then looked at myself in the mirror. I'm sure the bandage wrapped around my head made it look worse than it was, and I considered taking it off when someone decided they needed to wash their hands in my sink.

I knew from his scent, from the way he brushed up against me, and the warm timbre of his voice who it was.

"Who did that to you?" Marshall asked. He shook the water from his hands and met my gaze in the mirror. "Who was it?"

That hatred, the barely contained loathing, was in his eyes all right. It just wasn't aimed at me.

I wasn't sure what to make of that.

Before I could answer, someone walked in, and Marshall walked out without so much as a backward glance.

I went back to the tables my team was at, but I didn't even sit down. "Hey, guys, I'm out," I said. "Gonna Uber it home."

They half-heartedly protested, but they kept looking at my eye as if they understood. I ordered a ride home, pocketed my phone, and clapped Lleyton's shoulder.

"I'll call you in the morning to see if you didn't die," he said.

"Yeah, thanks." I gave them a wave as I turned to walk out.

"And don't worry about Burwood's number four," Connor yelled. "Bastard'll get what he's owed."

I glanced at Marshall on my way out and I knew he'd heard that. His smile told me he'd heard it just fine.

The air outside was bitingly cold and it kind of helped with my headache and my throbbing eyebrow. I only had to wait a few minutes for my Uber and when I climbed into the dark backseat, someone slid in right next to me.

Someone with a familiar scent and soft woollen sweater.

CHAPTER 9

MARSHALL

IT WAS A STRANGE THING SEEING VALENTINE WITH A banged-up face. He had a bandage wrapped around his head. His left eye was half covered but clearly swollen and there was already bruising.

Whoever had hit him had hit him hard. And it wasn't a typical knock from rugby. Lord knows I'd had my fair share of those. This was a deliberate hit.

And it bothered me in ways I wasn't quite prepared for.

In ways I couldn't quite rightly explain.

Because just a few days ago, I'd caught a quick glimpse of the bruises I'd put on his throat and, as disturbing as it was, I found it hot.

I'd marked his skin.

Imprints of *my* fingers when I'd gripped his throat while I fucked him. While I owned him, owned his body in animalistic ways.

Yes, it was fucked up. Me marking him? I was totally on board with that, and so was he.

But someone else?

Someone else hurting him?

Yeah, that didn't fly with me.

As soon as I'd seen him, a burst of fire flared behind my sternum, embers white hot.

No one else touches him.

No one but me.

And that feeling, that possessiveness and claim of ownership was a new and strange thing.

Because I didn't own him.

I mean, I did in bed.

But I didn't really. I had no claim on him. I had no business even caring what had happened. Before our agreement, if he'd copped a black eye from someone, I'd have found it funny and would have assumed he'd deserved it. I'd probably have offered to buy the guy who did it a beer.

Now I wanted to kill him.

Number four from Burwood. Second row.

No one touched Valentine fucking Tye but me.

God, it was so fucked up.

And so was sneaking out of the pub and slipping into the Uber with him. He was pale and clearly not feeling well. His friends should have noticed that. They hadn't.

But I had.

"What do you think you're doing?" he whispered, probably so the Uber guy didn't think I'd hijacked the ride.

"Making sure you get home okay."

He snorted. "Guess it saves you paying for your own ride in an hour's time."

God, he infuriated me.

Like saving a few bucks was the only reason I'd joined him.

"If you're not gonna say thank you for me checking on you, then just shut the fuck up."

He shot me a glare with his right eye, but given the

bandages and swollen left eye, it fell far short of menacing. It would have been funny if it didn't look so painful.

And if it didn't fucking bother me so much.

We made the rest of the trip in silence, got out at his place, and I followed him inside. We stepped into the elevator and he sighed as we went up to his floor.

"Does your head hurt?" I asked.

He nodded.

"And your eye?"

He nodded again, just as the elevator doors opened. He unlocked his front door and I followed him inside. He dumped his wallet and keys on the fancy cabinet thing, just as Enzo the cat came out to yell at him.

"Yes, I'm sorry," Valentine said. "I'll feed you. I'm sure you're starving."

Enzo yelled at him some more.

I pulled Valentine's arm and led him to the dining table. "You sit. I'll feed the cat."

I could see Enzo's bowl on the floor, and there were still some biscuits in it. I pointed to it. "You haven't eaten all of those yet."

Then the freaking cat yelled at me.

"All right, all right, Christ."

I opened a tall door I assumed was the pantry door and found some vet brand of cat biscuits. I held it up for Valentine to see. "This?"

Valentine damn near smiled. "Yes."

Enzo yelled at me again.

"You make a lot of demands for someone who doesn't pay rent," I said to him. He yelled louder, so I filled his bowl with his stupid biscuits just to shut him up.

I found the first aid kit from the overhead cupboard I'd seen Valentine get it from before, and there were some headache tablets next to it. I grabbed those too and pulled a bottle of water from the fridge.

"Make yourself at home," Valentine said flatly.

I shut the fridge door with my foot, took everything over to the table, and popped two capsules for him. "Take those."

I pulled a chair over and sat in front of him, our knees interlocked. He took the pills without argument, and I gently unwound the bandage from his head and peeled the wad of gauze off his eyebrow.

It'd stuck to the butterfly clip with blood, and it did pull a little even with me being gentle and slow. But he never flinched.

I had to wonder about his pain tolerance.

His eyebrow was swollen and his eye was almost fully shut. It was mottled and bruised with dark red and black near the bridge of his nose. The cut on the corner of his eyebrow seemed to be the least of it.

It looked sore as hell.

"Jesus," I breathed. "Do you have any pain other than the headache?"

He half shrugged. "No. The medic felt all along my orbital bones. Said nothing felt broken. It's just swollen. And I passed the HIA."

I stood up and went to the freezer for some peas or corn. There were none. "Do you not have frozen peas?"

"I hate peas."

There were exactly two bags in the otherwise empty freezer. Frozen mango pieces and a huge bag of edamame. I grabbed those. "You have freaking edamame and not peas?"

"I like it."

I wrapped the bag in a tea towel and gently pressed it against his eye. "Hold that."

Then I remembered how he'd been the other day when

I'd seen him at the office. He was pale and a bit shaky because he hadn't eaten. "Did you eat tonight?"

"No."

"Did you eat today?"

He looked away.

Christ.

"I had breakfast," he said.

I opened his fridge again, noticing now just how empty it was. Sure, there were bottles of water, a small tub of expensive butter, some chutney on the door, a block of some fancy cheese.

And nothing else.

Then I checked his pantry again and realised there wasn't much in there either.

"What do you eat?"

Enzo saw the open pantry as an opportunity for more food, so I scooped him up and held him. At least he wasn't yelling at me now. "There's more food in here for you than what there is for your dad."

I carried Enzo back to the table and sat down; Enzo sat himself down on my lap. "What kind of pizza do you like?"

Valentine looked at me, then at Enzo, then shrugged. "Any. I'm not fussy."

I took out my phone and ordered two pizzas. "I hope you like tandoori chicken pizza or meat lovers, because that's what we're having."

"You don't have to do . . . any of this," he said quietly. He let his hand drop, his swollen eye making him look more pitiful.

I lifted his hand and the bag of edamame back to his eye. "Keep it on there."

"I'm no stranger to pain," he mumbled.

Jesus Christ.

I didn't want to think about that.

"So," I said, giving Enzo a pat. He started to purr. "Number four on the Burwood team, huh?"

His good eye cut to mine before he looked away, and he sighed. "I really can't say for sure. I don't remember it. I woke up in the dressing rooms. But they said it was number four, and he was in the sin bin, so . . ."

I nodded slowly. "Kinda convenient that we play Burwood next week."

He snorted. "What are you gonna do? Get even?"

"Fuck yes, I am." I pulled on his shirt collar to get a look at his neck. The marks I'd left there were gone. "No one lays a finger on you but me."

He rolled his good eye and let his hand drop to his lap. "The fuck is that supposed to mean?"

I didn't know what it was supposed to mean. It sounded better in my head, less possessive and less . . . I didn't know what it was supposed to mean.

I pointed my chin to his eye. "This was a dog shot. A cheap, deliberate hit. So fuck the guy that did this."

He put the bag of edamame back to his eye and gestured to Enzo, who was now a black loaf purring on my lap. "What the fuck is this?"

"He likes me. Cats are a very good judges of character."

"He's a traitor, and he crossed enemy lines."

I laughed. "Enemies with benefits includes cuddles with the cat."

Valentine sneered at me but then winced.

"Why don't you go have a hot shower," I suggested. "Then the pizza will be here and then you can take more pills and go to bed."

He dropped his hand again. "What about our Saturday night arrangement?"

I almost laughed. "You think I'm fucking you with your face banged up like that?"

"Sorry I'm not pretty enough—"

"I don't give a fuck what you look like, arsehole. You're in pain enough as it is, and there ain't no way I'm pushing your face into the mattress or squeezing your throat when you already have a headache and a head wound. Jesus Christ, Valentine."

He sneered and made a low rumbling sound. It was possibly a growl, and maybe under different circumstances it would have been hot. "Then what are you here for?" he asked quietly.

Like it was a completely foreign concept that someone might want to make sure he was okay. "You weren't lookin' too good when you left the pub."

He raised his chin a little. "You can go once your pizzas get here."

"The pizzas are for you, arsehole. And I'm staying here tonight. I'll take the couch."

He looked stunned. "Stay?"

"You said you don't remember being hit, and you woke up in the dressing rooms. That means you got knocked out. Which means you need someone to check on you to make sure you wake up. For fuck's sake, did they say none of this to you?"

He shook his head and shrugged in an I-don't-know kinda way, which meant he had no idea what they'd told him because he got knocked the fuck out and couldn't remember.

He sighed, resigned, because he knew I was right.

"Anyway, me and Enzo are besties now." I gave him a few pats, making him purr louder. "I'm here for him, not you. It's not *all* about you, arsehole."

Valentine rolled his good eye, and damn, he almost smiled.

"Now go have a shower," I ordered. "You'll feel better. Then you can eat and go to sleep with a belly full of carbs."

It also wouldn't hurt him to see his face in a mirror.

Ignoring him so he'd go do what he was told, I picked up Enzo and went to the couch, found the remote, and turned on the TV. "Let's see what we can find to watch."

After a few minutes of scrolling and ignoring Valentine, he walked into his room. A short while later, I heard the shower and then I got a message that the pizza was here. I left his door ajar, and when I put the two pizzas on his coffee table, Valentine walked out.

He wore track pants and a T-shirt, his hair was washed and still wet. He looked cleaner and fresh, and his face still looked sore as hell.

"Oh, wow," I said. "Is that a new eyeshadow colour? I hear mangled plum is all the rage this season."

He sat down next to me. "Funny."

"Still got a headache?"

He made a *hm* sound that told me yes, of course he still had a headache.

"Eat up," I said, separating the pizza boxes.

He chose the tandoori chicken to start with and almost inhaled his first slice. The idiot needed to eat more.

"It's good," he said, taking another slice.

I spoke with my mouth full of meat lovers. "I shoulda ordered some Coke."

He stared at me, disgusted. "Charming."

I grinned at him. I didn't need to mind my manners around him; he already didn't like me. There was no reason to be on my best behaviour.

"Your Netflix selections are lame," I added, then bit into

more pizza. "You can tell a lot about someone by their recently watched list." I nodded to the thumbnails on his massive TV. "What the fuck is this shit?"

He chewed and swallowed before speaking. "I don't watch a great deal of television."

"I'm not surprised, because what you watch is shit." I scrolled down to the action movies and found the first *Expendables* movie. "This is where the good stuff is at."

"Don't click on—"

Too late.

"Now I'm going to have them recommend me more of this." He waved his hand at the screen. "Dear god, what even is this?"

"This is good," I said, again with my mouth full. I pointed my half-eaten slice at the TV. "It's got all the old-school action actors in it."

He sighed. I didn't know why, but annoying him made me happy.

He watched the first two minutes. "Have you ever considered watching something educational?"

"This is educational. If I ever need to know how to beat the shit outta someone, or blow shit up, or drive in a car chase, or fly a plane while getting shot at, I'll know how to do it."

"You do know how to beat the shit out of people," he said flatly. "I've seen you play rugby."

I chuckled and picked up another slice of pizza. "I don't hit people without good reason."

"You've tried to take my head off a few times."

"Yeah. Like I said. Not without good reason."

He smirked.

Arsehole.

Enzo came sniffing at the pizza boxes. "Enzo, get down," Valentine said.

I picked a piece of Italian sausage off my pizza and gave it to the cat, and when Valentine glared at me, I smiled at him.

"Pissing you off is my favourite thing to do," I said.

He did that growling thing again, but he sat back on the couch, clearly having eaten enough. I think he'd had two pieces.

"You need to eat more," I told him.

"You need to mind your own business."

I snorted and tried his tandoori pizza and spoke to him with my mouth full, for no other reason than he didn't like it. "Hm, this is good."

He stared at the TV. "Thank you for ordering it. I need to put a grocery order in. I usually do that on Sundays."

"That might explain why you have no food here," I said. "And why you went to work the other day without eating. Does that happen often?"

He shot me a glare. "You're awfully concerned about something that's none of your business."

"But it kinda is my business. If I'm gonna come here and rail you twice a week as hard as you like it, I need to know you can handle it."

He turned his glare to the television instead, but his nostrils flared. "I can handle it just fine."

It really did make me feel so much better to have him pissed at me.

I laughed. "Hm, yes, yes you can handle it."

He sighed, his voice flat. "You can leave whenever you're ready. I don't need you to stay."

"Oh, I'm staying. For no other reason than to piss you off."

EWB   117

"You've far exceeded my expectations in that regard."

I snorted again. "I far exceed your expectations in all regards. Otherwise you wouldn't have propositioned me to be your EWB."

"EWB?"

"Enemies with Benefits."

He sighed loudly. "Right."

"And you wouldn't have asked me to dick you twice a week if I didn't exceed your expectations."

"Are you done?"

"Not even close."

"But you refused tonight, so my expectations are not exceeded."

I gave the pizza crust to Enzo, earning another glare from Valentine. Then, to piss him right off, I patted him on the head. Valentine, not the cat. "If you're a good boy, I'll suck your dick before I leave tomorrow."

He seethed. "I hate you."

"I hate you more. But that's what I'm doing here, right?" I stood and picked up the pizza boxes. "It's what makes being your EWB so much fun."

I shoved the pizzas into the fridge and, after searching a few cupboards for a glass, I poured myself some tap water.

"Want another water?" I asked.

Valentine stood up. "No, thank you. I'm going to bed."

"Take some more pills," I said, collecting the headache pills from the table and offering them to him with my glass of water.

"No, thank you. I have . . . I have something stronger." He turned and walked to his bedroom door and paused. "I can't offer you a spare bed because I don't have one. I don't even have a spare blanket. If you get cold . . ."

"I'll be fine," I said. "If you start to feel sick or dizzy, let me know."

He frowned at the floor and gave a nod. "Good night."

He left his door slightly ajar, and a few moments later, I heard the toilet flush, and his light went out. I watched the rest of the movie with Enzo, hearing nothing but silence from Valentine's room.

I probably didn't need to stay. I was sure he'd be fine. But he'd had a pretty decent knock to the head, and by rights, someone should check on him. He'd said he was going to take something stronger than headache pills, so I was pretty sure he'd be out of it. I opened his door as quietly as I could, and he was on his side, sleeping on the not-banged-up side of his face. His mouth was slightly open, his chest rising and falling.

He didn't stir.

Leaving him alone, I found the main bathroom and took a piss, then decided to have a little sticky beak around his apartment. He'd said he didn't have a spare bed but there was definitely another door. I wondered if it was going to be some kinky sex room and was disappointed to find his spare room was set up with a treadmill and weights and a yoga mat.

A yoga mat?

Of course, he did yoga.

Then again, it probably explained his incredible core strength. I could bend him in some pretty impressive positions while I fucked him, and he managed them all. Plus, he had great abs and obliques . . .

I considered getting myself a yoga mat and closed the door.

His apartment was gorgeous, no two ways about it. And

expensive. Like holy shit. I didn't know anyone that could afford a place like this. Except him, of course. His furniture was all designer stuff and I'd seen his bed enough times to know it was the super-expensive kind.

But his apartment was decidedly empty. There was very little of him on display. No personal touches, nothing to make me say, *yes, Valentine Tye lived here.*

Maybe that was the real Valentine Tye.

Private, closed off, nothing personal, just showroom-vibes only.

It kinda tracked.

Having seen enough, I fell back onto the couch and decided to fuck up his recently watched list a bit more by clicking on the worst action movies I could find, and when I was bored with that, I checked on Valentine again.

He was now on his back, snoring softly.

So typical that he was even gorgeous when he slept with a banged-up face.

But then he mumbled and flinched in his sleep, immediately wincing at the pain and groaning. He didn't wake up though, so I went in and sat beside him. I touched his forehead with the back of my hand. He didn't feel hot, but the touch made him stir. His good eye cracked open.

"Just checking on you," I whispered. "Go back to sleep."

Hmm. Maybe I should keep a closer eye on him.

With that in mind, I peeled off my sweater and socks and, leaving my jeans on, I climbed into bed with him. I was on the other side of the bed, the side closest to the door, but it made him stir again.

"What are you doing?" he mumbled.

"Keeping an eye on you," I hissed back at him. "So shut the fuck up and go to sleep."

Even in the dark room, I could have sworn he smiled.
Arsehole.

I woke up before the sun to find Valentine using my arm as
a pillow, tucked into my side with his head on my chest. He
was sound asleep.

What the hell?

I was still wearing jeans and a shirt, which wasn't overly
comfortable. But his bed . . . holy hell, it was the most
comfortable bed I'd ever been in.

And him in my arms. His body heat, his weight.

It made for real deep sleeping.

Which I tried not to think about. I couldn't get my head
around the fact it was Valentine freaking Tye.

I was tempted to shove him off, but I remembered his
black eye, so I let him lie on me for a bit longer . . .

Not thinking about how good it felt. How comfortable it
was, how he fit against me so well. How I wouldn't mind
waking up like this with him more often.

I tried not to think about that the most.

Until I needed to pee.

I peeled him off me as gently as I could, rolling him
back over to his side, and I got out of bed. His ensuite door
was open so I went in and relieved myself. His ensuite bathroom was all charcoal grey tiles, black sink, cabinets, and
tapware.

Expensive as fuck.

The mirror above his vanity was one of those fancy
backlit ones and even his hand soap was some expensive
crap with a minimalist label. Then, because I couldn't help
myself, I cracked open his cabinet, surprised by what I saw.

Not the skin care retinols and sunscreen shit, or even his brand of deodorant or stupidly expensive cologne that I loved the smell of.

But the three orange prescription bottles with his name on them.

I didn't recognise the drug names, not that I expected to. Not that I cared. Because it wasn't any of my business.

But damn.

I was surprised to see it, but at the same time, I wasn't surprised he had them. He had issues, as I was all too aware. We had an agreement for me to hate-fuck him twice a week and he liked it when I told him he was a piece of shit and a whore.

So yeah, he had more issues than *Reader's Digest*.

And I remembered all too clearly when his father had turned up at work the other day. Valentine had been fine— he was always frosty and reserved, that was nothing unusual. Well, he'd been unwell and even thankful for the tea and crackers I'd given him. He'd even smiled.

But when he saw his father, I swear a wall of ice went up around him.

An ice wall as real as me standing next to him in the breakroom.

Now, if I hated Valentine with the power of a burning sun, then I hated his father infinitely more—with the power of every sun in the universes. I despised that man. Loathed him in ways I couldn't even begin to explain.

And I got the distinct impression that Valentine did too.

Hated him or feared him, I wasn't sure which. But his reaction, that visceral recoil, cold as ice, was a reaction of a truth untold. Valentine hadn't expected to see his father; that much had been very clear. Because I'd have thought he'd be better at hiding his reaction than that if he'd been prepared. And maybe if I hadn't spent time with Valentine over these last few weeks, I wouldn't have even noticed.

But notice I did.

I told myself it wasn't my business because I did *not* care.

I did *not* care about Valentine fucking Tye.

I closed the cabinet door and left his bathroom. He was still asleep and I could see the discoloured blotch around his eye.

I should have just left. I should have grabbed all my shit, called an Uber, and took my arse home, but something—and I don't know fucking what—but something made me stay.

I couldn't make him breakfast because he had no damn food in the house, but I could make coffee and heat up some leftover pizza.

Enzo met me in the kitchen. He sat there with his tail wrapped around his little front paws and gave me a judgemental up and down. Pretty sure he knew what I did to his owner twice a week, and he was not impressed.

"Good morning to you too," I mumbled.

I opened cupboards, looking for the coffee. Valentine used the pod kind in his two-thousand-dollar Italian machine. A far cry from my instant kind of supermarket coffee. But whatever.

As soon as I opened the pantry, Enzo weaved between my legs and meowed loudly.

"Oh, you wanna talk to me now," I replied.

He meowed again and again, seriously yelling at me, and then I spotted some small tins of fancy cat food on the side shelf. I picked one up and showed it to him.

"This? Do you get this for breakfast?"

He meowed again and did a figure eight around my feet, rubbing against me, which I took for a yes.

I picked up his dish and tipped the leftover biscuits into the bin, and as soon as I opened the tin, he jumped up onto the counter next to me.

"Well, I'm pretty sure you're not allowed up there," I said, spooning the disgusting sardine gruel into his dish. "But I won't tell your dad if you don't."

"Tell me what?"

Both Enzo and I looked up to find Valentine standing near the wall.

"Nothing," I answered. "Right, Enzo?"

He stayed silent.

I grinned at Valentine. "See? I'm his favourite."

I put his bowl back down on the little mat and Enzo jumped down and began scarfing his food.

"Why did you feed him?"

"Because he told me he has one of those cans for breakfast."

"He told you?"

"Yes. Right after he told me I was his favourite."

Valentine scoffed at me. "Okay, Dr Doolittle."

Ignoring his attitude, I got a better look at his eye. The swelling had gone down a little and his eyeball was visible now at least, but it was very black and purple, and the cut at the end of his eyebrow had bled a little during the night.

"Your eye looks better," I said.

"Hm."

"How's your headache?"

He looked annoyed, but he eventually shrugged. "It's fine."

"I think I turned your coffee machine on," I said. "Does it need to heat up or something?"

He shuffled over to it and pressed a button, then took two coffee cups out of a cupboard.

I took the pizzas out of the fridge. "Plates?"

Valentine went to another cupboard and pulled out a plate and put it on the counter. "So, are you just not a morning person?" I asked. "Or does your head hurt and you just don't wanna say? Or are you pissed because I'm still here?"

He turned around, leaned against the counter, and crossed his arms. "Yes."

I snorted and threw some slices of meat lovers on the plate, then threw them into the microwave. But of course I didn't know how to get it to work because his microwave was fancy and stupid.

He gave an annoyed sigh and did it for me. Then I found the coffee pods and went to put one in the machine, but that annoyed Valentine too, because he sighed and nudged me out of the way so he could do it.

By the time the pizza was reheated and the coffees were made, he was well and truly annoyed. Of course that made me happy.

He took his cup to the dining table and sat down, and I took my coffee and the pizza. I picked up a slice and pushed the plate to him. He turned up his nose. "I don't eat breakfast."

I managed to chew and swallow before I spoke this time. "You should. I saw what happened to you the other day when you didn't eat."

He glowered at me.

I pushed the plate closer to him. "Eat up."

"No, thank you."

"Eat," I said.

"No. I'm . . . I'm having lunch with my sister." He shook his head as if it annoyed him that he'd told me that.

"I didn't know you had a sister."

He glowered, divulging no more details.

"You're allowed to eat more than once a day," I added. "In fact, three meals a day has been popular for a while now. They call them breakfast, lunch, and dinner, though there are regional variations of course. And in-between-meal snacks are a thing. And given you play and train for a contact sport—"

"Are you done?"

"Annoying you? No. I could do it all day."

Annoying him aside, he still hadn't eaten anything, and this was clearly going to turn into a game of who could be more stubborn, so I played dirty. "Eat half a piece of pizza, or I don't suck your dick before I leave."

He stared at me, then looked out the wall of glass to the morning sun and let out a sigh. "You should get a job as a police negotiator."

I snorted, but then I looked at his still-uneaten pizza and sighed dramatically. "Such a shame. I really wanted to eat your dick. I mean, you've had mine twice and I haven't had yours even once. How is that fair?"

His gaze cut to mine and . . . was he trying not to smile? "Fine," he relented, snatching up a slice of pizza. "Christ."

I bit into my last piece and grinned as I chewed.

He rolled his eyes. "You're so gross."

But he did eat three bites of pizza, so technically I won. But I kept looking at his eye . . . it looked sore.

"Now you can take some ibuprofen," I said. "It helps with swelling. And you should get some aloe vera. Direct from the plant if you can. Slather it all around your eye. It helps with bruising."

"Are you finished telling me what to do?" he asked flatly.

Sore eye or not, I really did want some dick before I left.

"Nope. Telling you what to do makes me horny." I pushed the plate away and my empty coffee cup, making room on the table in front of me. "Get your arse over here and give me your dick."

His nostrils flared, but he put his coffee cup down and stood up. I pulled him into place, right between my knees, and pushed him so his arse was on the table. I spread his legs apart with my knees and pulled his trackpants down.

He was going commando, so I had easy access and he was already half hard. I wanted him to know he wasn't the only one who could suck dick like a pro. Why I wanted him to know this, I couldn't begin to say. I just wanted him to know that I could ruin him, leave him a shattered, sated mess, no matter which way I decided to take him.

I wanted him to be such a whore for me, to beg for it.

So I sucked him to within an inch of his life. I did him so good he had one foot off the floor and had his head back, his body arched, groaning like the whore he was.

I played his body like a finely tuned instrument, and I drank every drop he gave me.

When he was done, he all but collapsed on the table, lying back with his legs spread, panting and twitching.

He was so fucking hot.

And I hated that he turned me on so much. I hated that every little thing he did sang to me in ways no one else ever had. My dick wanted him 24/7, wanted to be buried inside him every minute of every goddamn day.

And with him lyin' out on the table in front of me like a damn feast . . . I could have so easily taken him. No lube, no prep; just lift his arse and sink all the way into him. He'd have screamed and he'd have loved every second of it.

I could have. So easily.

I got to my feet, unzipped my jeans, and pulled my cock out.

I was so tempted . . . he was laid out before me, his pants down to his thighs, his arse was *right there*.

He tried to sit up so I pushed him back down, my hand pressed to his chest. "Stay the fuck there," I said, gripping my shaft and pumping. "I should fuck you right now," I bit out. "I should make it hurt."

He opened his legs wider.

Daring me.

Tempting me.

Like the whore he was.

"You need to learn your place," I hissed at him, jerking myself.

So close already. So fucking close.

"And your place is beneath me, taking everything I give you."

He moaned, and I leaned over him, my balls on his junk. With my hand still on his chest, I held him down, and I shot my load, painting stripes of come across his belly and his chest.

God, it felt so good.

Like I'd just marked my territory, like I owned him. Like he was mine to do with whatever I wanted, and the more I treated him like shit, the more he liked it.

Because he knew his place.

I tucked myself back into my jeans and lightly tapped the uninjured side of his face. "Such a good whore." His dick twitched, so yeah, he fucking liked it. I spread his legs wider and pulled his arse onto my crotch. "You better have your arse ready for me on Wednesday night. Because I won't be so patient."

He smirked and arched his back, like my words struck something inside him.

Jesus.

I left him, still lying on his dining table with his track-pants around his thighs, covered in my come, and I walked out.

CHAPTER 10

VALENTINE

LUNCH WITH MY SISTER WAS ACTUALLY KIND OF NICE. She'd almost died when I'd pulled off my sunglasses and she'd seen my eye, and she proceeded to lecture me about the dangers of rugby.

Thank god, she hadn't seen it last night.

The swelling had gone down a lot, and the cut was healing. There was no need for the butterfly clip now. But the colours . . . black, purple, blue, and red.

But I could see okay, and feeling along the eye socket, it was tender but there was no sharp pain, so nothing was broken.

And apart from my sister's lectures, it was nice to have someone concerned about me.

Like Marshall was concerned. Sure, he sneered at me a lot and gleefully said things purely to annoy me. But he *had* been concerned. He'd come home with me, tended to my injured face. He'd fed me, and he'd slept beside me to keep a close eye on me.

He had surprisingly gentle hands. When he was cleaning my eyebrow, I was surprised by how deft his calloused hands could be. Normally he was rough with me, holding me down, gripping hard.

But not last night.

And him sleeping in my bed . . . I'd never slept so soundly. Maybe it was just that I wasn't alone, that for some strange reason I felt safe with him, which was ridiculous considering the things he did to me, things that I asked him to do to me. Perhaps the reason I felt safe with him, or the fact I trusted him, was a testament to how fucked up I was.

But god, I'd slept well. Even in my sleep, I'd had vague recollections of the warmth of his body, his strong arms.

Maybe that had been a dream.

Goddammit.

Marshall Wise.

I wasn't supposed to like that he'd stayed the night. I wasn't supposed to like that he'd threatened me to eat breakfast. Or how he'd sucked my dick or held me down and come on me.

God, how he'd done that. And then just walked out as if I was something to be used however he saw fit.

He was so good at it.

No. Stop thinking about him.

As long as he kept on despising me, we'd be fine . . .

"Valentine?" Brooklyn said. "I lost you for a while there."

"Oh, sorry," I replied, sipping my mineral water. "The sun's putting me to sleep."

She smiled skyward. "It's so nice, isn't it?"

It was nice. The warmth of the sun on a cold winter day. It'd been far too long since I'd sat and enjoyed it.

"Have you heard from Mum?" she asked.

I shook my head. "No." Not for months. "You?"

She sipped her spritzer and rolled her eyes. "A few

weeks ago. She was in London, I think. Or . . ." She waved her hand. "Somewhere over there."

"Looking for a gin distillery that will allow her to swim in a vat?"

She laughed. "Highly likely."

Our mother had never been interested in us. We were raised by nannies and au pairs, none of them ever staying long. Brooklyn was three years older than me, and she'd gone to a private girl's school; me to a private boy's school. We'd done all we could not to be at home, basically. Our lives barely coincided at all. Until university, adulthood, when we'd try and connect.

Like now.

I did like her. Loved her, even. In the way that you loved a sibling. There was a bond of sorts, a commonality. Ours was our terrible parents.

All the money in the world couldn't buy us love.

"What will you do about work?" she asked.

"What about it?"

She nodded pointedly at my face. "Your eye. Dad will lose his shit if he sees you like that. At work, no less."

"He can get over it." I sneered, a common reaction to any mention of my father. "I got it playing rugby. It wasn't like I got busted by the cops with coke and hookers and tried to fight my way out of it."

She laughed, which was the reaction I was hoping for. "Oh my god, have you heard the latest?"

Happy I was no longer the subject of her questions, I chuckled and sipped my drink. "No. What has he done now?"

Mattias, our cousin, was a constant source of scandal and family embarrassment. A guy who prioritised sex and booze over everything else, and someone who my father chose to pretend didn't exist.

Was my father proud that his own two children were better behaved? Not at all. He used Mattias against us as a prime example of what not to do, of how shameless it was, how crude and disrespectful.

If only he knew what I did.

God, he didn't even know I was gay, let alone about my perversion for humiliation and degradation.

It was cheaper and more productive than therapy, and god knows I'd tried that. They'd all talked about my relationship with my father, and I could probably see why they'd take that leap. He was half the parental disaster that shaped me into who I was, after all. But he wasn't the only reason; my mother had equal shares in the stock of failed parenting.

But I'd made peace with that mess a long time ago.

I didn't need closure or acceptance or to open dialogue with my parents for me to move on with my life. They weren't the reason I craved sexual degradation, and like one shrink tried to explain, the lack of love from my father was not the reason I was gay and sought comfort from men.

That had been a very short first and last meeting with that idiot.

I mean, Jesus fucking Christ. I should have had them struck from practicing. Probably would have if it wouldn't have outed me in the process.

But there was no cryptic psychological analysis required.

I had fucked-up parents. So what? Take a number and get in line. I was now an adult, and I made my own choices for my future and well-being.

And above all?

I just really liked getting held down and deep-dicked by a guy who was hung like a horse. If he called me names while he held me down, even better. And if I ached for a day afterward and could imagine feeling his dick still inside me, double bonus.

Marshall ticked all those boxes.

I required nothing more from him than that, and he required nothing more than that from me. It was the perfect arrangement.

Last night, with him staying and sleeping in my bed, had been an exception to the rule. Nothing more.

"So," Brooklyn said, having finished telling me all about Mattias. She sipped her drink, smiling. "Seeing anyone?"

Visions of Marshall Wise filled my mind. His body, his dick. The way he fucked me, the sounds he made when he came inside me. His hands on me, the way he held me, tight enough to mark me.

But also, how he spoiled Enzo, and how my arsehole cat adored him.

The way Marshall smiled.

The sound of his laughter.

Christ.

"No," I answered flatly. "You?"

She studied me for a moment, then shook her head and turned her face back to the sun. "Heavens, no. I'm too conceited and too comfortable with solitude and my own company for anyone else. Or so I've been told."

I laughed and, reaching over, tapped my glass to hers. "Cheers to that."

She smiled at me. "Thanks, Mum and Dad, for such a wonderful family trait."

I cracked up laughing, which hurt my eye. "Ow."

She laughed. "You need to get yourself some aloe vera."

I nodded and smiled as I sipped my drink. "Yeah. So I've been told."

———

I CONSIDERED NOT GOING to work, as Brooklyn had suggested, because my father would hate it and would think it'd reflect badly on his company, and god forbid his son be seen as anything other than perfect.

But I had work to do and didn't care what people thought.

If I had critical meetings or teleconferences with important clients, I'd have probably made other arrangements. I could understand wanting a perfect appearance with overseas buyers, but everything on my calendar this week could be done from my office. I didn't have to see anyone . . . except for the Monday morning site-manager meeting.

I walked into the conference room at exactly eight to a crowd that fell silent when they saw me.

I put my iPad on the table and gestured to my still-black eye, to which they were all staring at. I figured it was best to get it out of the way straight up. "Rugby union. I'd like to joke and say you should see the other guy, but *I* didn't even see him."

"Holy sh—" Harris said, clearly stunned. "Sorry. I didn't even know you played rugby."

"I do."

"Did you win?" Carl asked with a grimace/smile.

"My team? Yes. Me?" I gestured again to my eye. "Not so much."

Someone snorted.

Marshall.

"Have you considered wearing headgear?" he asked.

My gaze met his and he smirked as he tapped his pen on his notepad, but there was something in his eyes that told me perhaps he was serious. As if he wanted me to wear protective headgear so I wouldn't get hurt.

"I'll keep it in mind," I replied, holding his gaze for a beat. Then I changed the subject. "Okay, enough about me. This week's going to be busy enough without me keeping you longer, given the end of financial year is fast approaching. All invoices need to be lodged . . ."

I kept the meeting short and sweet, using bullet points to brush over topics of importance. I'd taken Marshall's advice to heart. These people weren't interested in the corporate wankery I was used to. They wanted fast facts so they could get back to work.

I liked that.

And the breakfast idea had been a good one too.

Last week I'd learned from Andrews about the changed traffic control, which had an indirect impact on his job site, and I might not have known otherwise. And today's breakfast chat with Harris when they mentioned, just in passing, they had firsthand experience with green energy solutions.

And that was something I'd earmarked for a potential job coming up in September.

Though the additional time with Marshall in a public, professional setting wasn't as easy as I'd thought it would be.

When I made myself a coffee, he was suddenly beside me. "Your eye looks a lot better," he murmured.

"Thanks. The aloe helped."

He grabbed an egg-and-bacon burger and pretended we weren't having a conversation. "Did you eat breakfast?"

"Having it now," I mumbled, stirring my coffee, pretending I didn't know him.

He grabbed a second burger and shoved it at me. "You need to eat."

And then he was gone, off talking to Carl and Jaman again as if this secretive exchange hadn't happened at all. Over the next half an hour, I saw him look my way once or twice, and then he stood with his back to me.

Was that so he wouldn't keep looking at me?

I'd have liked to think it was. That I bothered him. That he had to make himself *not* look at me.

That I messed with his head. That it annoyed him. That it made him mad at me or at himself. I didn't care which, as long as he took it out on me on Wednesday night.

When I looked the next time, he was gone.

I told myself I didn't care, that I didn't feel his absence. And that him making sure I ate food every once in a while didn't mean anything.

Because it didn't.

Marshall Wise meant nothing more to me than a mutually beneficial sexual agreement. He gave me exactly what I needed and letting him use my body for his own gratification was exactly what he needed, apparently.

It wasn't anything more than that.

It couldn't ever be.

We were too different, from two very different worlds. Aside from me being his boss, not forgetting one very important factor: Marshall Wise hated me. My family had hurt his family in ways I could never fully understand or appreciate. He would never forgive me for what my father did, nor should he.

And that stark realisation sat like a cold greasy lump of dread in my belly, a dull ache behind my ribs.

So I told myself that I'd let him fuck me extra hard this Wednesday. That I'd encourage him to do it.

And that I'd deserve it.

The fact I needed it and loved it was an added bonus.

Why I was starting to feel conflicted about that, I wasn't sure. Nor did I have any intention of unpacking that.

Nope.

I tucked that nonsense away and closed the lid tight. And counted the hours down until Wednesday.

CHAPTER 11

MARSHALL

VALENTINE'S EYE DIDN'T LOOK ANYWHERE NEAR AS BAD as I thought it would on Monday morning. It didn't look good, let me put it that way. But the cut was healing nicely, the swelling was mostly gone, and the dark purple was fading and would soon be that sickly green and yellow.

But he still didn't eat enough, and what possessed me to shove a breakfast burger in his hand at the manager's meeting, I'll never know.

I could tell myself that it was because if I was going to rail him a few times a week, he needed to look after himself. But his need to get called names while I fucked him hard made me question his self-worth enough as it was, and if he was going to add not looking after himself, then maybe he was on a quest for self-destruction, and that wasn't a ride I signed up for.

I understood the whole hold-me-down-and-fuck-me thing was hot. And I understood that some folks had a kink for getting degraded or praised, and I was completely fine with that.

But didn't those people have faith in their sexual part-

ners to look after them? To trust their sexual partners to
ensure *all* their needs were being met?

I didn't know enough about that lifestyle and maybe I
was a fool for diving in headfirst without asking questions or
setting boundaries for myself.

Making sure Valentine ate enough food was the bare
minimum, surely.

I didn't want to back out. I didn't want to bail on our
agreement. Because for all his faults, Valentine was right
about one thing.

It was fucking hot.

I'd basically had a permanent semi since this whole
agreement started. He had invaded almost every waking
thought. I found myself thinking about him when I was in
the shower, when I was stuck in traffic, when I was at my
parent's dining table for Sunday dinner.

When I was at home on Monday night . . . which was
why I also found myself googling shit like *mentality behind
sexual behaviours* and *behavioural traits of sexual
submission.*

What had Valentine said that very first time?

He'd tried BDSM clubs, but they weren't for him
because they didn't *really* hate him.

And he needed someone who *actually* hated him.

Christ.

Was I in over my head?

I was beginning to think I was.

Would I stop seeing him?

No.

I still didn't like the guy. In fact, he annoyed the hell out
of me, and it gave me great joy to piss him off.

But he wasn't the complete arsehole I'd thought he was.

There were more layers to him than I'd assumed, and he

certainly didn't have the perfect life I'd thought he had.
Sure, he had money. He was born into that, yes. But he
worked hard for it too.

I didn't pity him.

I could see now that he was a guy with issues and
demons, just like anyone else. He wasn't infallible. God, he
was far, far from perfect.

But I wasn't sure if I still hated him.

And the fact that we had sex without condoms . . . as
much as I could tell myself otherwise, that meant something
to me. It wasn't anything I'd ever done with anyone else,
and some weird-primal part of me loved the fact that I could
come inside him.

Him, especially. That it was Valentine Tye who took
my seed. That, like some fucked-up reasoning, I owned him.
A guy who had been an adversary my entire life would
bend over and take my loads because I owned him.

And that was kinda fucked up.

"What's up with you?" Noah asked. We'd finished
training on Tuesday night and were having a few beers at
the pub afterward. I'd missed drinking with these guys—my
last few post-game Saturday drinking sessions had gone by
the wayside—and it felt good to knock back a few and talk
shit with the boys.

But my mind had wandered back to Valentine. Again.

"You ditched us the last few Saturdays," Taka added.
"Don't tell me someone sunk their hooks into ya?"

I laughed. "Fuck no."

Taka shoved his face in mine. "Holy shit. You're blush-
ing! You *are* seeing someone!"

I gave him a shove and laughed it off. "Fuck off. I am
not. No one's got their hooks in me."

They all laughed, and I had to question my ability to lie.

Was it a lie though?

Jesus Christ, Marshall.

"You haven't hooked up with anyone the last few weeks, Wise," Millsy said, then took a swig of his beer. "You been leaving early, not drinking, not fightin' anyone."

I shook my head. "That's not true."

It kinda was and we all knew it.

Noah shook his head at me. "You are fucking whipped."

I pointed my beer bottle at him. "That is a crock of shit."

Taka laughed. "It might have been convincing if you were trying not to smile, my friend."

"Who is it?" Millsy pressed.

"No one."

"Come on, give us a name."

"There isn't anyone."

"Who's the lucky guy?" Taka asked.

"No one!"

"Who's the poor guy that has to take your dick?" Noah asked. "Can he even walk the next day?"

I couldn't help but laugh. I shared a locker room and showers with these guys. They'd seen me, and they'd all made jokes. I had a big dick. This was common knowledge and often the punchline of many jokes. It was hardly an insult.

I hid my smile behind by beer. "You guys are delusional."

Millsy shook his head sadly. "We've lost another one, boys." He made the sign of the cross with his beer bottle. "RIP Marshall Wise. The man-whore lives no more."

They all raised their beers like it was some farewell salute to the fallen.

I snorted and took a swig of my beer. "You guys are full of shit."

Millsy gestured around the bar. There was a decent crowd for a Tuesday night. "Then prove us wrong. Go pick up some random, right now."

I scoffed. "No."

"See?" he said like it proved some point. "It's not like you haven't fucked anyone in these bathrooms before, let's be real."

Well, that was true.

"Just because I don't feel like it, don't mean shit."

Millsy raised his eyebrow and Taka laughed. "Yep. He's a goner."

I gave another glance around the bar. I mean, there were a few guys who I knew would be up for it. And I technically could pick up . . . if I wanted to.

But I didn't want to.

And not because it was a rule to mine and Valentine's agreement.

I just didn't need to, because . . . well, because my needs were being well and truly met.

With Valentine.

Fucking hell.

The guys joked some more and I didn't even mind. If today was my turn to be the butt of their jokes, so be it.

But then on Wednesday at work the jokes continued as soon as Taka and Millsy walked on the job. Taka strode in, doing some sidestep dance to "Lover Boy" by Billy Ocean while Millsy laughed his arse off.

"You're not funny," I said.

Millsy replied by singing "Let's Hear It for the Boy" and Taka continued his stupid dance, both of them clearly thinking this was the funniest thing ever.

And maybe it would have been if I hadn't tossed and turned all night thinking about what they'd said. How I was a goner, how someone had their claws into me, and RIP to the man-whore.

I had to yell over the top of them so they could hear me. "Next person to sing today is on shitter-cleaning duty for a year."

They both shut up.

And then, because apparently when you sing about the devil, he turns up.

"Ah Marshall," Taka said, nodding to the carpark. "The boss is here."

I turned to find Valentine walking in. I let my head fall back with a groan. "Just fucking great."

Which, I then realised, Valentine heard.

"Do you have a problem, Wise?" he said as he got closer.

Shit.

"Aw, don't be too hard on him, boss," Taka said with his huge, lovable grin. "We were just teasin' him because he went and got himself a boyfriend."

Valentine's eyes shot to mine.

"Not something we thought we'd ever see in our life-times," Millsy added. "Gotta say, pity the poor man who tamed this one."

I ran both hands through my hair and let out a slow puff of air, trying to calm down. "Like I told both you boofheads last night, no, I don't. And this is not the place to bring it up, so if you could both shut the fuck up, that'd be great." Then I gave Valentine an exasperated look. "So no, no problem here. To what do I owe the privilege of this unexpected visit with impeccable timing today?"

His jaw bulged. "A word, please," he murmured, and turned on his heel and began walking back to his car.

I shot Taka and Millsy a thanks-a-fucking-lot look and followed Valentine. He walked all the way back to his car where he didn't even turn around. We just had some weird side-on conversation.

"What. The fuck. Was that?"

Okay, so it wasn't much of a conversation . . .

"That," I replied, "was a carry-over from last night where half my rugby teammates accused me of being under the thumb because I no longer got shitfaced and wanted to fight people after the game on Saturdays. I've bailed on them the last few weekends and they noticed. Apparently the idea of me being nailed down to one guy is funny as hell."

Valentine's nostrils flared and his jaw ticked, but he kept his eyes straight ahead. "You didn't tell them anything . . ."

"Are you insane?" I snorted. "Like I would ever tell them that. Or tell anyone, for that matter."

His gaze cut to mine with laser precision.

I cracked a smile. "They wouldn't believe me if I did."

He stared at me, studied my eyes, looking for what fuck only knew. "Hm."

I couldn't resist having a little jab. "Are you jealous? When they said I had a boyfriend, did you think it was someone else?"

He scowled at me. "Don't be ridiculous."

And another jab. "Did you think it was the end of our agreement? Were you sad?"

He seethed. "I would miss one part of you." His gaze drew down to my dick and back up. "And nothing else."

I laughed. "Liar."

"If you think—"

"Your eye looks good."

He shut his mouth and his nostrils flared as he tried for a breath of calm. "You're so infuriating."

"All part of the agreement."

He shook his head, and damn if that fucker didn't almost smile. "Your work crew are most likely watching."

"One hundred percent chance of that, yes. They're probably taking bets to see if one of us throws a punch. Odds will be in my favour, just so you know."

Valentine rolled his eyes. "You wouldn't be fast enough."

I scoffed out a laugh. "Oh really? Fucking really? Should we take that bet?"

"My place, tonight at seven."

"You wouldn't stand a chance."

"Oh, don't worry," he said. "I fully intend to let you win."

Now it was me who smiled. He was such a sonofabitch. "Did you come here for anything work related? Or just to see me? Did you miss me? Wanna make it three nights a week?"

His eyes met mine, daring, and he smirked. "I do like a challenge."

Jesus fucking Christ.

Was that . . . was that for real?

"But about work," he said, opening his car door. "I'll need all your reports by Friday, and the air conditioning team need to bring their calendar forward, so they'll be here next week. And your shipment of optic cabling came in; install starts today."

What the . . .

"What the fuck?" I gestured to the building where, yes, my crew was indeed watching. "How is that fucking possible?"

I might have yelled that, and my crew most definitely heard it.

Valentine smirked at me as he got into his car. "Have a good day."

His door closed, and the quiet purr of the stupidly expensive engine just pissed me off even more. He reversed out of his spot, smiling as he left the car park, and so god fucking help me I was reminded of why I hated him.

Yeah.

Seven o'clock tonight he was gonna fucking get it.

I stomped back over to where my team was waiting. "Well, that looked like a fun conversation," Taka said. "You swore at him, so are you fired?"

"If I'm gonna get fired by that piece of shit, it'll be because I punched him in his stupid fucking mouth."

His stupid fucking *talented* mouth . . .

They were still waiting for an explanation.

"Schedule change," I said. "Aircon install's come forward to next week. Optic fibre install starts today."

They stared.

I nodded. "That's why I swore at him."

"Shoulda punched him," Millsy said. "Next week? How can we have this ready by next week?"

I took a deep breath in and exhaled slowly. "We'll get it done. Because it'll be over my dead body that Valentine fucking Tye ever beats me." They all nodded, ready to go to work. Like I knew they would be. They'd never let me down yet. And if Valentine thought I'd fail, then he didn't know me at all.

And yeah, he was gonna get it tonight. I was gonna give it to him so hard he wouldn't be sitting down tomorrow.

Or—I thought to myself later on, after I'd had to call the electricians and beg them to drop everything and get done what they could in two days—if I really wanted to make

Valentine suffer, I should *not* fuck him like he wanted me to.

Yes. I smiled. *Perfect.*

If he wanted to play stupid games, he would win stupid prizes.

Bring on seven o'clock.

I WALKED into Valentine's apartment on a mission. And with takeout containers of Thai food because I knew he wouldn't have eaten.

"What's that?" he asked, looking at the bag in my hand.

"Dinner."

He turned on his heel and walked away. "I don't believe dinner was part of our agreement. I seem to recall the term 'walk in, fuck me, and leave' was the specification."

God, he looked good. He wore black lounge pants and a grey long-sleeve T-shirt that both probably cost more than my entire outfit, boots included. His hair was kinda damp and he smelled shower-fresh, and damn, I bet his skin was shower-warm . . .

Stay focused, Marshall.

I put the bag of takeout on the dining table. "Actually, I seem to recall the actual specification was 'walk in, put a load in you, and leave' but the sentiment's the same."

Enzo trotted over to me and wound himself around my leg. I picked him up. "Hey, little guy. This food is not for you."

He meowed, and I shot Valentine a look. "He tells me you haven't fed him yet."

Valentine rolled his eyes and sighed. "He lies."

I carried Enzo with me to grab some plates. If it

annoyed Valentine that his cat liked me, I was going to use it to my full advantage. I was pretty sure Valentine also hated Enzo on his kitchen counter, so that was where I put him.

Anything was ammunition in war.

I washed my hands in his kitchen sink using his fancy soap and wiped my hands on his fancy tea towel. I collected two plates and took them back to the table. All the while Valentine never said a word.

He stood there with his arms folded, watching me, his jaw clenched. "This is not fucking."

I grinned at him, then took his chin between my finger and thumb. "Not yet, it's not." I turned his head to the side, getting a better look at his eye. "Hm. You heal fast. Good to know."

His nostrils flared and his eyes flashed. "Is this payback for today?"

Smiling, I sat down at the table and took the takeout containers out of the bag. "I don't know what you're talking about, and"—I held up two fingers—"rule number two was no talk of work. Now sit and eat."

He took a few measured breaths, clearly pissed, and sat down slowly. I handed him some chopsticks, all too pleased that this seemed to annoy him as well.

"I wasn't sure what you liked," I said, dishing up a bit out of both containers onto my plate. "So I just bought what I liked and figured you could deal with it."

He sat unmoving for a few seconds. "And if I said I wasn't hungry?"

I ate a bite and swallowed. "Do you need me to tie you up and force feed you?"

"You could tie me up and force me to do most things," he answered aloofly. "Eating isn't one of them."

I shoved some chilli beef into my mouth and chewed it slowly. "If you don't eat your dinner, you don't get dessert."

He knew what dessert I was referring to.

"Hm. Spicy," I said, getting up. I fetched two glasses of water and put his in front of him. When I sat back down, I pulled my chair a lot closer to his.

He rolled his eyes, but he did eat a bite of the chicken and rice. And after he had that bite, he had two more.

"Mmm," I hummed, a low guttural rumble. I slid my hand up his thigh. "Good boy."

His gaze struck me, not with heat or fire but with pure annoyance. Maybe even a hint of hatred.

I smiled as I ate more.

This was going so well . . .

With my hand still on his thigh, I gripped his leg and pulled his thigh over mine. He wasn't sure what to make of it, obviously. Startled and unsure. But it left his legs open.

Those soft lounge pants hid nothing.

Damn.

When he realised the game I was playing, he tried to change the rules. Or maybe he just got off on it, I wasn't sure. But he began to eat with more emphasis on hums of pleasure, licking his lips. He toyed with the chopsticks in his mouth, pulling them out slowly. He sipped his water like it was nectar from the gods.

He never moved his leg off mine.

But he did roll his hips and arch his back a little.

Fuck, he was such a whore.

I slid my hand up his inner thigh to the bulge in his pants. But I ignored his dick and rubbed his balls instead. He liked it but it seemed to frustrate him, which made me smile. "Something wrong?" I asked.

"No," he breathed.

"Good." I picked up a piece of beef and put it to his lips. "Open."

He didn't.

So I took his balls in my hand and squeezed. "Open."

He grunted but complied, so I released my grip on his balls and fed him the beef. "Good boy."

He seethed, almost growling at me as he chewed.

I ate some chicken and rice, then tried to feed some to him. He pressed his lips together in defiance and I squeezed his balls again.

He opened his mouth.

So I rubbed his balls as a reward and gave his dick a slow pull. Just through his pants, not skin on skin.

He hadn't been *that* good a boy yet.

"If you want me to touch you properly, you have to eat more."

He glowered at me, but he ate two more mouthfuls, my grip on his balls tightening until he complied.

He kept his hands by his sides the whole time, and he kept his leg over my thigh. He could have stopped me at any time. He could have said the word no.

But he never did.

Until, after the last mouthful, he gave a small shake of his head. "I'm full."

I don't know why it made me happy that he'd told me he'd had enough food. He wasn't just going to comply to play this game; he'd had enough and he told me. I respected that.

"Do you think you've earned dessert?" I asked quietly, rubbing his balls and teasing with a gentle squeeze.

"Yes."

I slid my hand under the waistband of his pants and gave his silky shaft a few strokes. "You're such a whore."

And there it was. That slow blink, that subtle smile. That place he needed to go, needed me to take him.

And I was *going* to take him.

I stood up, his leg sliding off mine. I kept my hand around his dick, and with my other hand, I took a fistful of hair and forced his head back, and I kissed him, hard.

I shoved my tongue in his mouth, owning his tongue, as I stroked his cock and pulled his hair.

He grunted into my mouth, his cock pulsing in my hand.

Such a dirty whore.

I pulled my mouth from his and looked into his eyes. I reluctantly took my fist from around his cock. "Bedroom. Now."

It took him a second to register the words. His glazed-over eyes focusing on mine, then he disappeared into his room. I threw the containers of leftovers into the fridge, put the plates in the sink, and followed him.

The bottle of lube was on his bed and a folded towel. He was shirtless now, his pale torso teasing me, taunting me. God, I wanted to run my hands all over him.

He slid his lounge pants over the swell of his arse, giving me a glance over his shoulder as if he was asking permission. I gave a nod, and holy shit, he let them fall down his legs.

He was fully erect and fucking beautiful.

And I was still fully dressed.

I pulled my boots off and he spread the towel on the bed and knelt over it. Then he popped the lid on the lube and began to apply it to his arse, and I was stuck watching with my jeans open, unable to look away.

The fucker smirked, enjoying the audience, enjoying the hold he had on me.

God, if only he knew . . .

If he only knew the hold he had on me.

He slipped a finger inside himself and moaned like the fucking slut he was, and I remembered what I was doing.

Now, I'd fucked him plenty of times with my jeans still on—a quick fuck and go, like he wanted.

But tonight I was in charge of the rules, and I fully intended to do my best to piss him off. I wanted him angry to the point of losing his shit . . . before I gave him what he so desperately wanted.

So I stripped fully naked, keeping my shirt in my hands. It was pretty clear he wanted me to stand at the side of the bed and fuck him from behind. So I wasn't going to do that.

I went to him and gripped his wrist, stilling his hand that he was fucking himself with. "Turn around," I ordered. "The only thing that will be inside you tonight is me."

He smiled as he turned, still on his knees, still gorgeous.

"Give me your hands," I murmured.

He did, and I tied them together with my shirt. His chest rising and falling in slow, measured breaths, a calmness to him I wasn't sure whether I loved or feared.

Then I forced him onto his back and pulled his legs out, spreading them wide. I knelt on the bed between them and applied more lube. I fingered his arse, fucking him, stretching him slowly, and from the crease of his brow, I knew he didn't like it.

He didn't like the fact that I was being gentle.

He brought his tethered hands up to my chest, annoyed now. He even tried to fight me, to struggle, to ignite a reaction. So I pushed his hands above his head to the mattress and spread his thighs wider with my knees.

"You'll get it when I give it to you," I said, my nose close to his.

His eyes flashed with heat and frustration.

"I just don't think you want it bad enough yet."

He sneered at me, and I pressed my lips to his, slow and soft.

He didn't like that much either. He growled at me, frustrated, and tried to pull his hands free.

So keeping his hands pinned to the bed with one hand, I pinched his chin with my thumb and forefinger, opening his mouth so I could really kiss him. I tangled my tongue with his and he grunted, the fight leaving his body as he kissed me back.

He could tell me he hated it, but his body never lied.

Then he raised his hips, hooking his legs behind my thighs, trying to pull me into him.

He wanted my dick so bad.

But not bad enough. Not yet.

So I kissed down his jaw to his neck, scraping my teeth along the soft skin. God, he tasted incredible. I wanted to lick every inch of him.

He brought his hands down again. Still bound with my shirt, so much easier to control him. I pushed his arms back up above his head and held his elbows, pinning him so now I could lick more of him.

His collarbone, that hollow at the base of his throat.

That made him gasp.

Yeah, he liked that a lot.

I moved to his left nipple first. Flicking it with my tongue, sucking on it, pinching it with my lips. His whole body reacted. His legs came up, his back arched, his cock jerked between us, and he groaned.

"You're such a fucking whore," I mumbled, then went to work on his right nipple.

He groaned louder this time and brought his bound hands down to cover his face. He bit my shirt that was tied around his wrists and groaned again, but it was a sound of pure frustration now.

I pushed his hands back up over his hand and put my nose to his. "You want it?"

He nodded.

"Tell me you want it."

"I want it."

I kissed him and gently bit his bottom lip. "How bad do you want it?"

He growled in reply, and I laughed before kissing him again and plunging my tongue into his mouth. He lifted his hips, trying to position my cock at his hole.

I pulled back, standing to my full height beside the bed, taking in the view. He was sprawled out before me, his legs spread wide, his cock hard, his lips red and swollen. His bound hands were above his head, his chest heaving.

He was fucking beautiful. He was so sexy like this it took my breath away.

I ignored the thump of my heart, the knock against my ribs that should have given me pause. I should have called it what it was. That maybe I didn't hate Valentine as much as I used to . . .

Valentine fucking Tye.

God, Marshall. What are you doing?

I snatched up the lube and sneered at him. "You're such a desperate whore," I said as I slicked my erection. "You lie there like that in front of me, telling me how bad you need my cock."

I folded his legs up and pulled his arse to the edge of the bed and pressed the head of my cock against his hole. I leaned over him, staring him straight in the eyes. He tried to look away, so I grabbed a fistful of his hair and spoke against his lips. "Look at me while I fuck you."

His breath hitched, his lips parting. His eyes widened, gaze drilling into mine as I pushed inside him. That tight heat, the resistance, the glide home.

His eyelids fluttered, his breaths sharp and shallow, but he kept his eyes on mine.

"Such a good little whore," I rasped out.

I realised I was cradling the top of his head with both hands, still fisting his hair, pulling hard as I fought for control.

He felt so fucking good.

Like no one I'd ever had.

I pushed all the way in and he cried out, his back arched, his neck corded. Having his mouth open like that was irresistible. I crushed my lips to his, kissing him deep, delving my tongue in as I began to slide back and forth in his arse.

He grunted and groaned, and the sound curled around my spine. I was close to coming already and it was far too soon. This wasn't going to be some quick fuck. I wanted more this time.

I broke the kiss and ran my lips along his jaw to his ear, kissing and sucking, burying my face against his neck. Driving into him slow and deep, dragging out every ounce of pleasure.

This was how I'd fuck someone else.

This wasn't how I fucked Valentine.

I thought I'd do this to annoy him because he'd hate it.

But the sounds he made, the way he brought his tied hands down over my head, how he rocked into my thrusts . . . he wasn't hating this at all.

But I couldn't stop.

I wanted this to be measured and meaningful.

Meaningful?

What the fuck?

I shook that stupid thought out of my head.

Just enjoy it, Marshall. Forget about everything else. Nothing else exists except for the tight, wet heat . . .

"Fuck, you feel so good," I said, my voice fraught with restraint. I drove up into him, all the way in, and stayed there.

He moaned like a porn star and drew his legs up higher, and I wasn't sure I could hold back much longer. I was up to my balls inside him—most guys couldn't take it—but he rocked back and forth.

Fuuuuuck.

I pulled away and stood up, gripping his ribs and sliding my hands down to his hips, driving up into him.

He cried out, almost a scream, and he came, spurts of come covering his belly and chest. His body rigid and his arse clenching around my length.

Fuck yes.

Just like that.

I slid my hands under his shoulders, buried my face in his neck, and rammed into him over and over until it was too much, too hard to hold back, and I let my orgasm win.

I came inside him, pulsing and shooting, and he moaned and sighed as he felt it.

It took a few seconds for my mind to stop spinning, for my senses to float back into my brain. I was breathing hard. My bones were jelly. I laughed into his neck, then bit him for the fun of it.

He grunted and tried to push me off him. I pulled out slowly, my dick sensitive and somehow still not ready to quit.

I would never get enough of him. I wanted to fuck him 24/7, and even that probably wouldn't be enough.

I used the towel to wipe his come from our bellies and chests, and he rolled onto his side as if he was going to slide off the bed and get up.

"Yeah, I don't think so," I said, shoving him onto his front. I kneeled on the bed and dragged him further up so he was in the middle of the mattress. I spread his thighs with my knees and laid myself down on top of him.

I needed to catch my breath and I wasn't ready to leave yet.

Plus, I wasn't opposed to cuddles after sex. It felt . . . nice.

I didn't exactly want to cuddle Valentine, but the full body contact was warm and welcome. My chest to his back, his arms up near his pillows, his head turned to the side.

The fact my dick was wedged down to his arsehole wasn't exactly terrible either.

I ran my hands up his arms and kissed his shoulder. "Want me to untie your hands?"

"No."

I smiled into the back of his neck. "You're a naughty boy," I murmured.

He pressed his face into the mattress and lifted his hips a little.

Jesus.

I scraped my teeth along his nape, nipping the skin with a little bite, then kissed it better. I ran my hands up to his, over my shirt that bound his wrists, and threaded my fingers with his.

He stilled beneath me. "Are you going to fuck me again?"

I rolled my hips, jutting my cock down to behind his balls. "Yep. Wanna fuck you all night." I kissed his shoulder. "How much do you reckon you can take?"

He hummed. "As much as you can give me."

I rolled my hips a few times and he lifted his arse up. Urging me, desperate for more.

Christ. He was as insatiable as me.

I pressed my lips to the shell of his ear. "My cock has never wanted arse like it wants yours."

He gasped and tried to rise up. To his knees? To get away? I wasn't sure.

I didn't care.

I pushed his hands down and pinned him with my body. "You move when I tell you to move. If I wanna fuck you like this, I will. And you'll take as many loads as I give you."

He moaned, still trying to raise his hips. An involuntary curl? A deliberate roll? I didn't know. I didn't care.

I shoved my hand on his hip and held him down. "I told you not to move."

He whimpered.

He fucking whimpered.

With my other hand, I fisted his hair and gave it a tug, my lips at his ear. "You're a good-for-nothing whore," I whispered.

He smiled. He goddamned smiled.

Christ, my dick was ready again. Holding him down turned me on as much as being held down turned him on. Telling him he was worthless and that I was going to fuck him . . . it shouldn't have turned me on.

But it did. Like nothing I'd ever done before.

I wanted to be inside him all the damn time. I wanted my come inside him.

Mine.

I wanted to claim him, own him.

I pushed up off him and he was about to protest until he

heard the click of the lube bottle. Then he pressed his forehead into the mattress and raised one knee.

I gave myself a quick fresh supply of lube and was about to pour some down his crack . . . until I saw . . .

"Holy shit," I breathed. A small bead of my come was dripping out of his hole. "Oh fuck, that's hot."

I spread his arse cheeks and, using my thumbs, gaped his hole a little. "You don't need lube," I said. "You're already wet."

I'd never get tired of seeing it.

He groaned and tried to go to his knees, offering himself, urging me to take him.

So I pushed him down again, pressed my cock to his used hole, and drove into him. All the way in, in one long, hard push.

He cried out, trying to twist away from the intrusion so I held his arms above his head and held him still until he got used to it. "You can take it," I murmured behind his ear. I licked up the back of his neck, nipping the skin with my teeth.

Then I kissed his shoulder, his neck, nuzzled my nose in his hair until his breaths were steady and he relaxed. I could have so easily pressed my hands on his shoulder blades and fucked him hard, and I was sure he'd have wanted me to do exactly that.

So instead I rocked us slowly, a blissful glide, as slow and torturous as I dared. My come already inside him and he was about to get a second dose.

How could I not be sick of this? I hadn't even come yet and I was already looking forward to doing this again.

How could I still want more?

God help me, I wanted to do this forever. With him. With Valentine fucking Tye. Of all people.

I was slow-fucking him again and he was loving it. I dug in deep and hard, slow and sure, while I kissed every inch of skin I could reach. He grunted with every thrust, raising his hips to take it.

I wanted to stretch him thin, to iron out any knots and troubles, and hold him. I wanted to kiss him, make sure he ate properly. I wanted to make him smile.

I wanted to fix him.

So I held him tighter and fucked him slower. I lost myself to the warmth of his body, to the feel of him underneath me, to the sounds he made, to the gasps and moans.

I lost all track of time.

And maybe for the first time, I lost myself.

All that existed was him.

And when my orgasm took hold, I planted my seed in deep, and he arched his back to take it all.

I collapsed on top of him and neither of us made an attempt to move. I stayed inside him, right where I wanted to be, until he rolled us over. I was pure dead weight. I was a boneless mess and could barely keep my eyes open.

But Valentine got to his knees on the bed and put his hard dick in my face. "You forgot something," he said. With his hands still tied with my shirt, he took handfuls of my hair and shoved his cock in my mouth, and he proceeded to skull fuck me.

And I let him.

This was not part of our agreement.

This was not what I'd signed up for.

But I let him do it.

I wanted it. I loved it, and I took every drop.

He collapsed to the bed, twitching with the aftershocks of it. I laughed and pulled the shirt free from his wrists, then pulled him into my arms.

He fit against me perfectly, like a goddamn puzzle piece. He was warm. He smelled like himself but also like me, of sex and sweat.

It was divine; a scent made just for me.

I closed my eyes for just a second and my heart was thumping for different reasons. Not the exertion, not the cardio marathon we'd just done.

No, it was thumping, two-sizes too big, because of Valentine reasons.

Valentine fucking Tye reasons.

I was too tired to care. Too exhausted, too heavy, too comfortable.

Too happy.

"I THINK I'M IN TROUBLE," I mumbled.

Taka looked at me, head tilted. He'd just asked me what was wrong. We were in the dressing sheds before our rugby game. I was bouncing on my toes and getting myself psyched up. Apparently to him I looked bothered.

"What do you mean?" he asked with nothing but concern on his face. "I know you've been busy at work, gettin' it all ready for the aircon guys, and the paperwork reports and whatnot. But we got it finished on time. It's all good, man."

I bounced on my toes some more and shook out my arms. "Not work."

The penny dropped. "Ah. The new boyfriend."

"He's not my boyfriend."

"But you want him to be."

My eyes cut to his.

The last three days—since I'd left Valentine's apartment

before sunrise on Thursday morning—had been a total mindfuck.

"It can't happen."

Fuck.

Did I even want it to happen?

Pretty sure I did.

"Aw, why not?" he asked. See, the thing about Taka was he was a pure soul. A fucking unit of a man, he was huge, but he was gentle and kind and beamed fucking sunshine. Everyone loved him, his smile was contagious.

And he believed in things like falling in love and happily ever afters.

"If you want it to happen, you'll find a way," he added.

I stopped bouncing and deflated. "God fucking dammit." I shook my head, getting mad at myself for letting things get this far.

I hadn't stopped thinking about Valentine. About how my heart was beginning to betray my mind.

"It can't happen," I repeated. "I can't tell you anything more, and I'm sorry about that. But it was supposed to be a no-strings-attached thing, and . . ."

"And now there are strings."

"Just on my side," I admitted, and perhaps that was the part that stung the most. Because Valentine would never . . . I let out a long-drawn-out puff of air. "This feeling is fucked."

Taka gave me a clap on the shoulder. "Maybe you should be telling him."

I shook my head. "No. That'd be the end of it for sure."

"You sure?"

"One hundred percent."

Because the purpose of our fucked-up agreement was

for me to hate-fuck him. That was all he'd wanted. He'd even said pretend-hate wasn't enough.

Granted, I hadn't exactly hate-fucked him on Wednesday night, and as much as he'd probably try and deny it, he'd enjoyed it.

But if I told him I didn't hate him anymore?

He'd tell me we were done, and that was the reason for the lump in my belly and the strange tight ache in my chest.

I hated this feeling.

Taka gave me a bit of a shake. "Clear your head," he said. "We got a game to play. And Burwood go hard. We need you on your A-game."

Right.

Burwood.

I grinned at him. "Consider it brung."

We took to the field and won the toss. We kicked first, straight to their second row, their number four took the ball. I lined that fucker up and cracked him right across the nose with my elbow.

He went down like a sack of shit, his nose a bloody zigzag, and I went down on him, my elbow across his ribs. "For Valentine Tye," I spat.

Then I was pulled off him and a bit of a scuffle broke out, but it was all over pretty quick. I got a lot of what-the-fucks from my teammates and the referee sent me off for the game.

I hadn't even touched the ball.

But I didn't care. My work was done. Their number four got a trip to the hospital for his busted nose, but I didn't care about that either. That fucker got what he deserved, and I wasn't sorry.

My coach was royally pissed though. So pissed he couldn't even speak to me, and I knew I'd let the team

down. They'd fought hard for the win and deserved to celebrate their victory.

I wasn't exactly in a drinking mood but figured hanging
around and buying them a few rounds was the least I
could do.

No one really questioned my outburst. They were used
to me picking fights and being the reasons drunken weekends sometimes ended with fists thrown. They did shake
their heads and some of them laughed at me and my too-
short temper.

Except Taka. I knew he'd say something and I didn't
have to wait long. He put a beer in my hand. "So tell me,"
he said casually. It was just me and him, and the bar was
loud enough that no one else could hear. "The hit you put
out today didn't have anything to do with him bein' the one
to hit Valentine last week, would it?"

I damn near choked on my beer. "What?"

"Same guy apparently." He took a swig of his beer, not
looking at me.

Fuck. Fuckity fuck.

"Not that it'd be any of their business," he added, "but
these guys haven't joined the dots."

"The fuck are you talking about?" I asked. "There are
no dots to join. I dunno why I hit that guy today. He had a
stupid face, and I was pissed off."

Taka took another drink of his beer. "Yeah. Your
problem is you got feelings for someone you shouldn't."

I stepped in front of him, his eyes met mine, and all I
could do was shake my head. Just shake my fucking head
because I couldn't speak. My heart was hammering and I
almost felt sick. I wanted to tell him to shut the fuck up, but
I couldn't find the words—and I couldn't lie to him. He'd
been my best mate since high school.

Taka gave me a sad smile. "I won't tell no one," he mumbled, then put his bottle to his lips and smiled. "But I gotta say, ain't no one gonna believe me if I did."

I shook my head again, my mouth dry. "I don't know what you're talking about."

He laughed. "You're a shit liar, my guy. That look of *oh fuck* just gave yourself away." He smiled far too smugly. "I thought something was up with you two. First, you stopped pickin' up randoms. Then you been far too happy, smiling and stuff, so you definitely getting some on the regular. Then last weekend you basically followed him out of the pub. And he came to see you at work, where you two went off for your private conversation."

"That's not . . . that's not what it is."

His eyes met mine. "So it's like a work bromance," he said, nodding. "But the *b* is silent."

I would have laughed at that if I wasn't busy trying to remember how to breathe.

Taka grinned. "I saw him smiling at you by his car. I mean, you also swore at him." He shrugged. "Which kinda proves my point, because ain't no one else can do that and not get fired. And then you wanted to punch him in the mouth, so I'm thinking things are going well between you?"

"Taka," I said. I had no idea what I was going to say, because what could I freaking add that wouldn't incriminate me?

"I gotchu, bro," he said, knocking his bottle to mine. "Your secret is safe with me. Like I said, ain't no one believe me anyway."

When I still couldn't speak, he drained his bottle and handed it to me. "Your shout."

I was only too happy to buy him a beer if it meant I could walk away and try and think.

When I went back to him, he was with Noah and Millsy, and I was kinda glad any chance for conversation was over. I handed him his beer and drank mine, standing back a bit. I wasn't really up for conversation, just happy to listen to them spin bullshit and laugh, but when Taka waved his empty bottle at me again and asked me if I wanted a refill, I looked at my half now-warm beer.

"Nah, mate. I'm gonna go," I said.

A few of the others ribbed me for piking out again and Taka did a bit, but the look in his eyes told me it was okay.

I drove to Valentine's, parking down the street like that would disprove anyone's theory of who I was seeing.

Goddammit.

God fucking dammit.

I rang Valentine's buzzer with less patience than manners. No answer. I rang it again. No answer.

I checked the time. It was 8:54.

I waited a few minutes and buzzed him again in case he was in the shower.

No answer.

Where the fuck was he?

I scrolled for his number and reluctantly, hesitantly, pathetically, called him.

He answered on the second ring. "Hello."

"Ah, yeah, just um, just wondering if we're on for tonight?"

Why did I sound so unsure?

"I'm on my way home now. Two minutes away," he said, his voice that smooth, confident tone that gave nothing away.

"Oh, okay. Good. Fine." God, I was being pathetic. "You once told me never to be late. I assumed the same rule applied to you."

"You're early, so my not being there yet doesn't count."

"Pretty sure it does."

He snorted quietly and ended the call.

Arsehole.

About a minute later, he appeared at the foyer door, coming up from the underground resident parking lot, no doubt. He opened the door and stood aside. He had a takeout bag in his hand. "I thought I'd bring food this time."

I hit the elevator button, then shoved my hands into my jacket pockets. "Good idea."

We stepped into the elevator and he eyed me, a hint of a smile on his stupidly perfect mouth. "You seem nervous," he said.

The doors opened and I followed him to his apartment door, then followed him inside. He flipped on light switches and put the takeout on the dining table. Enzo came padding out with a sleek sway and a disgruntled meow that his servant dare be late with his food.

Valentine poured out some cat biscuits, grabbed some plates, and I was still standing there not knowing what to do or say.

Valentine put the plates on the table, but he was watching me. He looked really sad all of a sudden and spoke to the floor. "If you have something to say, Marshall, say it."

Oh hell.

Here goes nothing . . .

"Um . . . I think we might have a problem."

CHAPTER 12

VALENTINE

"WHAT DO YOU MEAN 'A PROBLEM'?"

I was sure I knew what he was talking about and what it meant for us. I knew this had been too good to be true.

My good mood, my intent on buying us dinner, and making a night of it, seemed so foolish.

What was I thinking?

That we had something more than what it was?

Christ, Valentine. This is why you keep your walls up.

I couldn't bring myself to look at him because of what he'd see in my eyes.

"Taka knows," Marshall said. "About us."

Well, I looked at him then. Shocked. "What? How?"

He put his hands up. "I dunno how. He . . . he put it together." He shook his head, then ran his hand through his hair. "He said he knows me too well. He reckoned I was seeing someone, but he didn't know who. I was leaving after our games and not getting drunk or picking fights. Then he said you came to our worksite and we talked. You smiled at me, whatever the fuck that means, and I swore at you and didn't get fired." Then he shrugged. "And then today I took out Burwood's number four, and Taka knew he'd got a cheap shot on you last week—"

"You what?"

He stopped and squinted at me. "I what to which part? Out of everything I said, which—"

"You took out their number four?"

"You damn fucking right I did. From the kick off, the ball went straight to him. I lined him up and cracked him right in the nose." He shrugged again. "I got sent off. Missed the whole game and will probably miss next week too. Which I realised after is against your team, and at first, I was pissed about that, but it's probably a good thing now."

"Why—"

"Because Taka knows! That's why. And if I run out there against you, then—"

"Not that." I cut him off. "Why did you hit their number four?"

"Because he deserved it. And I fucking told him too. When he was a puddle of blood on the field, I fucking told him it was for you. Because fuck him."

I squinted my eyes shut and sighed. "Christ, Marshall. Did it occur to you that's why Taka knows? Because you said that?"

"No one heard me," he replied. "And fuckface won't remember it. He was too busy being a groaning sack of miserable—"

"Marshall."

"He fucking deserved it and I'm not sorry."

I sighed again.

He shook his head, his jaw clenched. "He put a hit on you and no one fucking touches you but me."

Oh.

Okay, wow.

His hands were fists and he turned away from me and growled. "Fuck! Sorry, I shouldn't have said that."

I could see the torment on his face in the reflection of the wall of glass.

The truth was, I'd liked what he'd said.

I was just about to say something, walk over to him, I wasn't sure, when he spun around. "You know what? I'm not fucking sorry about that either. I am the only one who can touch you, and if any fucker thinks they can hurt you, I'll send them to hospital too. I don't give a fuck. I protect what's mine. That's who I am and it's what I do, and I won't apologise for it. If you don't like that, then . . . then fucking tell me now." Then he ran his hand through his hair again and growled. "Fuck! I should go. I shouldn't have come here tonight."

I protect what's mine.

He said I was his.

He went to shoot past me, but I grabbed his arm. I didn't even mean to, and I was as surprised as he was to find my hand on him.

He looked at me, his eyes burning fire into the side of my head, but I kept my eyes down.

"I dunno what I'm doing," he said.

"I don't either," I admitted in a whisper. "What I'm doing, what this is. I don't know." I swallowed hard. "Just don't go."

Christ, Valentine, could you be any more pitiful?

When did you ever beg anyone for anything?

I closed my eyes and shook my head, trying to silence the voice of reason.

He put his fingers to my chin and lifted my face. I didn't want him to see my eyes, to see the honesty, the vulnerability. The real me. But he kept staring until I had no choice but to meet his gaze.

His brown eyes were so warm, searching mine. Eventually his gaze went to my eyebrow. "Your eye looks okay. Did you play today?"

"Half a game," I murmured, surprised my voice actually worked at all. "The coach didn't want me to play. He made me wear headgear."

Marshall cracked half a smile. "Good."

God, my heart was hammering.

I couldn't take my eyes from his now, not even when I'd wanted to. His fingers still held my chin, but then he swiped his thumb along my bottom lip, and his gaze drew down to the movement and he let out a shaky breath.

He licked his own lips and moved in closer, and I knew he was going to kiss me.

We'd kissed before, but only during sex and usually when he was domineering and forceful. This was going to be neither of those things.

I couldn't remember the last time someone had kissed me nicely.

My brain was screaming at me. Did I want this to happen? Was I going to let him kiss me?

God, I think I am. I want him to. I want him to kiss me.

My heart was squeezing to the point of pain. A pain I wasn't sure how to fix, but needing to find out if Marshall knew the answer.

He closed the distance between us, his eyes fluttering closed, and he pressed his lips to mine. Soft and warm, slow and gentle. His lips parted and he kissed me again, his hand sliding up to cup my jaw as he angled us to deepen the kiss.

His tongue was teasing and forgiving and he hummed and sighed as he kept kissing me.

The sounds made my knees weak.

What the hell.

There was no rush, no push and pull, no fight for dominance. No rough hands, no demands.

I'd forgotten what it felt like to be kissed like this, how good it felt, how I needed more . . .

When I tried to deepen the kiss, he broke free, pressing his forehead to mine. We took a second to catch our breaths, to regain some control, and he put his forefinger to my lips.

"Goddammit, Valentine fucking Tye," he murmured, then stepped back and shook his head. "I must be out of my damned mind."

I put my hand to my forehead and let out a breath. "Same. Marshall fucking Wise."

His eyes met mine and he laughed. "Christ."

I felt marginally better knowing he seemed as conflicted as me about this.

He took a few steps backward to lean his arse against the back of the sofa. "What do we do about Taka?"

"I don't know any hitmen."

He rolled his eyes. "Not funny."

It kind of was. I almost smiled, anyway. "What did you tell him?"

"I denied it, of course. But he called me a terrible liar." He put his hand to his chest. "I *am* a terrible liar. I can't lie for shit, and I can't lie to him."

I nodded slowly. Taka was a nice guy. I didn't know one person who had a bad word to say about him.

What they said about Marshall was a different story, but for all his faults, Marshall was honest. Most people didn't like that trait in others, but personally, I loved it.

Honesty, no matter how brutal, was always better than a lie.

"He said he won't tell anyone," Marshall added. "Pretty sure he said something to the effect of 'no one would believe me anyway'."

"Then what can we do?" I asked. "I won't come to your worksite anymore, though I deny the claim that I smiled at you."

His eyes flashed to mine and he raised an eyebrow. "You absolutely did."

"And if they believe I should have fired you for swearing at me, perhaps I could issue a first warning citation, if that would help."

He snorted. "The fuck you will."

I chuckled and turned to the table. "Are you hungry? I got us some Japanese food."

He pushed off the back of the sofa and pulled out a chair at the table. "I can always eat."

I pulled the containers out of the bag and then considered drinks. "Want a wine?"

"Sure."

I grabbed the bottle of white from the fridge and two glasses, and Marshall had dished up some food from each container on two plates. I took my seat and poured us a glass each, and figured now was a good time as any to bring this up.

"Regarding Taka and him saying he won't tell anyone, I, uh . . . my personal life has never been up for discussion. My father has reminded us that our public profile is to remain *unscathed*, I believe was the word he used."

Marshall studied me for a moment. "Do you mean gay?"

God, I hated this.

"He doesn't know. He can't know," I admitted quietly. This topic of conversation did very little for my appetite.

God, even looking at food wasn't good. "I'm not out as a gay man. Not even my sister knows. My father would . . ."

"Hey," Marshall said. He put his fork down and slid his hand over mine. "Fuck your old man."

I looked at him and snorted. "Thanks."

"Taka won't tell anyone. You have my word." He waited until I met his gaze. "But Valentine, I mean it. Fuck your old man. And if he can't stand the thought of having a gay kid, fuck him even more."

"My father is . . ." I wasn't sure I had the time or the energy to go through the list.

"A piece of shit," he finished for me. "You're a better person than he'll ever be."

I gave him a sad smile. "He's not a nice man. That's no secret. I could never tell him I was gay. Not ever. He'd never understand. And if he had the choice of me being out and happy or closeted and miserable, he'd choose miserable without hesitation. Part of me actually thinks he knows. He knows I'm gay and he sees my unhappiness as loyalty to him, I think." I sighed. "I don't know. It's fucked up."

"I'm sorry," Marshall murmured. "It is fucked up and it's not fair on you."

I gave a bitter laugh. "God, I envied you in high school."

He stared. "You what?"

"I envied you. You were out and proud and didn't give one fuck what people thought. That took more courage than I'll ever have. God, I wanted to be you."

"Well, I dunno about out and proud. I got caught checking guys out and I got teased and called names." He made a face. "So I punched the shit out of them and broke a few noses and said they could tell everyone they got beat up by a gay guy."

I gave him a sad smile. "What is it with you and breaking noses?"

"Only if they deserve it." He stabbed some beef and rice noodle with his fork and I expected him to eat it, but he put it to my mouth. "Eat."

I rolled my eyes and opened my mouth. I hated that he did this, that he played the let's-feed-Valentine game, but damn, part of me loved it too.

Then he ate some, then he fed me some more, and by the time we were done having alternating forkfuls, our plates were almost empty.

He kept his hand on my thigh, and he did a fair bit of smiling, which did concerning things to my heart.

I hated that he could do that to me.

I hated that I let him. That I liked it.

He lightly pressed his finger between my eyebrows. "You get a line here when your mind goes somewhere you don't want it to. What's wrong?"

I shook my head, brushing off his ability to read me as pure luck. "Nothing. I—"

"Bullshit."

Great.

See, the problem with letting people in is that then they get to know you.

Yes, Valentine. That's generally how it works. But it's too late for that now, isn't it?

I sighed. "I, uh . . . I'm not sure . . ."

He slid his palm further up my thigh. "I think I know. You want to know what this means for our agreement. That if I can sit here and be all sweet with you, then that means I can't throw you down and fuck you hard. But, rest assured Valentine, I can do both."

My pulse kicked up a notch and I smiled despite myself. "Am I that easy for you to read?"

He chuckled. "Pretty much. You can be a steel trap when you want to be. But I think I got you figured out."

Oh god.

Why did that scare me so much? "You do, huh?"

His smile faded and he put his hand to my jaw and searched my eyes.

Never had I felt so scrutinised, so vulnerable.

He dropped his hand to my lap and squeezed my hand instead. "You need rough sex. That's how you like it, and I gotta be honest with ya, I like giving it to you. It's hot as hell, and fucking you bareback and coming inside you is the hottest thing I've *ever* done." He let out a breath and shook his head. "Not gonna lie, I think it's a primal, knuckle-dragging thing, and damn, my dick's been hard pretty much non-stop since we started this thing."

Oh, okay then. He was just going to say this stuff out loud.

"But you also need me to be sweet sometimes," he added. "It's nothing crazy or personal, it just is what it is. What it means to be human."

I didn't like where this was going.

I didn't like it at all.

"You mean it's something you need."

He glowered at me. "No. It's something everyone needs. You want me to throw you down and fuck you hard every single time, so be it. Only too happy to oblige. But don't tell me you don't like this." He waved between us, then at the empty plates. "Because you stopped me from leaving before. Whether you like it or not, something inside you didn't want me to leave. And yeah, it's confusing and a total mindfuck, because I spent my whole life hating you, and yet here I am. It is confusing. But for some fucked-up reason, I find myself needing to soften the barbs a little. Fucked if I know why. And I think you need me to."

I blinked a few times. My mouth was far too dry. I wanted to object and tell him he was wrong on all fronts about every single thing.

But he wasn't.

I was suddenly not feeling too well. I had the palpable urge to stand up and ask him to leave. To tell him maybe this whole thing was a bad idea.

He shook his head. "Don't do that," he said, half stern, half sorry. "I can see you retreating in your head and putting your defences up. You get this terrified look in your eyes. Christ, Valentine. I'm not asking you to come out or go public. Christ, I would never. I know how hard that is. You don't ever have to do anything you're not comfortable doing." He sighed. "All I'm saying is you don't need to put your walls up around me. You don't need to be on the defensive with me. Not anymore. You can just be yourself around me. No pretences, no bullshit."

I didn't know what to say. All I could do was shake my head. Because I was more myself with him than I'd ever been with anyone else.

Marshall shrugged. "I'm not asking you for anything more than what we have now."

"What we have now?"

"Yeah. Whatever this is. This agreement. Whatever the fuck it is. Nothing has to change."

"But it has changed."

"To include what? Dinner? Yeah, because like I said, if I'm going to fuck you like you want me to, I need to know you're up for it. That this isn't some downward spiral of self-destruction and you don't care what happens to your body. I happen to like using your body as a fuck-toy, and I need it in good working order. Christ." He let his head fall back with a frustrated sigh.

And I found myself smiling. "A fuck-toy? In good working order."

His head shot up and his eyes met mine. He sighed again when he saw me smiling, and the corner of his mouth lifted upward.

"Christ, Valentine. I don't know what I'm doing. I know outside of whatever this is, it can't be anything more. And that's fine. But inside whatever this is, maybe we can order takeout and not get weird about it. It's just food. If you really want me to do nothing but turn up, fuck you, and leave, then tell me right now."

Is that what I wanted?

It was in the beginning. It was all I had the emotional currency for. But now . . . well, now I wasn't sure . . .

My phone rang in that moment with either the best or worst timing, possibly both. I took my phone from my pocket and saw *Father* on the screen. Marshall saw it too.

I groaned because my father was the last person on the planet I wanted to speak to right now.

"Answer it," Marshall said.

Knowing if I ignored my father it would only make matters worse, I took a deep breath and answered. "Hello."

"The Melbourne integration is moving forward faster than expected and you'll be overseeing the project this week. Your flight leaves tomorrow at one o'clock, returning on the seven o'clock flight, Thursday night. Camilla will forward you the flight details."

I stood up and walked to the back of the sofa. "What? I thought you were in Melbourne for the integration this week."

"I was. Now I'm in Taiwan sorting out a supplier issue."

"I can't just up and leave. I have a busy week—"

"If your team cannot handle your absence for four days, you've failed as a manager."

Marshall's hand on my back surprised me, but I welcomed the touch. Warm and strong. His workman-hands, calloused and rough, were masters of touch. He massaged my shoulders and worked his way down, stepping in close behind me while my father droned on in my ear about my shortcomings as a successor to his empire.

Then Marshall's hands slid around to my front and unbuttoned my jeans. I tried to turn around to tell him no—because I was on the phone to my father!—but he held me still and pushed my hips against the back of the sofa.

My father started on about how industry dominance required a level of cruelty, how his success was because of his savage acumen. Meanwhile, Marshall slowly unzipped my fly, pulled my jeans down, then bent me over the back of the sofa.

I thought he was going to try and fuck me without lube, and there was no way I could remain quiet during that, but then I felt his warm breath before his tongue licked over my hole.

"Oh," I said.

My father stopped mid-sentence. I hadn't been listening anyway. "What was that?"

"Sorry, I dropped something," I managed to say.

"What are you doing?" my father barked. "Are you even listening?"

"I'm . . . eating," I said. "Dinner."

Marshall chuckled as his tongue flicked across my sensitive skin and poked it inside me.

I mean, I'd showered after rugby, but I hadn't been

expecting this. I worried I might not have been clean enough . . . but then he began to fuck me with his tongue. I sucked back a breath and tried to not make a sound on the exhale.

"Valentine," my father barked.

Good fucking god.

"Sorry. It's hot. Dinner, I mean," I said, my voice tight. "Melbourne tomorrow. Got it. Bye."

I clicked off the call, knowing my father would be *pissed*, but in that moment, I didn't care.

"Fuck, Marshall."

He laughed, his breath hot on my skin, his tongue wet and probing . . .

Sweet heavens above, what was he doing to me?

He stood up and pulled me upright by the back of my shirt, his lips pressed against my ear. "Every time your father calls you, I'm gonna eat your arse, because fuck him." He pressed his erection against my arse crack. "I would fuck you while you speak to him, but you make the most obscene noises."

I whined, and he laughed before tightening his hold on my shirt. It pulled against my throat, and he drove my hips against the back of the sofa with his body, the hard-on in his jeans making me moan.

"Look at your reflection," he ordered, giving my shirt a little tug on my throat. "Look at how fucking hot you are."

I turned my head to the wall of glass, to the full-length reflection of us. To my jeans under my arse, to him pressed against me, my back arched because of the shirt pulling on my throat.

To his muscular body, his strong arms.

His complete control over me.

"Want me to fuck you right here so you can watch?"

My knees almost gave out. "Yes, please."

Please?

Did I just say please?

He chuckled. "Go get the lube."

He let go of me and I almost wobbled on my feet, and I tried to walk slowly to my room, as if I was the one calling the shots here, but it was a concerted fucking effort not to run.

I came back and he'd cleared the table, putting the leftovers in the fridge. I put the lube on the back of the couch and began to pull my jeans off.

"Stop," he ordered, standing there with that impressive bulge in his jeans. God, I didn't know how it even fit in his pants.

I didn't know how it even fit in me.

But I did stop.

"I never said to undress," he murmured. He held my chin and turned my head to face our reflection. "I want you to watch."

Oh god.

He knew damn well what he was doing. My heart raced, and I tried to catch my breath. "I'll be away this week. No sex on Wednesday, so you better make this good."

He ran his nose up the column of my throat and smiled as he sucked on my Adam's apple. Then he ripped my shirt open, buttons popping and scattering to the floor, making me gasp.

He turned me around and bent me over the back of the sofa again. He took a fistful of my hair and made me look at our reflection, at him bending over me, pressing against me. Dominating me. Owning me.

"Watch me fuck you."

I didn't dare look away.

He poured lube down my arse crack and thumbed it inside me, setting my insides on fire. "How sore do you want to be tomorrow?" he asked, unbuttoning his own fly. He pulled his dick out, pumping the thick shaft. "Want to feel me every day you're gone?"

I spread my legs. "Please."

He pressed against me, into me, slow and to the hilt. I gripped the seat of the sofa and moaned into a cushion, almost falling forward. But he kept hold of my hips, keeping me right where I was. He was relentless and perfect, and our reflection was mesmerising.

His jeans were around his thighs, his hands on my hips, and he bent me over the back of the couch. The perfect height. The perfect fit.

His hips meeting my arse, his monster cock filling me completely, his head thrown back in ecstasy.

I couldn't take my eyes off him.

I'd definitely be feeling him every day I was gone. Wasn't that what he wanted? To remind me of whose cock owns me?

Fuck yes.

His rhythm got faster, his fingernails bit into my hips and his cock was impossibly harder, bigger, and with a raspy roar, he came inside me. I felt every pulse, every spurt.

I felt everything.

He dropped his forehead to the middle of my back, his breaths ragged, and he slowly pulled out of me. "Oh fuck, that was hot," he panted. He kept his hand on my lower back, keeping me bent over the sofa, and in our reflection, I watched as he inspected his handiwork.

"That's the hottest thing I've ever seen," he murmured. "Christ, look at you." He pulled me up to my feet, helping me stand, keeping his arms around me and his mouth on the back of my neck, kissing and humming. My eyes met his in the reflection. "You're such a slut for it, aren't you? Look at how sexy you are?" Then he pulled my hair, tilting my head so he could kiss my neck. "Full of my come. God, I wanna fuck you all night."

I moaned and my cock twitched, which he saw in the reflection.

He grinned and kissed the spot where my shoulder met my neck and I shivered. "I'll have you in the shower next, I think," he decided. "Any requests, Valentine?"

God, the way he said my name.

It shouldn't sound like that coming from him.

I shook my head. "Whatever you want to do to me."

He chuckled and nipped at my shoulder, sliding his hands around to my dick. He began to stroke me. "That's a dangerous thing to say to me."

I smiled as I dropped the back of my head onto his shoulder and leaned into him, letting him jerk me off. His spent cock pressing against my arse. One of his hands snaked up to my pec and he squeezed my nipple. "All night," he murmured. "All fucking night."

I boarded my flight to Melbourne the next afternoon on almost no sleep and with the sorest arse I think I'd ever had.

Ignoring that blooming warmth in my chest at him cooking me breakfast, ignoring the unfamiliar thump of my heart when I thought of his smile, and relishing the ache and painful twinge in my arse.

I hadn't stopped smiling yet.

CHAPTER 13

MARSHALL

OH YEAH. I WAS IN DEEP TROUBLE. DEEEEEP. LIKE Marianna Trench levels of deep.

And you know what?

I didn't fucking care.

Valentine fucking Tye had done a number on me, upended everything I thought I knew about him, about myself, and I was strangely okay with that.

"Your dad's a weirdo," I said to Enzo. He was in his cat carrier on the front seat of my ute.

Why? Because I was looking after him while Valentine was in Melbourne for four nights. It was too short notice for the cattery place, and Valentine refused to leave him at the emergency, short-notice stay at the vets. When I'd suggested I'd take him, Valentine was clearly uncertain.

"If you wanted to stay here instead?" he'd countered. "Or even just call past of an evening to feed him . . ."

"He can't be by himself for the rest of the day," I'd said, holding Enzo to my chest. "What kind of cat-dad are you?"

Enzo and I both gave him a look of horror.

Admittedly staying at Valentine's probably would have

been easier but would it be weird? Yes. Him giving me keys to his place would definitely be weird. Also, would I be more likely to get caught or questioned or found out coming and going from his place? Maybe, and that was a risk we couldn't take.

Taking Enzo to my place was just better.

Plus, me and Enzo were tight. The little guy loved me.

"Yeah, your dad's a weirdo," I said again. Enzo meowed. "Well, he's not too bad. Underneath that cold exterior, he has an inner whore with a kink for some weird shit. But he's not really the bad guy he pretends to be. We know this, don't we?"

Enzo meowed again.

First time in my life I'd ever had a full conversation with a cat.

First time in my life for a lot of things, apparently.

I got him settled into my apartment. It was much smaller than Valentine's, obviously, and nowhere near as fancy. Mine was in an old building, and it was just a one-bedder, but it was all I'd ever needed. My neighbours were nice and my landlord had been great.

Not sure why I felt the need to justify any of it to Enzo. He didn't appear concerned at all.

I put his carrier on my bed and closed the door, letting him get used to the scents and sounds, and after a brief inspection, he was surprisingly cool with everything. I set up his litter tray in my bathroom and then we watched TV for a while.

I did kinda cheat by feeding him some chopped up BBQ chicken though, piece by piece, while we watched crap on TV.

And because I couldn't help myself, I took a pic of Enzo perched on my lap watching the millionth rerun of *Rocky*, and when I was certain there was no way anyone could know it was me in the pic, I sent it to Valentine.

Giving your kid an education in film classics.

Well, they'd know it was me if they'd been in my flat before, which very few people had. Taka had, but he already knew about me and Valentine, so it made no difference. It wasn't like I was posting it to social media, and there was no way Valentine would share it with anyone.

His reply came through about five minutes later.

Is that . . . is that Rocky?

I snorted. *He likes it.*

He also likes rotten fish, so make of that what you will.

I laughed but wasn't sure what to say next.

Was texting for fun allowed in our agreement? Was it crossing a line?

Christ, after what I'd done to him in the last sixteen hours, it seemed anything was allowed. Our 'lines not to be crossed' were more like zigzags drawn by a squirrel on speed.

So I thought, *fuck it.*

And hit Call.

It rang three times and I could picture him sitting there staring at his phone, horrified that I would engage in conversation with him.

This was not part of our agreement, and I felt stupid, stupid, stupid. I was just about to end the call when he answered. "I wasn't aware phone calls were part of our arrangement."

I would have felt chastised if it didn't sound like he was smiling.

"Cat-sitting wasn't part of it either, and yet here we are."

He sighed. "I can't believe you're making him watch *Rocky*. I should call the RSPCA."

I snorted. "I'm not making him do anything. He's perched up on my knee like I'm part of the furniture."

There was a beat of silence. "So he's settled in fine, I take it."

"Very. Made himself at home the second he got here. Pretty sure I'm his favourite now."

"Was there food involved?"

"Of course there was. I'm not an idiot."

He scoffed and fell silent.

Wait. What did that mean? "Do you think I'm an idiot?"

He laughed then. "No."

"Just as well." I gave Enzo a pat. "How's Melbourne?"

"Cold and wet."

"Nice."

"Not really."

"Meetings tomorrow?"

He made a displeased sound. "Yes."

"My day's gonna be awesome," I said. "We usually have these team meetings on Mondays, but the reason I go won't be there, so I'm not going."

Another beat of silence. "The reason you go?"

"I'm talking about you."

"Yes, I got that part," he said. "Why am I the reason?"

"Well, first, the only reason I went was to annoy you."

"A good a reason as any." He was smiling, I could tell.

"Then I started going to see if you could actually sit down."

He barked out a laugh. "What?"

"Yeah. After what I did to your arse."

He snorted. "I told you, I like the reminder."

I realised I was smiling and told myself to stop. "How's your reminder feeling today?"

He hummed a little. "It's . . . enjoyable."

"That's fucked up."

"I like what I like."

"And I like that you like it."

Did I just say that?

Christ.

Think of something else to say. Think of something else to say . . .

"What does your recovery look like?" I asked, then regretted it immediately. "I mean, when we first started this thing, you said you'd prefer it to happen on Saturday nights because it gives you a day to recover. What does that mean?"

"A long hot bath, usually," he answered, his voice smooth as honey. "A relaxing day on the couch. Sometimes with a heat pack or an ice pack."

Jesus.

"It's more of a state of mind," he added quietly. "It's hard to explain, but being by myself at home, I'll wear nothing but my robe, and I let myself enjoy the aches and pains. It's silk, and the cool, soft fabric counters the discomfort."

I couldn't believe what I was hearing. "Uh, wow."

"Does this surprise you?"

"Ah, no. Not what you're saying, I guess. I wasn't expecting such an honest response."

He snorted. "Would you prefer I lie to you?"

"No. I don't want you to ever lie to me."

More silence then, and I was beginning to think maybe I'd said the wrong thing.

"I don't want you to lie to me either," he whispered, his voice so quiet I barely heard him.

Holy shit.

"Good. Let's add that to our agreement."

He chuckled, and Enzo chose that moment to do an elegant circle on my lap and curled himself into a ball, and he began to purr.

"Can you hear that?" I asked, putting the phone to the cat. "He's purring. See? I am his favourite."

I took a photo and sent it to him.

"Well, I hope you didn't have plans for the rest of the evening," Valentine said. "Because you can't move now until he gets up."

I snorted. "Yes I can."

"No, that's the rules of cat minding."

"Great. I'm supposed to be going to my parents' place for dinner."

He was quiet again.

"It's a Sunday thing," I added, feeling bad for mentioning family.

"Sounds nice."

"I'll leave *Rocky II* on the TV for my little new best friend. He won't even know I'm gone."

"Leave him food and a warm bed and he *won't* notice you're gone," he replied.

"You don't leave the TV on for him?"

"Uh, no."

"Why not?"

"Because he's a cat."

I covered Enzo's ears. "Don't tell him that."

"Oh, good Lord," he mumbled. It sounded like he was still smiling.

"What's your plans for tonight?" I asked. "Dinner in some fancy restaurant?"

"Heavens no. I avoid people when I can," he replied. "I'll be having a long, hot bath and ordering room service."

"Do they have robes there? Or did you pack your own?"

He chuckled. "Goodbye, Marshall."

"No, I was being serious! I want to know what mental imagery I'm supposed to jerk off to tonight. Is it a fluffy robe? Or silk? What colour is it?"

There was the sound of his quiet laugh before the line went dead.

Goddammit.

Now I'm gonna be wondering . . .

Damn, I bet silk felt good against his skin. I could imagine running my hands over him wearing a silk robe. Then again, a soft fluffy one would be good too.

My phone beeped with a message. It was a photo. A fancy bathroom, some exclusive hotel, no doubt, with a big mirror and low lighting. He'd cropped his head out of the photo, but it was Valentine. Absolutely no doubt. His back in the reflection, wearing an expensive-looking dark grey silk robe that fell around his shoulders, revealing a hickey and a bite mark I'd left on the back of his shoulder.

God fucking damn.

I replied with zero regard to my pride, or to our agreement.

You are so fucking sexy. My marks on your skin are hot.

He didn't reply, and he didn't have to. His photo was enough. Knowing he'd sent it to start with, knowing he wanted me to see the marks I'd left behind, that was all I needed.

If anyone else saw that pic, there was no way they'd know it was Valentine.

But I knew.

And that somehow made it hotter. It was just for me. He was just for me.

You're in so much trouble, Marshall. You're in way over your head.

I sighed and gave Enzo a scratch behind the ear. "Your dad isn't so bad," I mumbled.

I knew it wasn't the cat I was trying to convince.

"Hey, Mum," I said, giving her a kiss on the cheek as I walked into the kitchen. "Something smells good."

"Thanks. I thought some lasagne might be nice. It's a bit cold out there."

"Sounds perfect."

"What's that?" she nodded pointedly to the bag in my hand.

"Need to sew on some buttons."

She pulled her old faithful sewing container down from the cupboard. "Here you go."

I pulled out the shirt in question. It was one of my favourites. A tan button-down shirt with black palm trees on it that I'd bought at some trendy store. It was super comfy and it fit me just right . . . and I'd lost the top button when Valentine pulled it off me.

Granted, I'd popped every button on his shirt when I'd ripped it open. I wasn't sure how I'd only lost one. He said he'd take his shirt to a tailor to get fixed, but I told him I'd do it. He'd laughed when he'd asked me if I could sew on a button, and I was sure he didn't believe me when I said damn right I could; it was how I was raised.

But the reminder that we'd had very different upbringings made him quiet, so I'd shoved the shirt into a bag and didn't mention it again.

I threaded a needle and began sewing on my button, sitting at the kitchen table while Mum made some potato dish to go with dinner.

Until she saw what I was doing. "What are you using red for?"

I shrugged. "I don't care what colour it is," I said, poking the needle back through the hole. "And you've got a whole reel of red and only half white or black ones. Plus, one button with red cotton makes it look cool."

The black button with a red cross of cotton looked awesome.

I finished mine and pulled out shirt number two, then put all the buttons Valentine and I had managed to find on the floor into a pile on the table. Mum took one look at the expensive Polo logo.

"Well, that shirt's not yours."

"Uh, no." I grimaced. "But I . . . I might have popped the buttons on it, so instead of paying a tailor, I said I'd do it."

She pursed her lips and gave me her best mum look. "Were you fighting again?"

Fighting, fucking . . .

"Something like that," I mumbled.

"Oh, Marshall," she said, tsking her tongue. "I thought you'd have grown out of that nonsense by now."

"Grown out of what nonsense?" Dad asked as he walked in. He clapped my shoulder. "Thought I heard you come in."

"Hey, Dad," I said. "Yeah, just needed to fix a shirt."

"He was fighting again," Mum said, throwing me right under the bus.

"It wasn't fighting," I lied. "It was rugby."

She dead eyed me. "You were playing rugby in your good shirt, huh?" Then she nodded to the shirt I was holding. "And the guy you were fighting was wearing a two-hundred-dollar shirt playing rugby too, huh?"

Before I could answer, she noticed what colour thread I was using. "Oh, Marshall, you cannot use red thread on that good shirt." She tried to take it off me.

I pulled it away from her. "I absolutely can. I said I'd sew the buttons back on. Never said what colour thread I'd use. It's gonna be a button short anyway. If he doesn't like it, he can buy himself a new one. I mean who wears a two-hundred-dollar shirt to play rugby?"

Dad laughed. "How'd your game go yesterday?"

"They played well."

"They?" Dad questioned. "Did you not play?"

I groaned because I knew how this would end. "I might have got sent off."

My mother's sigh of disappointment was long and loud. "Oh, Marshall."

"He deserved it." I kept sewing on the stupid button so I didn't have to see the look I knew she was giving me. "It was payback for him hitting someone else."

"Still doesn't make it right," Mum said.

But Dad nodded as if that made perfect sense then. "If he hits one of your teammates, then he's fair game. That's how rugby works."

But he didn't hit one of my *teammates*. Not that I was telling my father that. I tied off the button and bit the thread with my teeth.

"Clear that away for now," Mum said, nodding to the sewing kit. "And help me set the table."

Mum's lasagne was delicious and I'd shovelled in half

my plate when Dad pushed his food around with his fork. "So," he hedged. "How's work?"

I was hoping to avoid this conversation tonight. Forever, if I could have. But here it was . . . I put my fork down and sipped my drink. "It's okay. Got a busy week. The Mercer job is almost at lock-up. Windows will be in this week."

That wasn't what he was really asking and we all knew it.

"And the new owners?" he asked outright this time.

I chose my words carefully. "Saw old-man Tye the other day. He's still a miserable piece of shit. But Valentine's . . ." God damn it. "He's not too bad. I'd always thought he was a piece of shit too, but he's not so bad."

Mum nodded and smiled. "We can't really blame the child for the actions of the father, can we?"

Dad chewed on the inside of his lip as he stabbed some lasagne. "Guess not. But . . ." He shrugged. "He's a Tye, right?"

And there it was.

"He is," I replied. There wasn't anything I could add or deny or argue or announce. There was no point in trying. But still . . . I felt an itch to defend Valentine, a burr under my skin to protect him.

Which was fucking absurd.

"I thought I'd see the Mercer job through and quit," I admitted. They both stared at me. "Maybe ask Mercer if they're looking for a site manager."

Dad put his fork down. "Because of Tye Corp. They just have to buy up everything at all costs, regardless of the collateral damage."

That might be true of his father, but it wasn't Valentine. I shook my head. "Maybe they do, Dad. But now I'm not sure."

"Not sure about what?"

"Not sure about leaving."

Mum reached over and gave my hand a squeeze. "You've worked hard for what you've achieved there. Don't let anyone ruin that, love."

Dad nodded slowly, a slight frown on his brow. "You have worked hard. You've proved yourself. If you want to stay, you should. Don't let them take that away from you."

Valentine wasn't taking anything away.

"I don't understand the merger details or none of that," I said gently. "That's not my business. And the hardware side of Tye Corp isn't my business either." My dad's gaze shot to mine and I shrugged. "I'm in construction. And the takeover has been as smooth as it could have been. I don't deal with the old-man Tye. I deal with the new construction division. And they're pretty good. So far, at least. It's only early days but what I've seen so far is decent. They listen, at least."

I shrugged again, feeling blown wide open for defending Valentine fucking Tye, of all people, to my father. Not that I'd said his name in that last part, keeping it at 'construction division' because if I had to keep saying his name, I wasn't sure I wouldn't give myself away.

"If that changes," I added, "if they show their arse, then I'll leave." I shovelled in another chunk of lasagne and changed the subject. "This is so good, Mum. Best one yet."

She smiled. "Want some to take home?"

"Hell yes."

"Don't give it all to him," Dad grumbled. "Leave some for me."

Mum rolled her eyes. "Like you don't get fed like a king every day of the week."

Dad gave her a cheeky smile that told her he knew all too well she spoiled him.

I laughed, glad the topic of conversation had moved on.

Mum finished sewing on the buttons of Valentine's shirt while Dad and I cleaned up the kitchen, but I couldn't stick around tonight. I had someone waiting for me at home . . .

That someone was a cat, but whatever.

It was kinda nice to know that someone would be there. I'd always thought myself as more of a dog person, but Enzo was cool. Maybe I should look at getting my own cat. Just a rescue from a shelter, not some expensive pedigree like Enzo. He had that same sleek air of superiority as Valentine, which made it funny, because they were both softies on the inside.

I was probably more of a moggie-bitzer-with-attitude kind of guy.

Enzo meowed at me as I walked through the door. I was pretty sure he was only interested in the lasagne because he seemed mad that I put it in the fridge instead of giving him some.

But when I crawled into bed, a few moments later I felt the gentle plop of soft paws landing on the covers, followed by padding up my body and then a purring furry circle wedged himself in the crook of my shoulder and neck, at the side of my face.

Great.

I grabbed my phone and snapped a pic, trying to not include my face and it was dark, but it was very clear that Enzo was asleep on me. I sent it to Valentine.

His reply came back immediately.

THAT TRAITOR

I fell asleep with a smile and purring cat on my neck.

I DIDN'T GO to the meeting on Monday morning. I had enough to do at work with the aircon crew anyway. I went to rugby training on Tuesday night where my coach made me do sprints until I almost puked, and then he had me holding the padded mats while the team took turns in hit-ups, and if that wasn't enough payback, he told me I was benched for the weekend's game.

I wasn't surprised, but it meant I wouldn't be playing against Lane Cove, against Valentine.

That in itself was probably a good thing, even though I was disappointed. Would I go easy on him? Would I tackle him harder than necessary? Would he aim for me? I wasn't sure . . . but I'd have liked to have found out.

I'd have liked to smile at him from opposing sides, to square off against him, to see which of us was faster, better.

I guess that competitiveness in me hadn't changed, despite how I felt about him now.

Which is how, Marshall? How do you feel about him now?

I . . . I don't know.

I wasn't sure. I certainly didn't hate him like I used to. I'd already established that. Hell, I even liked him. Was it more than that?

I didn't know.

I wasn't sure it could ever be more than that. Actually, the only thing I was certain about was the fact it could *never* be anything more.

And that sat in my belly like a rock. Like an anchor, keeping me stuck against the flow which I was trying to go with.

What I was . . . was confused.

Every night, I kept Valentine updated with a pic of

Enzo, either asleep on me or sprawled out in front of the heater. He'd follow up with a snarky reply.

On Tuesday night, I told him I was out of the game on the weekend. He'd replied it was only because I didn't want to lose to him.

On Wednesday night I sent him a pic of me and Enzo laying on the couch together watching *Predator*.

He'd replied almost immediately.

Hello RSPCA, I'd like to report a crime . . .

His sense of humour surprised me. Dunno why. I guess I was just surprised he even had one. He was always so serious, so aloof, so . . . cold.

Except he wasn't.

I already knew I'd miss having a reason to text him.

I wasn't going to ask, but it got the better of me . . .

How are we exchanging the child tomorrow night?

But he didn't reply with a text. My phone rang in my hand.

"Exchanging the child? Is this a ransom demand?"

I chuckled. "It could be. I like having him here." I gave Enzo a scratch under the chin for good measure.

"Is that him purring I can hear?"

"Yep. He likes me. And he likes action movies from the eighties. I'll be including a list when I drop him off."

"I knew this was a terrible idea. First you let him sleep on your bed, then you make him suffer through terrible movies."

"Okay, you seem to be under the deluded notion that I let or make him do anything. I don't *let* him sleep on my bed, he just does whatever the fuck he wants. He wants to lie on the couch with me and watch Arnie. It's his choice. I mean, can you *make* him do anything?"

Valentine chuckled. "No. I cannot."

"My point exactly."

"You seem to enjoy having him a little too much."

"I know. I'm now thinking I should get one."

"A cat?"

"Yep."

He made a happy sound, a sigh but as if he was smiling.

"And I'm gonna call it Arnie."

"Oh dear god."

"Or Rocky."

"That's worse."

"If by worse you mean awesome, then yes."

He laughed then. Actually laughed. It plucked at something inside me.

"Uh, about the drop off," he said. "I can call around and collect him. You've already been inconvenienced enough."

"What time's your flight?"

"I get in at seven. By the time I get home—"

"I'll pick you up from the airport."

I had no idea why I just said that.

"I'll bring Enzo along for the ride," I added quickly. "But I won't come into the terminal to get you, because that'd be weird, and I can't leave a kid in the car, so I'll wait for you at the express pickup spot. So don't be late."

He was silent for a long second. "You don't have to do that," he said quietly.

"Well, I kinda do," I replied, trying to play it cool. "See, tonight is Wednesday and usually by this time I'm up to my balls in you, and by the terms of our agreement, any delays should be rectified at the earliest convenience."

He barked out a laugh. "Is that right?"

"Yes."

"I don't recall that term."

"Believe me, by this time tomorrow night, you'll be very well acquainted with it."

He chuckled warmly. "I'll look forward to it then."

Hell freaking yes.

While I was on a roll for making demands, I said, "I think you should wear that robe. When you get home, not at the airport. Jesus. We wouldn't get out of the carpark before I nailed you."

He sighed, almost a moan. "I wouldn't mind."

I gasped. "We'll do no such thing. There'll be a child in the car!"

"Enzo isn't a child."

I put my hand over Enzo's ears. "Don't you listen to him, little dude."

"Christ," Valentine mumbled. "Pretty sure he saw what you did to me over the back of the sofa, so . . ."

I laughed. "That was some of my finest work."

Valentine chuckled again. "Yes, it was."

We were both quiet for a second, so I decided to end it before it got awkward. "Tomorrow night at seven."

"Terminal three."

"Let me know if you get delayed."

"I will."

I hung up before I could say something stupid like goodnight or sweet dreams.

I tried not to think about how I was smiling or how my heart was thumping funny. Instead, I thought about him wearing that robe for me and what I might do to him.

Tomorrow night couldn't come fast enough.

Chapter 14

Valentine

The Melbourne integration was moving fast and there were a few crinkles that needed ironing out. Nothing major, but the paperwork and legalities were tedious and time consuming, and it was good to have someone from senior management, being me, on the ground to oversee it. My father had been right sending me.

I could have spent my nights with old hook-ups or at discreet bars like I'd used to. I'd spent years here, moving in hidden circles to try and scratch an insatiable itch.

But I didn't need to do that anymore.

I yearned for nothing.

Every need I had was met, and it was met very well.

Marshall fulfilled every sexual desire, every sexual need, every sexual craving I could ever have.

He was also filling another vacancy in my life. It wasn't something I thought I'd ever want, but the non-sexual interactions were nice. I'd very deliberately avoided any such thing. I didn't deal well with emotional attachment, and I'd never needed the company of others.

But his texts every night while I was in Melbourne were the absolute highlight of each day.

I found myself smiling long after they'd ended.

I couldn't be one hundred percent certain, and I was hesitant to admit it, but it was beginning to feel a lot like happiness.

All my life I'd settled for being no more than contented. In my experience, disappointment accompanied hope, so settling for no-strings relationships was the safest option.

Until Marshall.

And now he was picking me up from the airport.

Granted, he was bringing Enzo back, but there was the promise of sex afterwards. How could I say no?

I didn't want to say no.

I wanted to see Marshall. To deny that would be a straight out lie. Though as I walked through the terminal to the pickup zone where he'd said he'd be, I felt giddy.

I had butterflies.

Which was ridiculous. I could lie and say it was in anticipation of getting railed so thoroughly. But the way he grinned at me when I got into his ute made my heart thump and stomach swoop. I had to bite the inside of my lip so I didn't smile right back at him.

It wasn't the promise of sex.

It was him.

"Melbourne okay?" he asked as he pulled out into traffic. "Did you get everything sorted?"

I nodded. "Yes. Thank you for coming to get me. I didn't expect you to."

"'S no problem. Me and the kid had a road trip. He likes my taste in music."

Enzo meowed from the backseat.

"See?"

I couldn't help but laugh. "Pretty sure that was a cry for help."

Marshall grinned as he drove. "We've had a boys' week. Hanging out, watching TV. It's been fun. He likes my mum's lasagne, just so you know."

I stared at him. "You fed him lasagne?"

"It wasn't so much as *fed him* as it was him trying to eat off my plate or off my fork." He shrugged. "He went a bit crazy for it, not gonna lie."

Oh dear god.

"I'm going to have to retrain him. He had manners when I left him."

He laughed. "Nah. Pretty sure he just knows he could walk all over me."

Enzo meowed again.

"It's all right, little guy," Marshall said. "We'll be home soon."

God, the way he talked to him . . . I hated that I liked it so much.

"Want me to go through drive-through somewhere?" he asked me. "Or do you want to go home and take care of business first and order takeout later?"

"Take care of business?"

"Sounds better than fucking." He shrugged. "Unless you'd prefer me to ask if you want orgasms or food first? Or want me to drill you first? Or—"

"I get the point."

"So? What's your answer?"

"No food through a drive-through will ever appeal to me, sorry."

"Not even Maccas?"

"Especially not."

He looked in the rear-vision mirror. "It's all right, Enzo. I'll get you some chicken nuggets."

"He's not eating chicken nuggets."

He shot me a quick look and made a face.

Oh, good heavens.

"You fed him chicken nuggets?"

He shifted in his seat. "See, here's the thing. I—"

"You're never looking after him again."

He gasped. "That's not fair. I already told him he can stay with me next time you're out of town. And he said he'd like that."

This was, by far, the most ridiculous conversation I'd ever had.

Why was I smiling?

"Okay, no drive-through food," Marshall said. "Orgasms, drilling, and fucking first. Food after."

The promise curled warm and low in my belly. "Good."

I carried Enzo into my apartment and Marshall took my bag, my messenger bag, and another smaller bag from his car. I opened the carrier and scooped Enzo out. He gave my face a welcome nudge and was purring.

"Oh, who's the traitor now?" Marshall asked. He dumped my bags near the door and put his smaller bag on the dining table. "I see how it is."

I gave him a smug smile and gently let Enzo to the floor. "What's in the bag?"

He pulled out my shirt and held it up. "Buttons sewn on by yours truly."

I looked closer at the shirt, then at him. "With red thread."

He grinned. "Yep." He pointed to the top button of his own shirt, which I now realised was also sewn on with red cotton. "We match. And the red matches the red Polo logo on yours, so it looks deliberate." Then he shrugged and chewed on the inside of his lip. "And if you wear this shirt, it's like you're saying Marshall did this, and no one but us will know."

What the hell?

I had no idea what to make of that.

"You want me to wear something that identifies me as yours," I asked, my voice quiet.

He made a face, his cheeks pink. "Sounds weird when you say it like that. And to be honest, it was just the cotton that Mum had, but I thought about it later. Seeing you wear it would kinda be like my stamp on you." He cringed again.

I let out a long breath, as steady as I could make it. "It actually sounds kinda hot."

His eyes flashed to mine. "You like the sound of that?"

"I like it when you mark me," I admitted. "Hickeys, bite marks."

His hand went to his dick and he rearranged himself. His very impressive bulge. That I wanted, needed, to feel inside me.

Enzo meowed at his empty bowl, and I shook my head. "I'll just feed him first," I mumbled.

In the kitchen, I put the bowl on the counter and took a can from the pantry and was opening it when Marshall stepped in behind me. His hands raked up my back and gently massaged my shoulders.

I resisted leaning back into him.

Barely.

Then he snaked his hands around my waist, up to my shirt, and slowly unbuttoned the top button. Then the second, slow and torturous, then the third.

I'd forgotten all about feeding Enzo.

With one slow finger, Marshall gently pushed the shirt

off my shoulder. He kissed the skin; his warm lips and hot breath sent a shiver through me. Then he pulled the shirt down and I knew what he was looking for.

The hickey and bite mark I'd shown him in the photo I'd sent him.

"They're faded," he murmured. "I need to do them again."

I groaned. "Yes, you do."

He ran his hand down over my arse and groaned. "I'll feed the cat. You go get ready. However you want me to do you," he murmured, nuzzling the back of my neck. "Your wish, my command."

My knees felt so wobbly, I don't know how I managed to walk away. I took my bag into my bathroom and took the quickest shower of my life but needing to get the airport grime off me and wash away the stress of the last four days.

I dried off and put my robe on because he'd said he'd like to fuck me in it, and I wanted to see his face when I walked out and he saw me wearing it.

I wasn't disappointed.

He stopped, stunned. His lips parted and he blinked, and his breath came out in a rush. "Jesus," he whispered.

I smiled far too smugly, but damn. I felt desired, wanted. Sexy.

He walked up to me, his eyes looking me up and down, but he stopped short of touching me. He studied my neck, and with a gentle finger, the barest of touches, he dragged his finger down my neck, under the collar of the robe, and he gasped.

"Your skin is so warm," he murmured.

"Scalding hot shower," I breathed. "Hot skin, cold silk."

He gently revealed one collarbone and kissed it, soft lips skimming up the column of my throat. His warm hands raked down my body, sliding the silk under his touch, and he undid the sash. The robe fell open and he looked down, inspecting me, my body, my half-hard dick.

He groaned. "You're fucking killing me." He put his finger under my chin and kissed me softly. "Where and how do you want it?"

"I don't care, as long as you give it to me."

He pinched my chin between his thumb and forefinger and kissed me again. But this time he opened my mouth with his own, plunging his tongue in, and walked me backwards to my room. "Get on the bed," he ordered. "On your knees and put your arse up for me."

Oh, hell yes.

I did as he asked, moving slow and relishing the swish and slide of the silk on my skin with every movement. He was stripping off behind me and I saw the bottle of lube land on the bed beside me, but I made no move to grab it.

My arse was hidden under the robe and I made no move to pull it up either. I wanted him to do everything. I wanted him to take complete control, to do whatever he wanted to me. To use my body however he saw fit.

Handing over that control was my favourite part.

In that moment, I never felt freer. Especially with Marshall, because I trusted him so completely.

It was total surrender.

He kneeled on the bed behind me, and I smiled as I raised my arse higher and let my arms fall loose by my sides, the tension already melting away.

His warm hand found the small of my back, sliding down my arse to the back of my thigh, sliding the silk over my skin. He drew it up, exposing my arse, and he let out a low breath.

"Fuck," he whispered. He rubbed the silk over my skin,

then draped it, skimming it over my arse and balls, back and forth, swishing, tickling, soft.

The sensation was exquisite and torturous, and I groaned.

"I was gonna try and take it slow," he said, his voice thick. "But I want you too much. Need to fuck you hard and fast."

The lube bottle lid popped and, a second later, cool liquid poured down my arse crack, his thumb smearing it, rough and probing.

"Need to put a load in you now," he said, replacing his thumb with the blunt head of his cock.

God, yes. "Do it."

But he didn't ram into me, he pushed and teased, he tapped my hole, and he groaned as he pushed the tip in a little before pulling back.

I shot up onto my knees and growled at him. "Stop fucking teasing me and do it. I swear to fucking god, Marshall."

He grinned at me, a sly feral look in his eyes as he gripped the back of my neck and pushed my head back down to the mattress. "Stay the fuck down," he bit out. He let go of my neck and kept his palm pressed flat to my spine, pushed his cock against my hole, and drove into me.

I should have kept my mouth shut.

I'd forgotten how big he was, how much of him there was to take.

I tried to squirm away and he pushed me down harder. "You wanted it," he grunted. "You fucking take it."

I gasped back sharp breaths, trying to find that place in my mind. That place that found me peace.

Then he pulled me back. He was on his haunches, caging me in his arms so I was all but sitting on his cock. His chest pressed against my back, his ragged breath hot in my ear. "Relax, and breathe for me," he murmured. "Just breathe. I know you can take it. You can take every inch of me. You're a slut for my cock," he whispered, kissing my neck. "You fucking love it."

God, he knew what to say. He knew just how to say it to make me relax. To make me melt. With his strong arms around me, one hand holding my robe to my chest, the other hand around the base of my throat.

His cock buried inside me.

"Fuck, you feel so good," he said. Then he groaned out a frustrated sound, as if he was trying not to come already.

I let my head fall back and he began to raise his hips up, hitting deeper inside. His fingers started to bite into my skin, and he pressed his face into the silk on my back, kissing my spine. "Fuck yes," he ground out. "Oh god." Then his grip on me tightened, he pulled the robe down, scraped his teeth up to my shoulder blade, and nipped the skin.

I'd be riddled with hickeys and bite marks tomorrow.

I couldn't wait.

Letting go of my throat, Marshall pressed his hand down my chest and stomach to my cock, and I let out a cry as soon as he wrapped his fingers around me.

I was overstimulated, every nerve on fire as he stroked my oversensitive shaft. He pistoned into me, slow and deep, as he held me in place, jerking me off in time with his thrusts.

I was unable to move, pinned and caged by his body, impaled and at the mercy of his hand. I wanted to fuck his fist, but he had full control.

I was in heaven.

"I'm gonna come inside you," he bit out, panting. "Can't hold it anymore."

I groaned. "Give it to me," I begged. "Please. Let me have it."

He let out a roar and drove up into me, holding my hips and ramming his thick cock in as deep as he could go.

I felt every pulse, every shot, every jolt of his body.

It was surreal and divine. That he could own me like this. Make me his, to do with me as he pleased. He rocked me, moaning and gasping, his hands sliding the silk robe against my skin.

And when I thought he might be done, he drove us forward, my face in the mattress and his hand on my shoulder, my arse still impaled on his cock. He pinned me like that, still buried inside me.

He kept fucking rough, hard, without mercy.

Just how he knew I needed it. He took me to that place only he knew. Where pain and pleasure became one.

"Yeah, you love it," he said as he slammed into me over and over. "Your arse full of my come, full of my cock, and it's still not enough."

I came with a cry, and he held me down harder, his hand, his hips, his cock.

My orgasm danced the line between pain and pleasure, intense and overwhelming. My whole body jerked under his hold, an orgasm so powerful I saw stars, and he kept fucking.

When my mind came back online, I couldn't tell if he was coming again or if it was my body twitching so much. I was breathless and gasping, torn between needing him to stop and never letting him go.

When I couldn't take it anymore, he collapsed on me, his weight heavy on my back, his breaths hot behind my ear.

I was still racked with uncontrollable convulsions, and when he pulled out of me, it made it worse.

"Fuck," I cried, my whole body recoiling, trembling. "The fuck did you do to me?"

He chuckled, kissing my shoulder. He pulled my robe down as best he could and nuzzled his nose into the back of my head until our bodies quietened. I was floating in that blissful place where nothing else mattered.

I was going to be sore tomorrow.

Hell, I was beginning to feel it now.

"I'm going to run you a bath," Marshall murmured as he kissed the back of my head. "Then order us some dinner."

"Mm." I wasn't capable of anything else.

He chuckled again and kissed behind my ear. "Stay right here."

"Mm."

I couldn't have moved if I'd wanted to.

He peeled himself off me, leaving a shock of cold air in his place. I tried to protest, but then he folded back the blankets to cover me. I hid my face to hide my smile.

I was so spent, so used and sore. I was also the happiest I could ever recall being.

I didn't try and make sense of it. I didn't try to pull it apart and examine the pieces. I didn't want to inspect the glue that was currently holding me together.

I was too scared of what I'd find.

I knew it was only a temporary fix. It was only ever supposed to be a temporary fix. After all, there was no way Marshall would want to play this fucked-up game forever. No matter how much I wished he would.

I startled when something warm touched my face. I hadn't meant to fall asleep . . .

"Wake up, sleepyhead," he whispered. He gently stroked my cheek again. "Your bath's ready."

"Mm-mm," I mumbled. I didn't want to get up. I didn't want to face reality. I didn't want this floating feeling to end.

"I've ordered dinner. It should be here by the time you get out of the bath." He slowly pulled the blankets off me and all but lifted me to my feet. The robe, now crinkled and warm, fell open.

Marshall groaned as he took my hand—he actually held my hand—and walked me to the main bathroom. He was dressed in his jeans and T-shirt, and I might have been disappointed if he didn't look sexy as hell. Those jeans were made just for him, his thighs, his arse, and the delectable ever-present bulge at the front.

The bathroom was warm, the tub was two-thirds full, and the dancing plumes of steam like fingers inviting me in.

Marshall stood behind me, and without a word, he slid the robe off my shoulders, revealing each sliver of skin like a prize. He let it slide down my back, catching it before it fell to the floor, and he pressed his lips to a tender spot on my shoulder blade.

Where he'd bitten me.

"Does it hurt?" he murmured.

"In a good way," I whispered. "It's tender and soft, and it reminds me of where you've been."

He put his forehead to my shoulder. "Valentine," he whispered, then he drew his nose up to my nape and pressed a warm kiss to the back of my neck.

It was such an intimate thing to do. Such a personal, sweet thing to do. How he could be so rough when I needed it and then be so gentle when I needed . . .

And I'd never needed softness before.

Not before him.

I'd taken care of myself and got through just fine. I was resilient and self-sufficient. I'd anchored myself to withstand any storm.

Until him.

He took my hand and helped me step into the tub, and he kept hold of me until I lowered myself in and leaned against the back of the tub, my head on the headrest. The water was hot, maybe a little too hot, but it brought to the surface every ache, every twinge.

Even the scars no one could see felt raw and ragged. Exposed.

As if my anchor was losing purchase and I was being set adrift. It was frightening and overwhelming all at once.

He let go of my hand and I quickly grabbed his fingers, fighting the sudden urge to cry. I suddenly felt as if I was drowning and he was my only lifeline. "Stay."

I hadn't meant to say that. I had no idea what pulled those words from me, but I had to swallow down the lump in my throat. I closed my eyes as if that somehow helped to hide my tears.

Why the hell was I crying?

Jesus, help me, what had he done to me? Maybe he'd think it was the steam or sweat from the hot water . . .

He wasn't an idiot, and he wasn't blind.

Marshall pulled his hand free, and I thought for sure he was going to bail. Why was I so emotional tonight? Emotions weren't something I struggled with. I normally just shoved them down until I couldn't feel anything . . .

But he pulled his shirt over his head and whipped his jeans off, then decided to climb in behind me. "Holy shit," he said, lowering himself down, his legs on either side of me.

"Fuck, this is like lava. Why didn't you say I made it too hot?"

I couldn't help it. I laughed and he pulled me back against him, his arm around my chest, and he held me like that until I felt better. Until the muscle aches were gone and the ache in my chest had subsided too.

Until dinner arrived, when he had to go down to the lobby and get it. I got out and dried off, opting for long lounge pants and a long-sleeve shirt. Marshall came back wearing his jeans and T-shirt and no shoes.

"Aren't you cold?" I asked.

"No, my internal body temperature is now forty-three degrees thanks to that bath."

He'd ordered pasta, which was absolutely divine, and as if he knew it was exactly what I needed. A hot bath, a belly full of carbs, and sleep.

I didn't even object when he pulled me to the couch and had me all wrapped up with my head on his chest. He chose some stupid show on TV, and I didn't even mind, because the circles he drew on my back and his fingers in my hair—his warmth, his strength—was sublime.

It was intimate and sweet and like nothing I'd ever experienced before.

Gentle physical touch without any prelude to sex.

Huh. Weird.

But oh, so nice.

I felt safe and cherished. I knew there was no emotional connection on his behalf, and I told my heart not to get too excited.

Just enjoy it for what it is. Enjoy this moment while it lasts.

I wanted to stay awake and enjoy it for as long as I

could, but my eyes kept betraying me. And I knew that meant he'd be leaving. I didn't know why that hurt so much. I didn't want to be alone.

God, emotions were fucking terrible.

"I'm so tired," I mumbled. "Can't keep my eyes open."

And as he knew exactly what I needed even if I didn't know it myself, he grabbed Enzo and flicked the lights off. "Then let's go to bed."

I stared at him. "What . . . what do you think you're doing?"

His gaze met mine in the half-lit room. "I'm not leaving you alone tonight."

My heart almost stopped before it kicked into high gear, and my nose burned and my eyes watered.

Christ. Why was I such a mess tonight?

"I was talking about Enzo," I managed to say. We both knew I wasn't talking about Enzo.

He put his arm around my shoulder and led me to my room. "He's coming to bed with us."

"I don't allow him on my bed."

"But I do." He gave Enzo a big smooch, then gently put him on the bed. "And I'm staying tonight, so it's a package deal."

But Enzo jumped right off the bed. Marshall deflated and I smiled.

When we climbed under the covers, Marshall quickly pulled me into his arms. He wrapped me up tight, my head on his shoulder, his leg over my thigh. I'd never been an affectionate person, never been one to cuddle.

But oh boy, this was nice.

"I can't believe Enzo let me down," he mumbled. "We had a deal. He spent every night on my bed with me, on my head, basically, purring his little motor out. And now I'm not good enough."

"I told you he was a traitor."

"I'm not buying him any more chicken nuggets."

I laughed. "Good."

Then there was a muted thud on the side of the bed and gentle cat pawsteps up to Marshall. "Yes," he said. "I knew you liked me, my little guy. I didn't mean it about the nuggets. Of course I'll get you some."

Christ.

Enzo started to purr as he made himself comfortable, and I was too tired, and too happy, to care.

Marshall tightened his arm around me and kissed the side of my head. I was warm and protected in his arms; no monsters would find me in my dreams tonight.

I smiled into the dark, wishing I knew what this was or why I wanted this to be real and not just some stupid agreement. Why I wanted it to be like this every night, and why the Marshall in my mind didn't glower at me anymore. He didn't shoot lasers at me with loathing and contempt.

Instead, he smiled.

Why didn't that bother me? Why did it make me happy?

Why did *he* make me happy?

Stop overthinking, Valentine. Enjoy whatever the hell this is while it lasts.

"What was that?" Marshall asked, half asleep.

It took a second for me to catch up. "What?"

"You mumbled something." He gave me a squeeze and snuggled in closer, his arms and hands holding me tight. "'S okay. I gotchu."

And it was that—that, right there—that scared the shit

out of me. Because he *did* have me. He had me in ways I wasn't prepared for.

I was so good at pretending I didn't feel anything. All my life, I'd put a lid on my emotions and locked it tight. But this felt too big to contain, too big to ignore.

And maybe, just maybe, I didn't want to ignore it anymore.

CHAPTER 15

MARSHALL

IT REALLY WAS A GOOD THING THAT I WAS SIDELINED for Saturday's game. I still went to the game, of course, and cheered the boys on. But I didn't have to face off against Valentine.

It was hard enough watching the game, watching him, and not being part of it. But my heart was in my throat every time he got tackled, every ruck, and I held my breath until he was back on his feet. If I'd have been on the field with him, fuck knows what I would've done.

And one time our lock, Simons, took him down. Now, Simons was a good guy, a teammate, a mate even. I'd known him for years but I had to shove my hands into my coat pockets so I didn't run out onto the field and take his head off for tackling Valentine like that. Everyone on my bench said things like 'good tackle, good tackle' and it probably was a *good tackle*, but I didn't like the fact he took down my Valentine.

My Valentine?

I was losing my damned mind.

Valentine wasn't *my* anything. Apart from my enemy

with benefits. Not that we were enemies anymore . . . My not-friend with benefits. A regular fuck. Someone I had an arrangement with.

Someone I cared for.

Someone I was beginning to care a great deal for.

Get a fucking grip, Marshall.

All that aside, it was a good game of rugby. North Ryde and Lane Cove were the only two teams undefeated so far, so it was always going to be a tough game. I thought Lane Cove might have had us in the second half, but my boys held their line and when Taka made a run for it, no one on their team could stop him. He was too big, too strong, and too good.

We won by four points.

I stood with the bench and clapped our boys off the field as they ran into the dressing sheds. I clapped a few of them on the back. Taka, of course. Not Simons.

But then I stood there and clapped the Lane Cove boys off too, because it was a good sportsmanship thing to do. I locked eyes with Valentine as he jogged past me, just for the briefest second, and there was the slightest smirk on his face. Along with sweat and a smear of dirt, and it could have very well been his mouthguard that made him smirk.

But I liked to think it was me.

And later, back at the pub, I stood with my back to where Valentine was sitting. I had to, to stop myself from looking for him every two seconds.

"Oh, for fuck's sake," Taka mumbled. "Dude, play it cool."

I paused, my beer bottle at my lips. "What?"

"You keep lookin' over there, you gonna give yourself away."

"Oh fuck off," I replied. "I'm not looking anywhere. I have my back to him."

Him.

I'd said *him* as if I'd just admitted it *was* Valentine, when last week I'd denied it. And at work, we'd been so busy we'd had no time for private conversations. And now, what? I just said *him* as if it was common knowledge?

Christ. Taka was right. I was gonna give myself away.

Taka smiled because he knew he was right. "And that makes it more obvious when you keep turning your head."

I rolled my eyes, but I knew he had me. Taka had a clear view over my shoulder. His gaze went from Valentine to me. "If it's any consolation, he's tryin' not to look at you just as much as you're tryin' not to look at him."

What?

I had to make myself not look. *Don't turn around. Don't look over your shoulder.*

"Hey, great game, man," one of the Lane Cove boys said to Taka on his way to the bathrooms.

"Thanks," Taka said, raising his beer bottle.

Well, now that I'd all but admitted it . . .

"I told him you knew," I said, then sipped my beer with my gaze fixed on the back wall. "But no one else can know."

"I won't tell anyone."

I cut my eyes to Taka's. I trusted him with my life, but now I was also trusting him with Valentine's. "No one can know, Taka. He's not out. His father would . . ."

His father would what? Kill him? Ruin him? Fire him? Send him away?

I shook my head. "No one else can know."

"It's cool," he said, his permanent smile in place. "No one'd believe me anyway."

I nodded because that was true.

"But thanks for saying it," he added.

I felt shitty for lying to him. "I never meant to keep it from you. It's just not my secret to tell, okay? He has his reasons for being—"

"An arsehole?"

"The way he is." Then I added. "And an arsehole. Except he's not." I shook my head at myself because this was ridiculous. "I don't know what the fuck he is."

Taka smiled as he swigged his beer. "Never thought I'd see the day."

"See the day for what?"

"Where you caught feelings."

"I haven't caught feelings." Christ, what a stupid thing to say.

"Where you got nailed down by one guy."

"I'm not nailed down."

He pressed his thumb on the bar like he was squashing a bug. "Under the thumb, my friend."

"Oh, fuck off."

Taka laughed just as someone tried to squeeze past. "Excuse me," a guy said, his hand lingering on my side as he got through the crowd. I gave him a brief glance and he was vaguely familiar. I think maybe I'd taken him home once. Maybe that explained the way he touched me . . . hopeful of a repeat.

A few weeks ago, that move would have seen me follow him to the bathrooms. Now I moved to let him pass without a second thought.

Taka gave me a pointed look. "My point exactly, bro."

I rolled my eyes.

Then someone else brushed up against me to get through. "Excuse me," he said, his voice warm and familiar. I turned this time, coming face to face with Valentine, his gaze lasered in on mine, and he smirked. "Maybe you shouldn't stand in the walkway."

I bristled, but then I noticed the shirt he was wearing. The white button-down with the buttons I'd sewn on with red thread.

And if you wear this shirt, it's like you're saying Marshall did this, and no one but us will know.

My gaze drew up to meet his, and I smiled. "Maybe you should go around."

His nostrils flared, but his friend Lleyton intervened and pushed Valentine past me. He looked at me with disdain. "Calm down, Wise," he said, then he smiled at Taka. "Hey, Taka, good game today."

Taka, of course, was now grinning. "Thanks, man."

My heart was hammering, blood pumping.

That little interaction was interesting.

He'd worn that shirt because I'd told him it was like saying I'd been the one to rip the last buttons off, how no one would know but us.

But I'd know.

He was wearing it for me.

When I finally met Taka's eyes, he laughed. "Yeah, no one will suspect a thing. Tell me, do you two hate-fuck each other or something? Because, Jesus." He shook his head.

I snorted and drained my beer. "Something like that."

"Hey, Valentine," someone said loudly, getting my immediate attention. "Happy birthday, man!"

I turned at that, because what the fuck?

He and Lleyton were talking to a group of guys near the bathrooms. They looked like typical rich private-school types, and Valentine shook their hands and did that fake laugh, and . . .

"Oh, thanks," Valentine said.

His birthday?

What the actual fuck?

How did I not know that? How did some fucking random dickhead in a bar know that and I didn't?

Anger spiked in my blood, a thousand stinging needles in my heart.

Valentine disappeared into the bathrooms, and I put my empty bottle on the bar.

"Don't do it, man," Taka said quietly.

I looked up at him. "Do what?"

"Don't go in there."

I was so fucking angry—irrationally and stupidly—and hurt.

I was hurt.

This was bullshit.

I fished a twenty out of my pocket and put it on the bar. "Next round's on me," I said. "I'm out."

I turned and pushed my way through the crowd, desperate for fresh air. I felt like I was drowning.

Over what?

Not knowing it was Valentine's birthday?

That he never told me. That it wasn't something he thought I should know.

That I wasn't . . . that we weren't what I'd stupidly fucking thought we were? And I'd have liked to think we were on the same page, especially after this last week, all the texts, me staying with him, getting into the bath with him because he was hurting when he'd tried to pretend he wasn't crying. Me staying the night and holding him while he slept because he wasn't as fine as he said he was. He was a mess and I wanted to make him better.

Me being in way over my head, and him . . .

Him being nothing more than he ever said he would be.

Christ.

I checked the time. It was half-past eight. Thirty minutes before our usual 9pm rendezvous time . . .

What I felt like doing was going back inside the pub, getting shitfaced, and forgetting all about him. Or going home to lick my wounds.

But what I needed to do was be a fucking grown up and talk to him.

I hadn't wanted to force his hand, to find out what the fuck we were, but apparently tonight was it.

We'd either be finished or we'd be . . . something else.

I'd only had a few beers, so I drove to his place and sat on the brick fence in the freezing fucking cold waiting for him. The longer I sat there, the more determined I was. I shot him a text.

Still on for nine?

My stomach was a massive knot, and my heart was squeezing tight.

I didn't want him to end this but by the end of the night, at least I'd know where we stood.

A knock on the glass foyer door startled me. It was Valentine, and he opened the door when I stood up.

"Waiting long?" he asked.

I shook my head and brushed past him. I hit the elevator button and we rode in silence up to his floor.

It was awkward.

And awful.

He opened his front door and stood aside for me to walk in first. Enzo came out to meet us and Valentine scooped him up, holding him like a shield for what he knew was coming.

I stood in his kitchen with my arms crossed.

"Just say it," Valentine murmured, his face a mask of sadness. "Clearly something's wrong."

"It's your birthday?"

He sighed. "Yes."

"Today?"

"Tomorrow, actually." He nodded slowly. "That guy . . . we were in the same year at college. It's his birthday too, that's how he remembered."

I scrubbed my hands over my face, trying to calm down, to put aside my hurt and get some answers. "I've been trying to think of why you didn't tell me," I said. "And the only thing I keep coming back to is that we're obviously on different pages here. Entirely different books, even."

He shook his head. "No."

"I think we are. Because here I am thinking maybe we had something, and it's pretty fucking obvious that you don't feel the same."

He shook his head again, but Enzo struggled to get down, and as soon as Valentine let him go, he began to meow at his bowl.

"I don't know how I feel," Valentine whispered. "I'm . . . confused. I don't . . . I can't . . ."

Enzo meowed and meowed, and Valentine groaned. "Okay, okay," he said, clearly flustered. He went to the pantry and got out the cat food and he fixed Enzo's dinner, agitated, his hands now shaking, and Enzo kept yelling at him until he put the bowl down. Then Valentine stepped back and shook his head, his hand to his forehead, fingers trembling. Enzo was finally quiet, but Valentine was pale, and he opened his mouth to say something, and he tried to speak, his eyes wide and watery. He gasped like he couldn't catch his breath. Over and over, he struggled to get enough air.

Oh my god.

He was freaking out.

Valentine Tye was freaking out.

I went to him and wrapped my arms around him, holding him. "You're okay," I soothed, though I wasn't sure he was.

"Sorry," he mumbled. "I'm sorry."

"Don't apologise," I whispered, rubbing his back. "I gotchu."

He nodded and then shook his head, still gasping for air. "Just need . . . to catch my breath . . . need my pills."

His pills.

The ones in his bathroom?

"I'll get them," I said, rushing into his room. I grabbed all the prescription bottles in his cabinet because I didn't know which ones he needed, and when I came out, he was getting a glass of water from the sink.

I put the pills on the counter and he opened one bottle, his hands shaking, and threw some back, chasing them down with water.

He shook his head. "Sorry. Sorry."

I took the glass from him, sat it down, then pushed him against the kitchen counter, my arms tight around him. His whole body was trembling, his breaths short and sharp. "Don't apologise."

"Panic," he mumbled, his face against my chest. "I have panic . . . attacks."

Christ.

Something else I didn't know about him.

"It's okay," I whispered, rubbing his back. "You're okay."

We stood like that for a long, long while, until his breathing evened out. Until the pills kicked in. "Haven't had one in a long time," he said, his forehead against my neck.

I rubbed his back some more. "You feel okay now?"

He nodded, barely. But when I went to pull away, his hold on me tightened. "I'm sorry," he said. "For not telling you. Birthdays aren't something I celebrate. Never have. Not really."

"Never?"

He shook his head and gave an uncertain shrug. "My sister and I . . . our parents weren't . . . no one . . ."

Parents? I couldn't ever recall the mention of his mother.

"Your parents are arseholes, and you and your sister deserved better."

"I know." He nodded, still not letting me go. "I didn't think to tell you because . . . because I forgot. Not forgot to tell you. I forgot it was my birthday."

Jesus Christ.

I squeezed him and kissed the side of his head. "I'm sorry I got mad. I heard that guy tell you happy birthday, and it stung. He knew and I didn't. And I . . . I don't know what I thought."

Yes, you do. You thought this was about you. You didn't for one moment stop to think about him.

"You're the only person who does know me, Marshall. Only you," he said. He pulled back now and his eyes were glassy. Glazed over. Yep, the drugs were definitely working. "I thought you were going to say we were finished and . . . I panicked."

Yeah, I saw that.

"I don't want to end this," I whispered, kissing him softly. "I thought you were going to tell me that this feeling wasn't part of our agreement."

He smiled sadly. "This feeling."

I nodded. "This confused feeling."

He snorted. "I have that same one."

"We need to talk," I said. "But maybe tomorrow."

He nodded. "Tomorrow. Please don't leave me alone tonight."

I cupped his face and pressed my lips to his. "I won't. Please don't tell me this is all one-sided."

He shook his head. "It's not. But I don't know what it is. I don't want anything to change. I can't offer you anything more than this. You showed me . . . things. Special things."

I frowned at that. "I showed you kindness. And it's a little bit fucked up that you think that's special."

"It's special to me. And you didn't just show me kindness. You showed me what was possible, and what I could have. And what I'll miss when you leave me. What I will never find again. All I wanted was for you to fuck me. I never asked for anything else, and now I don't know how to live without it."

"I'm not going anywhere."

"Not yet." God, he looked so damn sad. "I can't ever come out, Marshall. I can't ever be out."

"I know." I brushed my thumb over his cheek. "I don't expect you to."

He studied my eyes, and staring back at him was taking me places I wasn't prepared for. We really did need to talk, but tonight was not the time for this conversation. Not when he was like this, with his slow blinks and lazy smile.

I looked down at his shirt and tapped the first button. "Nice red coloured thread."

He smirked. "Thanks." Then he seemed to remember something. "Oh. That guy in the bar who put his hand right here," he said, sliding his hand down to my waist. "What was that?"

The guy who brushed past me? The one I'd thought the old me would have banged in the back alley, but the new me didn't even consider it? The guy I think I maybe did bang in the back alley once . . .

"I didn't like it," Valentine said, frowning.

I chuckled. "Is that why you came over and did the same?"

"I don't like it when other guys touch you."

He was jealous?

Well, I liked that way more than I should have, and I was about to take the piss, but then he smiled, his head lolled back and he tried to look at me. "Think I took one too many pills."

"How many did you take?"

He shrugged. "Two. Three?"

"How many are you supposed to take?"

"One."

Shit. "Do you need to go to hospital?"

He snorted. "Nope. Need to sleep. Make me tired. And wobbly."

Wobbly. Valentine Tye just said the word wobbly.

"Okay then, let's get you to bed."

He nodded and pulled his phone out of his pocket and slid it onto the counter, and I noticed a text on his screen.

Still on for nine?

My text.

Wait . . .

"Is that my text?" I asked. "Why is my name the pizza emoji in your phone?"

He laughed, and so help me god, his smile was incredible, high or not. "Pizza. Nine inches. Deep dick . . . I mean, deep pan."

I scoffed out a laugh. "What the . . . ?"

He laughed and he was heavy against me. "'S funny."

I mean it kinda was.

I chuckled, stunned. "You need to go to bed. I can assure you there will be no nine-inch-deep dicking tonight."

He whined and leaned his whole weight against me, resting his head in the crook of my neck. He fisted my shirt. "Don't go."

Oh god, Valentine.

"I won't leave. Me and Enzo can watch *Rambo*. He hasn't seen it."

He sighed, keeping his head down. "I haven't seen it either. I could watch it too?"

I reckoned he wouldn't even get past the opening credits, so why not? "Sure."

We got to the couch and he planted himself on me, between my legs, lying with his face on my chest. I gently ran my fingers through his hair until his eyes closed, and Enzo jumped up and joined us.

I could get used to this.

Real used to it.

So much had happened tonight. Things were admitted but not discussed. We definitely needed to talk, to clear the air, but for now it was enough.

I'd learned some things about Valentine tonight.

He'd said he had feelings for me. Feelings that confused him. He'd freaked out when he thought I was leaving him. He'd been overwhelmed and panic kicked in. He had pills to help him with that, so it was something he'd learned to live with. He'd never celebrated his birthdays because his parents didn't give a fuck. I didn't even know he had a mother, yet he'd said parents.

He'd said I was the only person to ever know the real him.

And maybe when I'd come here tonight, my feelings had been confused too. Leaving the pub, not knowing what anything meant. But lying there on his couch, with him in my arms and his cat purring beside us . . . my feelings were pretty freaking clear.

I didn't hate Valentine Tye anymore.

I hadn't for a while.

I didn't know what it meant for us or where we went from here. But he was on the same page as me. And, for tonight, that was enough.

I woke up around six o'clock, sunrise barely cracking through Valentine's bedroom window. He was lying on his side, facing me, sound asleep. His hair was messed up, his lips parted. He looked peaceful and so fucking beautiful.

And today was his birthday.

And if he'd never really celebrated a birthday before, then I should make this one he'd never forget. I'd make it all about him. Starting with breakfast.

"Why are you watching me?" he mumbled.

I laughed. "How could you tell with your eyes closed?"

He made a face and rolled over, burying his beautiful face into his pillow. "Don't be weird."

I kissed the back of his head. "Happy birthday."

He froze for a second, then groaned as he deflated. Did he just remember last night? "Mm."

"I'm going to make you breakfast," I said.

He groaned again. "Coffee."

"Breakfast."

"Breakfast coffee."

I laughed and smacked his arse before rolling out of bed. I pulled on my jeans and went to his fridge and found a whole lotta nothing. His pantry was the same. "Jesus Christ," I said, loud enough for him to hear. "Do you ever eat?"

His reply was half mumbled, half croaky. "Coffee."

I started his coffee machine and found two cups. Enzo decided to join me, jumping up on the kitchen counter. He meowed at me. "Morning to you too. Want some breakfast? At least there's food for you here."

I poured some biscuits into his bowl, and when the coffee machine beeped, I made us one each. I took it into his room. "Birthday coffee."

He groaned again. "Really?" He did sit up though, resting against the headboard.

I handed him his cup and sat on the edge of the bed. "Yes, because there's no birthday breakfast. I'm gonna have to go out and get something."

"Just have it delivered."

"For breakfast?"

"Sure. Why not?"

"Or we could go out to a café somewhere?"

His gaze shot to mine, and I realised I'd put my foot in it. No, we couldn't go out somewhere . . .

"We could go where no one knows you," I added. "Northern beaches or something."

"My sister lives up there."

Of course she does.

"We could drive up to Newcastle," I suggested, even though it was a stupid idea. "Or just drive and get something takeaway. We don't have to get out of the car. Maccas? I owe Enzo some nuggets."

Valentine almost smiled as he sipped his coffee, but he never said anything.

And this was the reality of seeing someone who was not out, who could never be seen in public with me. Not just any guy, but especially me. A guy who he'd had a somewhat public feud with for over a decade.

I was also an employee.

He was watching me. "Not so much fun, is it?"

"I just wanted to do something for your birthday," I murmured. "It doesn't have to be anything, really. We can order breakfast. Or I can make a quick trip to the supermarket."

His eyes met mine. "Just this is enough for me," he said. "It's more than I've ever had."

Christ.

It just made me more determined to do something.

"Okay, I'll make a dash to the shops. I'm going to make you breakfast. Actually, I'm going to cook you breakfast and you're going to help me. I'll be ten minutes." I stood up, not taking no for an answer. "And if Enzo tries to tell you he hasn't had breakfast, he's lying."

I pulled on my sweater and boots, grabbed my keys, and hauled arse to the closest supermarket. I bought all the breakfast essentials, then hit the cake section and even found some birthday candles.

Because fuck it.

I looked twice at the little balloons and decided that was too stupid, got to the end of the aisle, and went back for the stupid balloon because fuck that too.

And a stupid bouquet of stupid supermarket flowers at the checkout.

Because fuck that as well.

I made it back to Valentine's apartment with my arms full to find him freshly showered and smiling. "You took twenty minutes, not ten." Then he noticed what I was holding. "What did you . . . ?"

I took the flowers out first. "Happy birthday."

He stood there, stunned, maybe horrified. He didn't take them. He just stared. "Marshall . . ."

"They're only supermarket flowers. They were at the checkout. It was a stupid idea," I said, feeling like a grade-A fool.

Until he got all teary.

"No one's ever bought me flowers before," he whispered.

Oh shit.

Oh god.

"Well, to be fair, I've never bought flowers for anyone before. Except my mum, of course." Then, while I was being the biggest idiot ever, I took out the little balloon and shoved it into the bouquet and held them out for him.

He let out a breathy laugh and took them, his chin wobbling a little. "Thank you."

"Happy birthday," I said again.

He nodded and looked at the flowers as if they were some award-winning florist arrangement.

Then I took out the cake and candles. It was just one of those small ones, not much bigger than a muffin, to be honest. I quickly shoved a single candle in it and held it up. "And this." I shrugged. "I don't have a lighter."

He let out a teary laugh. "A cake?"

"Well, yes. It's what happens on birthdays, typically." I cringed, because god, this was all awkward. "But you have to eat your breakfast first. That's the rule. Well, that was the rule in my house growing up."

I cringed again.

Fuck.

Valentine laughed but he wiped a tear from his cheek. "Christ, this is . . . I don't know why I'm crying."

God, why did it hurt so much to see him cry? "I didn't mean to upset you," I murmured. This was all a bad idea . . .

He shook his head quickly, more tears welling in his eyes. "No, you didn't. I, uh . . . wasn't expecting this. It's just . . . maybe the nicest thing anyone's ever done for me."

Oh, goddammit.

I put the cake on the table and went to Valentine, putting my arms around him. "Don't crush my flowers," he mumbled into my sweater, holding the flowers out to the side.

Then, of course, Enzo decided to try and steal the cake. "No," I said, lunging for it. I saved it before he got his fangs in it. "Little dude, we had a deal. Remember?"

Valentine scooped the now-irate cat off the table and dropped him onto the sofa, and I took the cake and the grocery bag from the table into the kitchen. "Okay, break-fast-cooking time."

I pulled out the Turkish bread, eggs, bacon, vine toma-toes, and a jar of Hollandaise sauce, and began looking for a chopping board and different knives. Valentine stood back, leaning against the counter, arms crossed.

"You can help," I said.

He wore a strange smile. "But you're doing such a good job. I never realised how appealing it was to have a man who knows his way around my kitchen."

I took the short, sharp knife and handed it to him. "Roma tomatoes. Cut lengthways."

He smirked. "Mm, bossy. You know I like that."

I put a pan on the expensive stove top that I doubted had ever been used. "And I said no dessert until after breakfast." Soon I had bacon sizzling and badly sliced tomatoes frying, and I put him on coffee duty while I toasted the Turkish bread and cracked the eggs.

A few minutes later, we sat down at the table with a pretty good birthday breakfast.

He hadn't stopped smiling yet.

"This is really good," he said. "I can't believe you made this."

I sipped my coffee. "I can't believe you can't cut tomatoes."

He laughed. "I told you I don't cook."

"We'll have to make a dinner next. Something easy."

"Takeout is easy."

"Takeout is expensive."

He shrugged. "I have money, and honestly, I'd pay just so my kitchen wasn't a mess." He gestured to the pans on the stove.

"I'll clean this up," I said. "Only because it's your birthday. When we make dinner, we both clean fifty-fifty."

He was still smiling, and he ate everything on his plate. So much for only wanting coffee . . . But then that line between his eyebrows appeared.

"What's wrong?" I asked.

His eyes met mine. "Nothing. I was just thinking."

"I know. You get a line right here," I said, pointing above my nose.

He smirked wryly. "You know me so well."

I wasn't sure I did, but considering how private he was and how closed off he was towards others, maybe I did?

"When's your birthday?" he asked.

"August fifteenth."

"Any brothers or sisters?" He made a face. "You never mentioned any . . ."

I shook my head. "Just me."

"Longest relationship?"

"Ooh, straight into those kinda questions," I said. "Five months. His name was Kevin."

He frowned. "Five months . . ."

"I was twenty-two, he was thirty."

"Who ended it?"

"He did."

I wasn't sure if he was pleased or pissed. "Why? What was wrong with him?"

I chuckled. "Wasn't a good fit," I quoted. "Physically, I mean. He didn't like . . . he preferred a smaller dick."

Valentine laughed. "His loss, honestly. Yours is the best I've ever had."

Oh, Jesus.

"The best, huh?"

He nodded. "Easily."

"What's your longest relationship?"

He inhaled deeply and sighed on the exhale. "None. Us, whatever this is. I've only ever had physical arrangements. Sometimes repeats. Mostly not. I never wanted anyone around. I'm not exactly easy to be around, let's put it that way. It's just easier to be alone rather than explain my . . . life, my job, my family. And I never found anyone who was compatible." He shrugged. "Until . . ."

"Until me."

His gaze cut to mine, and he gave the barest of nods. But then he rolled his eyes. "Don't get smug. It's not all about you."

I chuckled. "No. It's about you too." I stood up and took

our plates to the sink. "You go do something. I'll clean up here."

He sat there for a few seconds, his brow furrowed again, then he began clearing the table. When I'd finished stacking the dishwasher, I ran some hot soapy water into the sink for the pans and suddenly Valentine stood behind me. He put his hands on my waist and pressed his forehead against my spine.

"Thank you," he whispered.

I smiled, not game to turn around in case he pulled away. I slid my hands over his to hold him right where he was. "Is this the first time you touched me first?"

He was quiet for a moment. "I told you not to get smug." Then he snorted. "And I seem to recall a bathroom stall incident that I initiated."

I laughed. "Oh, yes. When you shoved me into a cubicle so you could give me a blowjob."

"I shoved you into the stall so you wouldn't start a fight."

"And so you could suck my dick."

I felt him smile against my back. "I'd heard you had a huge dick. I needed to see for myself."

I laughed. "Oh, like a nine-inch-deep, deep pan pizza, right?"

He snorted and pulled his arms free. He leaned against the kitchen counter, kinda smiling, kinda not. "Yeah, I'm sorry about that."

I turned to face him. "Don't be. It's funny. I'm just surprised you actually have a sense of humour."

He made a face. "No, not about the pizza emoji. I'm . . . sorry about last night. I freaked out a bit." He nodded to the prescription pills still on the counter. I thought he might have put them away when I'd gone to the supermarket, but no, they were still there. Deliberately, I could guess, so he could bring up this conversation. "Do you want to know what they're for?"

Oh boy . . .

"If you want to tell me, then yes. You don't owe me any explanation." *Here goes nothing.* "To be honest with you, Valentine. I saw those in your bathroom cabinet a while ago."

His gaze met mine. "Oh."

"I totally snooped. Sorry. But like I said, you don't owe me an explanation. If you need meds, you take them. It's that simple. You don't need to feel ashamed or embarrassed."

"I'm not . . . ashamed." He shook his head, then crossed his arms and uncrossed them, then searched for pockets he didn't have.

I reached out and took his hand, giving it a squeeze. "It's okay."

"I'm not ashamed," he said again. "I just . . . it's not easy to admit weakness."

"It's not a weakness, Valentine."

He winced, and then he let out a long sigh before he reached for the first bottle of pills. "These are sleeping pills. I don't take them very often, but sometimes my mind won't stop turning. If I have a lot going on at work, or if I've had to deal with my father . . ." He shook off whatever line of thought that was. Then he picked up another bottle. "These are for anxiety. I don't need them very often either, but sometimes it sneaks up on me. If it's something big or something I can't control . . ."

Like the idea of me leaving.

I rubbed his arm and let him get his thoughts together.

"Sometimes it feels like everything's closing in on me and I can't breathe."

"Like last night."

He nodded. "I thought you were going to tell me . . ." He shook his head again and laughed. "Fuck. This got complicated, didn't it?"

"Not really," I said. "It doesn't have to be."

"When you . . ." He scowled like he was mad at himself. "When you fuck me, it makes everything stop. Nothing else exists. My mind goes quiet and nothing else matters."

Oh, okay. Not what I was expecting, but—

He licked the corner of his mouth and nodded. "I like the pain of it because it centres my attention, and I like it when you're rough and when you use me for your pleasure. I'm sure there's probably a shrink's list on why that's fucked up, but all I know is that I like it. All my life people have given in to me or yielded to me because of who I am, because of who my father is. Yes, Valentine. Anything you want, Valentine." He rolled his eyes. "But not you. You bend me over and hold me down and call me names, tell me I'm worthless and for some fucked-up reason it validates me. It reminds me that I'm not invincible, that I'm human."

Christ.

He folded his arms then and stared at the wall. Vulnerable Valentine was gone, proud and defiant Valentine in his place. "I don't want that to change," he added. "I don't want this agreement to change. And that might be selfish on my behalf because it's all about what I want, and I'm sorry. But it should come as no great surprise to learn that I'm selfish."

"So you still get what you want, you still expect me to yield, to give the Valentine Tye whatever he demands, even though you just said you liked it when I didn't?"

He winced. "No." Then he sighed. "Yes."

"Okay, just so we're not confused."

He sighed. "Marshall."

"No, I get it. It's all about you."

His eyes met mine and he raised his chin. "You're supposed to hate me, remember?"

I barked out a laugh. "Oh, so that's what this is about? Poking and prodding me to get a reaction. Well, let me tell you something, Valentine. You want me to hold you down and fuck you so hard you can't sit down for two days; you don't need to make me mad for me to do that. I know how you like it. You like it rough. You like me to own you, use you. I don't need to be mad at you to do that. I'll give it to you as hard as you can take it because that's how I like it too."

His jaw bulged and his nostrils flared, a familiar heat filled his stare.

"But I don't hate you," I admitted quietly. "I hope that's not going to be a problem. I mean, I don't particularly like you, Valentine."

He studied me for a second until he tried not to smile. "Good. Because I don't particularly like you either."

"Good." It didn't help that I was smiling back at him.

"So," he said. "Now we have that out of the way, I believe there was a mention of birthday sex. Well, you called it dessert, but you were talking about—"

"Ooh, cake," I said, remembering. I plucked the candle out of the cake, went to the gas cooktop, and pressed it on. The gas plate lit up, I lit the candle and carefully stuck it back in the cake. I held it up for him. "Make a wish."

His eyes went to mine, and his smile wavered a little. "A wish?"

"Yes, it's a birthday cake thing."

He stared at the flame for a second but then he very gently blew the candle out.

"Happy birthday, Valentine."

"Thank you," he murmured.

I put the cake on the counter. "You have to cut it and eat the first slice. That's another birthday rule."

"But it's eight o'clock in the morning."

"It's your birthday." I pulled a knife from the drawer and handed it to him.

"But I wished that you'd bend me over the sofa and nail me. That's what I wished for and it hasn't happened yet."

I laughed. "Oh believe me, I'm gonna do that too. But first you gotta cut the cake."

He rolled his eyes but he was smiling, and it might have been stupid, but no one had ever made a fuss over him on his birthday before, so what the hell.

I sang him the birthday song.

He was embarrassed, for me, I think. But he did take a bite of the first piece, then he made me have a bite, and it was far too much sugar, but then he leaned up on his toes and kissed me.

Just a peck.

And for all the filthy things we'd done together, that simple little peck was just the sweetest thing. It took me by surprise and made by belly swoop. He'd never initiated touch, and he'd certainly never kissed me first. Sure, I'd had his tongue down my throat, but this seemed by far the most intimate kiss.

"Thank you," he murmured, his cheeks tinted in the softest pink.

Damn.

"Don't get smug," I said, repeating what he'd said to me earlier and ignoring the thump of my heart. "Now, about that birthday wish."

Chapter 16

Valentine

Marshall left around lunch time. I wasn't sure on the exact time because he'd left me in a crumpled mess on my bed, and I'd been so thoroughly had, I'd fallen back asleep.

Well, he'd slapped my arse on his way out and told me to have a happy birthday.

Believe me, after what he'd spent hours doing to me, I was.

My best birthday to date.

My ringing phone woke me up. It was Brooklyn, and I assumed she was just wishing me a happy birthday, but no, she had something to do in the city and said she'd call in when she was done. We'd do a late lunch, she'd said.

Sounded good to me.

I stripped my bed and washed everything—my god, what a mess—and showered again, smiling at the ache in my arse. I smiled as I tidied the kitchen, remembering how Marshall had laughed at my attempt to cook anything. I smiled at the flowers on my table and at the silly little balloon.

I smiled as I recalled what he'd done to me. Once on the back of the sofa, and the second time in my bed. I swear I could still feel him inside me . . .

I smiled as I got into my sister's car.

"Happy birthday," she said cheerfully.

"Thanks."

She pulled out into traffic and glanced my way a few times. "You look happy."

I almost laughed. "Do I?"

"Mmm," she said. "Any particular reason?"

I snorted. "On grounds that I may incriminate myself, the defence rests."

She rolled her eyes and laughed, but thankfully let it drop.

She took me to a place on the harbour for our late lunch, and I was surprised by how much I enjoyed it. Enjoyed the outing, enjoyed the sunshine, enjoyed the company.

It was just nice.

"Heard from Mum or Dad?" she asked.

I shook my head. "To wish me a happy birthday? Of course I haven't. Are you surprised?"

She sighed. "No." She scowled at the view. "Honestly, fuck them."

I smiled at her. It was comforting to know we felt the same, that we had each other. Though it struck me as I looked out across the water that we really didn't know each other well at all, either.

I had no idea what her closest friends were up to or even if she still had the same closest friends. I had no idea what she even did in her spare time.

Just like she knew very little about me.

I'd never even told her I was gay. Would she be okay with it? Probably. Would she even care?

"So," she said, sipping her spritzer. "The other week you said you weren't seeing anyone, but you were awfully smiley when I picked you up."

"Am I not allowed to smile?"

She snorted. "Of course. It's just not . . . it's not a common look on you, that's all."

That was fair. I sighed and stabbed the fruit in my drink with the straw. "I might be seeing someone," I said.

No idea why.

No clue what possessed me.

"It's not serious though," I added. "Just a bit of fun. And very much on the down-low. I can't say much more than that."

"Aw, not even a name?"

"No."

"An initial?"

"No."

"So not fair."

"If it's any consolation, you're the only person I've told."

Her eyes lit up. "Ooh, so it's a big secret."

"Yeah, very much."

She sipped her drink and looked back out at the view. "So can I ask you something?"

Oh, fuck. I didn't like this at all . . .

"I can't tell you any more than what I've said already."

She chewed on the inside of her lip. "Would Dad disapprove?"

"Vehemently."

She laughed. "Then good. Even better."

I met her gaze and clinked my glass to hers, and both of us laughed.

She changed subjects then, talking about a work deal and another company contractor who was being difficult . . .

And all I could think about was telling her.

Five minutes ago, I'd have denied it and told her not to be ridiculous . . . and now I had to stop myself from blurting it out.

I wanted to tell someone.

No, not just someone. Brooklyn. I wanted to tell my sister. Not about Marshall, per se. Just the fact that the person I was seeing was a guy.

The words were right there on the tip of my tongue, but I choked them down with logic and fear. It wasn't something I could ever take back, and what if she didn't like it?

Then I guess I'd have no family at all.

The car ride home was quiet, and it was my fault because now I had these stupid thoughts in my head, and they wouldn't quit.

My languid, blissed-out state of mind that Marshall had left me in this morning was now well and truly gone.

"You okay?" she asked. I hadn't realised we were stopped, parked outside my apartment block.

"Oh, sure," I said quickly. "Thanks so much for lunch. I really enjoyed it. We should do this more often. Not just on birthdays."

She nodded but there was something in her eyes that looked a lot like concern. "Look, I didn't mean to push earlier. If you can't tell me who it is, that's fine. I'm just glad you're happy, that's all. At least one of us is getting some—"

"I'm seeing a guy," I blurted out. Fuck, fuck, fuck. "The . . . the person I'm seeing is a man. So now you know why it's a secret. It's always been a secret. Christ, I have no idea why I told you. I shouldn't have said anything."

Then I made the mistake of looking at her face.

Shock would've been an understatement.

Fuck.

I fumbled with the door handle and pushed the door open. "I need to go," I mumbled, getting out. "Thank you, again, for lunch or . . . whatever."

I closed the door and almost ran to my building. What had I done? What had I been thinking?

Christ, Valentine. That was stupid, stupid, stupid, stupid . . .

I thumped the elevator button until the doors opened, and my hands were shaking so bad, I struggled to get the key into my door. I closed the door behind me, leaning against it with my hands on my knees, trying to catch my breath.

This wasn't good.

Second panic attack in two days. This wasn't good at all.

I took a long, deep breath, trying to rein everything in.

But then my intercom buzzed. I could see Brooklyn on the screen. She was looking at the camera, her hand jammed to the button. The buzzing was like a drill, never ending. I hit the intercom just to make it stop.

"Valentine, open the door," she said.

I still couldn't speak.

"If you don't let me in, I'll yell what I have to say to you from here. Everyone in the building can hear me."

Fucking hell.

I pressed her through and watched her get into the elevator.

My chest felt all tight, my lungs were squeezing, and I felt cold and hot at the same time. I opened my front door for her and barely made it to the couch by the time she walked in.

I needed to sit down.

She took one look at me and frowned. "Oh, Valentine," she whispered.

"I'm not seeking your approval or validation," I said, my voice weak.

She came and sat down beside me and patted my knee. "You can relax," she said gently. "I don't care if you're gay. Actually, I always kinda wondered if you were gay or bi, but I never knew for sure. It's not my business anyway. It's not anyone's business."

I couldn't believe what she was saying.

"I've never told anyone," I managed to get out. I tried to take a deep breath in and let it out slowly. It took a few goes to get it right.

She waited for me to look at her. That took a while too. "Because of Dad, right?"

I laughed sardonically; tears burned in my eyes. "Right."

She growled under her breath. "Valentine, listen to me. You can't live your life in fear of him."

What the . . . ?

"Easy for you to say. I mean, thanks. If only I'd known that before."

She made a face. "I know. I'm sorry. What I meant to say was I don't want you to live in fear of him. You shouldn't have to. I know how controlling he is of you. And I know I got off lightly. I mean, I basically don't exist because his firstborn wasn't a son and I have the audacity to be female. He hates all women, especially in corporate. And yeah, that's shitty, but I got off easy compared to you. I know that."

I nodded, wiping a stupid tear from my cheek. "I hate him."

"Then quit."

I looked at her as if she'd lost her mind. "I couldn't. I don't even know if I'd want to. I like my job. I just . . . I hate him. I live with this constant disappointment. I'm on eggshells the whole fucking time, needing everything to be perfect because, god help me if it's not. He's priming me to take over one day and god, I don't know if I want that. I don't want that responsibility. That pressure." I shook my head. "And he'd flip his shit because I'd do everything different to him. I'm not like him. He wants me to be a replica, a mini version of him, but I'm not like him. I refuse to be."

Brooklyn put her hand on my back and patted me. It was awkward and she was uncomfortable having to comfort with physical touch. God, we were so alike, so emotionally fucked up, it would have been funny if it wasn't so sad.

"You're nothing like him," she said. "Nothing."

"I can't ever come out," I said, fresh tears welling in my eyes. "Not to him, and not in public, because it'd ruin his company's image." I imitated his voice. "God forbid."

She gave me a sad smile. "Valentine, let me ask you one thing." She paused for effect. "What does he know about you? About your personal life, that is. What does he know?"

I shrugged, trying to think. "Nothing. He knows I play rugby. That's it."

"Nothing personal, though. Not your friends, your favourite food, your hobbies. Even your birthday. Does he even know where you live? Has he ever been here?"

I shook my head. "No."

"So why would he know who you date?"

I stared at her. I mean, I knew what point she was trying to make. And it was valid. "Pretty sure he'd know if I was dating a guy."

She shook her head. "No, he wouldn't."

"I'd be photographed with a man. I can't go out on a date. I can't be seen in public. Christ, just this morning Mar—" Shit.

"The guy I'm seeing wanted to take me out for breakfast. But I can't. I can't even do that for him. And believe me, it'd be a thousand times worse if Dad read about the heir of Tye Corp on a date with a man instead of hearing it from me. I mean, could you imagine the fallout? He'd have a fucking stroke."

She gave me a sad smile and nodded because we both knew I was right. "I get it," she offered gently. "I'm just saying he wouldn't know. Dating in public, maybe. But what you do in private, he'd have no clue. So enjoy that, at least. And thank you for telling me. If you want to bring him for lunch at my place, you absolutely can. You don't need to hide from me, okay?"

I got teary again. "Thank you."

She let out a sigh. "So, Mar . . . You almost said his name. Mar, Mark? Martin? Is it Martin?"

I laughed. "No. And I'm not telling you." I put my hand to my forehead. "I can't believe I'm having this conversation with you. At all, to be honest. I never . . . I never thought I'd tell anyone."

She made a sad face. "No one knows at all?"

"No. No one knows. I mean, Lleyton knows I'm gay, has done since college, but not even he knows who I'm seeing. It's . . . complicated." I let out a long breath. "Actually, it's a whole big mess. Destined to fail from the start."

She studied me for a long moment. "But you like him."

My gaze cut to hers. "I, uh . . . I'm not exactly dating material. Let's be real."

She did the double-stare thing. "But you like him."

I slumped back on the sofa, my hands covering my face. "Fuck."

She patted my knee. "Then you gotta make it work. That's the only big sister advice I can give you. Like I'm a relationship expert," she snorted. "My longest stint was barely a month. How long have you and not-Martin been not-dating?"

I snorted and tried to think . . . "Uh, two months, maybe."

"Jesus, Valentine. That's practically married in gayville."

I wasn't even bothering to reply to that.

"So you have feelings," she said. "And you and I both know feelings are like . . ." She made a disgusted face.

"The worst thing ever?"

"Exactly. But who knows . . . they can't be all that bad. Other people seem to enjoy feeling . . . emotions."

I laughed out a sigh. "Don't believe the lie. The whole thing is completely terrible."

"I could tell by your smile this morning how terrible it was." She smiled and patted my knee before she stood up. "I should get going." She looked at the dining table. "Oh dear. Did he buy you those flowers? Those are dreadful."

I gasped. "Leave them alone. They're the only flowers I've ever been given."

"They're the blokiest flowers I've ever seen."

"He got them from the supermarket."

"I can tell."

"When he went there at sunrise to buy stuff so he could make me breakfast."

She pouted. "Well, that is sweet. But the balloon . . ."

"Is the best part, so shut up."

She laughed. "Yeah, okay. I can tell how much you don't like him."

I sagged, back to square one. I wasn't about to tell her about the cake in the fridge. And then my phone rang. I pulled it out, half expecting it to be Lleyton, when I saw the pizza emoji.

He was calling me?

"Is that him?"

"No."

"Answer it." It rang and rang again. She waved at my phone. "Answer it!"

Panicking, I hit Answer. "Hello?"

Before Marshall could say anything, Brooklyn leaned down closer to my phone. "Hello, is this Martin? Mario? Mark? I know it starts with an M."

"Christ, Brooklyn. Really?"

Marshall was quiet. "Uh, hello?"

"Sorry, it's my sister," I said. "She was just leaving." I pointed to the door.

She grinned on her way out, but as she opened the door, she looked me in the eye. "Make it work," she said, and was gone.

I sighed. "Oh my god, I'm so sorry about that," I said into the phone. There was only silence. I looked at the screen and it was still connected. "Hello?"

"Yeah, I'm . . . who the fuck is Martin and Mario?"

I laughed. "No one. I almost let your name slip earlier. I got the M out. Actually, it was more of a Mar—before I caught myself. She thinks your name is Martin. I'm so sorry."

More silence. "You, uh, you told her about me?"

I laughed again, starting to sound a little hysterical. "I came out to my sister today." More laughter, more tears. "Whew. Fuck."

"Holy shit," he breathed. "Are you okay? What did she . . . I mean, are you okay?"

I laughed and shook my head and fought ridiculous tears again. "I think I am."

"Would you like me to come over? I can be there in twenty minutes."

"No, it's fine. I'm good, actually. It went better than I could have expected. She was great."

"Are you sure? It's a big deal, Valentine."

"Yeah," I whispered. "It is. But I'm okay. I . . . I could use some alone time, to be honest. It's been a busy week, with work and with you. Sorry if that sounds harsh. I just need some time alone with this."

"No. Not at all. I get it."

I put my hand to my forehead. "I can't believe I told her. I was going to, then I wasn't, then I *absolutely* wasn't going to tell her, then I blurted it out."

"And you almost said my name?"

I groaned. "Almost. But she doesn't know who it is."

"Why were you talking about me?"

"She asked me if I was seeing someone. I said no, not really."

"Holy shit."

"She also said I was smiling when she picked me up at lunchtime. I had to tell her something. I could hardly say it was because you'd just reamed and creamed me."

"Oh my god!" He barked out a laugh. "Ream and cream. I'll have to remember that."

"Believe me, I won't let you forget it."

He snorted. "Right."

"So I had to placate her with something. I said maybe I was kind of seeing someone, but it wasn't public."

"Mm."

"Don't think for one second that it's because I like you."

"I wouldn't dare," he said. He was definitely smiling, I could tell.

I took a deep breath in and let it out slowly, trying to get my head around everything that had happened.

"How do you feel?" he asked.

I realised I was smiling. "I feel good. Lighter than I have in a long while."

He made a happy sound. "I'm happy for you."

I was happy for me too. And then I remembered that he'd called me. "Did you call me for any particular reason?"

"Well, I'm going to my folks' place for an early dinner—I'm in my car, that's where I'm driving to right now—and I wondered if you'd eaten anything. I assumed you wouldn't have, because you're you, so I was going to order you a birthday pizza. But do you know how hard it is to find a pizza place that will deliver a nine-inch pizza? Not an eight- or ten-inch, specifically nine inches."

I laughed at that.

"They think I'm weird."

"Can't imagine why."

He laughed. "So have you eaten? I wasn't even sure you'd be home."

"I had a late lunch. And yes, I'm home, and while I appreciate the sentiment, and a nine-inch-deep pan pizza would have been funny. Honestly, I'm not hungry. And if I feel peckish later, I have cake in the fridge."

He was quiet for a second. "Are you sure you're okay? If you want me to come around, just so you're not alone . . ."

His offer settled in behind my ribs, a warm feeling I wasn't quite prepared for. "I'm fine, but thank you."

"Okay," he said. "Just don't think for one second that it's because I like you."

I snorted. "Wouldn't dream of it."

He ended the call and I sat there for a good five minutes, smiling like an idiot. It made me feel all giddy and silly. Not feelings I'd normally appreciate, but for some reason, today, I didn't mind.

THE MONDAY MORNING meeting was short and to the point. It was a busy time for everyone, and I appreciated the full attendance. The little chats afterward were productive and informative, and it did foster a team environment.

Something I could thank Marshall for, though I wouldn't. I'd already told him it had been a good idea. If I told him again, he'd get a fat head.

Just like when my assistant walked in with a slab of cake with the candles lit. "A little birdie told me it was someone's birthday yesterday," she said.

I didn't need to ask who the little birdie was. Because he stood there at the back of the room with his arms crossed and a smirk on his face.

Arsehole.

It was horrifying when people sang happy birthday to me. *Horrifying*.

But it was also kind of nice.

Not that I'd ever admit that, and I sure as hell would never tell Marshall that.

He made a point of fixing himself another coffee beside me as I was handed the first piece of cake.

"I take it you're to blame for this?" I murmured.

Not looking at me, he smiled as he stirred his coffee. "Don't know what you're talking about."

When everyone was done and leaving, I helped clear

everything away, just catching Marshall as he was walking out.

"A moment, Mr Wise. In my office, if you don't mind."

I didn't wait to see if he followed. I knew he would. I held the door for him and closed it behind him. He sat in the chair opposite my desk. "Anything I can help you with? Mr Tye?"

"Hm," I said, fixing my jacket button as I sat down. "Wednesday night."

"What about it?"

"I thought perhaps we could meet at your place."

He looked around quickly, then eyed me cautiously. "Why?"

I knew he'd ask that and I had no valid reason. None that I'd admit, anyhow. "I thought people might begin to recognise your ute, seeing as though it's become a regular visitor."

He smirked. "Pretty sure no one notices a dual-cab work ute anywhere. Your car at my place would be a different story. It's gonna get noticed. And possibly stripped of tyres and rims."

I hadn't thought of that. "I can Uber it."

His gaze met mine. "You wanna see my place so bad?"

"No." I raised my chin, defiant and adept at lying, apparently. "Why would I care what your place was like?"

Or not so adept, because he snorted. "Yeah, okay, fine. You wanna come to mine, that's great. Be there by seven, because you'll be cooking us dinner."

"That was not . . . that's . . . we can order in."

He levelled his don't-try-me stare. "Seven o'clock, and we're cooking."

I sighed, hating that it actually sounded fun. God, what had I become?

Marshall made a face. "I thought we were to never discuss this at work."

"I could have texted," I admitted. "But I also wanted to not-thank you for telling Shayla it was my birthday."

He grinned. "You're not-welcome." Then he shrugged. "Feeling special is part of the birthday experience."

I rolled my eyes. "And I'll need your address."

"You could look it up. You have it on file."

"I could. But I won't. You either give it to me yourself, or I don't get it. I won't use anything, information or otherwise, that you're not willing to give me. I've told you that."

He tried not to smile. "Fine."

He took out his phone and thumbed out a message, my phone beeping a second later.

Then he held up his phone. "Oh, and I changed your name to the peach emoji."

I glared at him. "Nice."

He grinned at me. "You should be grateful. I wanted to make it the washing machine emoji, but there isn't one."

"A washing machine?"

"Yeah. I put loads in it."

I barked out a laugh. I had to make myself not smile, trying to seethe at him instead. "I hate you."

He stood up, and with both hands on my desk, he leaned forward, smiling. "I hate you more."

He turned and walked out, and I sat there smiling at my door. God, he was such an arsehole.

Shayla came in and stopped. "Everything okay, Mr Tye?"

I schooled my face. "Yes, it's fine." I opened my schedule. "Okay, this week . . ."

CHAPTER 17

MARSHALL

DINNER ON WEDNESDAY NIGHT WAS GOING TO BE easy. I was a simple man, truth be told. I didn't need fancy dinners in expensive restaurants. I knew in all likelihood Valentine and I would never be able to go out in public on a date, and yeah it kinda sucked, but it was what it was.

Him coming to my place though?

Kind of a big deal.

I wasn't sure why it was a big deal or why exactly he wanted to meet at mine. But it felt like a big step.

I could guess that he was curious, and wanted to see how I lived, that he wanted to know more about me. But he was also taking a huge leap out of his comfort zone.

He was letting his guard down. He'd come out to his sister the other day and that was a massive thing.

Massive.

And now he wanted to come to my place.

Yeah, Valentine Tye was beginning to thaw out. The ice-cold walls he had built around himself were starting to melt.

I didn't know where it would stop or what it meant for us, but I was happy to take it one step at a time.

Starting with dinner.

Right on seven, there was a knock on my door, and I opened to find him standing there, looking sexy as fuck, wearing dark jeans and a charcoal sweater, holding a bottle of wine.

Like a date.

Holy shit.

I grinned and stood aside. "Come in."

He took an awkward step inside and didn't take another. He was clearly nervous, and instead of taking the piss, I had to remember that this was very unlike him. It was new to him and it was, very probably, his first date.

If that's what this was.

"This way," I said, leading him through the small living room to the kitchen. "I hope you like Moroccan chicken pasta."

He looked at the ingredients I had on the kitchen counter. "To eat, yes. To make? Uh . . ."

"You'll be fine."

He handed me the bottle of wine and shrugged. "I, uh . . . it felt rude to turn up without bringing something."

"You should have brought Enzo. He likes it here."

Valentine looked around and shoved his hands in his back pockets. "It's a nice place."

I laughed. Not because my place wasn't nice, but just at how awkward he was. "It's okay," I said, looking around. "I've lived here for about five years. It's small. One bedroom, but the kitchen and the bathroom are good. The landlord's nice. Nothing's a problem, and he doesn't charge me a fortune. Pretty sure it's because I fixed the window jamb for him." I gestured to the living room window next to the balcony door. "And I replaced the washers in the laundry fittings. Took me five minutes. That was the month I moved in. He calls me *the nice boy*."

Valentine smirked. "So he doesn't know you at all."

"Shut up. I am the nice boy."

"You're making me cook dinner, so yeah, I'll go with a no on that."

"Speaking of which," I said, handing him the largest knife. "First thing we have to do is slice the eggplant and sprinkle it with salt."

"Like an exorcism?"

I snorted. "Yep. Just like an exorcism." I gripped the eggplant and, with my arms around him, held his hand with the knife, showing him how to slice it so he didn't massacre it like he'd done the tomato the other day.

"This is unnecessary," he whispered.

I kissed the back of his neck. "I disagree. Foreplay starts now."

He huffed out a laugh that sounded a lot like a hum. He certainly didn't mind when we cut the onion and capsicum the same way, or when I drew my nose across his nape, or when I pressed my dick against his arse.

Until it came time to slice the raw chicken thighs.

He dropped it and shuddered. "Oh my god, why does it feel like that?"

"Have you never touched raw chicken before?"

His eyes were wide. "Why would I do that?"

I laughed because we really had lived different lives. But he decided that filling the pot with water for the pasta was more his forte while I sliced the chicken. I did make him add the seasonings though, and I had him rinse off the eggplant and dice it, and then we fried it all up in a big pan, added some cream, and dished it all up together.

I watched him take his first bite. His eyes lit up and he spoke with his mouth full. "This is actually really good."

I laughed. "Classy."

He shovelled more in. "Shut up."

I was just happy to see him happy. Which I would never admit to him. God forbid.

"I've been to Morocco," he said, kinda out of the blue.

"You have?"

He nodded and sipped his wine. "I travelled after university. Did one of those crazy tours—see thirty countries in three months." He shrugged. "It was fun."

"Who'd you travel with?"

"Lleyton."

I nodded, resisting the urge to growl.

Valentine laughed. "Jealous?"

"No."

"Liar." He smiled as he sipped his wine. "He's a good friend. He's also very straight and has been supportive of my big dirty secret."

And then I felt bad.

Up until three days ago, before he told his sister, Lleyton had been the only person who knew Valentine was gay.

"I'm glad you have him."

He studied me for a long moment. "I'm trying to decide if that's sincere."

"It is. I am. I'm glad you had one person in your corner."

He smiled as he stabbed another piece of pasta and ate it. "I still can't believe I told my sister," he said quietly. "And I can't believe she was okay with it."

I studied him for a second, his fine features, dark hair, and dark eyes, and he looked happy . . . ier. Not happy.

Valentine Tye rarely looked happy. He was always so serious. Burdened, even. But right now, he looked happ*ier*.

"It must be a huge relief," I said. "Like a weight's been lifted."

He nodded slowly, his lips twisting in a half-smile. "Yeah. Was it that way for you?"

"Eventually. In the beginning, it sucked, but those who mattered stuck around. Those who didn't, didn't matter."

His eyes cut to mine and he nodded. "I like that. You're a lot braver than me. I can't even come out now, let alone when I was just a kid."

"Not coming out isn't about a lack of bravery. For some, not coming out is about survival. And don't judge your own story against anyone else's. It's gotta be the right time for you. Not anyone else."

He swallowed hard and seemed to consider my words. "How were . . . how did your parents take it?"

I let out a sigh. "They were okay. Shocked more than anything. I think they thought all gay guys were fem or did ballet or something." I rolled my eyes. "And I played rugby and wanted to work in construction. But at the end of the day, they just wanted me to be happy. I'm pretty close with my folks."

He nodded slowly.

"Can I tell you something?" I asked.

"Sure."

"We didn't use to be close. When I was a kid, my dad was never home. He worked at his store, open till close seven days a week. He never once came to a game or a tournament, never made it to any school event. It was always just me and Mum. And that was fine. He worked hard." I sighed. "And then Tye Corp came in and killed the store. My dad was devastated."

Valentine winced. "I'm sorry."

"Don't be. It certainly wasn't your fault. Even though I blamed you for a decade," I said with a bit of a laugh. "In the end it did us a favour."

His eyes met mine. "How?"

"Dad thought he'd failed us. He wasn't the great provider he'd set out to be. But he realised he still had what really matters. Me and Mum supported him and loved him, and we got him through it. He got a new job and they loved him—he's still with them after all these years—and we did okay." I shrugged. "Though we had to sell the big house and I changed schools."

"It still must have been hard for you. And your parents."

"Sure. But we came out of it okay. It made Mum and Dad stronger as a couple. The house they have now is smaller, sure. But it's a good home. It's my family home. And honestly, the public school system is better than that private shithole you went to. I met Taka my first day. Been best mates ever since."

He smiled a little sadly. "Taka's a good guy."

"He is."

He chewed on his bottom lip and frowned. "My parents . . ." He shook his head. "I can't remember the last time they were in the same city, let alone the same house. I haven't seen my mother in . . ." He made his thinking face. "Two years, I think. Last we heard she was in London pickling her liver in a gin factory. It was Paris before that. Or Singapore. I can't remember."

Oh damn.

"And my father . . ."

"Your father's an arse."

"Oh, he's more than that," Valentine mumbled. "He's conniving. I don't trust him. I think I love him in the way that a son might love his father, but I don't like him. He made me what I am today and that's not exactly a compliment." He sighed. "I grew up in a very wealthy house. I wouldn't say I grew up privileged because there was no privilege. It came at a great cost. I've been in self-sufficient, self-preservation mode since I was a child. I've been on my own since kindergarten, more or less. I had one nanny who took me to karate lessons. Until my father found out and fired her." He held up two fingers. "For five years she took me, twice a week, and he had no idea until I got my black belt and I stupidly told him, thinking he'd be proud of me." He rolled his eyes. "Imagine not knowing where your kid was two days a week for five years. He had no idea. I was ten."

Jesus Christ.

"But I know how to function. I know how to survive, how to push emotions aside, to never show weakness because that's what my father taught me." His smile was bitter. "For him, people are just a means to an end. Including me. I could never come out to him. Not now, not ever. He'd be . . ." His eyes met mine. "He'd cut me off, fire me, disown me. I'd lose everything."

"But you'd gain you."

Valentine smiled ruefully. "I have me. I'm very used to it just being me."

"Then don't ever tell him," I said. "Fuck him. He doesn't deserve to know the real you. He doesn't deserve any part of you. Especially if he's just gonna use it against you. Fuck that."

His eyes met mine and he smiled more genuinely. "That's exactly how I feel. And it's not about the money when I said I'd lose everything. I know it sounds like it is, but . . ."

"But what?"

"Do you wanna know what I really want to do?"

"What's that?"

"I just want . . ." He shook his head and laughed. "I don't even know what I want to do. I'm being primed to take over as CEO one day."

Jesus. Now he'd said it, it was kind of obvious, but it wasn't something I'd considered before. "Do you want that?"

He shrugged, which to me was a no. It certainly wasn't a yes. "I don't know," he replied. "But even if I did, boy, I'd do things very fucking differently. I like my job. I'm good at it. But . . . but I don't know. I was never allowed to consider anything else. It was just expected of me."

"I'm sorry."

He shrugged again. "It's okay. I do actually like my job. I have the construction division now, as you are very well aware. My father giving it to me is a litmus test for taking over the whole corporation when he retires, I'm sure of it."

I wasn't sure what to say, even less how I should say it. "Would you ever consider doing something else? Something on your own?"

He inhaled deeply and sighed. "I don't know. Probably not. I'm not entirely unhappy with my life. I just . . . wish some things were different."

"Your father."

"Yes. I wish he cared. I wish he wasn't so consumed with success and money. But wishing for impossible things is an exercise in futility. I don't need the disappointment or anguish. My life is what it is, and I am who I am." He met my gaze and smiled. "And what else could I do? I'm not cut out for anything else. I'm not good at anything else, and I'd rather not give my father the satisfaction of seeing me fail."

God, that was so unfair. "You'd be good at anything you set your mind to."

He snorted. "You should be careful, Marshall. You're starting to sound as if you like me."

I snorted. "Well, I fucking don't, so get over yourself."

He smiled and it seemed our serious conversation was over.

"So . . ." I hedged. "You have a black belt in karate?"

"A long time ago. I haven't practiced in fifteen years."

"And it only took you five years? So you're good at everything you do, right?"

He rolled his eyes and ignored the compliment. "I've started back at the Dojo on Monday nights. Just since I've been back here in Sydney. It's just for fun. I like the discipline. It's good for my mind."

I smiled at him. "Karate, huh?"

"It's not serious."

"But you *could* fight me," I added. "When I push you around and hold you down. You could actually stop me if you wanted to."

He laughed. "Why on earth would I want to stop you? You and I both know I beg you for it."

I grinned at him, then I gave it to him.

He didn't even have to beg.

⸻

WE WON our game on Saturday and Valentine's team did too. We'd heard he'd had a great game, apparently, and he was named player of the match. That usually meant a few drinks back at the bar, so I wasn't surprised when my phone buzzed with a message.

Be late. Sorry. Drinking.

That was at half-past eight, so I figured getting at his place around half nine would be plenty of time. There was no answer when I rang his doorbell, and he didn't reply when I texted him.

How late?

I sat on the brick wall in the shadows, wondering if I should just go home. He could hardly blame me for bailing when he was the one who was late and not communicating.

I sent him another text at 9:40.

Strike one, Valentine. I'm going home.

Because fuck him. It was freezing cold and I was sitting in the dark outside waiting for him like a thief in the night. I could have stayed at the pub with my team and had some drinks with the boys instead of being on call to give Valentine what he wanted.

I was mad at myself for giving in to him.

I jumped off the wall just as my phone rang. It was him, of course.

"Heyyyy," he said, clearly very drunk.

"Where are you?"

There was a ruffling sound and a muted thud, and I could hear someone's muffled voice. "Jesus Christ, Valentine. Where are your keys?"

It sounded like he fell over?

"Where are you? I'll come get you," I said, starting to walk back to my ute.

There was another voice and it sounded like laughter . . . but I realised then I wasn't hearing it through the phone. I turned around, back to the entrance of Valentine's building, and there he was.

Well, there he was unable to stand up, being half carried, half dragged by Lleyton.

Fuck.

I stood there with my phone to my ear, and Valentine laughed as he swayed towards the ground. He didn't see me, but Lleyton sure as hell did.

Valentine tried speaking into the phone. "You still there?" His voice echoed from my phone and Lleyton clued in immediately.

"What the fuck?"

Valentine looked up, saw me, and laughed, swaying in Lleyton's hold. "Well, fuck," Valentine said. "'S awkward."

He went to gesture to me but lost his balance and I went to help him. I took his other arm and put it over my shoulder. "Christ almighty, Valentine."

"Need his keys," Lleyton said.

I patted down Valentine's pockets and found them. "Come on, let's get you inside."

We managed to get him into the foyer and I pressed the elevator door button, and guessing we were past the point of wondering how I knew where Valentine lived, I hit the button to his floor.

"What the hell was he drinking?" I asked.

"Tequila," Lleyton answered. "He just had a few too many, then he couldn't stand up."

"It's because he doesn't eat," I replied as the doors opened. We got him down the hall and I opened his front door.

I knew which door was his. I knew where the light switch was. I knew the way to his bedroom.

There was no denying shit now.

We dumped him on the bed and he groaned and closed his eyes. I took his shoes off and pulled the covers over him. Lleyton stood there, his jaw bulging and his gaze steel. "You wanna start explaining?"

Enzo chose that exact moment to run in, come

directly over, and yell at me. He meowed and meowed and I picked him up. "Enzo, my guy. We've talked about this." Ignoring Lleyton, I took Enzo out of Valentine's room and headed towards the kitchen. I knew what he wanted, and the little shit wouldn't shut up until I gave it to him.

I put him on the counter, went to the pantry and got Enzo's biscuits, and filled his bowl for him, putting the biscuits back.

Yeah, I knew my way around Valentine's kitchen too.

Christ.

"You're awfully familiar with his place. And his cat," Lleyton said. He had his arms crossed now. "Wanna tell me what the fuck's going on?"

I sighed. "Me and Valentine . . . we . . . we have an agreement, of sorts."

His eyes narrowed. "You? You're the guy he's been seeing?"

Wait . . . "You knew he was seeing someone?"

"I could guess. But never in a million fucking years would I have guessed it was you."

I snorted. "Same."

He shook his head slowly, clearly disbelieving. "You?"

I nodded.

"You hate each other."

I laughed. "I know. It's what makes it work."

He blinked a few times. "What the fuck?"

I sighed with a shrug. My immediate response was to be defensive, but he was Valentine's best mate, so I needed to rein in my temper. "Are you pissed that it's me? Or that you didn't know?"

He clamped his jaw shut and stared. "Both."

"Sorry to break it to you, but it's not about you, Lleyton. It's about him. You know why he can't tell anyone, and you know why you can't tell anyone about me being here."

"He could have told me."

"Why would he? It's not like we're dating or seeing each other for real," I replied. It didn't sit well with me to say that out loud, but it was unfortunately the truth. "We meet each other to fuck. Nothing else."

Valentine mumbled from his room, followed by a rather large thud. I raced to his room to find him trying to figure out how the door worked. It swung inward and he swayed, almost falling, but I caught him.

"Hey," he said, smiling up at me.

Christ, he was drunk. Cute but drunk.

"What are you doing?" I asked. "Go back to bed."

"'M hungry." He tried to aim for the kitchen and then he saw Lleyton. He straightened up but overcorrected and I caught him again. "Shit."

"Yeah, shit," Lleyton said, gesturing to how I was still holding him. "What the fuck, Valentine?"

Valentine tried to be serious but he looked at me and laughed. "D'jyou tell him?"

"I didn't tell him shit." I took Valentine to the dining table and sat him down. "Stay there. I'll get you something to eat."

I went to the kitchen and checked his fridge, found nothing but condiments, the bacon and eggs I'd bought the other day, and a tub of butter.

But in the freezer beside the frozen edamame, there was a package of Turkish bread, so I took that out and nuked it. I had to wonder if he'd bought some to try and replicate what we'd made on his birthday.

When the bread was thawed out, I threw it in the

toaster and fried him some bacon and eggs. I put a glass of water in front of him. "Drink that."

Lleyton was sitting across from Valentine, and Valentine sighed. "He's mean," he mumbled, but at least he sipped some water. "Argues a lot 'n' makes me eat."

I ignored the way Lleyton looked my way. I plated up the scrambled eggs and bacon, buttered the Turkish bread, and put it in front of Valentine. "Eat."

Valentine snorted. "See?"

He managed to hold the fork and get a few mouthfuls in, but god, it was not a pretty sight.

"Who the hell let him get this drunk?"

Lleyton shot me a glare. "I've seen you in worse shape than this." I could see the moment he remembered. "When he took you home. That night in Bondi."

Yes, that long ago.

I stood there, my arms crossed. God, this was a huge mess. It all seemed so complicated. It was never supposed to get complicated.

Valentine spoke with his mouth half full. "Had enough," he said, pushing his plate away. At least he'd eaten something. He stood up, swaying as he found his feet, and I was quick to catch him.

He laughed and took a fistful of my sweater as he tried to pull me in for a kiss. "Hey, you."

I instinctively looked at Lleyton, which made Valentine look at him. He let go of my sweater. "Shit."

Yeah, shit.

"Fuck'm drunk," he said. "Tequila's no good."

"You need to go to bed," I said.

"Mm."

I led him to his room and put him back to bed. I found a bucket in his laundry and put it beside him and threw a towel on the mattress near his pillow. I filled a glass from the kitchen tap, all while Lleyton sat there and watched me, and when I put it on Valentine's bedside and closed the door, Lleyton was still sitting there. He had his arms crossed and a neutral expression.

"I'll take the couch," I said. "In case he vomits in his sleep." Lleyton still stared at me, so I gestured to the sofa. "Unless you want to?"

He still said nothing.

"What?" I asked. "If you got something to say, fucking say it."

"You said this"—he waved his hand in my general direction—"was just fucking. Nothing else, huh? Not dating or anything."

"No."

"Sure looks like it to me."

I didn't care what it looked like to him. "Well, it's not."

"Looks to me like you actually care about him."

I rolled my eyes.

"You know your way around his kitchen like you live here. God, you knew where the cat food was. The cat knows who you are!"

"Because I babysat him for five days," I said, then realised my mistake.

Lleyton stared at me. "He trusted you with Enzo?"

Fuck.

"Enzo likes me."

"Because you're here all the time." He shot me a look that dared me to argue. "Because you make Valentine cook, you make sure he eats. You watch movies together. You bought him flowers, for fuck's sake." He gestured to the dying flowers still on the table. "Sounds like dating to me."

"It was his birthday. And nobody's ever given one single

fuck about him on his birthday before, so I . . . I tried to make a big deal out of it."

"Because you care about him."

I shook my head. "That's not . . . you don't know shit."

He ran his hand through his hair and chuckled, looking at the glass wall. Then with a sigh, he turned to face me. "Marshall—"

"Why do you care who he sees?"

"Because he's never dated anyone before. He's never had any kind of relationship before. Ever."

"That you know of."

"No." He shook his head. "I know he hooks up. I know he'd line up one-nighters, because he'd tell me. And I don't care who he fucks. Honestly, he could be fucking the pope for all I care. As long as he's happy, good for him. That's his business and none of mine."

"Glad we agree on that."

He scoffed. "Christ, Marshall. You still don't get it. He'd tell me about the men's club and the random fucks, but he never once mentioned you. Why do you think that is?"

"I don't know. Because . . . well, because there's nothing to tell."

"Bullshit. He'd tell me about the randoms because they meant nothing. But he didn't tell me about you because there *is* something to tell. Whatever the fuck this is between you actually means something to him."

I shook my head, not daring to believe it.

"He's never opened himself up to anyone," Lleyton said, his voice quieter. "He's never let anyone into his world, into his life. In all the years I've known him. Except you."

I looked at him then, not sure what he wanted me to say.

"And you can't tell me you don't care about him." He

gestured to Valentine's bedroom door. "Because it's pretty fucking clear that you do."

I shook my head, ran my hand through my hair, and let out a deep breath. "It can't ever be anything else. He can't . . . we can't . . ."

"Pretty sure yous already are."

I shook my head again because this was ludicrous. "Look, I'm sorry he didn't tell you. We agreed not to tell anyone. His father would . . ."

"I know."

"Just don't be pissed at him. If you wanna blame someone, blame me. Not him. He needs you in his life. He needs . . ." Fuck. "He needs people in his life who actually care about him."

Lleyton studied me for a long moment before nodding slowly, like I'd just proved his point, and that was the end of the conversation. "Open his door so you can hear him if he pukes," he said, and he left.

I stood there in the mostly dark apartment, in the silence, wondering how the ever-loving fuck it had all come down to this.

CHAPTER 18

VALENTINE

I WOKE UP TO VOMIT, SURPRISED TO SEE A BUCKET beside the bed.

Grateful.

I had no idea how the bucket came to be there or who had put it there. I had no recollection of going to bed. Everything was a blur, and my head felt like it had been hit with an axe.

I fell back into bed with a groan and closed my eyes, hoping the pain would kill me quicker. Please have mercy.

The suffering.

Christ, the suffering.

I woke up to vomit again, only realising after I lay back down that the bucket was clean.

I slept again, unable to do much else, and woke again. Not to vomit, thankfully. The bucket was clean again and I hadn't imagined it. It meant someone was here.

Someone was looking after me?

I had flashbacks of Lleyton taking me home. I'd fallen out of his car. I remembered him helping me up, helping me walk.

God, I would owe him big time.

Especially if he'd cleaned up my puke buckets. Christ.

I managed to sit up on the side of the bed, wondering how it was possible to still be alive with such a blinding pain in my head. I had to walk out there, even though the bright sunlight would probably kill me.

I held the door frame and groaned. The brightness, being upright, walking . . . none of it was good.

"How's your head?"

Not Lleyton's voice.

Marshall?

"Not good," I whispered, trying not to think about vomiting again. "Why are you . . . what are you doing here?"

"You don't remember last night?"

I shook my head, regretting that immediately. I managed to get to the kitchen with my eyes half closed to shield the sunlight. "Curtains. Please."

Marshall laughed but a moment later the curtains drew closed, and the room was blessedly darker. "Thank you."

He was beside me then, a glass of water and some headache pills in his hand. "Take these."

I took them, though my stomach was undecided on the offer.

"Christ."

He snorted. "Well, now I've seen that you survived, I should get going."

"Did you . . . the bucket?"

"Yes, I cleaned it."

I closed my eyes at the horror. "Thank you. And I'm sorry. God."

"You were incredibly drunk."

I nodded, my eyes still closed. "Sorry."

"It's fine, but you might wanna give Lleyton a call. Let him know you're still alive."

I looked at Marshall then. "I don't . . . I don't remember much."

"He knows about us," Marshall said. "I was here when he brought you home."

Oh god.

I closed my eyes and sighed. "Fuck."

"He's okay," Marshall said quietly. "Probably more hurt that you didn't tell him. I mean, he won't be signing up to my fan club any time soon, but he's not mad at you."

I put my hands on the kitchen counter and let my head fall forward. I couldn't even get my mind around any of that because of the throbbing in my skull. I'd have to deal with it later.

I couldn't think about anything.

"I need a shower," I said. "Thank you for staying. Thank you for cleaning up . . . after me. I can't believe I . . ." Ugh. My stomach wasn't happy. "I need to have a shower. Maybe sit on the floor and try not to die."

Marshall laughed and all I could think about was getting to the bathroom.

I took a hot shower and let the water pummel the back of my neck, my face. I didn't vomit again, thankfully. But god, it was not good. I did feel marginally better when I got dressed and I expected to find Marshall gone.

But no, there he sat on the couch with his feet on my coffee table, Enzo on his lap. "Figured I should stick around to see if you actually died in the shower. Someone would need to let the paramedics in."

I walked to where he was, fell onto the couch beside him, folded myself up with my head on his shoulder. "Death would be merciful at this point," I mumbled.

He laughed. "You know what you need?"

"A sniper."

He laughed again. "You need a burger and fries and full-sugar Coke."

I groaned. "Oh no, I really don't."

"It will fix you."

"It will kill me."

"Well, fix or kill, either way you win. Let's go."

"Now?" I groaned again, though it sounded like a wail. "Do you really hate me that much?"

He snorted. "Yep. Come on, let's go."

But, but . . . "I'm wearing tracksuit pants."

"Where I'm taking you, no one will care."

He got up, dumping Enzo and me on the couch, and he came back with a hoodie and my slides. Then, when he realised I couldn't participate in getting dressed, he did it for me.

He shoved the hoodie over my head, shoved my feet into the slides, and pulled me up. "Come on. It'll make you feel better."

He grabbed my wallet and keys and dragged me out the door. I was in his ute and halfway along Lane Cove Road before I realised what was happening. "Where are we going?"

"To the best burgers in town. You'll thank me."

"Pretty sure I won't."

Never in my life had I left the house in my old track-pants and hoodie. I guessed it would help with going incognito, because no one I knew would ever look twice at me like this.

It also helped that no one I knew would ever be at the place he took me to. It was a small corner takeaway shop straight out of the 1960s. There was a newspaper stand by one side of the front door and a rack of fruit and vegetables on the other. The Coke sign on the drink fridge was faded, the floor was old linoleum, and the few tables were old cheap pine. The menu boards behind the old counter were blackboard and chalk, filled with messy handwriting.

It was nothing I was used to. No expensive anything. If I'd been with anyone else, I'd have turned around and walked out.

But a short, older woman took one look at Marshall and grinned at him. "Oh my, Marshall, look at you."

"Mrs Younis," he said. "How've you been?"

"Good, good, very good," she said. "How's your mother?"

"Fit as a fiddle."

She beamed. "Good to hear. Tell her I said hello. I will have eggs for her this week."

"I'll let her know."

"What can I get for you today?"

"A hangover cure."

She then looked at me. "Oh. One works burger, yes?"

Christ. Did I look that bad?

Marshall laughed. "Make it two."

She nodded and waved us off. "I'll bring it to you."

We sat at the far table and Marshall put a bottle of Coke in front of me. "Drink up."

I had a vague recollection of Marshall putting food in front of me last night and telling me to eat. "Did you make me eat last night?"

"Yes. I cooked you some bacon and eggs. You ate some. It wasn't pretty. I gave Enzo the leftovers."

I squinted and shook my head. Horrified, embarrassed. "God."

"You had a good night, huh?"

I looked up at him and went back to squinting my eyes shut. It hurt considerably less. "I did. Up until someone said everyone has to buy the MVP a shot, and then it went downhill considerably fast."

"Were they trying to kill you?"

"I don't think so. I was the one stupid enough to drink what they gave me."

"It was kinda stupid, yeah." He was quiet a long second. "So, MVP, huh?"

I shrugged one shoulder. "I played okay."

He snorted. "Well, at least you scored yesterday."

It took a second for my ache-splitting brain to catch on. I looked up at him. He was smiling, but yes, I'd defaulted on our agreement. "Ugh, yeah. Sorry. I wasn't in any shape for anything last night, and to be honest, I don't think anytime today is looking good either. I'll owe you a catch up or—"

He barked out a laugh. "You don't owe me anything. I'm not keeping score. Jesus. I was just joking."

"I do owe you," I replied. "For last night. For making me eat something and the bucket . . ."

He held up two fingers. "Twice."

Oh dear god. "I'm so sorry. And thank you, and Christ almighty, I'm so embarrassed. I feel terrible."

"You look terrible."

I pulled my hood up and sank back into my chair. "I wonder if there's a level of terribleness to succumb to before death."

"Well, I'm glad you're not one to be melodramatic or anything," he said with a smirk. "Stop being pitiful."

I whined. "Please be nice to me."

"I have no sympathy for self-inflicted wounds."

"But I'm suffering."

"Tequila will do that to you."

I almost gagged. "I will pay you to never say the T-word again."

He laughed again just as Mrs Younis brought over two takeout trays. She sat them on the table and patted my shoulder. "Eat up, will help. Alcohol is no good."

"Alcohol is very bad," I said. At least *she* was being nice to me.

Marshall, on the other hand, seemed to relish my misery. He nodded to the mountain of food in front of me. "I'm telling ya, saturated fat, salt, sugar, and caffeine will fix any hangover. And these are the best burgers in Sydney."

It didn't look particularly appetising, but it smelled good. It was a tall burger with everything: a huge beef patty, fried onions, a fried egg, beetroot, tomato, and melted cheese. The fries were stacked at the side, covered in chicken salt. I wasn't sure I could eat any of it.

Marshall picked his burger up and somehow managed to take a bite. He groaned and burger juice ran down his hand. "So good."

He was right about one thing. It would either fix me, or kill me, and I didn't care at this point which way it went. And I was kinda hungry.

I managed a small bite and washed it down with a sip of Coke.

"Oh, come on," he said. "You can open your mouth wider than that. I know you can. I've seen it firsthand."

I glared at him, opened my mouth like a python, and took a huge bite.

He laughed. "There you go."

It was the best thing I'd ever eaten.

I'd smashed half of it and some fries before I'd even realised. I hated that he was right. I sat back in my seat and rubbed my belly. I didn't dare to overdo it.

Marshall wiped his mouth and finished chewing. "Better?"

I nodded. "But I'm done."

He looked at what was left but nodded. I don't know what his fascination was with me and eating. As if he actually cared if I did or not . . .

I wasn't in any state to be thinking about that. "You know the woman behind the counter?" I asked.

"I played rugby with her son in high school. We've been coming here since I was fifteen." Then he shrugged. "My parents live a few streets over."

"Oh."

So someone could see us here . . .

But no one did. People came in and out of the takeaway shop and never looked twice at us. Not that anyone would recognise me in these old house clothes with the hood pulled up, though I thought they might recognise Marshall.

But no one cared.

If we'd driven my car, it'd have been a different story perhaps. Or if we'd actually cared to get dressed properly and hit up a nice café in Bondi or the northern beaches, then yes, maybe someone would have looked twice.

But here, wearing trackpants and driving a work ute? No one cared.

I liked it.

He drained the rest of his Coke. "Ready to go home?"

Not really. I didn't want my time with him to end.

"Sure."

He grabbed a sports drink from the fridge on the way out, I paid the tab, and we went back to the ute. And for some stupid reason, I didn't want to say goodbye.

The thought of going home by myself made me uneasy.

It made me sad.

He drove for a few blocks and glanced my way. "You okay? Feeling any better?"

"Much, thank you," I admitted. "You were one hundred percent correct. Now I just need to spend the day on the couch staring at the television and I'll be right."

He smiled but didn't take the bait.

Christ, I was going to have to ask.

Would I?

God, what if he said no?

My stomach felt all tight and it had nothing to do with the burger or being hungover. This was nerves. I didn't just have butterflies. I had the entire zoo.

It was ridiculous.

No, I could go home and clean everything, put a small grocery order in for some more coffee and some of that Turkish bread Marshall got the other day, and chill out for the rest of the afternoon by myself.

As I did every day. As I had done my whole life.

Except now I didn't want to.

Marshall pulled up at my place and cut the engine, and I still hadn't said anything.

"You sure you're okay?" he asked, his eyes warm as honey.

I nodded. "I'm fine," I replied automatically. My auto-pilot response.

"Bullshit." My gaze shot to his and he sighed. "You can't lie to me, Valentine. You've got that thinking line between your eyebrows and you squeeze your fingertips when you're nervous."

I stopped squeezing my fingertips. "I do not."

He laughed. "Just say whatever it is you want to say."

I opened my mouth, wanting to ask so badly, but I couldn't push the air out to make the words.

"Valentine," he said softly.

"Did you want to come up?" I asked in a rush. "You don't have to. I know you've probably got things to do or places to go. But I . . ." Fucking hell. "I'm not sure I want to be alone today." I let out a long breath, not believing I'd just admitted that out loud. To Marshall Wise, of all people.

Why him, of all people? You say that as if that's a bad thing?

He's the only person who understands you, Valentine. The only person who's ever understood you. You have feelings for him and you know it.

I shook my head at the stupid voice of reason. "Never mind," I said, opening the door and getting out.

"Wait up," he said. "Christ, you're impatient. Let me get out of the fucking car." He got out and fell into step beside me. "Was it that difficult to ask me?"

God, if he only knew. I unlocked the foyer door. "Yes, it was, actually. And don't think for one second it's because I like you."

He laughed and pulled the door open, holding it for me. "Yeah, of course not." I didn't make eye contact with his reflection in the elevator but I knew he was smiling. "I'm picking what we watch on Netflix."

Arsehole.

Once inside, he pulled me onto the couch. Him on his back, lying down, me between his legs with my head on his chest. This seemed to be our thing. I sipped my sports drink every now and then, and he rubbed circles on my back and played with my hair. The warmth of his body, his touch, his huge dick pressed against my belly, was every bit the comfort I needed. I ignored the way my heart craved this, craved him, and the contentment made me more relaxed than I'd felt in a long time.

Then Enzo joined us, and I might have dozed off.

Until my phone beeped with a text. It was Lleyton.

Did you survive?

I sighed. I'd blissfully forgotten about him finding out about us, about him being here, and about him bringing me home.

"Don't reply," Marshall said.

I looked up at him. "What?"

"Don't reply with a text. Call him. You need to speak to him, Valentine. He deserves that much."

Ouch.

I sat up, still between his legs, and ignored the ever-present bulge in his jeans. "Whose side are you on?"

He chuckled. "There are no sides here. He's your best mate and you kept something from him and he found out. Like me and Taka."

"Exactly. I'm not the only bad guy here."

"I apologised to Taka, face to face. And you're not the bad guy . . . well, you will be if you reply by text. Call him."

I glared at him.

He raised one eyebrow. "Want me to call him for you?"

I huffed. "I liked you better when you didn't interfere."

He laughed at that. "So you do like me?"

"No. I hate you."

He grinned as if he'd won a prize. "I hate you more."

I snarled at Marshall and hit Lleyton's number, which clearly surprised him. I could tell by his voice when he answered. "Uh, hey, everything okay?"

"Yes," I said, giving Marshall another glare because this was his fault. "Everything's fine. I just wanted to call you to say thanks again for getting me home last night." I cringed. "And that I'm sorry for not telling you about . . . Marshall."

Marshall chuckled quietly and I shot a shut-up glare at him.

It sounded as if Lleyton scrubbed his hand over his face. "Gotta say, I was surprised."

"So was I."

Lleyton laughed and let out a sigh. "What surprised me more was the way he looked after you."

"What?"

"He cooked you food. He fed Enzo. He told me to keep it a secret to protect you. He put a bucket beside your bed, and he slept on the couch in case you spewed in your sleep."

I know.

I know he did these things.

I looked at Marshall, where he lay before me with Enzo now on his chest. He was staring at the TV, trying to ignore me having this conversation.

"So he's not the jerk we always thought he was," Lleyton added.

"No, he's not," I mumbled.

Marshall looked at me then and I rolled my eyes.

Lleyton snorted. "You might wanna watch yourself though," he said. "I dunno what agreement you think you have—he mentioned something about just fucking—but from what I saw, it's more than that. I know relationships aren't your deal, Valentine, so I hate to be the one to break it to you, but you're in one."

I snorted out a laugh. "What?"

"In case you're as oblivious as he is, he's got it bad for you. That man is in deep."

I shook my head. "Don't be ridiculous."

Lleyton laughed. "What time did he leave this morning? Did he cook you breakfast?"

Fuck.

Fuck.

Fucking fuck.

"Oh my god," Lleyton said. "He's still there, isn't he?" Then he roared, laughing. "Tell him I said hi."

"No."

He laughed some more. "My case in point. And for what it's worth, I'm happy for you. So are the rumours true about his horse-dick?"

"I'm hanging up now."

He laughed and I clicked off the call, tossing my phone onto the coffee table. I pouted, and Marshall snorted. "So that went well?"

"He said to say hi."

Marshall smirked at the TV, still stroking Enzo behind the ear. Enzo looked very smug on Marshall's chest.

"Hey, cat," I mumbled. "You're in my spot."

Enzo didn't move and Marshall chuckled but didn't move him either. I pouted some more. "I liked it better when you were just here for sex. When you'd walk in and fuck me, and when I was Enzo's favourite."

Marshall laughed. "You're cute when you're hungover and sulking. But if you keep pouting like that, I'll find a better use for that mouth."

A jolt of warmth rushed through me. "Don't tease me." I looked down at his dick. "Though to be very honest with you, I don't know how much I'd trust my gag reflex today, so you might need to shut me up another way."

He sat up, dumped Enzo onto the couch, took my hand, and dragged me to my room. He took my face in his hands and kissed me, slow and sensual, tongues tasting. And Lleyton's words came back to me.

In case you're as oblivious as he is, he's got it bad for you. That man is in deep.

Oh god.

The way he was kissing me, I thought Lleyton might have been right. And it struck me how I wasn't horrified or even scared. Instead, it made my heart race and my belly warm. It made my skin prickle all over, in a good way. In a way that felt alive.

It struck me how happy it made me.

But then Marshall shoved me onto the bed, folded me in half and fucked me good and hard.

Like he loathed me.

Like he couldn't get enough of me.

Like he loved me.

CHAPTER 19

MARSHALL

I LEFT VALENTINE'S WITH JUST ENOUGH TIME TO PICK up some groceries on the way home, shower, and be at my parents' place for dinner.

I hadn't planned to spend most of my weekend with him, but I wasn't mad about it.

In fact, I kinda liked it.

And when he'd been so nervous to ask me if I wanted to come back to his place . . . how could I say no? It was sweet.

He was sweet, whether he wanted to be or not. He liked to cuddle, whether he ever wanted to admit that or not. He liked the company, as much as the old Valentine would dispute that.

But this new Valentine? And he *was* a new Valentine. He wasn't the cold and distant arsehole he'd pretended to be anymore. Not with me, anyway.

And I wasn't mad that Lleyton knew about us. I kinda liked that too.

It was less pressure, less stress, and I trusted Lleyton to keep the secret for Valentine's sake. And I think part of Valentine needed Lleyton to know.

He'd covered some personal ground in the last few weeks. First telling his sister he was gay, then Lleyton finding out about us . . .

I'd heard most of their phone conversation. It had been hard to *not* hear it with him sitting between my legs. I'd heard Lleyton admit I wasn't a jerk, that he liked how I'd looked after him.

I'd heard him say something about a relationship and then I'd heard him say, "He's got it bad for you," and my heart damned near stopped. I expected Valentine to get defensive or mad, even.

At least deny it.

But he just shook his head, his cheeks red. Then he'd pouted, that perfect bottom lip, the colour still heating his cheeks, and damn . . .

Every part of me wanted him.

My dick always wanted him. That was nothing new. But now my heart was leading the race.

I knew he'd never be prepared to give this thing between us a name. Lleyton had said *relationship*, and I'd be only too happy to call it that. Valentine had called it an agreement, which it was.

I guessed all relationships were an agreement of sorts.

But we were well past the enemies-with-benefits label now.

He'd been his usual professional self at the Monday morning manager's meeting, like he hadn't taken my cock for hours just the day before, like he hadn't begged me to come inside him, and I was disappointed he didn't call me in for a private meeting afterwards.

But he did come to my place on Wednesday night instead of me going to his. We cooked dinner again, which was basically an hour of foreplay, and after we'd eaten, I

took him to my bed where I drove him crazy, mapping out
his body, taking him torturously slow, and drawing every
drop of pleasure out of him.

On Saturday, after our rugby matches, all teams went
back to our local pub. Me, Taka, and the boys were already
there, them being mostly drunk and rowdy. I was sober and
laughing at their stupid arses when the Lane Cove boys
came in.

Lleyton walked in with Valentine one step behind him,
and I did my best to ignore them. Lleyton's eyes met mine
and I gave him a small nod and turned back around.

After a while, Taka nudged my shoulder. "What did
you do?"

"To who?"

He glanced over my shoulder, then back to me. "Who
do you think? Just wondering why his best friend keeps
looking at you."

I sighed. "He knows. He found out last week. Valentine
got maggotted, Lleyton took him home, and I was there.
Kinda no hiding from that."

Taka laughed. "Oh, to be a fly on the wall."

I laughed and sipped my water. "It went okay.
Surprisingly."

He stared at me for a while, kinda smiling.

"What?"

"Bro."

"Bro, what?"

"How long you gonna pretend you hate the guy?
Because I'm pretty sure the reason you been smiling these
last few weeks is the opposite of hate."

I rolled my eyes, dismissing what he was implying, but
deep down I knew he was right. Hell, it wasn't even deep
down anymore. It was just under the surface.

I sipped my drink. "Like I said before, it's complicated."

"And like I said before, it doesn't have to be."

Except it was, and it did.

In the end, I sighed. "Yeah, I dunno. It just is what it is."

"Hey, Wise," a voice said.

I turned around to find some guy I didn't recognise. He was with the team we'd played against and beaten. He looked drunk and messy, holding a rum and Coke, staring at me like I was shit on his shoe.

So I returned the favour. "What?"

"You think you can just put a hit on someone and get away with it?"

I snorted. "A hit? The fuck you talking about?"

"Wallace," he said with a sneer. "You busted his nose."

Wallace? I tried to recall, with no luck. *I didn't break anyone's nose today.* "Who?"

He now had two friends beside him and clearly felt a whole lot braver. "You know who."

"I really don't. But if I did, then he deserved it."

Taka nodded beside me. "Wallace. Burwood, second row. Number four."

Ohhh.

I laughed and locked eyes with Drunk McIdiot. "Oh, yeah. He deserved it."

He bristled immediately, puffed his chest out, clenched his jaw, frothed at the mouth a little. One guy beside him held his arm and mumbled something, and we had quite an audience now.

"You wanna fucking go?" he said, being held back by his friends. He had the crazy eyes, spilling his drink. "I'll fucking give you what you deserve."

Not taking my eyes off him, I put my glass of water on the bar. "Look, mate. I'm really not in the mood to fight tonight, but because you asked so nicely." I took a step towards him, my fist clenched and ready . . .

Then security stepped in and shoved the idiot towards the door. His friends went with him and some of his teammates ushered him outside, offering an apologetic wave on the way out. The other half of his team ignored him, so that told me all I needed to know.

The crowd around us, mostly my team who had my back, all seemed to exhale and relax, going back to their conversations. Except for Taka. He still stood at the bar with his drink in his hand, laughing. "Asked you nicely," he repeated, laughing again.

I risked a glance at Valentine and he was watching me. So was Lleyton. Actually most of his team were. Mostly curious, none seemed disgusted or angry. But Valentine was smirking.

I turned back to the bar.

"Tell me," Taka said quietly. "What's gonna happen between you and your man when we play them again next time?"

"My man?"

"Want me to say his name out loud?"

"No."

He held up two fingers around his beer bottle. "Two weeks, my friend. We play Lane Cove in two weeks. And we're undefeated and they've only lost to us. You know what that means."

It wasn't a question, because of course I knew.

It was going to be a North Ryde, Lane Cove final.

Me against Valentine.

"And let's not mention work," Taka added. He was getting far too much enjoyment out of this. "The Mercer contract will be finished in two months. Whatcha gonna do about that?"

"About what?"

"You were gonna quit or burn down head office. I can't remember which."

I snorted and let out a sigh. "Fuck. I dunno." I met his gaze. "I don't know."

He clapped my shoulder, bumping me into the bar. "You ain't leaving me and you ain't leaving him. Deny it all you fucking want. I know you, bro. And I know you ain't ever been like this with anyone else."

Goddammit.

I took a twenty out of my wallet and held it up for the barman. "Get Taka whatever he wants," I said. "And some superglue so he'll shut the fuck up." I clapped Taka on the back. "See you Monday."

I stepped out into the cold night and headed towards my ute parked up the street. There was a figure in the shadows and for a second I thought it might have been Scrooge McDrunk looking for that fight he so badly wanted. My heart rate kicked up a notch, but Valentine stepped out of the dark.

My pulse quickened for a whole different reason.

"Evening," he said smoothly.

Grinning, I unlocked the doors and caught him trying not to smile as he got in. And funnily enough, all the uncertainty about what we were and what kind of future we did or didn't have didn't seem to matter.

That smile, that giddy feeling, that was all I needed.

"So you were popular tonight," he said as I began the drive to his place.

"Who? The guy who wanted me to break his nose?"

Valentine chuckled. "I think he liked you."

I snorted. "What can I say? I have that effect on people."

His phone buzzed a few times and he pulled it out of his jacket. I saw a quick glimpse of a lot of messages, but he sighed and switched his phone to do not disturb.

"Not gonna deal with any of that?"

"It's all work," he said. "And no. There is nothing that can't wait. It's Saturday night." He let his head fall back onto the headrest. "It never stops."

"Fun, huh?"

He shook his head and looked over at me, his face half-shadow, half-blue in the light of the dash. "Not really."

"Did you have a good game today?"

"Mm, I played okay. No MVP this week though."

"No shots of tequila?"

"God no." He made a face. "Why would you even say that?"

That made me laugh. "You're cute when you're hungover."

He glared at me for that. "I thought we agreed to never speak of it again."

I chuckled. "You know Taka brought up a good point tonight," I said. "We're rostered to play against each other in two weeks."

"Do you need to mentally prepare yourself for losing? Is two weeks long enough?"

I scoffed. "Oh, please. We'll flog you. But you know what that's like, right? We have beaten you twice this year already."

He smirked. "Only one of those games counted. So why did Taka feel the need to bring it up now?"

"I think he thought I'd forgotten." I shrugged, trying to

play it cool. "And he thinks I'm gonna let my team down by taking it easy on you."

That made him laugh. "He clearly doesn't know that you taking it easy on me is not what we do."

I snorted. "Ah, no, he doesn't know that."

When we walked into his building and then into the elevator, I smiled at his reflection, and he smiled back before he ducked his head. And damn, if his cheeks didn't turn pink. It rattled my heart and my lungs felt too big for my chest, and suddenly the elevator seemed so small it was a relief when the doors opened.

He unlocked his door and held it for me. Enzo ran over, yelling at us and winding himself around my feet. I picked him up. "Look, little dude, I know you're not starving, so you can quit the act."

I put him on the kitchen counter, despite knowing it annoyed Valentine, got his biscuits out of the pantry, and filled his bowl. I slid the bag of cat food back onto the shelf, just thankful for the silence, and when I turned around, Valentine was standing there, smiling at me.

His arms weren't crossed. He had his hands on the counter behind him, and he looked relaxed and sexy as fuck in that black sweater. And wait . . .

I went to him, my fingers under his chin, and inspected his cheekbone. "Is that a bruise?"

He laughed. "It's a slight bump. You know, because I play rugby."

I tried to tamp down the flare of anger. "Who did it?"

He raised his eyebrows and laughed. "As if I'd tell you! So you could line him up sometime and take his head off."

"I don't like the idea of anyone else's hands on you."

His eyes sparked with amusement and fire. "I hate to break it to you, but I get touched a lot during a game."

I growled. "I'll do the manhandling, thanks."

He seemed to like this game. "Just like you get manhandled. In tackles, rucks, scrums. You don't see me complaining."

"Maybe you should."

"Oh god." He rolled his eyes. "Then you're really not gonna like this." He grinned as he lifted his sweater, revealing his abs and . . . a scrape of sprig marks across his ribs.

I knew these were common in rugby. I'd had them countless times and I'd given my share too. I knew they didn't really hurt too much . . . but it rankled me to see them on him.

That anyone would do this to him.

I gently touched the reddened skin. "Are you okay?"

"I'm fine."

"Do your ribs hurt? Who did this to you?"

He smirked at me. "I don't know." He laughed when I glowered at him. "I mean it. It's hard to see who's stomping when you're the one on the ground."

Yeah, that kinda wasn't helping.

He pulled his sweater back down and took my hand. "You going all Neanderthal and wanting to take down anyone who hurts me is very caveman of you."

He was probably expecting me to burr at the word caveman and maybe throw him over my shoulder and take him to bed . . . but he was still holding my hand. I couldn't stop staring at how his long fingers interlocked so perfectly with mine. How nice it felt.

"This is the first time you've held my hand," I murmured.

He dropped my hand and shoved my shoulder. "Until you made it weird."

I snatched his hand back, clasping it in mine. "I didn't make it weird."

His dark eyes met mine, full of light and something I didn't dare name. Then he leaned up on his toes and gently pecked his lips to mine.

Holy shit.

"Second time you've kissed me," I murmured.

"Are you keeping tabs?"

Had I really been keeping tabs on that?

Apparently I had.

He studied my eyes. "Want me to kiss you some more, Marshall?"

"Yes."

He took his hand from mine and slid it up to my jaw. His palm was warm, his touch electric—his eyes intense, flickers of fear and fire—and he brought my lips to his as his eyelids fluttered shut.

Soft and warm, I inhaled sharply at the sweetness. He took my bottom lip in between his, gently tugging me closer so he could deepen the kiss. I let him lead, let him do whatever he wanted.

There was a tenderness to Valentine I wasn't expecting, and it squeezed my heart, made my knees weak. His fingers tangled through my hair and slid down my back, pulling me flush against him.

I wanted to hold his face and devour his mouth, but I didn't want to ruin this . . . whatever this was. When he pressed his forehead to mine and took a few deep breaths, I half expected him to demand I fuck him hard.

But no, not this Valentine.

"I want to ride you," he murmured, trailing his nose along my jaw until his lips met my ear. "Marshall."

My breath hitched and sweet mother of god, how he said my name.

It took every ounce of control I had not to grip him, take him, and fuck him. "Say it again," I whispered.

He breathed in my ear. "Marshall."

A shiver of cold fire ran through me.

Holy fuck.

He chuckled. "Will you let me ride you?"

I'd have let him do anything he fucking wanted to me at that moment. "Anything you want."

He grinned like a demon, but then he took me to bed. He stripped me slowly and pushed me onto the mattress, and he did exactly what he said he was going to do.

He sank himself down on my cock and rode me, slow and deep. He was in charge, and he was glorious. Seeing him on top of me, seeing his head thrown back in pleasure.

He controlled everything: pace, touch, the way he kissed me. He controlled me like a puppet on a string. I fully surrendered to him, to his power over me, and when he begged me to come inside him, I surrendered that as well.

—————————————

I woke up facing him. He looked so peaceful in the dark room, faint light coming in from the hall and the door we'd left ajar. He looked younger, his long lashes, his pale skin and pink lips, his dark hair tousled.

I could stare at him forever.

You're supposed to hate him.

Yeah. But I don't.

I haven't for a long time.

"Are you watching me sleep?" he mumbled, a smile

tugging at his lip. His eyes cracked open. "'S fucking creepy."

I chuckled and pulled him into my arms, his head on my shoulder. He protested for half a second, but I held him tight, and he sighed into submission.

"Still don't like you," he mumbled as he snuggled in closer.

"Still don't like you either."

I WAS ALREADY LOOKING FORWARD to Wednesday night. From the moment I left him on Sunday, I was already counting down the minutes until I saw him again. Was alone with him again.

He was fine on Monday morning at the manager's meeting. Trying not to smile and trying his hardest to ignore me, not look at me, and definitely trying to *not* make eye contact.

It was a rush. A thrill that made my heart gallop. That made me happy, walking around with a dumb-arse smile on my face, and not even giving one single fuck about all the jokes Taka threw at me.

I was too happy to care.

On Tuesday after work, I texted Valentine in hopes it would lead to an early invitation to come over.

What are you cooking for dinner tomorrow night?

His reply came through about an hour later.

A nine-inch-deep, deep pan pizza. Scheduled for delivery around 7pm. It better not be late.

I laughed and my dick started to fill at the mere thought. I was hoping he'd take the bait and ask me to come over. But nope.

You can have it delivered tonight if you'd prefer.

I wish. I'm in the city tonight for a meeting.

Bummer. My dick deflated.

Fun?

No.

So Enzo's at home by himself?

My phone rang. "Are you more concerned about him than me?"

"Yes. You have the ability to feed yourself." Then I thought about it. "Even though you don't. Have you had dinner?"

Valentine sighed. "I know you might find this difficult to believe, but I'm capable of eating. Yes. I'm at a restaurant right now. Well, I'm outside speaking to you. I told them I had an important call to make."

"This is an important call."

He chuckled. "It's a dinner meeting. Budgets and finance."

"Sounds terrible."

"It's supposed to be a low-key informal thing."

"Ah. The greasing of wheels."

"Something like that."

"Well, I'll be greasing your wheels tomorrow night. Seven o'clock. I think there'll be two courses of your deep, deep pan pizza. I'll be feeding you twice. First course, then you can feed me actual food. Your second course will be served after."

"Christ. Now I have to go back inside with a semi. This is great, thanks for that."

I laughed and disconnected the call. Making him suffer a little bit was all part of the fun. The anticipation, the desire.

And Wednesday at work almost killed me. It was supposed to be anticipation for him, not me, but holy shit, I wanted inside him so bad. I had to jerk off in the shower before work so I didn't have a hard-on all day. Short of strapping my dick down with duct tape, it wasn't something I could easily hide.

By the time we'd called it a day and I got home, I considered jerking off again, but remembered I'd offered him a double dicking so thought it was best to save the first one.

Except when I was getting ready to leave for his place, I got a text.

Sorry to cancel. Tonight's not a good idea. I'm sorry.

I read it and read it a dozen times. I waited for the punchline. I waited for another text, an explanation.

I got neither.

I hit Call.

It rang and rang and I wondered if he'd answer at all.

If he was okay.

He certainly didn't sound it.

Tonight's not a good idea. What the fuck did that mean?

He answered just before it rang out, but he said nothing.

"Hey, Valentine?" I asked. "What's wrong? Are you okay?"

He sighed. His voice was distant, quiet. "It hasn't been a good day. I'm not up for . . . anything. Sorry . . . I'm sorry, Marshall."

"Don't apologise," I said. "Are you okay?"

I heard him swallow. "I wouldn't be very good company tonight." His voice cracked on the last word, and he let out a long breath. "Can we just forget about tonight, please? It wouldn't be anything good. I'll call you tomorrow or something."

"Valentine."

"I'm fine."

I hated those two words. Because he was *not* fine.

"I have to go," he mumbled, and the line went dead.

I grabbed my keys, pulled my door shut behind me, and made it to his place in record time. I pressed his buzzer, and when he didn't answer, I kept my hand on it. I knew he could see me. I looked up at the camera and kept my hand on the buzzer, and a few seconds later the door clicked.

I thumped the elevator door button and cursed every second it took to get to his floor. Though he opened his door when I got to it, so at least I didn't have to break it down.

He was still in his work suit, his head down.

"What are you doing here, Marshall? I asked you not to come."

"Because something's wrong. Because you need some-one, that's what I'm doing here."

He scowled and turned for his kitchen. "I don't need a babysitter."

"No, you don't. You need . . . a friend."

He got to the kitchen counter and sighed. "Is that what you are?"

Oh boy.

Okay, here goes nothing. I probably wasn't ready to do this but it was now or never. I was putting my cards on the table, consequences be damned.

"I . . . I don't know what I am. I don't know what we are. But you sounded so miserable I just couldn't stand the idea of you being alone. We don't need to do anything tonight. But just let me stay with you. If you need to talk—"

"I don't need to talk!" He raked his hand through his hair, frustrated and angry. "Christ, Marshall. I had a bad day, so fucking what?"

A bad day.

I'd seen him have bad days before. Hell, I'd even enjoyed his misery. I'd walked in here before, saw that he'd *clearly* had a bad day, and made him get on his knees and suck my dick.

He'd loved it, and I'd left him with a smile on his face, but still.

Now, I wanted to heal him in other ways.

"You can talk to me," I tried again.

His eyes were wild, bewildered. "I don't need to fucking talk. You know why I cancelled on you tonight? Because what I wanted so fucking bad was for you to hurt me. Like really hurt me, Marshall. And I knew it'd be fucked up. I didn't want you to have to go through that."

Jesus fucking Christ.

"Valentine," I murmured, reaching for him.

He took a step back, as if touching him right now was a bad, bad idea. He put his hand up, telling me not to come any closer.

"I know what you're gonna say," he whispered. "Christ, Marshall, why did you have to come here tonight?"

"Because you need me."

He scoffed. "I do fucking not. I don't need anyone."

"That's not true," I offered gently. "You need to speak to someone, Valentine."

His eyes flashed with anger, his nostrils flared. I'd struck a nerve. Clearly. "I do not need a shrink." He was seething mad. "I don't need some pretentious doctor to autopsy my trauma once a week. Been there, done that, and fuck it all to hell. I know what my faults are. I know how I am isn't my fault. I'm a product of my parents' fuckups. I know the public scrutiny doesn't help. I know all this. I know every line a shrink can throw at me, and I know how to deal with it."

"Valentine . . ."

"I know how to deal with it, Marshall, for what suits me best. I know what works for me. I've been on my own forever, and that's how I like it. I know how to function. I know how to survive, how to be on my own."

I put my hand to his cheek. "You don't have to be on your own anymore."

He pulled his face back. "I don't need you."

"Well, too bad. You've got me."

"I don't want you."

"I said too fucking bad."

He pushed me backwards, shoving me hard. "Marshall, I swear to god, don't start this with me."

He needed to break. He needed me to push him past his limit, to let the pressure out before he exploded.

So I got in his face, gripped his shirt. "Or what?"

Valentine pushed me, ripping my hand from his shirt and shoving me backwards. "Or I'll fucking end it. This, whatever the fuck this is."

I pushed him back so hard he took a step back to brace himself, then he launched at me, trying to tackle, wrestle me. Trying to hurt me. Hurt me like he was hurting.

But I was bigger and stronger. I countered his attack, using his swinging arm to turn him around and shove him against the wall. His arm bent behind him. I used my entire body to pin him to the wall.

I breathed against the back of his neck. "You won't end us," I murmured. "Because you need me. You need this as much as I do."

He struggled and I held him tighter, pressing him

harder against the wall. "I don't . . ." he said. "I don't want you."

I never budged, never lessened my hold. "No. You don't want to want me. You don't want to need me. But you do."

Valentine shook his head. "No."

"And I don't want to want you either," I murmured. "But I do."

He struggled again but I held him firm. "Let go of me," he hissed.

"No."

"We're finished. This agreement is over."

"No it's not. We're far from over."

Valentine pushed and fought, trying to twist out of my hold. So I spun him around and pinned his arms to the wall up above our heads, our faces just an inch apart.

He was livid. Furious and . . . and scared.

"The fuck are you doing, Marshall?"

"I'm trying to make you see."

He struggled again. "See what?"

"To see that you're worth it. That you're—"

"Enough!" he pushed me hard, for real this time, with fire and fear in his eyes, and it honestly scared me.

I let him go.

There were a few feet between us now, both our chests heaving, the air charged with static between us.

He sneered at me. "You don't know shit about me. You think you can come into my life—"

"I know what you need. I know what you think you need, and I know you're wrong."

"You don't know shit," he spat. "I just like rough sex. There's nothing fucking wrong with that. I like to be held down and—"

"I'm not talking about sex!"

Valentine stopped. "Then what the fuck are you even on about? That's all this is."

"It is not and you know it, Valentine. Jesus fucking Christ." I ran my hand through my hair, pulling at the strands. I wanted to rip it out of my head. Goddammit. "You and me, we're way past that, don't you think? You need me in your life, and that scares you because you've had your first taste of something good and it scares the fuck out of you."

He shook his head, his eyes wide and glassy. "No."

"Bullshit. You cannot lie to me."

"I don't need anything—"

"You need me!" I yelled at him. Every ounce of frustration, of emotion, burst inside me. God, I wanted to throttle him, to wrap my hands around his throat, to pummel the shit outta him. But he was so broken.

I wanted to hold him. To kiss him, to hold him tight and tell him it was okay.

My voice was just a whisper. "You need me to love you and it terrifies you."

Valentine shook his head, tears in his eyes. "You're supposed to hate me. That was the deal. You're supposed to hate me."

"I do," I murmured.

Valentine recoiled, confused.

Close to breaking.

"I hate a lot of things about you," I said quietly. "I hate that you think so little of yourself when I think you're kinda great. I hate that your parents cast you aside and use you, and they make you feel worthless when everything you do is for them. I hate that you put up these walls of ice like you need to protect yourself. I hate that you—"

Valentine thumped his chest, a tear spilling down his cheek. "Me. You're supposed to hate me!"

"I hate that I don't hate you anymore."

Another tear fell and Valentine scrubbed it away. "You know what? Fuck you."

I wrapped my arms around him, and Valentine tried to struggle out of my hold but there was no fight in him. No fight in him at all.

So I held him tighter, and Valentine sobbed in my arms. He cried and cried and let me take his weight. "Fuck you," he mumbled through his tears. "Fuck you for doing this to me."

I nodded. "I know."

He wriggled in my arms, trying to break free, so I gave him some room but kept my hands on his shoulders. He wouldn't look at me. "You were never supposed to do this. I was doing fine before you came into my life. I knew how to not feel anything, and I had a lid on it, then you fucked it all up."

He needed to vent. He needed to get this out.

Valentine scrubbed another tear from his face. His eyes met mine and he sniffled as he thumped his fist to my chest. "Who the hell do you think you are? You were just supposed to be a regular fuck. Nothing else. You were supposed to hate me."

"I used to," I whispered.

"But you don't anymore," he asked. It wasn't a question.

I shook my head.

Valentine's chin wobbled and fresh tears fell. "Then we're over. This is done. Whatever the fuck this was. It won't work."

I shook my head and put his arms back around him.

"We're *not* finished. Not until you give me a better reason. A *real* reason."

"I don't want you. I don't need you," Valentine mumbled.

"I don't believe you."

"I'm better off without you."

I sighed. "If you really want me gone, if you really don't want me to love you, then *tell me* you don't want me to love you and I'll go. I'll walk out right now."

Valentine sobbed. "I don't want you to love me," he whispered as he cried.

I dropped my arms, letting him go, and took a step back, ready to turn and walk away. Not wanting to.

Leaving him was the last thing I wanted to do.

But if Valentine didn't want me . . . if he didn't think we had anything left to salvage . . . Maybe he wasn't ready. Maybe he'd never be ready.

"Okay," I whispered, tears in my eyes. "I can't make you love me. But I can love you. I know you think you're not loveable, or you're not worth worthy of it, but you are." God, my heart hurt so damn much. "I wish I could make you see that."

I took a reluctant step away, and he grabbed my shirt, fisting it tight. He kept his head down, but he shook his head and sobbed.

Oh, Valentine.

"I don't know what I want," he whispered, crying.

I put my hands to Valentine's face and made him look at me. "You'll be okay."

Valentine nodded, more tears falling. "I don't know what . . . I don't know what I'm doing. I don't know how to do this. This is your fault. I was fine before you came along. I never needed anyone until you."

I pulled him into my arms, wrapping him up tight and kissing the side of his head. He was letting himself feel emotions, giving into them. It was hardly surprising that he was confused and felt exposed and vulnerable. But, piece by piece, those ice walls were slowly coming down.

"I know," I murmured. "But I'm not sorry. And I'm not going anywhere."

Chapter 20

Valentine

I felt foolish. I was a fool. I'd let myself become vulnerable, exposed like a wound open for infection.

It was never supposed to be like this.

I was never supposed to be like this. My life was so much easier before Marshall fucking Wise came into my life. Before I'd grown accustomed to him being around, to him looking after me. To him caring about me.

I'd almost wept when I'd seen him on the intercom screen, when he must have sped the whole way from his place to mine, because he cared about me.

I knew letting him in was a bad idea.

Because I needed him.

I'd never needed anyone or anything in my life.

Marshall Wise ruined me.

He made me feel things. He made me want things. He showed me what happiness was. He showed me what it felt like to be important to someone.

A glimpse of what love felt like.

And so help me fucking god, I wanted it.

As much as it scared me.

I never realised I needed him to fight for me.

And fight for me he did.

Standing there in my kitchen with his arms around me, with my heart a beating mess, he held me while I cried. While I finally admitted that I was not as unbreakable as I pretended to be.

Admitting that I needed him was one of the hardest things I'd ever done.

Admitting I needed anything was hard for me. But giving my heart to someone, trusting them not to hurt me, was terrifying.

"You're okay," he whispered, kissing the side of my head again. "I gotchu."

And he did.

He had me. All of me.

I knew I needed to talk, but I wasn't even sure where to start. At the beginning seemed like a good place. I wiped my snotty nose with the back of my hand. "I'm a fucked-up mess."

"I know," he said.

I snorted out a laugh. "It's true. I'm selfish and detached."

"I know. I know who you are. I know what I'm getting myself into." He pulled back and cupped my face, wiping my cheeks before kissing me softly. "But I also know who you are when it's just me and you. I know the real you."

"I say horrible things just to hurt people. I don't mean to, I just . . ." I shook my head. "It keeps people away."

"It's a self-defence thing," he offered. "But you're worth it, Valentine. You're worth it. You deserve something good in your life. And that's me, if you haven't guessed. I'm the good thing you deserve."

I relented a teary smile and nodded. "You're the *only* good thing in my life."

"No I'm not. You have your sister, you have Lleyton. And Enzo. And your whole rugby team. Those guys have your back too." He brushed the hair from my forehead and searched my eyes. "You have you. And you're stronger than you realise."

My eyes welled with more tears, and I swallowed thickly. God, I was so sick of crying.

"I can't offer you anything more than this," I said again. I needed him to understand. "I'm not out. I don't know if I'll ever be out."

"That's okay, Valentine."

"It's okay now. But it won't always be. I can't expect you to say it's okay. And what if in six months or a year from now you realise it's not okay and you want more than I can give? What do I do then?"

"I won't ever rush you to do something you're not ready for. Is it going to be easy? Not always. But I don't expect it to be. I'm pretty sure nothing with you is going to be easy."

I snorted out a laugh. "That's probably true."

"Now, about the whole sex thing," Marshall said.

I opened my mouth to counter some argument, but he shushed me. "I know. I know how you like it. You like me to walk in, bend you over and put a load in you, and walk out. I know you like that. And I'm still on board with that because it's hot as fuck. But sometimes I'll slow-fuck you and put a load in you. And other times I'll make love to you for hours and—" He shrugged. "—put a load in you."

I gave a teary laugh, but I nodded. I thought he was going to say it couldn't be like that anymore and I was relieved to hear otherwise. Because he *did* understand me. "Thank you."

"But I won't hurt you," he added. "Not pain for the sake of it. You want a good dicking, fair enough. You want it slow, great." He kissed my forehead and whispered, "You just gotta talk to me. I know it's not easy for you. But if you're having a bad day, tell me. If you need cuddles on the couch, tell me. If you need me to leave you alone for a day, just say that."

"I told you to leave me alone today and you refused."

"Time alone to breathe and time alone to recharge, not demanding I stay away because you're hurting. There's a difference. I'll help you learn that."

I nodded again and let out a shuddering breath, trying to get my head around everything and not knowing where to start. "What do you need? Out of this. From me?" I had no idea how this should work. "I don't even know what I should ask you."

"I just need you to talk to me." He kissed my forehead again. "And the occasional pizza, and every now and then, just to walk in, bend you over and put a load in you and walk out."

I laughed, wiping my nose again. "Sounds perfect." I swallowed hard and collected myself a little. "I like what I like. It's not some fucked-up psychological thing. I've discussed it at length in therapy."

Marshall made a face. "Well. Therapy could be a good thing. Maybe?"

I frowned. "Therapy can't fix my childhood or what my parents are. Therapy can't take back every hurtful thing they've done and said."

"No. But it helps to talk about it. To understand why you might feel certain ways."

"I know who I am," I said flatly. "I know my faults. I know my shortcomings, and I know my strengths. If you want me to go to therapy, if you absolutely do, I will consider it. I'm not opposed to it. I've just tried it before and it was a waste of my time. I know who I am. Sometimes people are just fucked up."

He kissed my lips softly. "I just want you to be happy. I want you to know how important you are to a lot of people. How important you are to me."

I smiled sadly. "I don't know what I ever did to deserve you."

"Uh, you shoved me into a toilet cubicle and sucked my dick."

That made me smile. "And if I got a redo, I'd do it again."

But knowing it was time for honesty, I sighed. "I've never needed anyone like I need you. In my whole life, I've never had anyone. Until you. I . . ." I shook my head, new tears welling in my eyes. "This isn't easy for me to talk about. And I will get things wrong more than I ever get them right, but I want to try. Marshall, you have to promise me you won't leave me. Even if I push you away. I've never trusted anyone like I trust you, and if you throw that back at me, I'm not sure how I'd survive that."

"You won't push me away, because you're going to talk to me, remember?"

I nodded. "I won't always get it right."

"I don't expect you to. I won't get things right all the time either. But we'll try. And we'll talk like adults." Then he shrugged. "And fuck like animals."

I barked out a teary laugh. "Deal."

Marshall slid his hand along my jaw, kissing me softly, before pulling me in for a long, warm hug. "I don't hate you, Valentine."

I nodded into his neck. "I don't hate you either."

And so we stood there in my kitchen for a long while, him holding me and me not letting him go. My god, it felt so good. How was a hug so healing? I'd been so touch starved, so affection starved, kindness starved for so long that a simple hug felt like oxygen after struggling to breathe.

Eventually Marshall pulled back, his eyes on mine. "Want to tell me what happened today?"

I shook my head because my immediate reaction, my knee-jerk reaction was to recoil and say everything was fine. But it wasn't fine, and I had to learn how to talk to him, to admit things, and be vulnerable. "My father," I mumbled.

Apparently it was all I needed to say because Marshall growled. "I know he's your father and I'm trying not to—"

"I hate him. He just makes me so fucking mad. And it's not one thing in particular, it's everything. Every little jab, every poke, every prod. Every snide comment, every sniff of arrogance. He wears me down, and I used to just ignore it. I used to be able to tamp down every emotion and pretend it didn't hurt, or hell, that I even deserved it, and I don't know why but I can't do that anymore."

Well, that's not true.

"Actually, I do know," I added. "I'm pretty sure it's your fault."

His eyes went wide. "Me? What did I do?"

"You made me feel things, Marshall. You made me deal with shit that I never had any intention of dealing with." I had instant tears in my eyes, and my nose burned, and my chin wobbled. I gestured to my stupid face. "See? What the fuck is this?"

He laughed but was quick to pull me back in for a hug. "Come here."

I let him hold me tight because apparently I needed that now. "God, emotions are so fucking terrible."

He chuckled quietly and rubbed my back. "So terrible."

I stayed right there, taking in his warmth and his scent. His strength. "If I quit now, my father will think it's because I couldn't handle it. He handed the construction division to me as a test, and he'll think I'm a failure."

Marshall sighed and pulled back. He put his palm to my jaw, his thumb gently swiped my cheek, his eyes on mine. "You didn't fail anything."

I shrugged because I didn't know what else to do. "I don't want to leave my job. I like what I do. But I don't know how much longer I can deal with him for. He was such an arsehole today. It's embarrassing and demeaning."

It really hadn't been one thing today that set me off. By god, I only had to see my father and it set my teeth on edge. It put my defences up.

In the end, I sighed. "And you know what? Maybe that's the point. Maybe I'm not cut out for it. Because the mega-corp world is full of people just like my father. It's how he became so successful. He's ruthless and gives not one thought to people he trampled in his climb to the top." I didn't have to tell Marshall that; he knew all too well. "But all those huge corporate execs and CEOs, they're all like that. It's just business, they say. It's not personal. What a crock of shit. It *is* personal, every fucking time."

He nodded, frowning. "It is."

I knew he'd get it. "I'm not like that. I can't do that. I thought I could. I thought I could just squash it all down and pretend it didn't matter, but I can't." I shrugged again, though realisation was dawning on me. "So maybe he's right. I'm not cut out for it. I did fail."

Marshall shook his head. "You didn't fail. In fact, I'd reckon this is you doing the opposite of that."

"I don't know what to do," I admitted. "For the first time in my life, nothing's mapped out for me."

He put his hands to my face. "So," he said. "How about you take it one day at a time? There's no need to rush into anything or do something that can't be undone. I think you made a pretty big decision already today. How about we let the dust settle for a bit?"

I knew he had a point, but . . . "Maybe I should do it now."

"Do what now?"

I shrugged. "I don't know!"

Marshall smiled and kissed me softly. "Maybe having a plan of action in place first would be a good idea, yes?"

"Or maybe jumping in with both feet into the unknown is my plan?" I put my hand to my forehead because, holy shit, that was daunting as fuck. "Or maybe not."

Marshall took my hand from my forehead and kissed my knuckles. "Whatever you want to do, I'm one hundred percent okay with. As long as you're happy."

I had no idea how much I needed to hear that until he'd said it. "Thank you."

"Just let me know if you're not gonna be my boss anymore," he said. "Because I was totally gonna quit and tell you to shove the whole company up your arse when this Mercer job was over."

Wait, what? "You were?"

He nodded. "Back in the beginning. When Tye Corp took over and you walked in. I had absolutely no intention of staying. I only stayed because I didn't want to let Mercer down. I was actually going to ask them to hire me."

Jesus. "And now? What are you saying, Marshall?"

He smiled. "Now I went and caught feelings, and leaving don't feel right."

Oh god, he was just saying this stuff out loud to my face. "Caught feelings, huh?"

He nodded. "I mean, I had feelings the first day too. More akin to rage and loathing though. Man, I wanted to strangle you that first day. I was so fucking mad."

"I remember," I said, recalling his face when he heard the news. "You looked at me with pure disgust in your eyes. It was so fucking hot. I pretty much knew then I wanted your hands on me."

He laughed. "Oh, really?"

I sighed. "Yes."

He ran his hands over my shoulders and up my neck, so gentle and warm. "Like this?"

I ignored the heat in my cheeks. "Sometimes."

He laughed and, holding my face, brought me back in for another hug. He wrapped me up tight and sighed. "How about we organise some food and hit the couch and watch some dreadful TV?"

"Will you stay tonight?" I asked, beyond sounding desperate. If this entire night hadn't been an exhibit of pitiful, then what's a bit more? "I really want you to stay. I want you to wreck me tonight."

He hummed and lifted my chin for a kiss. "I'm happy to wreck you, Valentine. But there'll be no hurting tonight. It's gonna be slow and deep, and you're gonna feel everything I feel for you."

I leaned into him, melting in his arms. And that's exactly what he did. He fed me, then took me to bed and wrecked me in the very best of ways. In ways I'd never been wrecked before. He made love to me, slow and deep, just like he said he would. Every emotion in every kiss, every thrust, every touch. He shattered me, splintering me into tiny pieces and then he put me back together again. He reassembled me, more complete than I'd ever been.

And in case I thought for one minute that this was how he was going to task sex with me from now on—lovemaking instead of the hard fucking I craved—before he left for work the next morning, he flattened me on the bed, held me down, and rammed another load into me.

Then he slapped my arse and walked out.

I smiled into my pillow, stretching my used muscles, relishing in the feel of where he'd been. My body sang. My heart was happy. *I* was happy.

I'd gone and fallen in love for the first time in my life.

I was in love. *So* in love.

With Marshall fucking Wise.

God help me.

CHAPTER 21

MARSHALL

THE GAME AGAINST PENRITH ON SATURDAY WAS MESSY but we managed to hold the win. Barely. We made the long trip back to our pub for drinks, but it was quiet, no one really in the mood to celebrate.

I had somewhere else to be, anyway.

Apparently Lane Cove had smashed Warringah, and Valentine was in a good mood when I got to his place at nine.

He ordered Japanese food and we drank a few cans of Asahi while I made him watch *The Expendables* on Netflix. It was a very boyfriend-ish thing to do, and while I was too scared to ask if that's what we were, it felt right.

I'd told him I basically loved him on Wednesday when he'd had his big meltdown. *If you don't want me to love you, tell me right now.*

That's what I'd said.

He hadn't voiced any great declarations in return, but his entire spiral was because he felt things he'd tried to ignore.

And he could deny it till he was blue in the face, but I knew he loved me.

Valentine didn't have a lot of love in his life, and he said he wasn't sure what it even meant. But the way he looked at me, the way he smiled at me.

It was love.

And how he'd cleared away dinner, then curled up against me, my arm slung over his shoulder as we watched the rest of the movie. The way he took my hand and led me to bed, the way he kissed me, the way we made love, and the way he fell asleep in my arms afterwards.

This was love.

I knew we'd have challenges and bridges to cross. I knew it wouldn't always be easy. When it was just us? Easy as breathing. When we factored in the outside world, how our friends and families might react?

Not so much.

I just didn't expect it to happen so soon.

Because on Wednesday night he came over to my place. I'd been to the supermarket for ingredients for him to cook because we certainly couldn't go to the supermarket together.

Like we couldn't go out for breakfast on his birthday.

Because we couldn't be seen together.

Because he wasn't out, and we were supposed to hate each other. Because he was also technically my boss.

There was no way we could explain it without incriminating us, without exposing us both. And it was fine. I had no problem with keeping us on the down-low. It was safer that way. It was more private and personal, and I kinda liked that.

Until we were in my kitchen, and he was gagging trying to touch the raw fish and I was laughing at him . . .

And there was a knock on my door.

We both stopped and stared at each other, silent. My heart was thumping against my ribs and Valentine paled.

Fuck.

Another quick knock and a familiar voice. "Marshall? It's just me."

My mum.

I almost told him to go wait in my room, but that felt a stretch too far. I didn't want to hide him. He shouldn't have to hide like we were doing something wrong.

"Stay here," I whispered, my hand on his arm. The kitchen was hidden from the front door. He'd be fine. "She won't come in here."

I went to the door, wiping my hands on a tea towel, and opened it. "Mum," I said. "What are you doing here?" I hadn't meant it to sound rude, but a little notice would have been nice.

She was holding a tray of eggs. Of all the fucking things. "I went into Mrs Younis' shop for fresh eggs like you said. She wanted me to give you these, and I was just on my way home," she said, looking past my shoulder. "I thought I heard you laugh."

I almost told her it was the TV, but the damn thing wasn't on. "Oh, I, uh . . . um."

She zipped past me. "I'll just put these in the kitchen—"

"Mum, wait!"

She stopped in the entryway, seeing Valentine. "Oh." Then she shot me a bewildered look. "You have company."

Fuck, fuck, fuck.

"I do . . . I, uh . . . Mum, now's not a good time. I'll explain later . . ."

Valentine was standing there in the kitchen, awkward as I'd ever seen him. He was still a shade pale and was gripping the kitchen counter, looking about ready to run. Or puke.

"Hello, dear," Mum said, making a face. This wasn't good. She handed me the eggs and did a half-wave thing that was weird and just as awkward. "I'm Penny. Marshall's mum."

Fucking fuck.

I had to introduce them. I didn't expect Mum to recognise him. She wouldn't have seen him for almost twenty years . . .

"Ah, Mum, this is Valentine." My mouth was so dry I couldn't even swallow. "Valentine Tye."

Mum's eyes cut to mine, wide with surprise, and I didn't miss how Valentine steeled himself. "Oh," Mum managed.

"Nice to meet you," Valentine said, his voice tight.

Mum seemed to collect herself. "Yes, nice to meet you too, dear. I didn't recognise you after all this time." Her eyes drew down to his shirt. The white button-down shirt with the buttons with red thread. She looked at me, realising that we'd sewn those damn buttons on weeks ago.

And I'd never said anything.

I put the stupid eggs on the counter and stepped in closer to Valentine, almost shielding him from view. He needed to know he had my support, that I was on his side. "Mum," I said. "Valentine and I are . . ."

Well, shit. I didn't really know what we were.

I raised my chin and put my arm around his waist. "We're kinda together, but it's complicated, and I'm sure you understand why I never said anything. It's . . . well, it's . . ."

"Me. I'm the reason," Valentine whispered. "I'm not . . . I can't . . ."

"It's for both of us," I added, not wanting Valentine to have to shoulder this on his own. I pulled him a little closer and looked him right in the eye. "It's not just you, Valentine."

Christ, he looked miserable and scared as hell.

Thankfully, Mum seemed to clue in. "It's okay," she said with a sad smile. "It's not anyone else's business. And I should have called first but I was driving, and you know I can't use that Bluetooth thing. I'm sorry for just turning up. I should get going or your father will worry."

I cringed. "Yeah, uh. I dunno about Dad—"

"I'll take care of your father," she said, giving me that don't-argue-with-your-mother look. "He'll be fine."

I wasn't sure about that.

"I'll let you get back to your evening," she said. Then she studied Valentine for a beat. "You okay, love?"

He blinked a few times. "I'm really sorry."

She put her hand on his forearm. "You have nothing to apologise for. I'm sorry for interrupting your night. You make sure Marshall looks after you, okay? And you let me know if he doesn't."

That was clearly an attempt to lighten the mood and maybe even get Valentine to smile. It worked, kind of.

He nodded. "I will."

Her eyes met mine, wide and apologetic, before she went to the door. I followed her, seeing her out. "I'm sorry," she whispered. "He wasn't ready."

"No one can know," I replied quietly. "He's not out. You can't tell anyone. Dad—I don't expect you to keep this from him, but he won't understand."

"He doesn't have to," she said. "He just wants you to be happy."

"I am happy, Mum."

She nodded, a little teary. "I'm sorry you felt you couldn't tell us."

"Me too."

"We'll talk about this later," she said. Then she spoke loud enough for Valentine to hear, telling us both, "But I'll call before I just turn up next time. I promise. Have a good night, boys."

She left and I closed the door, not sure how this night would now end. Like my mum had said, he wasn't ready.

I walked straight up to him and collected him in for a crushing hug. At least he couldn't make a run for it if I was holding him. "I'm sorry," I said. "I didn't know she'd just turn up. I mean, she just turns up sometimes. But she won't tell anyone. She understands that all too well."

His hands were at my sides, fisting my shirt. "I'm sorry too," he mumbled.

I pulled back and took his face in my hands. "You have nothing to apologise for."

He looked so fucking sad. "Your dad's gonna hate me."

"No he won't. He'll be surprised, let's put it that way. But you're not your father, and he'll see that. He'll get to know you, and . . . he'll see how much I love you and then he can't say shit."

Valentine's eyes went wide and I realised what I'd just said.

Well, it was out there now.

"You . . ." He began to smile and cry at the same time. "You said . . ."

I pulled him back in for another hug, mostly so he couldn't see my oh-shit face. "I said it, and you know what? I'm not sorry. And it's your fucking fault. You made me fall in love with you with the whole I-want-you-to-come-inside-me thing. Like what was I supposed to do? *Not* fall in love with you?"

He barked out a snotty laugh. "Oh my god."

I wasn't letting him go because I didn't want to own up to anything I'd just said, but he pulled back. His arms were around my waist, his eyes met mine. "Marshall," he whispered as if he was out of breath.

"It's okay. You don't have to say anything, and I don't expect you to say it back to me. But you should know." I knew my face was red, but whatever . . . "You should know how I feel. You deserve to know."

"And you do too," he whispered. "I've never loved anything or anyone, and it scares the hell out of me but—" He shook his head. His voice was just a breath. "I love you too."

Holy shit.

Holy fucking shit.

I was smiling like an idiot and kissed him. "Was it because I came inside you? It was, wasn't it?"

He burst out laughing. "Pretty sure it was, yeah."

"I knew it."

His smile faded. "I'm going to fuck it up, I know I will. I just ask that you try and be patient with me. I'm sorry your mum found out like this. I was hiding in your kitchen, for god's sake. I'm sorry you had to keep this a secret from your parents."

I put my hand to his jaw. "You know what? I'm glad she knows. And she'll tell my dad and then we'll have to do Sunday dinners with them, and it'll be embarrassing and awesome. And I'm glad Lleyton and Taka know, and your sister knows . . . Well, she knows you're gay, and that's amazing because now the most important people in our lives know. The rest don't matter. I don't care about anyone else. We can just be us now, without worrying about people finding out."

He inhaled deeply and nodded into my palm. "Besides the whole work thing."

I conceded a nod. "Well, yeah. There's that."

"And our rugby teammates."

I snorted. "Could you imagine the look on their faces?"

"When they find out I'm gay? Or when my team knocks your team off the top of the ladder?"

That made me laugh. "You wish. And god, no. They'll just bypass the whole gay thing when they find out who your boyfriend is."

He froze, his eyes meeting mine. He blew out a breath and shook his head, fighting a smile. "Christ. It's a night for big announcements, isn't it?"

I snorted. "Apparently."

"Maybe we could forgo the cooking tonight and just skip right ahead to the wine and fucking."

Laughing, I turned him around to face the fish, my hands on his hips, my chin on his shoulder. I let out a long breath and kissed the top of his shoulder. "Nice try. Food first. Then wine and fucking."

I WAS PUMPED for the game on Saturday. Valentine had been smug about how Lane Cove was going to thrash us and knock us off the top of the ladder.

I couldn't wait to see them try.

It was going to be a hard game. They were in fine form while we'd barely managed to scrape together our last win. But we were undefeated, and they'd only ever lost to us.

"We're going to rectify that today," Valentine had said

before he kissed me goodbye this morning. Then he looked me right in the eye and smirked. "I'm taking you down."

That smugness, that arrogance. My god, I used to hate it.

Now I saw it as a challenge.

"You gonna be cool today?" Taka asked me. We were in the dressing sheds, warming up before taking the field. We were T-minus two minutes until kick off and my pregame nerves were bordering on nausea.

"Yeah, I'll be fine." I bounced on my toes a few times and shook out my hands. "But we gotta get the W today. He'll never let me forget it if we don't."

Taka laughed and wet his mouthguard before putting it in. "Good luck with that."

We took the field, running out to where Lane Cove were already waiting. They had the home field advantage, and the full crowd was a mix of cheers and boos. I blocked that shit out and focused on one thing.

Valentine Tye.

I hated that he looked so fucking hot in his rugby gear. He grinned around his mouthguard at me, and I grinned right fucking back.

He was wearing headgear and I knew it was to avoid another serious knock like before. But rest assured, no one was getting near him today.

If anyone was taking him down, it was me.

"You're going down, Tye," I yelled out.

"You fucking wish, Wise," he yelled back.

Lleyton's eyes almost bugged out of his head and Taka laughed behind me. The referee told us to behave right before he blew the whistle. They kicked off and it was game on.

We got the ball and they held their line, defence tight. They hit hard and my first touch of the ball, I fumbled it.

Like that wasn't bad enough, but someone laughed.

I got to my feet, fist closed, ready to get my fight on, only to see it was Valentine.

Would I have swung at him?

Undecided.

Taka pulled me back by my jersey. "You don't wanna do that," he said, shoving me back into my line.

But a few sets later, when Valentine made a run for touch, I got a clean tackle on him, smearing him into the ground with an oomph. I laughed for the spite of it and tapped his headgear. "Who's laughing now?"

One of his team pulled me off him none too gently, and the referee was soon between us, telling us to cool it.

But I hadn't had this much fun playing rugby in years.

Then they scored and it made me focus. Head back in the game, dignity on the line.

I made a break pass, feeding Taka a sweet ball and he steam-trained across the line.

We went into half-time tied on seven–all. We knew it was gonna be a tough match, and they weren't giving us a second to let us catch our breath.

Two minutes into the second half, Simons got a tackle on Valentine. It was fair, a good tackle even, but it rankled something in me. I pulled Simons off him, earning me a "What the fuck, Wise?" from someone in my team, but I just pointed to our defence.

"Hold the fucking line," I bit out.

Valentine got to his feet and grinned at me, and it spurred me on even more. And the next time I got my hands on the ball, I tucked it under my arm and ran like a man possessed.

I could hit harder, I could bulldoze harder, I could dig in harder and hold a whole fucking scrum.

But he was faster than me.

He took me out across the sideline. We slid on the grass, the try line just a few feet away, and he got pulled to his feet by his team with cheers and slaps on the back. I got to my feet and wanted to kill him.

By some grace of fucking god, we managed to score on the next set. But then with five minutes left on the clock, hit up after hit up, they went across the line again.

Thank fuck they missed the kick for goal, the whistle blew, and we'd somehow managed to hold our title of undefeated.

Barely.

It meant we'd have next week off getting a walkthrough to the final, while Lane Cove played again for their spot against us for the shield.

It also meant we'd be heading back to their pub for after match drinks. As usual, their team hung out in one corner, my team hung out in the other, rarely intermingling. Sometimes meeting at the bar or passing through to the restrooms.

Like it always was.

I kept my back to Valentine like I always did so I didn't stare at him and get caught smiling like a lovesick schoolboy with hearts in my eyes.

Until I caught Taka smiling at someone behind me.

"Good game," Valentine said.

I turned then, smiling, because I was a total goner. "Thanks."

"I was talking to Taka," he said casually. "Though the way you fumbled the ball was outstanding."

I had to take a deep breath and try counting to ten while also trying not to laugh and not strangle him. Or kiss him. I put my drink on the bar and stepped in closer, still trying to decide. "Is that right?"

"Ah, jeez," Taka said quietly. "Got yourselves an audience, fellas."

Valentine laughed, found my gaze, and held it. He was baiting me, goading me. But then he clapped Taka's arm. "Good win." Then he threw a fifty on the bar and ordered some drinks for his table.

I had to make myself take some deep breaths, and when I looked around, both our teams were watching us like they were holding their breaths. Waiting for a fight to start, waiting to jump in.

Valentine was going to get it when we got back to his place, and I knew without doubt that's what he was doing. He was trying to piss me off enough so that when I walked into his place at nine o'clock, I'd make him pay. I'd be rough and ready. Unforgiving.

And I would. I'd give him exactly what he wanted, exactly how he wanted it.

He was such a whore.

He was *my* whore.

I snatched up my bottle and took a swig, turning my back on Valentine and lasering my gaze on the far wall instead.

"You okay, bro?" Taka asked me quietly.

"Oh, yeah. Him goading me like that? It's like foreplay."

Taka almost choked on his beer. "And you both trying to flatten each other in the game today?"

I nodded. "Yep. Foreplay."

He laughed. "Bro, that is fucked up."

If only he knew. "You have no idea."

Then someone bumped into me from behind, kinda hard, kinda deliberate, knocking me into the bar. I thought it might have been someone looking for a fight, so I turned around, ready to go.

It was some random guy who was quite drunk. And familiar. Maybe I'd fucked him once . . .

He smiled and fell into me. "Oh, hey there, stranger," he purred. And slurred.

I tried to set him on his feet. "Yeah, okay, steady as she goes, sailor. You got wobbly boots on."

He laughed and tried to fall against me again. "Wanna take 'em off for me?"

I pushed him back to arm's length. "No. I don't."

He lifted his finger, to do what, I had no clue. "You played so well today."

Then, appearing outta thin air, Valentine was there. He stood at the bar, closer to me than he probably should have been, and he glared at Wobbly Boots McDesperate. His gaze was cold, his voice like ice. "He said no."

Oh boy. Holy shit.

Some of his team were watching.

I tried to whisper as inconspicuously as I could. "What are you doing?"

Valentine put his hand to his forehead and looked away. "I don't know."

"You okay?"

Valentine shook his head just as the dumbest drunk guy on the planet decided to pipe up. "Dunno what your problem—"

Valentine turned to him and got in his face, smooth and lethal. "My problem is you."

Aaaand then half of Valentine's team were on their feet —glaring at me because most of them hated me and I happened to be near Valentine when he was about to get his fight on—which was hot as fuck, by the way—and their reaction towards me made half my team take notice.

I put my hands up because I was just a bystander in this. "I didn't do anything!"

Which of course made Valentine spin to face me, shooting daggers of ice from his eyes.

It was kinda hot.

Taka laughed until Valentine's glare landed on him. He straightened up. "Yeah, okay. You're on your own with that one." He clapped my shoulder and sidestepped away.

Connor and Paul, two of Valentine's teammates who I knew didn't like me, came to stand beside him.

"What's your fucking problem, Wise?" Connor said. He was the guy Valentine once said wanted to fight me, the reason Valentine shoved me into the toilet cubical that time all those weeks ago.

Dunno what I ever did to piss him off. Was probably just better than him at something.

"I don't have a problem," I replied. "Yet."

"You know what I reckon?" Paul added. "I think we might need to take this outside."

I laughed. For two reasons: one, because they thought they could fight me. And two, just to piss them off. "You wanna lose twice in one day?"

Connor bristled and tried to puff himself up like a fucking pigeon.

Then Valentine stood in between us, facing me. His eyes were wide and wild. Was he on my side? Or was he on theirs?

"What are you doing?" I asked quietly.

"I don't know," he breathed. "I don't know what the fuck I'm doing." He put his hand to his forehead, his fingers shaking.

Ah, jeez.

I'd seen this before. Right before he got too over-whelmed and freaked the fuck out.

I grabbed his wrist to pull him to the door. He needed fresh air. The cold fresh air would do him a world of good. But apparently grabbing Valentine's wrist wasn't the right thing to do because Paul grabbed my arm.

"Let him go," he said, trying to shove me backwards.

I almost lost my footing and Valentine pulled his arm free, and while Connor and Paul were trying to get to me, I was trying to get to Valentine. "Get the fuck off me," I said, shoving Connor as Paul grabbed my collar.

"Let him go," Valentine yelled, then he was in front of me, his hand on Paul's wrist, his knuckles white. "I said let him go."

"What the fuck?" Paul cried, pulling himself free. "Whose fucking side are you on?"

Then Taka was in the middle of it all with his huge arms out. "Okay, fellas, cool it, yeah?"

Valentine's hands were still shaking, he took a step back, and he gasped for breath. "Can't . . . I can't . . . ." Everyone was staring at him. His eyes met mine. "Marshall. Marshall . . ."

I fought free and grabbed him and all but carried him outside, Lleyton right behind us. I burst through the front doors, got him into the cold air, and put my hands to his face, making him look into my eyes. "Breathe, okay. Just breathe." I took deep breaths with him. "Nice and deep."

Valentine blinked a few times, but he managed a lungful of air and then another, keeping in time with me until he nodded and sagged. I pulled him against me and he came without protest.

"What was that?" Lleyton asked.

"He just has trouble catching his breath sometimes," I answered. I was a little surprised that he didn't know about Valentine's anxiety, but then again, the fact Valentine hadn't even told his closest friend didn't surprise me at all. I kept my hand on the back of Valentine's head, his face in the crook of my neck. "You okay?"

He nodded but made no move to pull away. He was heavy, exhausted. Embarrassed. "Sorry."

I rubbed his back. "Don't apologise."

Hearing voices behind me, I turned to see quite a crowd outside. Mostly his team, some of mine, probably wondering if Valentine and I were fighting, shocked to see me with my arms around him.

"Nothing to see here, folks," Taka said, his voice always so calm and disarming.

Lleyton walked back and both he and Taka kinda shielded us.

"You're okay," I murmured. "Wanna go home?"

He nodded against me, still breathing heavy. "I feel so stupid."

"You're not stupid."

"That guy was all over you."

Which one? The first one? Where Valentine intervened?

"He was a dick. I told him no."

He looked up at me then. "I know you did. I don't blame you. I just . . . I couldn't handle seeing him touch you. Anyone touch you. I wanted to stand with you, touch you, and then he thought he could touch you. Like it lit a fire under me or something, and I was in his face before I knew what I was doing, and I know how that looked. I know . . . People will know . . ."

I put my hand to his face. "It's none of their business."

"I wanted to tell him. God, I almost came out. I almost did. I almost said it in front of everyone. That you were mine and that guy needed to back the fuck up. And then Connor got in your face, and my god, Marshall, I've never had anyone to defend before. No one's ever been mine. If he punched you, I would have killed him."

I put my hand to his hair, to his face, unable to keep from smiling. "That's kinda hot."

He sighed and closed his eyes. "I can't keep doing this."

"Doing what?"

"Hiding. Lying. Lying to my team, lying to myself. Hiding who I am. I don't want to hide in your kitchen anymore."

"Oh, babe."

"I want to come out, Marshall. I need to. For me. I need to stop being such a fucking coward."

"You're not a coward," I said firmly, my forehead to his. "Like I said before, everyone's story is different. If you want to do it for *you*, then great. But don't let yourself feel pressured."

"I'm sick of hiding. I'm sick of not being me. Not being able to do what I want, be what I want." He shook his head. "Lleyton knows, and Taka. Brooklyn knows, kind of. Your parents know. And it's such a fucking relief. I can't begin to explain . . . I don't need to explain because you already know. Fuck."

"No one else matters."

His eyes searched mine. "Then why should I care if they know?"

"Your father—"

"I don't care. If he fires me, so be it. Makes my decision about what to do easy. If he disowns me, he'd be doing me a favour."

Oh, Valentine . . .

His eyes searched mine. "You once said what I'd lose by being true to myself doesn't matter in the end because I'd gain me. And back then I thought that was stupid." He shook his head, his eyes glassy. "But I'm worth that, aren't I? I deserve that, don't I?"

I could have just about cried. I could barely nod. "Yes."

"Then fuck everything else."

I laughed, took his face in my hands, and kissed him.

He laughed, a little teary, and put his forehead to my shoulder. "I feel better already. Even just making the decision. I haven't even told anyone yet."

Uh . . .

"Well, about that," I said, turning his head to the audience we still had out the front of the pub.

"Oh shit." Valentine stared at them, then at me. He took a small reflexive step back, but then he blinked a few times, then he laughed. "Fuck. Well . . . fuck."

"Still wanna go home? Or wanna go back in for another beer?"

He looked back at the guys outside, then back at me before he let out a shaky breath. "I don't know if I'm ready . . ."

"Then we don't go in there. We'll go home." I took his hand and went to lead him to my ute.

He stopped. "Wait."

I stopped and waited for him to talk.

"If I leave it, it'll be worse. In my head. I won't be . . . I won't be able to face them at training." He looked back at the pub as if he was sizing up a fight. "If I do it now, it'll be done. Like ripping off a Band-Aid, and if anyone's got a problem with it, then at least I'll know. Before training.

Knowing is better than . . . not knowing. I'll get all up in my head and it'll be bad, and I want you with me—"

I squeezed his hand. "Hey. I'll be with you. The whole time. Every second."

His eyes met mine and he nodded. "Okay."

"You ready?"

He let out a rush of breath and nodded. "Yes."

Okay then.

I led him back to the pub, to the crowd, still holding his hand. He was gripping mine so tight I thought he might have been trying to break it, but every breath he let out was long and shaky. He was still trying not to freak out, still oblivious to the courage it took to do what he was doing.

"You all good, bro?" Taka asked me. Ignoring everyone else, ignoring the silence.

"All good."

He held the doors open. "Good. Then get your arse inside. It's cold out here and it's your shout."

Leave it to Taka to break the ice. There was a reason why everyone loved him. But inside we went. Everyone stopped and stared as we made our way to the bar, and I swear you could have heard a pin drop.

Valentine still held my hand.

Now, no one in their right mind would have dared say anything. We had Taka in front of us, Lleyton behind us. And I'd have flattened anyone who dared say shit to Valentine.

So I was surprised when Connor was the first to come up to us. I hoped he had dental in his private health insurance because he was about to fucking need it.

He didn't look at me, but he gave a weird smirk to Valentine. "Really?" he asked. "Out of all the guys, you picked the enemy?"

Now, I still wasn't sure if this was an olive branch or a stick of dynamite. My instinct was to go with the latter, defend Valentine and take Connor's head off. But I knew my reaction had to depend on Valentine's. He had to take the lead here, and I didn't want to make things worse.

Valentine raised his chin, his eyes darted to mine, and eventually he smiled. "He's actually not that bad." His grip on my hand could be measured in PSI, but he sighed unsteadily with a shrug. "I mean, enemy's a strong word."

Connor smiled and there was some silent agreement between them, and just like that, it was done. Valentine relaxed immediately and let out a deep, shaky breath, and after a second, Connor pointed his stare at me. "This doesn't mean I have to like you or anything, does it?"

I snorted. "Fuck no. I don't have to like you either."

He smiled. "Good." He took a swig and shook his head. "Gotta say, Valentine. You have terrible fucking taste."

Valentine laughed and leaned into me a little. "I know."

Then Connor must have realised . . . "So, about the grand final? What happens—"

"When we flog you?" I asked, slinging my arm around Valentine's shoulder. "When we go through the whole season undefeated?"

Valentine's eyes met mine, though his cheeks were pink, he was smiling. Genuinely, truly happy. "You fucking wish."

My entire team went to Lane Cove's next game, and like a dutiful boyfriend, I cheered from the stands. He played really well, and I was so proud of him my chest hurt. Also no one hurt him, so I didn't have to kill anyone.

Always a good thing.

They won, of course, and it meant I'd be facing Valentine in the grand final. We always knew it would come down to this. And I might have spent the week spruiking off and being a smartarse about how we were gonna win, win, win.

Rival against rival. Boyfriends off the field, enemies on the field, right down to the final whistle.

Except my whole team played like a busted arse, me leading the parade. Like we'd never held a rugby ball before. The one time I managed to make a break for the line, Valentine drove me into the ground and I lost the ball. He got up, patted my back, and laughed.

I would have been fucking livid if he wasn't so damn happy.

We lost, and lost spectacularly.

The scoreboard was humiliating. Nowhere near how humiliating going back to their pub for post-game defeat celebrations was going to be. And after my cockiness and big fat mouth for the last two weeks, I was going to deserve every single bit of it.

We walked into their bar, limping and wounded, to rounds of applause and jeers. Valentine's grin was breathtaking, his eyes only on me.

I fucking hated that I loved him.

He handed me a beer with a laugh. "You played terribly."

I ignored the bursts of laughter around us. "I don't wanna talk about it."

Valentine laughed so hard he snorted. "This is gonna be so much fun."

EPILOGUE

Boyfriends With Benefits

Valentine

COMING OUT WAS THE MOST FREEING THING I'D EVER done. I couldn't begin to describe how light I felt after not having to carry around such a burden. I actually hadn't realised how heavy it was until I didn't have to carry it anymore.

Coming out wasn't something I thought I'd ever get to do in my lifetime. But Marshall changed all that.

Little by little he showed me it was possible.

That I was worth it.

That I owed it to myself to be happy.

All the people in my life that mattered knew, and those who didn't know didn't matter.

And the thing that struck me the most? No one really cared.

If any of my teammates had an issue with it, they never said anything. They all treated me the same. Granted, I was never *great* friends with most of them. I didn't have many close friends.

But as a whole, people just didn't care.

I could remember back to when Marshall had poked fun at me, saying I wasn't actually as popular or famous as I thought I was. That the media or corporate world didn't think about me as much as I thought about them.

And I'd rolled my eyes because he didn't know. *How could he possibly know?*

Well, he was right about that too.

No one caught wind of it.

No one cared.

If Shayla caught on, she neither reacted nor cared. She treated him coming to my office as she treated any other visitor, though she did tell me she noted his birthday on my calendar . . .

So she knew.

And she didn't care.

And working with Marshall had been flawless. We didn't flaunt anything, and we didn't behave unprofessionally in any way. Though I knew it wouldn't always be the case, and yet . . . I still wasn't sure what the solution would be.

The thing was, he deserved to keep his job.

He was very good at it, and as the Mercer job drew to a close, I'd already told him of the next project for his team.

He'd once said the Mercer contract would be his last under Tye Corp, but now he was happy to stay.

He'd stay because of me.

But I felt if one of us should go, it should be me.

Which he said was ludicrous because it was my company, my family's company. But oh boy, leaving was a dream. To do what, I had no clue. I had no idea what I'd do with my life, or what would be the reason for me to ever pull the pin.

I just didn't know.

And then if I did leave, would he even want to stay? Would my leaving be for naught?

So many questions we didn't have answers to.

We were just happy with how things were.

We'd had dinner and weekend lunches with my sister. She loved him. We'd even had a few dinners with his parents. It'd been awkward at first, but Marshall's parents were really good people. His father had been unsure, which was completely understandable, and that first time I'd been so nervous I'd almost vomited.

But they were kind and welcomed me into their lives with open arms. It was more than I could have ever wished for. We just made a point of never speaking about work around his dad. Apart from the very first time, when Mr Wise had wanted to clear the air.

"Your father," he'd began.

"My father is a terrible person," I'd replied, because it was the truth, and we all got along fine after that.

And for a few months, everything was amazing. I was the happiest I'd ever been. The most thoroughly sated too. Every aspect of my life was a fucking dream.

Except one.

Except that one dark cloud I could never be rid of.

Shayla knocked at my office door before slipping inside. "Sorry to interrupt," she whispered, "but your father's here."

No warning, no meeting, no schedule.

No consideration for anyone but himself.

I gave her a smile. "Thank you."

"Should I bring tea or coffee?"

"No, he won't be staying long."

He never did.

He walked in without so much as a knock, his familiar scowl and hard-set eyes zeroed in on me.

"Dad," I said, not getting to my feet. I put my pen down and closed my laptop, aiming for a pleasantness I didn't feel. "This is unexpected."

I *expected* him to make some snappy reply about always *expecting* him, but he said nothing. He sat across from me and, like always, went straight to business. "I've just seen the projection figures for the next financial year," he said. "If you want to stay viable, you're going to need to cut costs."

Cut costs?

"We've barely been operational for one year," I started. "Ten months. That's hardly—"

"We knew it was risky and we bargained to carry the cost of incorporating the construction division, but interest rates . . ."

And so he went on about interest rate rises, increased manufacturing costs, shipping costs, incorporating Melbourne. The list was extensive, and I understood that financial decisions needed to be made.

But without explanation, I also knew that my father's idea of cutting costs was firing staff.

The expendable cost, the collateral cost.

The human cost.

It was always the first on his list.

Now, before that moment, I didn't know what the catalyst for me would be telling my father what I thought of him, but apparently this was it.

I'd accepted my departure from Tye Corp would be a long game, and even knowing I'd be leaving one day in the future had been enlightening. I felt good about my decision.

I'd told Brooklyn about my plans to leave *one day*, and it was exciting to think of a new life starting over.

One day.

Well, *one day* came around quicker than I'd thought it would.

My father wanted to cut costs, which always meant cutting staff. And that meant cutting Marshall. He just told me to ruin some more lives as if he were stomping ants into the ground.

I never knew I had a hard limit line, a point of no return, but apparently that was it.

"Or," I said, looking my father dead in the eye, "have you considered not taking millions in dividends and using that funding to cover costs instead?"

He stared. Cold and disbelieving. Calculating. He smirked as if he was dealing with a defiant calf before he called for its slaughter. "You dare question me?"

I didn't care. I no longer depended on his approval. "I dare question sound financial decisions."

"What do you know about financial decisions?" he barked. "We have shareholders—"

"We have nothing without staff," I snapped. "You want to treat your precious company like a machine, but you keep eliminating all the cogs and soon enough none of the wheels will turn. Who do you think runs your company? You?" I scoffed. "I'll tell you who makes your machine run. People. It's the people on the ground. Every single time. All those inconsequential little ants you despise. Without them you'd have nothing."

Well, that was not the correct answer, apparently. The dark storm in his expression erupted. The old me would have been terrified by the cold darkness aimed at me, but not anymore. "You'll do well to remember your place," he whispered. "Lest you find yourself in the unemployment line with your staff."

I almost laughed. "I know my place very well. Though it seems you've forgotten yours."

I wondered if that vein in his forehead would actually burst. I kinda wanted to find out.

I smiled at him. "You know what happens to the queen ant, Dad, when all her drones realise she no longer has the colony's best interest at heart. They stop serving her and she starves. You think the queen is the most powerful in that colony, but no, she is nothing without her little drones."

"You . . ." he seethed. "You ungrateful—"

"I am many things," I said, speaking over him. "Not that you'd know. You have no idea who I am. You have no idea who your daughter is. You have no idea *where* your wife is. You might be a successful businessman, but you suck at everything else. Though I will say if you thought giving me the construction division would help me see what I could become, you were right. Because I want to become nothing like you."

My hands were shaking but damn, this felt good.

"If you want to fire the best construction teams you have, then you can be the one to do it because I will quit before I do that. And I'll make it known why in my resignation letter to the board. If you want to hire cheaper subcontractors, then go right ahead. Cut your budgets, cut all the corners, and enjoy the lawsuits that come from dodgy construction, because that's what you'll get. I'll not have my name attached to that. And your shareholders won't either."

That vein was looking precariously close to bursting.

"I don't know who the hell you think you're speaking to," he whispered, his voice like volcanic ice. "I raised you better—"

"You didn't raise me at all," I said.

I was so close to telling him. I wanted to tell him I was gay just to watch the look on his face, to see if that vein would actually burst, to see if steam would come out his ears.

But I realised then, sitting across from him in the empire he had built, that he wasn't worth it.

He didn't deserve to know.

He didn't deserve the very best part of me.

"Just know this," I added. "Me leaving has nothing to do with whether I could handle it. I can handle it just fine. What I can't handle is being the one to do your dirty work. If you want to strip budgets and fire people, you do it. You go out there and look those good people in the eye and tell them."

I picked up my pen. "You promised this division two years to meet target, and you're pulling the rug at ten months. And every financial report I've given you has been better than expected, so the real problem here is that your projection team that told you it would work missed the mark. Fire them instead."

"They couldn't have foreseen a second global financial—"

"That is exactly what you pay them to do. That is their one fucking job. To evaluate risk assessments and have contingency plans for every possible scenario." I tilted my head. "Unless the incompetence wasn't theirs? Did you make that call?"

And that was it.

The final straw that broke the camel's back.

He stood up, placed both hands on my desk, and glowered pure rage at me.

Then he fired me.

And I laughed.

And that was how I knew I was really done.

Done with his shit. Done with living under his cloud of expectation. Done living in his shadow. Done with every other cheesy cliché I could think of.

I was fucking done.

I called Marshall on my way home and he followed me into my apartment by about two minutes. He raced in, saw the box of my office things on the table, his eyes wide and he grabbed my shoulders. "Holy shit, what happened?"

"I'm done," I said, still smiling. I think I even laughed. "I told him I was done. I told him everything I wanted to say to him my entire life. I told him he was a terrible father."

"Holy shit."

I laughed again, probably sounding a little manic. "And if he wanted to fire everyone and close the construction division, he could damn well do it himself, because he's a fucking coward. Okay, well, I didn't say that exactly, but it was implied."

"Holy shit."

"And I told him . . . I can't remember everything I said because I kind of unloaded on him." I put my hand to my forehead. "But then he fired me. But I think I quit before that, so I dunno."

Marshall stared, then looked around the apartment, his eyes still comically wide. "Holy shit."

"You keep saying that."

"Did you tell him? That you're gay?"

I shook my head. "No. I was going to just really put the boot into him, but you know what? He doesn't deserve to know. I'm not giving him the satisfaction of taking the one good thing in my life and ruining it. Fuck him. I'm done. I'm so done, Marshall."

He laughed and gave me a hug. A kind of bewildered hug, but it still felt great.

"I'm proud of you," he said. "For sticking up for yourself."

"I stuck up for everyone." I was still smiling like an idiot. "I feel so good. I don't expect that's gonna last. When reality kicks in. And I don't know what it means for Shayla or any of the staff there. Or you and your team. I just don't know." My smile died, and *oh look, here comes reality* . . .

Marshall shook his head. "This isn't about me or anyone else. This is about you. You needed to do this. For you, to finally be free of all that bullshit."

I nodded because he was right. "Once I started telling him, I just couldn't stop. I probably should have stopped at the ant colony analogy."

"The what?"

I snorted. "Never mind."

He put his hands to my face and pulled me in for another hug. He was smiling, still bewildered, still disbelieving. "So he's getting rid of the whole construction division?"

"I don't know." I shrugged. "Maybe I should have offered to stick around so I could find out for you. I'm sorry about that."

He chuckled just as my intercom buzzed. "I'll get it," he said, walking over to the screen. "It's Brooklyn."

"Well, there's nothing wrong with the Tye Corp grapevine," I said. "Let her in."

Ten seconds later, Brooklyn barrelled in like a whirlwind, tossing her handbag onto the table and pulling me onto a dining chair. "Tell me everything."

I relayed the story, filling in more details for Marshall's benefit as well. Marshall made us coffee and he cuddled Enzo while Brooklyn hung on every word.

354   N.R. Walker

When I was done, she sat back and sighed. "What will you do?"

"I don't know," I said. "For the first time in my life, I don't know."

She smiled. "And how does that feel?"

I laughed. "Kinda awesome."

Marshall looked a little worried, and that was hardly surprising. He'd had to worry about future plans and finances his whole life. I understood where his concern was coming from, and the uncertainty moving forward.

I slid my hand over his. "Sorry. I don't mean to sound insensitive. And as soon as I hear what he's planning to do with the construction division, you'll be the first to know. I promise."

"We can worry about me another day," he said. "I'm just glad you're okay. And I'm proud of you."

Hearing him say that, knowing he meant it with his whole heart, made me tear up a little. "I love you," I whispered. "I wouldn't have had the courage to do what I did today if it weren't for you."

My sister put her hand up, making a face. "Ah, please pity the single person in the room."

Marshall chuckled warmly and squeezed my hand. "Well, don't thank me yet. You're unemployed and I probably will be soon."

Shit.

"It's not a bad thing," he added. "It just means some things might have to change, that's all."

"Like what?"

"Where I work, travel times, my unit." He made a face. "I've got a bit of money saved."

"Move in with me," I said. Both Marshall and Brooklyn

stared at me. "You basically live here anyway, and I own this place so there'll be no rent."

He stared at me. "You own it outright?"

I winced. "Uh, yeah."

Marshall sat back and ran his hand over his face. "Jesus Christ."

I turned to face him, taking both his hands. "Move in with me. If I won't see you at work, then I'll need to see you here."

"You rarely saw me at work."

"Marshall."

"Valentine."

"Uh, hello," Brooklyn said. "I'm still here. Still single. Which has never been more apparent than it is now."

Marshall laughed at that and kissed the back of my hand. "How about we just deal with one big life change at a time?"

"Stop being sensible."

He snorted. "One of us probably should be."

"I can't believe you're saying no."

"I'm not saying no."

"Then it's a yes."

"An eventual yes. Not a now yes."

I smiled at him. "I'll take that."

Brooklyn groaned. "For the love of god you're going to make me download Tinder."

I laughed and threaded my fingers with Marshall's. "Don't do it. Men are terrible."

He snorted and kissed the back of my hand again, not taking his eyes from mine. "They're the absolute worst."

Brooklyn stood up. "Oh my god, I hate you both." She grabbed her bag. "Valentine, I'll call you the second I hear any news."

We laughed as she walked out, closing the door behind her, and the room filled with silence. "Are you sure you're okay?" Marshall asked me gently.

I let out a long breath, taking stock of how I felt, waiting to see if doubt or regret reared their ugly heads. I waited for the tightness in my chest, for my breath to feel short, for anxiety to claw at my insides . . .

It didn't come. "I feel . . . free. Like I kicked down the door to my cage. I know there'll be times when I will question if I made the right decision, and I'll need you to remind me of how I feel right now."

He smiled, his eyes warm and full of love. "I will." He fixed a strand of my hair and studied my face before his gaze met mine. "Do you need anything? Tell me what you need."

I laughed. "You're expecting me to say a good hard fucking, aren't you?"

He smirked. "Well, I wouldn't be surprised."

I shook my head. "You know what I really need?"

"What's that?"

"Tacos. And a margarita. In the city. We'll take my car so people look. I want them to look. So they can see me hold your hand, and I don't care who sees, Marshall. I want them to see."

He laughed. "You want to go on a date?"

I nodded quickly, so freaking excited. "A real date. In public. I know that probably sounds stupid to you, but it would be my first date, actually. In public. With a guy. And I want it to be with you."

He made a sad smiley face, cupped my jaw. "That doesn't sound stupid. That sounds perfect." He paused, gesturing down to his work clothes. "I'll need to go home and get changed."

"You have jeans here. You can borrow a shirt."

"Your shirts won't fit me."

"They'll be tight, and honestly, I'm okay with that."

He rolled his eyes. "My boots have cement on them."

"Even better. I don't care what you wear. We're not going anywhere fancy."

"Valentine, your idea of a fancy restaurant and my idea of fancy are very different. Fancy to me is when a waiter comes to your table instead of ordering at the counter."

I laughed. "All I'm hearing is reasons for you to move in with me."

"What . . . how? That's quite a leap."

"Because if you lived here, your clothes would already be here and we'd be on our way to eating tacos instead of arguing about the definition of fancy."

He huffed at me and turned for my bedroom. "Feed Enzo while I get changed."

I did that and found him in my bathroom, raking wet fingers through his hair. "Our first public date and I look terrible," he grumbled.

I grabbed his arse. "You look great."

Jeans, one of my white polos, considerably tight, and his work boots. Perfect.

"I'm wearing this," I said, looking down at my suit pants and a fitted button-down, sleeves rolled to my elbows. "Or should I change too?"

"Oh, please. You look like a million dollars every day of the week," he said. "With your perfect hair and your perfect face."

"Hm. You might wanna be careful, Marshall. I might start thinking you actually like me."

"Well, I don't." He shoved me out of the bathroom. "Come on, let's go on a date."

I grabbed my phone and keys. "Wanna drive my car?"

"Aaaaabsolutely fucking not."

I laughed as we walked to the elevator. "Well, you'll be driving it home because I'm having a margarita. Or several."

He winced. "Christ. Why do you have such an expensive car, anyway?"

"Because it's beautiful."

"It's pretentious."

"It's pretentiously beautiful."

He laughed at that but then in the parking garage, as we walked to my very pretentiously beautiful car, he came to the driver's side with me. "What are you doing? You want to drive into the city?"

"No. I'm opening your door. It's a date. We need to do it properly."

I unlocked the car, he opened the door, held my hand for me to get in, and once I was safely inside, he closed the door. When he got in and put his seatbelt on, I was still looking at him.

"What?"

"You're just really sweet."

"Might wanna be careful," he murmured. "I might start thinking you actually like me."

I chuckled and started the car, the engine purring, and I caught the way he smiled. He could complain about my car all he liked but it was hard not to be a little impressed.

"So, this first date," I said. "If we're doing this properly, you'll have me home by nine and expect no more than a kiss on the porch when you drop me home, right?"

He nodded seriously, "Oh, absolutely. Just a kiss."

I drove out of my spot to the security gate. "You better fucking not. I have great expectations, Marshall." Then I thought I should clarify. "And I'm not talking about the book."

HUSBANDS WITH BENEFITS

FROM FIRST DATES TO HIM BEING MY FIRST BOYFRIEND, to Marshall's first night after moving in, there were a lot of firsts.

Our first fight, which was more about me needing to pull my head out of my arse. Apologising and admitting I was wrong sucked enormous balls, but the making up part was fun.

Or the first time Enzo fell sick and we rushed him to the vet. It was nothing some antibiotics didn't fix, but it was scary as hell, and I'd never needed Marshall more in my life. He was an absolute rock of support and level-headed and perfect, while I was nothing short of a hot mess.

Kinda summed us up though, really.

And then there was my first day in a new job.

It was with a big tech firm and their mission ethos about putting people first seemed a good fit for me.

I'd never had to interview for a job before, and it was daunting and nauseating but also exciting. I had a degree, a long and varied experience with data analysis, risk assessment, and resource management, and a solid employment history and a great portfolio. Granted, that employment history was in a family business, but it was at a national level. I was capable and willing, and with Marshall's unwavering support, I also believed in myself.

He was more nervous than me, pacing when I returned from the interview. "How'd it go?"

My grin told him all he needed to know, and he threw his arms around me and lifted me off my feet. "I'm so proud of you!"

I was proud of me too.

And so my slide into the IT world began. It was long hours—no longer than I was used to—Monday to Friday, and it paid very well. It was also proof for my father that I could do just fine on my own.

I'd spoken to him exactly three times in the last year. So not really any different to how things were before, though now we didn't have the cushion of work to soften the stark reality of our relationship.

And I was okay with that.

Marshall was still at the same job. There'd been some structural changes and technically it was still under the parent company of Tye Corp, but his construction division was now one branch removed on the fuckery tree. He was happier with that, and the truth was, he had worked hard to get where he was.

He deserved to stay.

Plus, he worked with his mates, there was minimal travelling, the pay was good, though he never went to another Monday morning manager's meeting.

And me?

I was so much happier. I hadn't even known what true happiness was until I no longer worked for my father. Sure, Marshall showed me what happiness was, but this was different. This was freedom and self-worth. I'm sure Marshall had a lot to do with that, and I'd probably never have had the courage to do half of what I'd done without him.

I was out of the shadow of my father, basking in the sunlight for the first time. I laughed more. I went out more. I was free. I was free to be the real me for the first time in my life. I still did Karate on Monday nights, still played rugby, still gave as good as I got.

It'd been a meandering path in finding the real me, each step a milestone.

But I was out and proud, living with a man I loved. A man who loved me.

And two years later, life was damn near perfect. There wasn't one thing I'd change.

Meeting our friends at the pub for a Saturday lunch had been a thing we did in the off season.

Taka was there with his now-wife, Rhea, bouncing his six-month old son on his knee, the chubbiest, cutest kid you'd ever seen. Lleyton was sitting next to Brooklyn.

Yes, my sister.

They'd started talking at our usual get-togethers and dinners in town, and to be honest, they were a good match. He knew all about our fucked-up family and I knew all about his. He'd been my best friend for years, after all.

But then they began hanging out together without me and Marshall, for the occasional private dinner and trips to the beach, and then it became almost every weekend. That had been going on for a while now, and I quite happily pretended it wasn't happening at all while Lleyton looked at her as if he was ridiculously in love. Pretty much the same way she looked at him.

It was gross.

I loved my sister, and over the last few years, we'd become incredibly close. I just didn't have to know about what my best friend did to her. Or what she did to him.

No thanks.

"Oh, before I forget," Lleyton said. "Sign-ups for this season start next week. Don't forget."

I made a face. "Ah, yeah, about that . . . I have an announcement."

His eyes went wide. "What announcement?"

I grimaced. "I won't be playing this year. I'm retiring from rugby."

Marshall's hand slid over mine on my thigh. "Me too."

Taka put his hand up. "Ah, same. I was gonna tell you guys today. My knee hasn't got another season in it."

"What?" Lleyton cried, his head falling back. "You're all soft." Then he lifted his head up and stared at me. "Whyyyy? Come on. We have another few years in us yet."

"We all turned thirty last year," I replied. "My body is very well aware." It was true. Sure, rugby was fun and I loved it, but my body didn't love it as much as my heart, that was certain. And honestly, I'd rather save the body aches and pains for the bedroom. "Man, we're out there against eighteen-year-olds. You remember what it was like when we were eighteen. We used to laugh at the old guys we played against."

"We're not that old," Lleyton cried. Then he pointed his beer bottle at me. "It's because you're 2–1 up on him, isn't it? You don't want him to even the score."

I snorted.

Lane Cove had beaten North Ryde twice in the last three years, North Ryde taking the shield last year. It had become a joke between us, between our teams, that it was Marshall against me, and the rivalry had always been fun.

But Marshall had hurt his shoulder last year and it put him off work for a few weeks, and it wasn't something he wanted to go through again. So we made the decision, together, that it was time for both of us to hang up the boots.

"As if North Ryde would beat us this year anyway," I joked. "We'd kick their arse."

"You fucking wish," Marshall said.

Lleyton got his hopes up. "So does that mean you'll play?"

We shook our heads. "No."

He groaned. "You all suck." He threw his bottle top at me. "And the way you said you had an announcement, I thought you were gonna say you were getting married or something."

I threw his bottle top back at him. Hard. "As if. Jesus Christ."

Taka's gaze shot to Marshall's, and Marshall gave the tiniest shake of his head.

What the . . . ?

"What was that look for?" I asked, pointing between them. "I saw it."

Taka put his hand up. "I didn't do anything." He suddenly found his kid very enthralling, avoiding eye contact with anyone.

So I turned to Marshall. I didn't even have to say anything. He shifted in his seat and made a face. "Would getting married be so terrible?"

I stared at him. Because what the actual fuck? "Ah, yes. Marriage *is* terrible."

His eyes met mine. "So you wouldn't . . . ?" He smiled sadly and sat up straighter. "Well, that's good to know."

"No," I blurted out. God, the look of hurt on his face struck deep in my heart. "I mean, marriage, in general, is not great. A legally binding contract tied to a religion I don't believe in doesn't make any sense."

"That's so romantic," Marshall said. His smile didn't look right.

It didn't look right at all.

Jesus.

Did he really want to get married?

I think he did . . .

Oh holy fuck.

"But getting married *to you* would be fine," I added, trying to salvage something yet somehow making it worse. "Better than fine, probably. If it didn't involve a church or my parents, or . . ."

Lleyton began to laugh.

"Better than fine," Marshall repeated slowly.

"Well, no, it'd be great, actually. It'd be great. I mean, we already live together and you're a great dad to Enzo. Though if you want me to wear a ring so people know I belong to you, then there's really no point, because anytime we're together you kinda growl at anyone who looks at me, so there's no mistaking—"

Marshall patted my leg. "Stop talking."

I stopped talking, and everyone was staring but also trying not to look at us. Except for Lleyton. He was still laughing.

Christ.

Goddammit.

"Fucking hell, Marshall. Well, now you better fucking ask me," I snapped. "Since you brought it up and made a whole scene."

Brooklyn snorted behind her bottle of beer. "This is the best thing I've ever seen."

I huffed at her. "Oh, zip it." I pulled my hand from Marshall's. "I hate you."

He laughed and took my hand back into his. "No you don't. Not anymore." He sighed. "We've done the whole enemies-with-benefits thing before. Then we tried the boyfriends with benefits thing. It was fun."

Was?

"Was?"

Why was he talking in past tense?

His smile was lazy, his eyes were warm in the fading summer sun. "Yeah. I thought maybe we could try the husbands-with-benefits thing. One day."

"It's fiancé first," Brooklyn added. "Fiancé with benefits, then husbands." She grimaced. "Technically."

I stared at her, because god, this was actually happening . . . then back to Marshall. "What are you saying?"

"Well, I was saying maybe we could get married one day, but if you think marriage is terrible, then . . ."

"No. I mean, yes. I mean, yes, I'd marry you. And no, marriage isn't terrible. I mean, it kind of is, but not marriage to you. That'd be kind of wonderful."

Brooklyn laughed, her hands to her face. "Oh god, this is a train wreck from start to finish."

I ignored my sister because I couldn't take my eyes off Marshall.

"So, is that a yes?" he asked.

I nodded, my heart so full it could burst. "Y-yes."

His grin was spectacular as he pulled me in for a kiss and everyone at the table clapped and cheered.

"I told you he'd say yes," Taka said. "Kinda fitting that you asked him in the very place it all started."

Oh god.

"It started here?" Lleyton looked around the pub.

Taka laughed and pointed his chin at the door. "In the bathrooms."

I shot Marshall a look. "You told him?"

Marshall grinned at me proudly. "Hell yes, I did."

Lleyton groaned. "Oh god. The bathrooms? Really?"

I raised my chin, trying to recoup some level of decorum. "I don't think I need to answer that."

Brooklyn laughed, reaching over to clink her bottle of beer to mine. "Classy."

I slid my hand over Marshall's, threading our fingers. This man, this perfect man wanted to marry me. I still couldn't quite believe it, and my mind was spinning.

"You okay?" Marshall asked.

I barked out a laugh. "Uh, yeah. I'm just trying to decide if I deliberately don't invite my parents, or deliberately *do* invite them just to see my father's face when he sees I'm marrying a man."

Marshall smiled. "That would be kinda funny."

I sighed. "Are you sure you want to marry me? I mean, you know what you're signing up for."

"Fuck yes."

I still couldn't believe it. But wearing his ring, promising forever, that sounded pretty damn good to me.

He'd clearly talked about it with Taka, so . . . "How long have you been planning to ask me . . . since when?"

His eyes were smiling. "Remember when we were in the Under 10s at that rugby carnival and you smashed me over the sideline to win the game?"

I laughed. "Liar. You have not planned it since then. You *hated* me for that."

He chuckled. "Okay, so maybe it was that night when you shoved me into the bathroom stall."

I snorted. "You hated me for that too."

He sighed happily. "I don't hate you anymore," he said, lifting our hands to his lips to kiss my knuckles. "But don't get any ideas. Just because I wanna spend forever with you and don't hate you anymore doesn't mean I like you or anything."

I laughed, so much in love. "Good, just because I said yes doesn't mean I like you or anything either."

THE END

About the Author

N.R. Walker is an Australian author, who loves her genre of gay romance. She loves writing and spends far too much time doing it, but wouldn't have it any other way.

She is many things: a mother, a wife, a sister, a writer. She has pretty, pretty boys who live in her head, who don't let her sleep at night unless she gives them life with words.

She likes it when they do dirty, dirty things... but likes it even more when they fall in love.

She used to think having people in her head talking to her was weird, until one day she happened across other writers who told her it was normal.

She's been writing ever since...

nrwalker.net

Also by N.R. Walker

The Dichotomy of Angels

Throwing Hearts

Pieces of You - Missing Pieces #1

Pieces of Me - Missing Pieces #2

Pieces of Us - Missing Pieces #3

Lacuna

Tic-Tac-Mistletoe

Bossy

Code Red

Dearest Milton James

Dearest Malachi Keogh

Christmas Wish List

Code Blue

Davo

The Kite

Learning Curve

Merry Christmas Cupid

To the Moon and Back

Second Chance at First Love

Outrun the Rain

Into the Tempest

Touch the Lightning

TITLES IN AUDIO:

Cronin's Key

Cronin's Key II

Second Chance at First Love

Outrun the Rain

Into the Tempest

Series Collections:

Red Dirt Heart Series

Turning Point Series

Thomas Elkin Series

Spencer Cohen Series

Imago Series

Blind Faith Series

Missing Pieces Series

The Storm Boys Series

Free Reads:

Sixty Five Hours

Learning to Feel

His Grandfather's Watch (And The Story of Billy and Hale)

The Twelfth of Never (Blind Faith 3.5)

Twelve Days of Christmas (Sixty Five Hours Christmas)

Best of Both Worlds

Translated Titles:

Italian

Fiducia Cieca (Blind Faith)

Attraverso Questi Occhi (Through These Eyes)

Preso alla Sprovvista (Blindside)

Il giorno del Mai (Blind Faith 3.5)

Cuore di Terra Rossa Serie (Red Dirt Heart Series)

Natale di terra rossa (Red dirt Christmas)

Intervento di Retrofit (Elements of Retrofit)

A Chiare Linee (Clarity of Lines)

Senso D'appartenenza (Sense of Place)

Spencer Cohen Serie (including Yanni's Story)

Punto di non Ritorno (Point of No Return)

Punto di Rottura (Breaking Point)

Punto di Partenza (Starting Point)

Imago (Imago)

Imagines

Il desiderio di un soldato (A Soldier's Wish)

Scambiato (Switched)

Tallowwood

The Hate You Drink

Ho trovato te (Finders Keepers)

Cuori d'argilla (Throwing Hearts)

Galassie e Oceani (Galaxies and Oceans)

Il peso di tut (The Weight of it All)

Pieces of You - Missing Pieces 1

French

Confiance Aveugle (Blind Faith)

A travers ces yeux: Confiance Aveugle 2 (Through These Eyes)

Aveugle: Confiance Aveugle 3 (Blindside)

À Jamais (Blind Faith 3.5)

Cronin's Key Series

Au Coeur de Sutton Station (Red Dirt Heart)

Partir ou rester (Red Dirt Heart 2)

Faire Face (Red Dirt Heart 3)

Trouver sa Place (Red Dirt Heart 4)

Le Poids de Sentiments (The Weight of It All)

Un Noël à la sauce Henry (A Very Henry Christmas)

Une vie à Refaire (Switched)

Evolution (Evolved)

Galaxies & Océans

Qui Trouve, Garde (Finders Keepers)

Sens Dessus Dessous (Upside Down)

La Haine au Fond du Verre (The hate You Drink)

Tallowwood

Spencer Cohen Series

German

Flammende Erde (Red Dirt Heart)

Lodernde Erde (Red Dirt Heart 2)

Sengende Erde (Red Dirt Heart 3)

Ungezähmte Erde (Red Dirt Heart 4)

Vier Pfoten und ein bisschen Zufall (Finders Keepers)

Ein Kleines bisschen Versuchung (The Weight of It All)

Ein Kleines Bisschen Fur Immer (A Very Henry Christmas)

Weil Leibe uns immer Bliebt (Switched)

Drei Herzen eine Leibe (Three's Company)

Über uns die Sterne, zwischen uns die Liebe (Galaxies and Oceans)

Unnahbares Herz (Blind Faith 1)

Sehendes Herz (Blind Faith 2)

Hoffnungsvolles Herz (Blind Faith 3)

Verträumtes Herz (Blind Faith 3.5)

Thomas Elkin: Verlangen in neuem Design

Thomas Elkin: Leidenschaft in klaren

Thomas Elkin: Vertrauen in bester Lage

Traummann töpfern leicht gemacht (Throwing Hearts)

Sir

THAI

Sixty Five Hours (Thai translation)

Finders Keepers (Thai translation)

SPANISH

Sesenta y Cinco Horas (Sixty Five Hours)

Los Doce Días de Navidad

Código Rojo (Code Red)

Código Azul (Code Blue)

Queridísimo Milton James

Queridísimo Malachi Keogh

El Peso de Todo (The Weight of it All)

Tres Muérdagos en Raya: Serie Navidad en Hartbridge

Lista De Deseos Navideños: Serie Navidad en Hartbridge

Feliz Navidad Cupido: Serie Navidad en Hartbridge

Spencer Cohen Libro Uno

Spencer Cohen Libro Dos

Spencer Cohen Libro Tres

Davo

Hasta la Luna y de Vuelta

Venciendo A La Lluvia

En la Tempestad

El Toque del Rayo

Corazón De Tierra Roja

Corazón De Tierra Roja 2

CHINESE

Blind Faith

JAPANESE

Bossy

PORTUGUESE

Sessenta e Cinco Horas

Made in the USA
Columbia, SC
28 May 2024

36280783R00231